Habits
ANNA B. DOE
USA TODAY BESTSELLING AUTHOR

Habits

Liz,

Eyes on me ♥

XO,

ANNA B. DOE

USA TODAY BESTSELLING AUTHOR

ISBN 978-953-8511-39-4

Habits by Anna B. Doe
Publisher: Wild Heart Publishing d.o.o.
Lukarišće, Croatia, 2023
Print on demand

Copyediting by Emerald Eyes Editing
Cover Design by Najla Qamber Designs
Illustration by Marina Kaya

Created with Vellum

"We become what we repeatedly do."
— Sean Covey, The 7 Habits of Highly Effective Teens

Blurb

All Jeanette Sanders wanted to do was escape her past and forget everything that has happened. Coming to Greyford was supposed to be her new beginning, a clean slate. Only it seems like her past doesn't want to let her go. As her old insecurities start to return in full force and lies grow bigger than ever, the only thing left is the hope that her broken heart will survive this time around.

Andrew Hill has been betrayed one too many times in the past. Cynical and cold-hearted, he closed off his heart for good and doesn't plan on letting anybody in ever again. Especially women. But his heart doesn't seem to care and starts beating faster every time a particular black-haired beauty gets in his way and puts him in his place.

He wants her body, not her heart. She tries to resist him, but the pull is too much.

They know they're all wrong for each other, but some habits are too sweet to give up.

Prologue

JEANETTE

One month ago

"You are one big jackass, Andrew Hill," I say, watching two girls walk away in a hurry.

He managed to upset one of them and get the second angry at him, as well as piss off his best friend and my brother. It has to be some kind of record for the number of screw-ups in one night. Or more precisely, ten minutes. But who's counting?

"Just figuring that out, Princess?" He shakes his head mockingly. "Sorry to disappoint you, but you are late and I've heard worse."

My eyes leave the darkness and concentrate on him. We're sitting in the shadows between the shelves in the school library. I can't see him clearly, but I don't have to see him to know the lines of his face. Not that I'd ever admit that out loud.

Andrew Hill is one handsome devil. I can't deny it, no matter how painful it is, even if I only confess it to myself. I would never utter it in the light of day.

His face is made of strong lines. High cheekbones and square jaw. His lips are full and reddish. They're pouty, stubborn and oh-so-kissable. A little bump on his nose—most likely the result of years of playing hockey—the only imperfection he has. Well, the only physical imperfection because God knows it, his personality has much to be desired.

Like you're one to talk.

And then there are his eyes. His big, piercing green eyes surrounded by thick eyelashes. The rich, dark green of woods and fields just after a perfect summer storm. Eyes that charm women into dropping their panties only to have their hearts shattered a moment later.

His brown hair is disheveled, as if he just ran his hands through it or got out of bed after a heated hook-up. It's not dark brown, but lighter, warmer. Streaked with honey strands when the sun hits at the right angle. It's longish, and the ends curl against his neck.

As I said, Andrew Hill is one handsome devil.

If only he was less of a jerk.

The school organized this senior sleepover. I don't get why they even bother, but my brother wanted to come, so here I am.

Max has been acting strange since we moved here. More accurately, since he met Amelia. So there is no way I'll leave my twin alone. We aren't as close as we were before, far from it, but that doesn't mean I don't care about him. He's not just my brother; he's my other half. My twin. When we are at our worst, our bond is stronger than some other siblings at their best.

Hill takes a pull from the bottle of Jack he stashed here for our little game and offers me a bit that's left. His green eyes look at me intensely.

Daring me.

Mocking me.

I don't think he's aware of what he's got himself into. I'm not like the other girls he usually has around. The ones that'll let him do and say whatever he pleases. The ones that'll do anything to please him. The ones that'll bat their eyelashes and smile stupidly, sighing at how good-looking, rich or dreamy he is.

There is nothing dreamy about Andrew Hill.

Just one big douchebag who thinks he knows everything.

Newsflash—he doesn't.

Yeah, he's rich. Correction, his father is rich. But so is mine. And yeah, you can say he's handsome. If you go for a big, bulky body, messy hair and pretty face. But there is nothing dreamy about the guy. He's cruel, cold-hearted and mean.

I take the bottle from him, my fingers brushing against his as I curl my hand around the glass and bring it to my lips.

The liquid burns in my throat. I've already drunk so much I'm starting to feel it. The numbness of my body. The warmth in my belly. The rush of blood in my veins.

I haven't drunk in so long—almost two years—that I forgot how it feels.

Nothing seems difficult anymore. There is no heaviness in my heart. Dark thoughts are pushed to the back of my mind.

Just for a little while.

I want to roll my eyes at the voice inside my head. Like I need a reminder that nothing can keep my demons at bay for long.

"Don't be absurd. I know exactly what you're hiding behind that mask of yours, Andrew Hill. I just like to remind you so you don't forget."

"You think I'm hiding?"

I tilt my head to the side, thinking. All this alcohol is making me warm and dizzy. My head is all over the place, and my mouth seems to have a mind of its own.

"Aren't we all?" I ask, the corner of my lips tilting in a small, taunting smile.

His eyes find me in the darkness and hold on.

Tick. Tock.

Tick. Tock.

The seconds tick by, and we just stare at each other.

We don't say a word.

We don't breathe.

Just look.

Something passes between us.

An understanding, maybe. And now, while his eyes are connected with mine, I feel peace wash over me.

A sense of belonging.

The boy I can't stand. The boy who irritates the hell out of me. The boy I want to strangle at least once daily. In this silly, unexpected moment, he gives me something that I haven't felt in so long, something I was afraid I'd never feel again.

Maybe it's the influence of alcohol, or just simple craziness. I don't know. And to be honest, I don't care.

I don't know how it happens, but he's suddenly right there in front of me. Or maybe I'm in front of him?

He stares at me, and my heart kicks up a notch.

Andrew takes the now empty bottle out of my hand and puts it on the floor by his side. His fingers curl around mine.

Intertwining.

Gripping hard.

I feel my teeth bite into my lower lip nervously. I want to pull away, but his hold, his pull, is too strong.

His eyes look down at me tormenting my lip. His pupils dilate, and a low growl comes out of him. A growl that I'll realize later is my name.

Then he's kissing me.

Andrew's hands go to my waist and pull me closer so I'm sitting firmly in his lap. His lips land on mine, and with the first touch of soft skin against soft skin, I feel a zap of electricity run through my whole body. I inhale sharply, my lips parting slightly before they're covered by his again.

The kiss is harsh, commanding, overpowering. Andrew nibbles on my lower lip, swollen and puffy, before he sucks it into his mouth, making me moan.

It's overwhelming. His closeness, his scent, the feel of his skin on mine.

So overwhelming, that for a second, I forget how to breathe.

My body shudders under his hands, relishing in the play of smooth and rough.

I kiss him back as fiercely as he's kissing me. My hands cup his cheeks and hold him close. The soft ends of his hair taunt me, so I let my fingers run through his locks.

Just like silk, as I knew they would be.

His tongue enters my mouth, mine meeting it halfway. I murmur incoherently in approval as our tongues mash together in a dance so synchronized, you'd think we'd done this before.

Long, frantic kisses that make my whole body hot and needy.

Plunging my tongue deeper into his mouth, I rub my body against his. My hands dig into his scalp, trying to control our kiss.

Andrew groans into my mouth. The sound is low and almost painful. I can feel his hard cock growing even harder between my legs. Big and imposing, just like its owner.

I want him, and there's no resisting it. I rub against him, my head falling back in pleasure.

"Drew..."

His lips don't stop for a second. They leave small, open-mouthed kisses down my neck and over my collarbone. He sucks lightly at the hollow between my shoulder and neck, and I know it'll leave a bruise.

Fucking barbarian. Not that I have it in me to care.

I continue rocking against him. One of his hands goes to my ass, passing the barrier of my pants and meeting naked skin, as he helps me move against his hardness. The other cups my breast through my tank top and sports bra.

In a hurry, he pulls the material down, revealing my breasts. For a few heartbeats, he simply stares at the revealed flesh, then his heated eyes meet mine.

"This is insanity."

Andrew doesn't wait for my response. His mouth suckles on my hard nipple, his tongue teasing circles around the tip.

My back arches, looking for more of his warm touch. More of his hands. More of his lips. More of him.

And there's nothing that can stop this madness—all I can do is close my eyes and moan his name.

Beg him for more.

I can feel him tremble under the palms of my hands, so I increase my rocking. Pressing harder against his rigid length.

Andrew doesn't leave me hanging. His hips push upward, meeting mine. We're dry-humping almost manically, losing control as we fight for dominance over each other. Pushing and pulling and biting.

There are too many clothes between us, but I can still feel his hardness pressing against my pulsing clit. His big hands are on my waist, holding me, pulling me down more firmly and helping me move and rock against him until I can feel the world crumble beneath me.

As we come down from our high, our breathing and heart rates slowing down, the silence that fills the room is palpable. I get off his lap and rearrange my clothes in a hurry, suddenly aware and embarrassed by the whole situation.

"This wasn't supposed to happen."

I don't dare look him in the eyes, afraid of what I'll find there. Turning on the balls of my feet before he can say a word, I let the darkness surround me.

Chapter 1

JEANETTE

Now

With disgust, I look at the water bottle in my hand. It's hard being one of the only people who's sober in a room full of drunk teenagers, but if there's one rule I never break, it's that I don't drink and drive. And tonight, the role of DD fell on me. Happy, happy times.

Frustrated, I lean against the wall, blending in with the shadows. My eyes scan the room full of people in different costumes before they finally land on a witch and a hockey player. I smirk at them, but it doesn't last long.

Max was right after all. Bringing Amelia to this party was the right choice. Hopefully, she and Derek will work through whatever shit they have going on and get it over with. They've been moping around for a couple of weeks. Amelia even went as far as to lock herself in her bedroom for days after she found one of the school's hussies on his doorstep while he was practically naked.

Not that I witnessed the event or anything, but you would be surprised how much you can find out if you only stand on the sidelines and listen. People tend to forget you are there and blab their big mouths. Or maybe they like to gossip way too much and don't care if somebody's listening.

There's also the fact that Max told me all about their plan. I was skeptical, but I went along with it. Because of my brother. Not Derek. Not Amelia. My brother.

I scan the crowd for him and find him with some of his hockey teammates. They're talking and laughing.

The weight I didn't even realize was there disappears, and my insides soften immediately.

I was worried how everything would affect him. He's hung around Lia almost since the day we stepped foot in this town. He's always with her, following her like a little, enamored puppy. He tells silly jokes to make her laugh and teases her. He does his best to help her and always acts like a gentleman when she's around. I was ready to bet he was falling in love. But if he was in love with her, wouldn't he do something about it? Wouldn't he form a game plan to win her over once Derek screwed up? Instead, he was helping *him* get her back.

Either he's one really big, masochistic idiot, or he's not as in love with Lia as the whole school would like to believe.

I should probably know it. Sense it somehow. We are twins, for God's sake. Two beings that came from the same cells. We spent the first nine months of our lives cramped in a small space, and in our seventeen years on this planet, we've only been apart a handful of times. I can feel when he's hurt. I can sense his mood swings. And sometimes, unintentionally, my subconscious brings me to him. But I don't know this.

I don't know if my brother is in love with Amelia or not.

Probably because lately, we have lost our way. Everything changed before we moved, and now, now we're trying to deal with it. Trying to find our way back to what we once were.

My thoughts are interrupted when *he* joins them.

Andrew Hill.

Partier.

Womanizer.

Daddy's golden boy.

Hot-shot hockey player.

Cocky, presumptuous, but I have to give it to him, one smart son of a bitch.

He joins the rest of his teammates and friends, swagger oozing from every pore of his body.

His brown hair is messy and curls at the base of his neck. His lips curl into one of his well-known, arrogant smirks, revealing straight teeth. I'm standing too far from him to clearly see the color of his eyes or the lines of his face, but I know them.

I've touched them.

Andrew would look almost perfect if there wasn't a slight bump on his nose. That small imperfection makes him look more rugged. More real.

His eyes always have this gleam in them. I've heard what people say. They call it mischievous, but I know better. I can see behind it.

I can see his darkness.

Because it matches my own.

He and his buddies are overly preoccupied with whatever they've been discussing, so I keep looking at them. It always amazes me how easy guy friendships are.

For years, I've watched my brother be the center of the group. He's the funny one. The easy-going twin. The jokester. People have always gravitated toward him, and he always had a bunch of friends.

And I have always been his polar opposite. Max never left me to fend for myself, but I never really felt like part of the group, either. Friendships and opening up never came easy to me.

Then high school happened. Things changed and here we are. Lost in the limbo of guilt, hurt and betrayal.

You could try opening up to Lia and Brook.

I ignore the little voice inside my head. Or at least try to, but it's been getting louder and louder the last couple of weeks, since that night I spent at Lia's house.

I don't want friends. Don't need them. I tried once and look where it got me. You open your heart to people, willingly give them power over you, and you'll lose the most essential part of who you are.

Loud laughter startles me out of my dark thoughts.

Max and his friends are laughing hard at God only knows what. Drew's head is thrown back, his neck exposed. My tongue darts out to wet my suddenly dry lips.

I've kissed that skin once, and I can still feel the texture of it on my lips.

A group of girls walks toward them, all of them wearing revealing costumes. Extremely short skirts and hooker heels. Even from here and in the darkness of the room, I can see that their hair and make-up are done perfectly because they shine in the dark.

Andrew turns to the girl closest to him. Her blonde hair is curled, and she's wearing a bunny costume with a plush tail and everything. No kidding.

Just looking at her makes me want to puke in my mouth and roll my eyes all at the same time.

I'm not sure if it's that Diamond girl that messed with Lia and Derek or one of her minions. They all look like clones, so it's hard to guess.

Whoever she is, she curls her hand around Andrew's and whispers something in his ear. He gives her one of his lazy I-am-gonna-bang-you-and-you-are-gonna-beg-for-more smiles, but the easiness that was there when it was just the guys is gone. In its place, a dark shadow looms over him.

The girl takes the drink out of his hand and sips from the red Solo cup. She flirts with him shamelessly, batting her eyelashes and giggling as she twirls a strand of her hair around her finger.

I feel my jaw tense, but I don't make a move. My eyes stay glued to them.

As if he can feel my stare, Andrew lifts his head and his eyes find mine through the crowd.

We are fixed on each other.

Not breathing.

Not blinking.

His smile widens.

Without breaking our eye contact, he lowers so that his lips touch the girl's ear. Goosebumps rise on my skin. It almost feels like he's doing it to me, like I can feel his lips on my earlobe and his hot breath touch my skin.

Silly, silly girl.

She giggles. I know because it's obnoxiously loud and fake, even in the crowded room with music blasting.

Whatever he said to her, she agreed to because I can see her locks bounce as she nods her head. Grinning, he pushes her out of the room.

Toward the stairs.

To his room.

Suddenly, I feel sick, the need to puke real. And at the same time, I feel ridiculous. Ridiculous and stupid. Why did I let him get to me? He knew I was watching, so he must have done it on purpose.

Andrew Hill isn't the hearts and flowers kind of guy. He doesn't do romance or relationships. He's a dick. Asshole with a capital A, and I don't understand why I let his behavior affect me. It's not like I haven't seen this same thing before.

Trust me, I know all about fake friendships, lying assholes and the disaster that is high school. Different school, different names, same personalities. But this time, there is something else that's different—me.

I look around the room, searching for my brother, but I don't see him. He was just there. Where did he go?!

Brook, Lia and Derek are also nowhere in sight. Where the hell did everybody go? They have to be somewhere around here. We came in the same car and I'm the one with the keys in my purse, so there is no way they left.

I grab my phone and shoot a quick message to my brother:

Me: Where are you?

Then my eyes fall to the bottom of the list. The bright screen taunts me in the darkness. I nibble at my lip, debating what to do. I know I shouldn't, but my fingers are faster than my brain, typing the message and hitting send before I can rethink my decision.

Me: Collecting your BFs leftovers. How classy.

I read it again and again, my breathing uneven as panic, cold and unforgiving, runs through my veins. I already regret my decision, but there is no taking it back now.

One more look at the screen assures me I have no new messages, so I decide to go outside. Maybe the cool night air will ease the pressure off my chest and let me breathe more easily.

Moving through the haze of kids, all in different costumes and states of drunk and undress, I find the door leading to the back terrace. It's wide open, but there is nobody outside, for which I'm grateful.

It's freezing out, and my Wonder Woman costume doesn't help much in keeping me warm, but I prefer it that way. At least in this moment. November coldness helps keep me grounded.

The terrace is illuminated with the dim light of the lamps and moon trying to shine through the dark clouds.

Tilting my head back as I sit on the ground, I let the crisp night air kiss my cheeks. Stars are scattered all over the inky sky, playing peek-a-boo with the clouds and light.

Closing my eyes, I inhale deeply. The icy air entering my lungs, relaxing my muscles and letting me breathe.

I don't know how long I stay like that—eyes closed as I simply breathe—but something interrupts my quiet. My eyes snap open and I see it, a shadow looming over the edge of the balcony.

Even in the darkness, I can recognize his face.

His hands are gripping the railing of the fence, his whole body tilting slightly forward. His head is bent, those taunting green eyes closed.

I keep quiet, observing his face in silence. In the darkness of the night when he's relaxed and unguarded, so different from his usual, everyday self, his face doesn't look as hard as it does in the light of the day. His lips aren't curled into a sneer, nor do his eyes throw icy daggers at me. No, in the darkness, traces appear of the boy he used to be.

What happens next, I'm not sure. Maybe I moved or murmured something without realizing it. His eyes snap open suddenly. Even in the dim light of the moon, they shine brightly, like those of a cat.

He looks at me, and I look at him.

Not breaking the stare.

Not uttering a word.

There is intensity in his gaze. Need and desire mix with resentment but even that doesn't make me break the contact.

It's like there is something inside of him that's holding on to something inside of me. Not letting either of us break free.

"There she is!"

My head snaps to the door as soon as I hear the words. Amelia is there with Derek on her heels.

"She's here, Max!" Lia throws over her shoulder before her dark-chocolate eyes settle on me again. "We've been looking for you. Ready to go?"

I stand, and without looking back up, turn toward the door. "Yup. I just needed some fresh air."

Chapter 2

ANDREW

An irritating, noisy alarm blasts through my room once again, and all I can do is groan loudly and cover my head with the pillow.

Every day it's the same old story. I turn off alarm after alarm until I can barely put my clothes on, take a piss and brush my teeth. Then I have to step on the gas if I want to get to morning practice on time.

Coach hates when we're late. It happened once, my freshman year. It was the first and the last time I did it. The drills he made me do were so fucked up, my whole body ached for *weeks* after that.

Groaning, I throw my legs over the edge of the bed as I rub my face. My temples are still pounding from partying all weekend, but that's nothing new. I press the snooze button to quiet the damn thing that's making my headache worse before getting up and putting on a baggy pair of sweats and a hoodie.

Yawning loudly, I go to the bathroom. It's five thirty in the morning, but for me it feels more like the middle of the night. After taking a piss, I grab my stuff and run down the stairs.

I start toward the garage when a slightly ajar door and light coming from the gap catches my eye.

He's home.

The door was closed and the light was off last night before I went to bed. I'd know, because it's one of the two rooms I enter only if I'm being summoned. And that happens if I screw up in gigantic proportions. Otherwise, he's too busy for me.

Work always comes first to my dear old pops. It's basically the only thing he does. It wasn't always like that. There were happy times. Times when my father was actually *Dad* and liked to spend time with me. But that was in another lifetime.

I stand there, looking at the dull light shining through the small gap. My hands are clenched into fists by my sides.

He's been away for two weeks. He never said where he was going. He never called and asked how I was or to let me know he was okay. For all he cares, I could be dead.

Sometimes I wish I am. It can't be any worse than being completely and utterly alone.

I lean against the locker, my hands stuffed in the pockets of my sweats.

The girl standing opposite me—Sophie? Suzie? Sammy? fuck if I know—twirls a strand of her honey hair around her finger. Pale, shimmery nail polish shining in the sunlight peeking through the windows.

She smiles at me, color creeping up her cheeks. She's trying to be all shy and mysterious, but I can see the predator look in her brown eyes. My lips curl into a knowing smirk, which she takes as a sign to lean in, put her hand on my chest and bat her eyelashes.

The urge to roll my eyes and yawn in boredom is strong. My palms itch so hard to shove her away and tell her to get some dignity and self-respect and not just crawl all over some random guy.

I know, I'm an asshole. A hypocrite. The biggest womanizer in this godforsaken town giving lessons on dignity and pride. Irony at its best.

Because of that, I don't say a word. I smile and take what's being offered to me. And she's giving it to me on a silver platter.

They always do.

Years ago, I learned that it doesn't matter how you treat people. If you are good-looking, if you are rich and have connections, you can do anything you want. You can insult, you can act like a complete jackass, and everybody will still try to crawl up your ass. Everybody will still try to be your best friend. As long as you can give them what they want.

So I do what I do best. I take what they offer. I use them, and then I throw them away. And they don't even mind.

Now both of her hands are on my pecks, grabby fingers holding on to my shirt. Her glossy lips are so close to my ear, I can feel them on my skin.

"You feel like—"

"Yo, Hill! You going to lunch?"

My eyes snap up and look at my friend and teammate, Max Sanders. His gray eyes take me to another day and time when a matching pair of stormy-gray eyes were staring at me with so much heat, I was afraid I'd catch on fire. His frown is soon replaced with his well-known grin.

"I'll be there in a sec."

I disentangle her fingers from my shirt and push her away from me. She's pouting, clearly unhappy with how everything's playing out, but I don't give a fuck about what she thinks.

All she can give me is a temporary oblivion. But it's not enough. What I need is something more. Something stronger. Something that'll make me forget about all the shit that's happening in my life. Something that will keep at bay the demons that haunt me.

"Maybe la—"

I don't wait for her to finish, just turn on the balls of my feet and walk away.

People move out of my way as I pass by. Some pat me on the shoulder or high-five me, congratulating me on our latest game or party. They want to be noticed, want to be known as a friend of Andrew Hill.

I play their game—after all, it's one of the things I do best.

Inside the cafeteria, I quickly grab something to eat and then start walking toward my friends. They are all sitting at the table in the far corner of the room, the secluded one that in the past seated only Amelia and Brook but is now full.

Since this school year started and the Sanders twins moved to town, nothing has been the same. They both joined their table the very first day, and now with my best friend, Derek, dating Amelia, it kind of became our table. Some guys from the team even join us every now and then.

Sliding into the first available chair, I look at my best friend.

"Dude, you have to stop doing this shit. Some of us are trying to eat here."

Derek lifts his face from the crook of Amelia's neck, where he's been doing God only knows what, to look at me.

His blond hair is messy, and his blue eyes have a spark in them. The goofy grin on his face makes me want to throw up, but at the same time, I'm happy for him. It's strange really. I don't remember the last time I felt happy.

Over the years, I've acted like a jerk to Amelia. Other girls I use, but I always went out of my way to be mean to her.

When we were younger, Amelia always looked at Derek like he was some kind of superhero. And he always snuck glances and smiles her way when he thought nobody was looking. But I saw it, so when everything with my family played out the way it did, I didn't want to lose my best friend, too. I was mean and pitiful toward her for years, and Derek was always on the side. Looking but not getting in my way. Until the moment he wasn't.

I watched them go around their feelings the last few months. When Diamond and her friend messed everything up for them because I was blabbing my mouth when I should have shut up—and because she's one crazy, fucked-up bitch—I grew a pair and did the right thing. I talked to Amelia and asked her to give him a chance. Something I should have done years before.

In righting my wrongs, I gave him an opportunity to win his girl back. It was selfless and so not like me, but I couldn't stand looking at his broken-hearted, ugly mug a second longer. What can I say? Even the devil himself isn't one hundred percent evil.

"No way." He shakes his head, and his chin settles on her shoulder. Lia's sitting on his lap, and his hands are around her middle. "We have a lot of catching up to do." The look he gives her makes her blush. "*Years.*"

I roll my eyes at the same time Brook, Lia's best friend, fake-gags on the other side of the table. She doesn't even lift her face out of her notebook to acknowledge them.

"You're just jealous," *she* whispers by my side.

Her voice is low and husky, her words only meant for me to hear. Creating a barrier between the two of us and the rest of the table.

Pulling me in.

I knew Jeanette was there. I saw her before I sat down, but this was the only place left open, so it's not like I could choose where to sit. But I *could* choose to ignore her. So I did. After all, it's something I do best.

Girls are just an irritation for me. A necessary evil if I want to lose myself, even if only for a short time. Forget. They don't mean anything to me.

When my mother left she taught me one lesson—don't trust anyone, especially women. They are manipulative, secretive liars. So I use them and leave them before they can do the same to me. Before they take everything away from me, leaving me with only a broken heart.

But there is something about this girl.

She's different.

The calm before the storm.

When I look into her eyes—those piercing gray eyes—I see something. A recognition maybe? And it scares me. It scares me because if I look too long, she'll see it. She'll recognize it, too, and then I'll be left wide open for her to see *me*. The real me. The guy hiding behind the mask.

Jeanette Sanders could be my undoing.

And I'm not ready for that.

So I do the only thing I can to pull away and break any connection she thinks we might have before it even forms.

My hands curl around the first girl I see passing in my peripheral vision. I tug her and she stumbles on her feet, her hand falling to my chest to steady herself and prevent the fall. Without waiting for her to realize what's happening or asking for permission, I plant my lips on hers.

She gasps in surprise, and I use that moment to push my tongue into her mouth. I have to give it to her; it doesn't take long for her to return my kiss. Now steady enough, her hands run through my hair, pulling me closer as she returns every swipe of my tongue inside her mouth with eagerness.

Predictable.

All of them.

My hands dig into her ass and pull her down on my lap.

My motions are practiced to perfection.

Every move sure and steady.

Fake.

Bored.

Disgusted.

I'm disgusted with myself, but I keep on doing it because the show must go on. And there is no greater stage than my own personal life.

It doesn't take long to hear the scratching of the chair against the floor and loud footsteps moving away. Once I'm sure she's gone, I break the kiss and push the girl off my lap like the nuisance she is.

"What the ..."

Turning back to my tray and the stunned faces of my friends, I wave her away. "You're no longer needed."

She stands there for a few moments longer, her chest lifting with heavy breaths before she screams like an angry toddler and stomps away.

"That was ..." Max looks at me, intrigued. "Interesting."

I shrug, pulling out my phone.

Me: Jealous much?

Me: It doesn't matter to me either way. Willing pussy is a welcome pussy as long as it's hot and makes herself scarce after the deed is done.

What can I say? I can be one charming fucker when I want to be.

Chapter 3

JEANETTE

Slamming the front door shut behind me, I stomp up the stairs to my room. The only thing that greets me is silence, and for the first time, I welcome it. Nobody deserves to see my temper tantrum. Not even my shitty excuse for parents.

Usually, I'd try to hold it in like everything else, all the other secrets I'm hiding. But today, I can't seem to reign in my emotions. They're overflowing all my senses. My mind and body alike, and if I don't let just a part of it out, I think I'll drown.

That stupid, motherfucking jackass.

I let my bag slide off my shoulder with a loud thud before I throw myself face down on the bed, fluffy pillows jumping in the air with the force of the impact.

The phone is still clenched in my hand. His message hidden behind the dark screen still taunting me silently.

Fucking Andrew Hill.

Asshole: Jealous much?

Asshole: It doesn't matter to me either way. Willing pussy is a welcome pussy as long as it's hot and makes herself scarce after the deed is done.

How much of a jerk can one guy be?

Presumptuous, self-centered bastard. That's what he is.

I knew he'd be trouble from the moment I laid my eyes on him. I know his type well. Rich daddy's boy with a house full of issues hanging off of his shoulders.

He thinks he's a godsend to women. Phew, not even in his dreams is he that good.

Frustrated, I turn on my back and stifle my groan with the pillow over my head.

How does he manage to do that? How does he get in my head and mess with me even when he's far away?

Giving up, I pick up my phone, which ended up tangled in the sheets during my fit, and look at the message once again.

I know I shouldn't do it. I should ignore him and his arrogant, patronizing behavior and just let it go. Just like I knew I shouldn't have sent that other message at the party. And just like then my fingers don't want to stop. When it comes to Andrew Hill, my brain acts on its own and doesn't listen to reason.

He makes me do crazy things.

Impulsive things.

Things I wouldn't do otherwise.

Me: Only in your dreams, douchebag.

I want to write more. Say more. Comment on his small, shrinking dick or something equally as awful, but at the same time, I don't want him to think I care one way or another. So I stop myself, and once the message is sent, I bury the phone under all the blankets and pillows so I don't look at it every few seconds waiting for the small light to start blinking, indicating a new message.

Then I sit at my desk and dig out my books, ready to start going through all the homework that's waiting for me. But after I stare at the same math problem for thirty minutes without making progress because I'm too preoccupied with calming my restless feet and consciously keeping my gaze on my notebook, I give up.

I lean back in my chair, my eyes falling on the violin box that's carefully leaning against the nightstand. For a moment, I contemplate taking the instrument out of the box and getting lost in the music, but I dismiss the idea almost instantly.

I'm still high on adrenaline and the anger rush from before and I know I won't do shit if I don't get rid of at least half of it, so I change into a pair of leggings and a sports bra with a tank top over it and go the basement.

When my parents realized that hockey wasn't just a passing fling for Max and that he's actually good at it, Dad decided to make a gym for him so he could exercise at home. You'd think the talent is enough, but you'd be wrong. He spends every free moment of his time either in this gym or on the ice, practicing and shaping the natural talent he has.

The gym isn't as big as a professional gym, but we do have a treadmill, bike, elliptical, a set of weights and a boxing bag.

As soon as I get down there, I turn on the lights, and the radio starts to play with some kind of heavy music Max likes to listen to when he works out. It's usually not my jam, but since this is Max's space and I'm feeling on edge, I let it be.

I quickly tape my fingers before I pull the gloves over my hands. I've done it so many times that I could probably do it in my sleep by now. I don't think I actually need double protection, but Max always insists. He doesn't want me to damage my "musical prodigy" hands, as he likes to call them.

I do a few test punches to check that everything is okay before I turn toward the bag hanging off the ceiling, and that's when I unleash everything.

My frustration.

My anger.

My disappointment.

Punch after punch, I let my gloved hands connect with the bag, enjoying the feeling of pounding into something. Two jabs from my left hand, one from my right, left, right, right, right. I do different series of punches, trying to keep my feet moving the whole time.

If you think about it, boxing is a lot like dancing. You have to keep moving with elegance, grace and speed. And although strength is important, being fueled by anger will not lead you to the win. You have to keep focus, have a cool head on your shoulders. Your mind has to be sharp so you can predict your opponent's next move and strike before you get knocked out.

And although my opponent is imaginary, or maybe it's myself I'm fighting, I don't let the anger rule over me. I get it out, but I'm the one controlling it, unleashing bits and pieces at a time.

One jab at a time.

One hook at a time.

As my legs move across the mat, I slide in a dance known only to me, punching and kicking until my eyes are blurry from the sweat coating my face.

With one final ounce of strength, I grit my teeth and lift my leg in the air. In a perfect arch, I swing my leg and focus all the energy I have left into that kick. My foot connects with the bag and makes it swing as I fall onto the mat, a sweaty mess.

"Who pissed you off?"

My head lifts and I turn toward the door, surprised by the audience.

"Max!" I scold. "You scared me!"

He grabs the towel and water bottle off the shelf and throws them to me. Grateful, I dry my face before I take one long swig from the bottle, downing half of it in one go.

"I called you when I got home, but you were too busy locked down here to hear me."

I look at the clock hanging on the wall. "It's already that late?"

I was so concentrated on my training that I didn't notice the time pass.

"Yeah, I got home a while ago." I nod my head, getting on my feet. They feel wobbly from all the work, but it's a pain I'll welcome every time. "So, will you tell me what demons you've been slaying down here for the last two hours?"

My eyes lift to his, our gazes connecting for a long while. Stormy grays meeting stormy grays. We might not have the same interests and abilities, but we're the exact replica of one another. As much as two fraternal twins can be. We have the same olive skin, dark, almost black hair and gray eyes.

I blink, breaking our stare, and offer him a weak smile. "No demons. It's just been a long day."

Slowly, I walk toward the door, intent on going back upstairs and washing off the workout before I attempt to work on my homework again. But of course my brother doesn't let it slide that easily.

Max stands in the middle of the doorway, not letting me through. His cool fingers brush against my cheek softly before he lifts my chin in the air, making my eyes meet his.

I can see worry play in his irises that makes me nibble at my lower lip.

"Are you really okay, Anette?" He gulps down slowly. Painfully slowly. "If there is something ..."

"I'm fine." I stop him before he can finish his sentence. "Really. It's just been a long day."

"If something were wrong, you'd tell me, right?" He doesn't let it go. Another thing about my brother? He has the biggest, most caring heart in the whole universe. It's something I'm starting to realize again.

Sometimes he's clueless. He isn't perfect; nobody is. He

made mistakes. We both did. Mistakes that lead us in different directions for a while. Mistakes that had a big price tag. No one got out of paying without scrapes. Not Max, and certainly not me. But we love each other, even after all the hurt.

With our family the way it is, it's always just been the two of us against the world. And being the male, bigger and stronger and a few minutes older than me, he takes the role of my protector very seriously. Always has and most likely always will.

I guess that's why the guilt's been eating at him. Why he's always looking at me like I'm a ticking bomb ready to explode. Because the first time he didn't see the signs. The first time, his actions were partly responsible for pushing me into the darkness.

The first time, he couldn't help me.

Couldn't protect me.

Couldn't save me.

But the reality was way different. No matter what he did or didn't do, he wouldn't have been able to save me. I was way beyond the point of saving.

My brother was always there for me. My brother. My best friend. My confidant. My protector. My everything. My *twin.* We were inseparable when we were kids, but things change. People change. And when he needed me to be strong, I couldn't do it.

I couldn't succeed on my own.

I wasn't strong enough.

And when the world around me came crashing down, I spiraled along with it.

Before

"Are you sure you don't want to come? The guys won't mind it." I lift my gaze from my phone and look at the stormy eyes of my twin. He's waiting for my answer, but I can see how he threw a quick glance over his shoulder to check on his friends.

"I'm fine, Max. Really. You should go with your friends."

"Are you sure?" He nibbles at his lower lip.

"Yes, I'm sure." I give him a small smile.

I don't really want him to go, but I don't want to go with him, either. Our freshmen year of high school started just a few weeks ago, but everything is different.

Max is already popular and well-liked by everybody. And me? I'm just his little, invisible sister.

It's not that I can blame them. Max is kind, good-looking and the only freshmen who got to be on the school's varsity hockey team, something that has never before happened in this district. Girls want him because of his good looks and uniform, and guys worship him because of his talent on the ice.

Me, on the other hand, I'm just the girl who got stuck with all the brains and bad genes. While he's athletic, I'm on the chubby side. All the years of hanging out with Max and his friends made me a tomboy. I'm always wearing pants and baggy shirts.

Puberty also hasn't been kind to me. It seems like every time one pimple disappears, another one pops up somewhere on my face, bigger and angrier than before. His black hair is glossy while mine is usually a big mess. His teeth? Pearly white and straight despite years of playing hockey, while I got stuck wearing braces.

We may be twins on paper, but in real life, we can hardly pass as siblings.

Max and I, we've always been inseparable. And I have to

give it to him; he hasn't changed. He still always asks me to join him and his friends, but I see the looks they give me over his shoulder.

Pity.

Annoyance.

I can't take it. They don't want me. They want him. And I won't, under any circumstances, rob him of that. So I decided to stay away. Let Max shine brightly and enjoy high school. We could still do our own thing when we're at home, but not here.

That doesn't mean Max will let me stay on the sidelines. He makes friends easily and expects other people to do the same. But it's not as simple for the rest of us as it is for him. People gravitate toward him. They *want* to be his friend. It's different for me. Kids our age, hell, people of any age, are scared of smart people. I get it. It's not something they find often, and they don't know how to deal with it.

"If you want, we'll be over there just tossing the ball and shit." He waves in the general direction of the open space where his friends disappeared.

"Don't worry. I have to write this music down anyway before I forget it. A little peace and quiet will do me good."

Max nods, but his gaze lingers on me a few moments longer. Finally, he leans down, kissing the top of my head like he always does, and walks away.

Sighing, I pull my headphones and music sheet out of my backpack.

Last night I worked on some new music. Usually, I record every time I play. I don't like to stop to write down the notes because it's too distracting, so I record it and then play it later over and over again, working through the music and writing down the final melody.

Max likes to joke that I'm a musical prodigy, but in reality, I just like to play violin. Mom wanted me to learn how to play the piano, but even before I sat down, I knew it would bore me to death. I was just never patient enough to sit for hours. But the first time I heard the violin, I fell in love with the beautiful, haunting sound it produces. I begged her for months to let me switch my classes until she finally did.

I learned to play all the classical masterpieces—Bach, Mozart, take your pick—but what I really love to do is create something of my own. Something that reflects who I am as a person, how I'm feeling.

I feel the rawest when I play because in those moments I put my every thought and every feeling out in the open. Leaving myself bare for people to see, hear and hurt. So I play for myself. Hidden behind the four walls of my bedroom, where nobody can hear me.

For a while, I write in peace, but then a shadow falls over me. I wait for it to pass; after all, I picked the most secluded spot in the whole yard to be left alone. But when the shadow doesn't move, I finally let the music sheet fall into my lap.

Lifting my gaze, I take her in. She's wearing high-heeled booties and knee-length socks. Her skirt is shorter than what the school policy allows, but it's not like anybody in the school cares. After all, this is a private school, and all of our parents pay big bucks for us to be here. Uniform means prestige, not equality.

Her tight, white shirt is tucked into her skirt, the top two buttons left undone, revealing her ample chest.

Finally, my eyes reach her face. Blue eyes look down at me with interest. She blinks a few times, long lashes fluttering and drawing my attention. Her skin is creamy and she's wearing full make-up, but on her it looks elegant, not slutty. Pink eyeshadow makes her eyes stand out and lipgloss accentuates her already plump lips. Her brown hair is long and silky, falling in a straight line down her back.

Maddaline Adams.

The hottest freshman.

The Queen Bee of the first year.

Future Queen of the school.

I'm not even exaggerating.

She opens her mouth and starts talking, but the music still blasting in my ears prevents me from hearing her. Pulling the headphones out, I look at her.

"Yes?"

"Jeanette Sanders, right?" Her smile widens. "It's so nice to meet you. I'm Maddaline and this is Lana and Nikki. Mind if we sit down?"

Maddaline doesn't wait for me to answer. She simply sits down next to me, her hand covering mine.

"What were you doing?" Lana asks, peeking at my lap.

I look down at the music sheet and swiftly start straightening my papers before I put them safely in my backpack. "Oh, nothing. Just some school stuff."

I rarely talk about my music with anybody except Max. It's not that I'm ashamed of it or anything like that. I've never had friends close enough that I wanted to share my music with. And then there is the fact that not a lot of people—even musically talented people—can read and write their own music. Being school smart is hard as it is, but being school and *music* smart is something completely different.

Maddaline looks at me for a second, but then joins in on her friends' conversation. They gossip about the school's faculty members and students. I mostly keep quiet, because to be honest, I don't know what to think. What to say.

I've never hung out with other girls. Never had girlfriends to talk to, gossip with, discuss boys with, paint our toenails and have sleepovers. And to think that the most popular girl in school just came to me to hang out ... it's just surreal.

"What do you think, Jen?"

"Huh?"

"Milkshake after school?" Maddaline tilts her head to the side as she looks at me.

I nibble at my lower lip, thinking it through. I could be quiet as a mouse and keep to myself, always looking at the others and waiting for something. Or I could take this opportunity. My eyes find Max across the yard. No matter how far away we are, I can always feel him. Our twin bond is so strong, I feel him at all times.

"Why do you want me to come?" I ask, my gaze returning back to the three girls.

They're all so pretty, I don't know why they would even want to hang out with somebody like *me*.

"Because we want to be your friends, silly." She winks at me.

A sense of awareness makes me lift my gaze. Looking over her shoulder, I can see Max looking at me, and then his gaze switches to the girls sitting next to me. Smiling widely, he waves at me. He looks so happy. And almost relieved. I know the last thing he wants is for me to be alone while he hangs out with his friends. And to be honest, I don't want that, either. I want to have friends. I don't want to just stand on the sidelines and look at the others enjoying their high school experience while I'm all by myself.

Maddaline notices my distraction, so she throws a quick glance over her shoulder before her light blue eyes find mine. "That's your brother, right?"

"Yes." I smile softly. "That's Max."

She nods her head. "Cool. Milkshakes?"

My smile widens. I expected her to continue talking about Max and maybe even invite him to join us, but she didn't. Maybe she really wants to be *my* friend.

You can do this, Anette. You can do this.

"Yes, sure."

The naïve little girl I was didn't know how some schemes could be calculated. She believed people were good. Well, she was wrong, and she eventually paid the price.

"Anette?" Max's tentative voice breaks me out of my thoughts.

I lift my eyes toward his. "Yes, of course." I lie because this time, it's my turn to protect him. When my world crashed down, instead of holding on to the people who love me, I did everything to blame them and hurt them. And Max, being the brother he is, took it without a complaint.

Even after all this time, that hurt lingers in his eyes every time he looks at me.

So it doesn't matter if I have to lie, pretend or cheat. It doesn't matter if guilt is eating at me from the inside out. This time, I'll do better. I'll be better. For Max.

He sighs in relief, pulling playfully at the tip of my ponytail. "You hungry?"

I don't get to say a thing before my stomach announces itself. Laughing, I shake my head. "I guess I could eat something."

Max takes a step back so I can get past him. "Great. Get your smelly ass in the shower and I'll call the delivery." He swats said ass as I pass by him.

"Hey!" I try to punch him, but he dodges it easily. "Look who's talking! The guy who wears the smell of the guys' locker room like it's the most exquisite of perfumes."

"I don't know who you're talking about." He lifts his hands in the air. "I smell like a rose."

I roll my eyes and start climbing back up to my room. I grab my stuff for the shower when my eyes fall to the rumpled bed in the middle of my room. Stopping in my tracks, I nibble at my lip as I debate on what to do.

To look or not to look?

If I look, the chances are high I'll get frustrated again. But if I don't look, I won't be able to think about anything else.

After another few minutes of internal debate, I finally give in.

Slowly, I walk to my bed and find my phone under a few pillows and a blanket. Just as I turn it in my hand, the small purple light catches my attention.

Asshole: It's not only in my dreams that you rub against my cock until you make yourself come, screaming my name. You want me, Princess. We both know it.

My cheeks grow warm as I reread the message, stunned. I'm not a pure little girl. Far from it. But there is something about Andrew's dirty words that makes me squirm in my seat. Every time he opens his mouth, chances are something inappropriate will come out. He makes my heart race and a blush creep at my cheekbones.

The memories from that night in the library assault my brain hard and fast, and I feel my body react to his words.

Frustrated, I throw the phone back on my bed and stomp into the bathroom.

"I won't let him affect me."

I chant those words over and over again, not even sure who I'm trying to fool, because I, for sure, am not fooling myself.

Chapter 4

ANDREW

I walk into the class, stopping the teacher mid-sentence.

She frowns at me, her forehead wrinkling in disapproval. I lift my eyebrow, daring her to say something, but of course she doesn't. Her lips press in a tight line as she watches me pass by. Even if I wasn't one of the Wolves, I'd still be Andrew Hill. And you don't mess with Hills.

Smirking, I leave my pink pass on her desk and walk to my seat.

Although morning practice is usually spent in the gym lifting weights, today coach asked a few of us to stay behind so we could discuss this week's opponent and some new plays he created. We got some new additions to the team this year—our most valuable being Max Sanders. So the coach is trying to come up with something new and unexpected that we can use as leverage in the upcoming season.

The Wolves are stronger this year than they have been for a long time, and since this is the final year for some of the key players, me included, we'll do everything in our power to bring the trophy back home. So a free pass on some classes for the greater good is the least coach could do.

Guys fist-bump me as I pass by and girls giggle if our eyes connect for more than two seconds. So predictable, all of them.

Well, all except for her.

Jeanette Sanders.

She looks straight ahead, her face impassive. Her stormy eyes don't stray my way. She doesn't blink or give me a side gaze. She doesn't smile or twirl her shiny black hair.

Jeanette Sanders is something else.

My fingers itch to touch that hair, dark as night and soft as silk. But I clench my hand into a fist by my side to stop myself. If I didn't know better, I'd say she isn't breathing at all. And since that's not possible, I can only assume she's good at keeping herself in check.

I pass next to her, and imagine that, slide into the only available spot that's right behind her.

It's my lucky day.

I don't know what it is about her, but her calmness irritates me almost as much as all those other girls throwing themselves at me.

I let the backpack slide off my shoulder with a loud thud, and I watch her shoulders stiffen.

Jeannette knows exactly who's behind her.

Good.

Our teacher gives me another dirty look before she resumes with her class. Rolling my eyes at her, I pull books out of my backpack and open them on today's lesson.

Leaning forward, only enough so she can hear me but not enough to touch her, I whisper softly, "Hey, Princess, let me see your notebook."

Jeanette doesn't acknowledge me, but I can see her shoulders getting even stiffer, if possible.

Which is the complete opposite of her skin. She's wearing one of those big sweaters that falls off one shoulder, revealing the thin, lacy strap of her bra and her skin. Lots of creamy, sensitive, covered-in-goosebumps skin.

"I know you can hear me."

She continues staring forward, scribbling in her notebook and completely ignoring me.

Despite my better judgment, I trace her exposed skin with the back of my fingers. The current of electricity *zings* between us, burning my flesh, but I swallow the hiss.

I try to pretend I don't remember, but there is no way in hell I could ever forget that night in the library with Jeanette Sanders. Her soft, toned, curvy body draped over my lap. The silkiness of her skin beneath my hands when I traced her naked thighs to pull her closer so her heat could press against my groin and release some of that pent-up tension in my body. Little did I know in that moment that having her in my arms would be like all the missing pieces falling into place. That having her, kissing her, being with her would bring a lot of things but not what I need.

"Princess..." I drawl in warning, my voice dangerously low.

She pulls her shoulder out of my reach, pulling the fallen material to cover her exposed skin. Gray eyes, pissed and stormy, look at me over her shoulder.

"Get the fuck out of my personal space, Hill," she hisses, not caring who hears her before she turns back to look at the teacher.

I catch some chuckles and catcalls from behind me, but I ignore my asshole friends.

For the rest of class, I don't do anything to provoke her. I sit in my chair and listen to the teacher, although she's boring me into an early grave. But before the class ends, I can't help myself; I have to taunt her.

"You can say whatever you want, baby, but we both know you can't escape the way I make you feel."

She doesn't reply, not that I expect it, but I know she heard me.

Just like I know she saw my message but decided to ignore it. Something I should do when it comes to her. This girl messes with my head like no other. If that's not a clear sign to stay away, I don't know what is. But no matter how hard I try, she pulls me in. Taunts me. Even in her silence, she demands my attention, and I can't ignore it.

I can't ignore *her*.

The bell rings, drawing my mind out of the gutter. Jeanette collects her stuff and runs out of the classroom, not once turning to look at me.

I put my junk in my bag, listening to my classmates joke and talk shit.

When I get out into the hallway, I collide with Max.

"Hey! Is An..." But he doesn't get to finish the sentence, because Jeanette's voice travels down the hallway, making everybody stop and stare.

"Get a grip, girl. Just because my brother felt the need to arrange one play date doesn't make us besties."

Even from here, I can see the hurt flash on Amelia's face as she takes a step back. Brook, on the contrary, wants to lash out at the girl hurting her best friend, but Amelia's hand stops her from doing so.

"What the hell..." Max starts toward them, but I hold him back.

"Don't."

There is nothing he can do to make it better, and Jeanette is lost in the sea of students anyway.

Chapter 5

JEANETTE

Once the bell rings, signaling the end of class and the end of the school day, I grab my stuff in a hurry, not even bothering to close my backpack after I dump everything inside and run out of the classroom like my butt is on fire.

This guy will be the death of me.

Stupid Andrew Hill.

Who the hell does he think he is? Sending me those kinds of messages. Making me flustered and so not me while at the same time irritating the hell out of me. Coming into my personal space and demanding attention in front of the whole fucking class. If he wants to be the main clown, so be it, but he doesn't have to drag me into his little show.

Just when I think I'm in the clear, I hear my name being called. Ignoring it, I continue down the hallway, but the footsteps soon come closer.

"Anette!"

"What?" I turn around abruptly, facing a winded Amelia. Her breathing is hard and her cheeks flushed from the exertion.

"Hi." She smiles one of her sweet, innocent smiles, taking a deep breath in. "So I was thinking, maybe we could hang out this weekend? Go to the movies or ..."

I tune her out, my eyes busy scanning the crowd for a mop of dark hair, an arrogant face and that over-the-top swagger that makes me want to punch something. Preferably him.

"Anette?" I guess I'm so preoccupied with trying to avoid Andrew, I don't notice that Amelia is done. Her hand touches mine, a frown appearing between her brows.

Irritated, I pull away from her.

"Get a grip, girl. Just because my brother felt the need to arrange one play date doesn't make us besties."

Lia gasps loudly and Brook's teeth clench hard as she takes a step forward, but I ignore both of them as I turn around on the heels of my feet and start walking toward the exit.

Somehow we attracted attention, so a large group of students has gathered around us. Gritting my teeth, I push through the crowd, their condescending eyes following me as I go. Taking me in. Measuring me. Judging me.

Cold-hearted.

Bitch.

Snobby.

Ice Queen.

I can hear them talking behind my back. They always think just because you're quiet you won't notice, but the quietest people, the ones who stand on the sidelines watching but never participating, are the ones who hear the most. They probably know most people's deepest, darkest secrets, and those same people aren't even aware of it. Because they don't notice the quiet ones in the first place. Because they don't *care* enough to notice.

Yes, I'm all of those things they think I am. And more. So much more than they're aware of. Worse than they can even imagine. But who are they to judge me?

Did Amelia deserve my attitude? No, she didn't. Stupid Andrew Hill threw me off my game, and I lashed out at her because it was easy. She's so damn good that being in her company makes me want to puke.

So innocent.

So pure.

That's because you were once her.

Not anymore.

They have no right. Just a few weeks ago, they were the ones treating her horribly. She was bullied and made fun of for years by those same people who now judge me. But since Lia and Derek started dating, she was magically accepted by the whole school.

Hypocrites.

All of them.

I want to hate them. I want to tell them to fuck off and leave me alone. To look at their own pitiful, miserable lives and stop meddling in mine, but all of this is too much.

Their whispered words.

Their side glances.

Their judgy eyes.

All of it takes me back.

Back to the moment I wish I could forget.

The moment I wish I could change.

The moment I was too weak and I let them break me.

The moment everything changed.

Before

"Have you seen what she was wearing at the party last weekend?" Nikki asks, and they all burst into laughter.

I join in, but it's weak.

I've never been interested in the gossip scene. I've never cared how people dress or who they hook-up with. But these girls do.

We're in my kitchen, having another one of our group study sessions. Usually we switch it up between our houses, but lately we've been hanging more and more at my house.

It was actually my idea, but now I'm kind of regretting it. After the milkshake, I thought things would return to normal. I thought I'd be left alone and Maddaline, Nikki and Lana would be their popular selves, but no. The very next day, they found me in the cafeteria and joined me at my table. I could feel people's eyes on my back. Staring. Thinking. Judging.

What could The Queen Bee and little Jeanette Sanders have in common for them to sit together during the lunch?

I still haven't found the answer to that question, and it's been a few weeks, but they keep me in their group. That day, we exchanged phone numbers, and although we didn't have the same classes, they made a point of sitting with me during lunch and inviting me with them after school. We would go to all the "in" hang-outs. Mall, café, diners, parties... you name it, they—and by extension me—were invited.

After a few weeks of hanging out, I noticed my grades slipping. I spent so much time with them, it didn't leave me enough time to do my homework, so I suggested we have a study group. They agreed, and so every Tuesday and Thursday, we'd meet up at someone's house and do homework.

At first, they even put some effort into it, but lately all they do is gossip. And all I want to do is finish this damn math homework that's been kicking my ass. Yes, even smart people have to study. Smarts don't come easy to anybody; we all have to work for it. You'd think after a while Maddaline and the others would run out of things to talk about, but it seems like the list of gossip topics is endless.

Trying to concentrate on the problem in front of me, I tune them out as much as I can, but it's impossible. They're loud, giggling and talking a mile a minute, their comments snarky and some downright mean. Not that I would say any of that out loud.

Sometimes it's still hard to believe they want to be my friends. We have so little in common. I'd probably have given up by now, but the smile Max gives me every time he sees me hang out with them is so big and promising, I don't want to break his hopes that I'm doing better. That I'm making an effort to expand my horizons and make friends instead of keeping to myself.

"I have to grab something from my room," I say to no one in particular.

They wave me off, not stopping the discussion on whatever topic has them so preoccupied.

I run up to my bedroom and go through the mess that is my desk. It takes a while, but finally I find the paper with all the formulas I've been looking for. Closing the door, I return downstairs. As I near the kitchen, I can hear them laughing. It's one of *those* laughs. The one they have when they're being mean, so I linger in the hallway, not wanting to participate.

"Like seriously, how stupid can one person be?" Nikki snickers.

"They even have a name for her," Lana adds. "D.U.F.F. Like that movie."

"Designated ugly fat friend." Nikki laughs even harder. "I haven't heard that one, but I can't say they're wrong. Have you seen those thighs in the leggings she wore the other day? They're like two trunks of a three-hundred-year-old tree."

All of them burst into laughter. I lean against the wall, nibbling at my lower lip as I look down at my legs, still listening.

I have to know, although I already have a feeling I do ... I have to know. For sure.

"Quiet." This time it's Maddaline who interrupts their laughter. "She could come down any moment, and then everything will go to shit."

My legs are wobbly, so I press them together. My thighs, my *fat* thighs, touching.

"Jeanette may be in all those fancy AP classes, but she's dumb when it comes to people and hierarchy," Lana states, and I can imagine her rolling her eyes at the obviousness of the situation. "Why would she otherwise think we're hanging out with her? She's not even worthy of wearing the title of our D.U.F.F."

"How much longer do we have to pretend anyway?" Nikki whines. "It's embarrassing. People are staring at us. *Talking* about us."

"Not much longer," Maddaline reassures them. "I've been talking to Max, and I have a feeling he'll invite me to the winter formal in no time. After all, he's the school's king, and every king needs his queen. Which is me."

Max has been talking to them? When? And why didn't he say anything?

Although we don't spend as much time together as we used to—with him playing hockey and spending most of his free time with his friends, and me trying to stay on top of my studies and spending time with the girls—we try to have dinner together a few times a week and watch a movie or simply chat to catch up.

And since when is he taking Maddaline to the winter formal? The last time we talked, he hadn't even planned on going.

Nikki interrupts the slight pause. "Do you seriously think

she's that clueless? I guess you have to be not to notice the difference between someone like us and someone like *her*. The only thing she has going for her is that Max is her brother. Otherwise, she'd be useless."

My hands clench into fists by my sides, and I feel the burning in my eyes.

I won't cry.

I won't cry.

I won't cry.

I chant those words over and over in my head, but nothing can stop them from falling when I hear Maddaline's next words. "Max told me she didn't have many friends."

"Shocker," Lana interrupts her.

"And that he's happy she's finally found some girl company. He thanked me for reaching out because she's really shy."

The tears roll down my cheeks. Why has he been talking to them? *Thanking* them? Like I'm some charity case.

"If only he knew he's the only reason we're hanging out with her in the first place ..."

The front door opens and closes. Quickly, I swipe the tears away as best I can before I lift my gaze and find Max standing in front of me.

"Hey, Anette!" He smiles. "I didn't know you were home."

"Stu..." My voice breaks, so I clear my throat before trying again. "Study group."

"Oh ..." He looks over my shoulder in the direction of the kitchen, where we can still hear quiet chatter. "I'm so happy you all are hanging out."

Would you still feel that way if you knew you're the only reason they're pretending to be friends with the fat, clueless girl? I want to ask him so badly, but I bite my tongue. For the first time, he seems genuinely happy.

I know it's been hard on him. Hard on *us*. With our mom

always preoccupied with her board meetings and friends and country club and Dad busy with his medical work, it's been just the two of us against the world. For years it's been us, and when you're as close as we are, it's hard to let go. But I can see it. He wants to let go. He wants to be his own person and not just my twin, but at the same time, he doesn't want me to feel left out.

So no matter how much it pains me, I have to let go. Because if I tell him what I just heard ... he won't do that. I know he'd never do that.

"Yeah, we're almost done though."

Max nods his head. "I'm going to take a shower. Dinner and movies later?"

My eyes fall down, and I look at my body.

D.U.F.F.

Fat.

Clueless.

Ugly.

Trunks of a three-hundred-year-old tree.

The words resound in my mind over and over again until I feel like my head will explode. I switch my weight from one foot to the other, and my thighs brush together.

For the first time in my life, I feel disgust wash over me. I feel fat and ugly and all I can think about is taking a shower and scrubbing that feeling off my body.

"No, I have some homework to finish. Sorry."

His brows furrow in confusion. I've never before rejected the opportunity for us to hang out.

"Okay. I'll be in my room."

I nod once, watching him climb the stairs. With Max out of my sight, I take one deep breath and go back into the kitchen.

"Was that Max?" Maddaline asks as soon as I pass the door.

My eyes meet hers, and for the first time, I can see the real her.

Calculating.

Cold.

Manipulative.

When she says Max's name, her eyes have that special gleam in them. She wants him. Badly.

How did I not notice it before?

"Yeah," I say swiftly.

I can feel their eyes on me.

Watching.

Assessing.

Judging.

As I walk to my seat, I can feel their gazes following me, and the earlier feeling of disgust returns in full force. What are they thinking? Are they disgusted with me as much as I am with myself? Can they see my belly spill over the edge of my jeans? Can they see my thighs touching? Can they hear the sound of my jeans brushing as I walk? They must. I can hear it. It's so loud.

"I'm so sorry to cut this short, but I just remembered we have a family dinner tonight so ..."

I let the rest of the sentence hang in the air.

The look they share between each other would be comical if I had it in me to laugh. "Yeah, of course."

They grab their stuff and start toward the door. "We'll see you tomorrow?"

"Yeah, sure ..." I agree, not even listening.

The last thing I want to do is continue hanging out with them, but I can't stop doing it without raising suspicion. Without giving some reason why. And I know if I tell the truth, I'll break Max's heart. So for my brother, I'll keep up with this charade, even if it kills me.

That night, when I get out of the shower, I let my towel fall to the floor as I look at my reflection in the mirror.

I let my gaze take it all in. My round, chubby, always slightly red cheeks. My full breasts. My soft, round belly. My wide hips and thick thighs.

Those damn thighs.

I was never too preoccupied with the way I look. I knew I wasn't skinny like some girls, but at the same time, I never considered myself fat.

Not until today.

I stare at my body for God only knows how long.

I stare and stare.

Stare until goosebumps cover my bare skin.

Stare until my eyes become dizzy.

Stare until I can finally see what they have been seeing all this time.

Fat and ugliness.

Imperfection.

Monster.

A knock on the door interrupts my thoughts, and I turn away from the mirror. I can't look at myself.

"Y-yeah?"

"You sure you don't want to have anything for dinner?" Max asks from the other side.

My belly rumbles at his words. When was the last time I ate? Probably snacks I pulled out when the girls were here.

Those same girls who think I'm fat.

"N-no. I'm not hungry." My stomach answers in protest, but I ignore it.

"If you're sure." I can hear Max's footsteps as he walks away from my room. Pulling the towel back around myself, I exit the bathroom and go to my closet. I grab a pair of leggings and a baggy shirt to put on before I go down to the basement to Max's home gym.

Their words are in my brain as I climb on the treadmill, the distorted picture of my body in my mind as I make myself run.

Run until my body is a sweaty mess.

Run until my legs are so wobbly I can't stand.

Run until the monster is at bay.

Run until the picture and words haunting me are pushed to the back of my mind.

At least temporarily.

Chapter 6

JEANETTE

Music has always been my saving grace.

My safe haven.

My quiet in the middle of the storm.

The sweet, tormented melody of the violin always finds a way to wrap me in a bubble. Isolate me from the rest of the world.

When I play, when a piece of delicate wood is tucked in between my shoulder and chin and the bow glides over the strings creating the melody that's laying in my heart, I let myself feel all those feelings that are hiding deep in my soul.

The regret.

The pain.

The guilt.

The sorrow.

I like to pretend that I don't feel, that nothing can get the best of me. They think I don't hear them whisper, but when you don't talk much, you have all the time in the world to listen.

Ice Queen, that's what they call me, but they can't be further from the truth.

I would give anything not to feel. And I try. I really do. But the thing is, I'm the complete opposite of what they believe me to be.

I feel.

So much and so fierce it's painful.

The rejection and disappointment from my parents. The ice cold between my family members. The distance with my twin. The loneliness because of my lack of friends.

I feel it all.

I wear this mask of indifference because it's easier that way. If people think you don't feel, they won't try to hurt you.

But there is no escaping hurt.

It finds you when you least expect it, and it tears you down to the ground.

And people who shouldn't hurt you, hurt you the most.

After my encounter with Lia and Brook, I got out of that place and drove straight home. I needed some peace and quiet. I needed to escape from my own cruelty. Get lost in the only place that makes me feel whole.

"Still playing?" Mom's voice breaks through the haze of the music.

I let the last note hang in the air just for a second longer before I lower the instrument and turn to look at her.

Even in her late forties, she's still beautiful. Jane Elizabeth Davies Sanders. Her beauty is timeless, and unlike some other women from her world—a world of old money, debutante balls and arranged marriages, where the only important thing is how far back your last name goes and how old your money is—she doesn't have to work or pay for it. Her silky black hair is collected in a neat, low bun. Not a strand out of place. Her make-up is tasteful and flawless, matching her pencil skirt, blouse and jacket. Pearls, her trademark accessory, hang around her neck. The whole look is accompanied by three-inch stiletto heels that add to her already tall frame.

"Yes." I don't offer explanation or justification.

The only reason I'm in the sunroom—fancy word for back living room, because yes, you need to have a back and front living room—is because I thought I'd be alone and I wouldn't be bothered. If I'd known somebody was home, I'd have stayed closed in my bedroom.

When I was younger, my mother tried to make me be like her. A collected and composed young lady, a spineless creature who would do what's expected without a mind of my own. Instead, she got me. Beauty pageants, tea parties, and piano lessons didn't last long because I couldn't keep still to save my life. I wanted to run around with Max. I wanted to skate, climb trees and play in the park. I didn't have it in me to sit still like a statue and play some crazy old tune written by a musical genius. But there was something about the violin that drew me in.

She assesses me—my ripped black jeans and silver top, messed hair, dark lipstick and chipped nail polish, she sees it all —disapproval written clearly on her face.

"Do you have to dress like such a hooligan, Jeanette?" Her red lips press in a tight line.

"It's called the fashion of the twenty-first century, Mother."

She looks down her body and then pointedly at me. "Well, I suppose they're still capable of producing clothes that are in one piece even in these fashionably horrendous times."

I try to hold in the eye roll, I really do, but it comes out anyway. Thankfully, she's already in her own little world, so she doesn't catch it. When it comes to her children, she notices only the things she wants to see. "I'm heading out. I have a meeting with a few ladies from the board."

At eight p.m.? Meeting my ass, more like a drunk fest at the country club but whatever.

"Sounds fine to me." I shrug indifferently.

I scroll through my phone until I hear the front door close behind her. Only then do I return to playing.

Tucking the instrument under my chin, I close my eyes and let the bow slide over the strings.

There is no introduction, no slow start, not today anyway. I get right down to it.

The bow glides hard and fast over the strings creating a frantic, almost angry melody. There are no rules or finesse to it. This piece is new, the production of my messed-up feelings and anger still running through my veins.

The melody fast-paced.

Explosive.

Skillfully, my hand slides with grace and precision, despite the fact that the music is quick. My whole body moves with the rhythm.

I don't know how long I've been playing. When I take the violin in my hand, time ceases to exist. It's only me and the bow gliding over the delicate strings. Just me, spiraling in the abyss of music. Deeper and deeper into the darkness where nothing except the next note matters. Where I can be whomever I want to be. Where I'm strong enough to fight my past. Strong enough to fight my demons.

Slowly, oh-so-slowly, subtly, the anger is gone. And as my movements slow, the only feelings that are left are regret and loneliness.

All that remains is this beautiful, haunting melody.

The one, that no matter how hard I try, I can't escape.

The one that makes me feel open.

Exposed.

Vulnerable.

The one that makes me feel like—me.

Chapter 7

ANDREW

Pressing the doorbell three times in succession, I take a step back and wait. Again. The sound echoes through the house, but there is no sign of life on the other side of that door. I've been out here for a good ten minutes, ringing the doorbell and knocking, but no luck.

Where the fuck is everybody?

Taking a step back, I tilt my head up to look at the house. It's not as big as mine, but close enough.

Just like me, the Sanders family lives on the outskirts of Greyford. The place where all the rich families live.

Secluded.

Wealthy.

Privileged.

Where the houses are more like mansions and the yards so big, there is no way you'll ever see your neighbor arriving home, much less walking around the house naked.

The thought brings out the hazy image of Jeannette grinding against my hard dick in the library and all the possibilities if our houses were closer than they actually are assault my brain.

Pity.

I probably shouldn't think about my friend's sister like that, never mind that he's my teammate, as well, but I never said I was an honorable bastard.

I decide to take a look around the house before calling it quits.

Max should have been home by now, but I guess he took a detour. Or maybe he stayed at school. Fucker is almost as dedicated to hockey and bringing the trophy back home as Derek. And that's saying something since Derek has lived and breathed hockey for years. I wouldn't be surprised if both of them end up in the NHL.

Sighing, I move backward until I can see the whole house. Except for the front light, all the others are turned off.

Where the fuck is Jeanette, though?

She ran away from the school as soon as class ended, and after her little lash-out at Lia, nobody's heard from her since.

Did she even come home?

Still deep in my thoughts, I start walking around the house.

The good thing about living in isolation? There are no noisy neighbors who can see you sneaking around the house, thinking you're a criminal or serial killer.

As I walk, my eyes scan the surroundings.

The grass is green and neatly cut. A few trees are planted strategically around the yard, but behind the fence is where the real woods start. A couple of rock gardens are in the backyard. They look dull and abandoned, but I guess in the spring when everything blooms, they give this place a certain... *charm.*

I shake my head, murmuring quietly, "Get a grip dude."

Deciding I've already wasted enough time, I quicken my pace. There was no actual reason for me to come here in the first place. Or I could have asked Max if he'd even be home when I left the practice but ...

I shake my head once again. A blunt. That's what I need.

Motherfucking Mary to take off the edge. My hand slides into my back pocket, and I take out the baggy. Making quick work of rolling the joint, I return the bag back to my pocket and grab the lighter. The lone light flashes in the darkness of the night. I watch the tip burn before I bring the blunt to my mouth and inhale.

My eyelids fall shut as I savor the first hit of sweetness. There is nothing quite like it. I hold it in, let it burn in my throat, my lungs, as long as I can before I slowly let it out. My eyes snap open, watching the little white clouds lift in the air.

"Two minutes, then I'm out."

Right next to the house there is a big open terrace. It's currently empty, just like the covered pool not far behind it.

I turn around, looking for ... something. But the only thing that greets me is darkness.

Running my fingers roughly through my hair, I take another long pull off the joint.

I'm not sure what I was expecting. What I wanted to find here.

Why am I even here? Why?

Just as I turn around to go back to my car to drive home, where I can get stoned in peace, I hear it.

At first, it's soft. So soft I almost miss it. I almost write it off as a product of my Mary-induced imagination.

I stop in my tracks. Staying still and just listening.

There is music flowing through the air.

Light. Almost inaudible.

I tilt my head to the side, listening carefully. Once I'm sure I hear it, I slowly start to move toward the sound.

I've never been a big fan of music, going with the flow of what everybody around me is listening to at the moment. When I'm in the car or working out, I turn on the radio and pick the loudest station there is. Music filled with the sound of heavy drums and the deep wail of guitar. But this is something else.

Something completely different.

Something I've never heard before.

The melody is slow, tender. Almost like a lullaby. It's gliding through the air, like it's from another world.

Beautiful, alluring, *haunting*.

It's pulling me in, like a lost sailor on the ocean.

Like the howl of the wind.

My heart squeezes painfully in my chest. And I have to grip harder the little that's left of my blunt so I can steady my hand enough to bring it to my lips.

I move as quietly as possible, following the music. The sound becomes more painful and heart-wrenching as I get closer.

Following it until I come face-to-face with Jeanette-fucking-Sanders.

She's standing in the darkness, but it's like she doesn't even notice it. Her eyes are closed, her head tilted to the side, chin holding the tiny piece of wood tucked between her shoulder and chin. The bow she's holding in her other hand glides over the instrument. Like a lover's caress bringing out the most beautiful of sounds. Her body sways with the motion, her short, black hair brushing against her shoulder—which is completely naked if we exclude the tiny strap of her bra.

I swallow hard, watching her play. It feels intimate somehow, even though she's fully clothed. Even though she's playing in the darkness of her living room. Watching her like this, without her knowing, feels more intimate than looking at her naked.

Seeing her like this, it's like I can actually *see* her for the very first time. See beneath her cold, sophisticated exterior. See beneath her bullshit and bravado. Because when she plays? She's a completely different person. She opens up, bares her very *soul.*

I stare at her.

Without blinking.

Without moving.

Without *breathing.*

I stare and stare, listening to that song that has me knotted up inside. Listening to her shattered, bleeding heart that she's hiding from everybody.

Hell, maybe even from herself.

Maybe you have more in common than you thought.

As I try to shush that annoying voice, her eyes snap open.

I don't know if I did or said something to get her out of her music-induced haze, but now her eyes are set on me.

The gray of her irises is lighter than ever before. Open and vulnerable. Her mouth falls open in a silent gasp of surprise as we stare at each other through the large, floor-to-ceiling window.

I'm not sure how long we stay like that—it could be seconds, it could be days—before she gently lowers the instrument and puts it back in the box that's been sitting on the couch behind her.

My Adam's apple bobbles as I swallow down my nervousness. I'm not even sure why I'm nervous. It's not like I did anything wrong. But the way she acts, the way she moves, it tells me all I need to know.

I'm in some deep shit.

As soon as the instrument is out of her hands, she turns around and comes straight at me.

JEANETTE

I'm fuming with rage so hot, I'm surprised I don't burn everything that's in my path.

Andrew Hill included.

Ever since I met him, the guy's been one huge pain in my ass, but now this? Sneaking up on me when I'm at my most vulnerable? Listening to me play. Staying behind the window like some creep ...

As I go outside, the door slamming shut behind me with force, I go straight toward him.

Andrew takes a few steps back, but doesn't manage to put much distance between us before he stumbles over his own feet, almost falling on his royal douchebag ass. Is this guy for real? And he plays hockey?

"You." My voice is low, scarily so, as I push my finger into the middle of his chest so hard it'll probably leave a bruise.

Ask me if I care.

"Look—" He lifts his hands in the air. "Let me ex—"

I shush him with another hard stab of my finger. "What the hell do you think you're doing, sneaking around my backyard in the middle of the night?"

"It's not actually..." He rubs at the nape of his neck, his lips curling in a looped smile.

"Do I look like I care?" I cross my arms over my chest, tapping my foot in time with my rapidly beating heart. "What the fuck are you doing here, Hill?"

I will myself to calm my breathing and slow down my racing heart, as I don't want to have a heart attack at seventeen.

He scratches the back of his head, mussing the hair as a smile spreads over his lips. He looks almost ... *boyish*. Not that I ever thought I'd use that word to refer to Andrew Hill.

"Well, funny story ..." He chuckles.

Fucking Andrew Hill chuckles.

"Are you drunk? High?"

Andrew chuckles again. "I wish."

Tilting my head back, I take one deep, *calming* breath in. Not that it actually helps, because I'm close enough to sniff the air around him.

"You're actually high!" I exclaim. "What the fuck, Andrew? What if somebody figures it out and they toss you off the team? Scratch that, I don't care. What I do care about is what are you doing in my backyard?"

He waves me off like what I'm saying means nothing. "I was here to see Max."

I lift my brow up in question, putting aside the subject of his intoxicated ass. For now. "Really?"

That one word is filled with so much sarcasm, even a fool couldn't miss it.

Andrew tries to hold my stare, but breaks down. "Okay, not really."

He takes one deep breath in before his eyes meet mine again.

I nibble at my lip as I wait for him to continue. I don't want to let him see it tremble, even if it's from the cool November air. I hug myself harder, rubbing my upper arms to keep them warm. The yard is covered in darkness, but I can see my breath form into small clouds as I exhale. It's been like this for a while now, and we're all just waiting for the first snow to fall.

"I—" Andrew opens his mouth, his eyes zeroing in on my face, but nothing else comes out.

My lips press in a tight line as I shake my head. In resignation? Disappointment? Hell if I know. I turn around on the heels of my feet to go back into the house, but his hands grab my wrist.

Precisely.

Securely.

With one pull of his strong hands, he turns me around and makes me stumble into his arms. I crash into him, chest to chest. Heaving, I lift my gaze to meet his.

"An—" But I don't get far, because his lips are on mine.

What the actual fuck?

Stupefied, at first I can't do anything. I just stand there like a statue as his calloused hands grip my face, digging into my scalp. As his lips, so soft and plump against mine, ravage my mouth.

The way his mouth feels against mine is in complete contrast to the way he turns my world upside down.

His eyes are closed as his mouth devours mine, a little furrow set between his brows.

Andrew nibbles at my lower lip, and I can't help but sigh, opening my mouth, though unintentionally, to his expert tongue. It slides between my lips, interlocking with mine, and I feel my whole body shudder at the contact.

Like a jolt of power suddenly runs through my veins and wakes me up.

My hands that were settled on his hard pecks grip the material of his hoodie between my fingers tightly as my tongue meets his in a dance for control.

A loud moan interrupts the silence of the night.

His? Mine? I'm not sure that I even care.

His fingers, intertwined between the locks of my hair, pull harder. The sting of the motion burns brightly as he tilts my head back, exposing my naked neck and shoulder to him.

"Andrew ..." I pant softly, but he hushes me without uttering a word.

His teeth graze the soft, exposed skin of my neck, making the goosebumps rise on my skin.

Once again, I shudder under his touch. When he gets to the

hollow of my shoulder, he bites softly into the flesh, making me hiss. My fingers run up his pecks and into the soft strands of his slightly long hair, pulling him away.

His lids snap open and our eyes collide.

Forest-green fields meet the dark gray sky.

He blinks away the blurriness and gives me one of his mischievous smiles before his lips attack mine again.

Only this time, I'm ready.

I'm waiting for his invasion, and I meet every swipe of his mouth with one of my own. He wants to plunge his tongue into my mouth again, that sneaky bastard, but I don't let him pass. Instead, my hands grip harder at the silky strands of hair between my fingers as I pull his head back, giving his lip a quick nibble in warning.

Andrew's loud groan fills the night as my tongue gets past his lips and meets his in a sensual dance.

Plunging and pulling, we fight for dominance. One of his hands slides down my back, cupping my ass and pulling me closer.

So close I'm pressed firmly against his body.

So close I can feel the throbbing heat of his cock against my lower stomach.

So close I'm surrounded by his intoxicating smell. The smell of clean, hot male and some sexy cologne and that bloody Mary.

The sweet, offensive smell brings me back out of my passion-induced haze.

What the hell am I doing? I can't go down this road again. I can't. And being with Andrew, doing whatever the hell we're doing right now, can't possibly result in anything sane. I don't have the luxury of going back to my old habits. Not again. Never again. I promised.

That's why I abruptly break the kiss. My hands, that only a second ago were pulling him closer, push him away.

"What ..."

"You better go home, Andrew," I interrupt him quietly, before I turn around and walk back into my house without sparing him another glance.

Chapter 8

ANDREW

Forcefully shutting the door behind me, I listen to the bang echo around the empty house as I stride through the dark hallways without bothering to turn on the lights. It's not like anyone will notice or be grateful for it anyway.

My body is still shaking uncontrollably, both from repressed anger and sexual frustration.

This girl ...

This fucking girl ...

My hands still tremble with the need to grab her and make her melt under me. To crush my lips over hers and hear her moan my name loudly as I subdue her to my will.

I shake my head, trying to erase from my mind the image of Jeanette Sanders in my arms. Nothing good will come of it. Not only is she my teammate's sister, which makes her strictly off limits, but also thinking of her only makes my cock throb stronger and my irritation grow bigger.

Growling in frustration, I go straight to the living room and the bar Dad keeps stocked with alcohol at all times. Grabbing one of his fancy crystal glasses, I fill it with vodka to the top. Throwing my head back, I down it all in one go without blinking.

The crystal *clinks* as I slam it down on top of the bar. Pouring a second glass of vodka, I urge myself to chill the fuck out. I take a small sip, this time intent on savoring the drink instead of throwing it down my throat like it's a glass of water.

The drink burns in my throat, warming me up from the inside out. My hands still shake as I lower the glass to the hard surface. Inhaling slowly, I let the air leave my lungs in a controlled hiss. Only then, slowly, do I will my fingers to relax from their stiff position. They're still shaking, but at least they're not clenched tight.

Knowing there is only one way to relax fully and forget this fucked-up day, I let my hand slide into my back pocket. Grabbing the baggy inside, I take it out and let it dangle between my fingers for a few seconds.

My eyes follow it as it slides though the air before I give a virtual 'fuck you' to the whole world and roll a joint. I put it between my lips and light it up, taking in a deep, shaky breath. Inhaling the sweet scent, I finally feel my body relax.

Fucking Jeanette Sanders. Making my dick itch and then brushing me off before I had her scratch it. For the second time, no less.

I don't remember the last time I hooked up with the same girl without getting my happy ending.

Never. That's when.

N.E.V.E.R.

Wham, bam, thank you, ma'am. That's been my motto since I've known what to do with my dick, and now she's messing with my head. No pun intended.

Running my hand through my hair, I throw myself onto the couch, taking one deep pull and holding it in before I let the smoke out.

My eyes zoom in on the little puffy clouds lifting in the air as my thoughts turn back to *her*.

The way she was standing in that room, completely immersed in her music. The way her shirt fell off her shoulder, revealing that sexy, smooth skin. The way her beautiful, haunting melody called to me.

My chest tightens at the thought, but I push it away.

My fingers grip the cool crystal harder before I bring the glass to my lips and take one long pull, emptying what's left.

I bring the blunt to my lips just as a cool, collected voice murmurs from behind, "Surrendering to your vices, as usual, I see."

A soft chuckle escapes me. Without gracing him with even a side glance, I get off the couch and go to the bar. This night is getting better by the minute, and the only way to keep even the slightest bit of sanity is to keep drinking.

"Good evening to you, too, Father."

John Hill enters the living room, his tall, imposing frame dressed in a top-notch, three-piece suit that probably costs more than the average income of a middle-class household. And that's without including his shoes or watch.

His cold, green eyes take me in, jaw tightening in irritation. Even though he's in his early fifties, he still looks good. Golf and the occasional visit to the gym keep him in shape. Light brown hair, peppered with grays, is neatly cut, thanks to his sacred first-Monday-of-the-month haircuts. A light five o'clock stubble colors his cheeks and taut jawline.

"It would have been even better if I didn't find my underage son intoxicated in my living room. I guess I should be thankful you're at home and not wandering around the town, where only God knows who'd see you. Marijuana, Andrew, really?"

My soft chuckle turns into a full-on laugh. I'm laughing so hard, the freshly poured drink spills over the rim of the glass. "Trying to play Daddy of the Year suddenly, John? What gives?"

"Can't a father just be worried about his son?"

His face is so straight, collected and composed, almost ... almost worried even. For a minute, I actually believe him. I let myself believe him. The image of the guy he once was enters my mind. The way his big, light smile could brighten a room. How his laugh was so strong it echoed all around. Whether I wanted it or not, I would eventually crack a smile myself. How he used to take me to the park and to the rink, where we would play for hours. Then I blink and remember who my father is. First-class lawyer. Con. Politician. Liar.

Taking a pull from the blunt, I put it out in the ashtray. "Try again, old man."

"Okay." He walks toward the bar, where he pours himself a glass of Scotch. Only the best for daddy dearest. "If you want it that way."

"If I want it that way?" I take a swig of my drink, pointing a finger at him, suddenly fuming with rage. "You're the one who's never around. You left, just like she did, and now you have the gall to act all worried?! Well don't bother, because you're so beyond repair they wouldn't give you the Worst Father of the Year award, much less anything else."

My chest is rising and falling violently. And here I thought this day couldn't get any worse. Five minutes in the same room with John Hill is all you need to remind you there is always worse.

"Don't you talk to me like that, young man. No matter what, I'm still your father."

"And a shitty one at that." I can't resist biting out.

"Andrew," he drawls, his voice irritated and resigned at the same time. "You should know by now that the elections are next year and I'm a strong candidate for mayor. This year will be crucial for me. For us."

I roll my eyes at his melodramatics. There is no 'us.' Hasn't been for years. He just needs me to play the part so he can get what he wants. Typical John Hill.

"Taking that into consideration, I need you to stop acting like a spoiled rich kid and step up to the Hill name." He looks pointedly at the glass still crushed in my hand and the blunt already forgotten in the ashtray. "No more wild parties. No more drinking. No more drugs. No more causing problems and fights. Keep clean. Focus on school, hockey and college."

I smirk. "And what if I don't?"

His face becomes grim, a shadow falling over it. "Then we won't have a nice chit-chat like we're having now. We're Hills, Andrew. Failure is not an option."

"Of course not," I deadpan.

We Hills do everything we have to—steal, lie and cheat—just to get to the top. And if you're in our way? God have mercy on your soul.

"Are we done here?" I don't wait for his answer. I have to get out of here. If I don't, I'll punch him in his presumptuous, pompous face.

Just as I reach the door, he stops me yet again.

"Oh, and Andrew?" I stop, not turning around to look at him. "There will be some events I'll need you to attend. It'll look good in the press."

"Of course," I mutter, stalking away.

Because why else would a father want to spend time with his son?

Chapter 9

JEANETTE

"Ouch." I wince, looking as one of the Wolf players slides down the Plexiglas. He was just pushed by the opposite team's player, who skated away like nothing happened.

"That's a foul!" Brook screeches next to me.

For a girl who didn't follow hockey until a few weeks ago, she sure is opinionated.

"There are no fouls in hockey." I roll my eyes at her.

Before the game, I went to Lia's house, where I knew I'd find them. Since Lia and Derek started dating, she hasn't missed any of his games, so I knew she wouldn't miss this one, either. I apologized for my behavior the other day, and being the girl she is, she accepted it before I was even done.

"How can there be no fouls?! The guy practically broke half of his bones with how hard he pushed him into the glass. I'm surprised it didn't shatter!"

"Everything is fair game until the gloves come off." I shrug, my eyes following the game.

The score has been tied for two periods, and now, with just a few minutes left on the clock, the tension in the rink is high.

My eyes follow Max as he intercepts the player from the

rival team, his stick effectively taking control of the puck and sending it to Derek.

It's like the guy has known all along that Max would manage to snatch the puck, and he rushed to be there, close and ready. The connection these two have on the ice is incredible. I've been cheering on Max for years, and there has never been a team he meshed so well with until now. Max and Derek are so in sync, you'd never guess they can't stand each other in real life. Or maybe they can, now that Derek is dating Amelia and all that.

Derek takes control of the puck and starts skating like the devil's at his feet. Defensive players clear the path for him, and just when I think he'll do it, just when I can taste the sweet victory, I hear Amelia's loud gasp on the other side of me. She jumps to her feet, her hands clenching hard against her chest just as I see a player bulldoze into Derek, making him fall face first.

An audible gasp followed by utter silence spreads through the rink as we wait for him to get up.

Everybody except *him*.

Andrew, the last part of the trio, throws his gloves on the ice and launches at the guy still on the floor next to Derek. Andrew lifts him in the air, like the guy weighs nothing, and shoves him into the Plexiglas so hard, the whole rink echoes with the force of the impact. I kid you not.

Nibbling at my lower lip, I suppress the wince when I see his fist connecting with the guy's face without mercy.

You can hear flesh hit flesh, followed by the sound of bone cracking. The rink is that silent.

Through the entire game, you could see that he's been on edge, anger radiating off of him in waves. No matter how hard I tried to ignore it, ignore *him*, I simply couldn't. My eyes still found him in the mass of players scattered over the ice.

He called to me, almost as strong as the call of a warm fire in the middle of a winter blizzard.

Andrew's movements have been faster, his shots harder. Even the slightest misstep of the opposite team irritated him, and he was already thrown in the sin bin twice for hard game.

Well, harder game than usual.

Both teams react pretty quickly, pulling Andrew off the guy since the ref was too busy helping Derek get on his feet.

Amelia sighs in relief, her squeeze on my hand—when did she even get a hold of it anyway–loosening.

The poor girl is so pale, the freckles on her skin look even darker than usual.

"He's okay." I return her squeeze reassuringly. "It's just a bad hit. He'll be okay."

Amelia nods her head, not uttering a word. I'm not sure she believes me.

Together, we watch as Derek gets on his feet, and after a quick discussion with the ref, his eyes scan the stands. When he finds Amelia, he lifts his hand in a wave, smiling. It's weak at best, but I can feel Amelia relax next to me a little.

The team doctor comes to the ice, helping Derek off. His body is stiff as he skates away, but he's standing, so I guess things can't be that bad. He'll most likely have one nasty bruise for a while, probably a concussion, too, but that's it.

The ref turns his attention back to the players on the ice and starts barking orders.

"Do you think they will let us see him?"

Brook and I exchange a knowing look over her head. "We can try."

ANDREW

Looking as my teammate fills my glass full of brown liquid, I tilt my head back and down it all in one go, letting the Scotch burn my throat. Once I'm done, I put it down violently.

"It's time to paaaaarty, assholes!"

My teammates and classmates holler in agreement before somebody turns the music to the max.

Liam, one of the juniors on the team, manages the bar tonight. He starts filling my glass, but I wave him off, grabbing the whole bottle out of his hand and taking a long pull.

Not even the alcohol-induced numbness can help me keep the angry monster at bay.

Once Derek was escorted off the ice, the ref threw the guy who ran him over into the sin bin for the last couple of minutes of the game. But he also threw me in there for coming after the guy while Derek was down. Stupid prick. But whatever. Coach called in another guy to replace Derek, and with retribution still burning in our veins, our team managed to score the game-winning point just in time for the final buzzer to signal the end of the game.

I expected the coach to bite my head off for all the fighting and unnecessary time in the bin, but he was too preoccupied with Derek and his injury. Apparently, my best friend has a mild concussion that will keep him out of the game for at least a week, if not two, and a bruise over half of his body that will grace his skin for a month or so. Fun, fun times.

The chair next to mine screeches, bringing me out of my thoughts.

"How are you holding up, man?" Derek sits down, wincing slightly. With his hand, he's holding on to his ribs.

"I should be the one asking you that." I tilt my chin in the direction of his chest. "What's the verdict? Anything broken?"

Although the team doc didn't think anything was broken, the coach didn't want to take any chances, so he insisted Derek go to the ER. Thankfully, his mom was working, so he was admitted immediately and everything was sorted out extra fast.

"Just bruised. But I'll be out for two weeks. They don't want to risk me re-injuring myself and this time actually breaking something."

I nod in agreement, taking a pull from the bottle. "I'd offer you some, but I don't think it'll go well with those fancy pain meds the doc gave you."

Derek laughs, but his smile soon turns into a grimace. "I guess not. But I'm sure you'll drink some for me, too."

Lifting the bottle in the air in salute, I wink at him playfully. "You know it."

"But seriously, dude, how are you holding up? What was your old man doing at the game?"

Just the mention of him makes my smile fall and a frown deepen between my brows. "I don't want to talk about it," I mutter through clenched teeth. The irritation that was just boiling softly under the surface raises back up.

Digging my hand into the pocket of my jeans, I grab the baggy that I thrust inside after I took a shower and start rolling up a joint.

I noticed it almost as soon as I stepped onto the ice. This new buzz around the rink that hadn't been here. As we took the ice to warm up, doing circles around the rink, my eyes found his instantly. The future mayor cheering on his son to victory. I could have assumed something like this would happen after what he told me a few days back, only I didn't think he'd get into politician mode so quickly.

He waved at me in passing, cheering my name like nothing was wrong. Like he's my dad and I'm his son and everything is perfect in our world. Only it's not. He's never around, always too busy with his next case, his next campaign and next assistant half his age he's screwing behind the closed doors of his office. And I'm all alone in our big family house, throwing parties or drinking myself into oblivion. So perfect. So fucked-up. So like Hills. Both of us.

With shaky fingers, I bring the blunt to my lips and inhale deeply, letting the sweet scent enter my lungs and spread through my body.

"You can talk to me." Derek leans forward, his blue eyes searching mine. "You know that, right?"

"I said I don't want to talk," I say through my clenched teeth. Why is he so insistent? Why is he even here? Shouldn't he be home resting or something?

"Andrew ..." He drags out, and just when I think I'll have to pull a douchebag card and tell him where to shove it, slender fingers wrap around my biceps, drawing my attention.

Inhaling what's left of my joint, I put out the rest before turning around. Slowly, my eyes take the girl in. They travel from high-heeled boots up her long, toned legs and narrow waist. Her ample chest is pushed up and filling the tight, skimpy purple dress that's leaving almost nothing to the imagination. Brown hair is straight, falling down her shoulders to mid-back.

"You were amazing out there today, Drew!" she squeals in her pitchy voice as her fingers dig into my forearm harder. "A real hero!"

I exhale what's left of the smoke directly into her face, not caring one bit that it's making her cough and her eyes water.

If only she knew, I chuckle dryly. There isn't a heroic bone in my body. Nor anything that can come close to it, for that matter.

She continues her chatter, not bothered in the least with my disinterest. I take a few more pulls off the bottle that's now almost empty as I watch her mouth move a hundred seconds a minute. I nod my head and smile when necessary, but my mind is far from whatever is leaving her mouth. What interests me is what I can get into her mouth.

Even without closing my eyes, I can imagine her on her knees in front of me. That silky mass of hair wrapped around my hand as I help her navigate that pouty mouth and take my cock all the way in until her eyes water.

My dick stirs as the images assault my brain. Taking one last pull off the bottle, I finally decide to call it quits. Now, I have other things on my mind.

I lean forward, my hand going to the back of her neck and pulling her closer. Losing my balance, I stumble forward, and instead of plunging my lips onto her mouth, they fall onto her neck. My tongue darts out, swiping over her collarbone and nibbling at the hollow of her neck, making her giggle. The sound is irritating as hell.

Jeannette wouldn't do it. She wouldn't giggle like some hormonal middle-school girl fantasizing about the lead singer of some cheesy boy band when my lips are on her skin.

The thought comes out of nowhere, making me stop.

Where the fuck did that come from?

Jeanette Sanders is just a tease.

An off-limits tease at that.

Shaking my head to clear my mind, I return to the task at hand. My palm goes down the girl's back until I get to her ass. Squeezing the flesh, I pull her closer. My mouth traces a path up her neck, getting ready to kiss her profoundly before I take her up to one of the guest rooms and fuck her brains out.

"Wow..." The quiet voice breaks through my haze, but not enough for me to stop doing what I'm doing. "Is that ... Jeanette?"

Until I hear that one word. One name that shouldn't mean anything, shouldn't make a difference.

But it does.

It so fucking does.

"Yup."

Hearing it is like a cold shower. In the blink of an eye, I disentangle myself from the startled girl, almost letting her fall on her ass as I turn around, looking for what's got my best friend and his girl's attention. When did Lia come anyway?

The girl finds her balance, straightens her skirt and looks around. I find Jeanette the same moment she does.

"Looks like the Ice Queen isn't as icy as we thought after all."

And then?

Then I see red.

Chapter 10

JEANETTE

"Why do I have to do this again?" I grumble, looking up at my twin.

His hand is pressed against my lower back, pushing me through the house as he greets his friends in passing, everybody congratulating him on the latest win.

"You promised you'd make an effort, and besides, Lia is here."

I roll my eyes at him. "Yeah, right. With Derek all beaten and bruised?!"

"He texted there isn't anything broken, but the doctors advised him to try and stay awake because of his concussion, so he said he'd stop by for a little while to hang with the team before Lia drives him home."

"Sanders!" One of the guys hollers over the sound of the music. He comes closer, the two of them doing one of those man greetings with bumping fists, slapping backs and whatnot.

"Where is the rest of the team?" Max looks around, searching for the guys in familiar white hoodies with a blue wolf on it. It seems like that's all they wear, their jerseys and hoodies.

"In the game room." He waves his hand over his shoulder in what I know is the general direction of the game room. Friday and Saturday night parties always happen at Andrew's house since it's the biggest one in the whole town. There are no neighbors close by, nor any adults present, and since Max insists on bringing me along, I've become quite familiar with it. "Some are playing beer pong while others are trying that new game. Well, except Drew and Derek."

That tidbit of information makes me tilt my head to the side if only the slightest bit. Not that I'll actually ask anything, but with Max present, I don't have to.

"Why not?"

The guy shrugs. "Drew is still in one of his moods."

Well, that explains it. Daddy's boy is being a prick. What's new about that?! I want to roll my eyes, but somehow manage not to.

"You wanna join?"

Max looks over his shoulder at me, lifting his brow in question.

"Go." I shoo him away. He opens his mouth, but I give him a pointed stare. "I'll be fine. I'll look for Lia."

Maybe. Probably not.

"If you want to go home, come and find me, okay?"

I nod my head in agreement and watch them both walk away.

Sighing in relief, I look around, deciding on what to do and where to go to be left in peace. I'd probably go outside, but it's freezing cold and my inner California girl won't be able to handle it. Why did we have to move from California to Michigan of all the places?!

It always the same, wherever you go. People mingle around with red Solo cups in their hands. They chatter and they laugh, some dancing, some hanging in groups. Guys trying to appear cool by making fools of themselves—dude, we really don't want to see you do a keg stand and then barf soon after—while the girls look around, judging and gossiping about who wears what and who they hang out with.

Different people, same scene. Always the same.

Before

"Damn girl." A loud whistle makes me drop the hanger and turn around to look at Lana. "What the hell happened to you?"

I look down my almost naked body, without actually looking. In the past weeks—since the kitchen reveal, that's how I refer to it in my mind—I've become an expert at that. Skimming past my reflection in every way possible has become my specialty.

"What?" I ask, dumbfounded. Squatting down, I pick up the dress I was looking at.

Patrick, one of the guys on the hockey team, is organizing a party tonight at his place to celebrate tonight's win. Usually, we just meet there, but this time Maddaline invited all of us over to her place to get ready together.

Giving the dress one last look, I decide it probably won't fit. Putting it carefully back where I found it, I skim through a few more hangers.

When Maddaline suggested I use her closet to find something to wear, I wanted to laugh in her face. Seriously, how cruel can she be? Suggesting little Miss Fat Pants wear one of the Queen B's short, skinny dresses. But I wanted to humor her nevertheless. Let the anger boil in my veins so that when I get home tonight, I remember why I'm going down to the basement to sweat my ass off for hours on end.

"When did you get so skinny?" she blurts, but I can see by the way her lips press in a tight line that she regrets her choice of words.

"Skinny?" I burst into laughter. "Yeah, right."

What kind of game is she playing? Only a month ago she called me fatty, and now she wants me to believe that all that weight magically disappeared? No way am I believing that.

"You should totally wear that dress," Lana continues, walking into the room and taking out the dress I just put back. "It'll look good on you."

She puts it in front of me and turns me around so I can face the mirror. Chatting animatedly, she doesn't even notice how rigid my body is.

My own reflection assaults me before I can think of zoning out. It's always harder to avoid your own reflection when you face the mirror straight on. When you're facing the monster, looking it straight in the eyes.

For the first few seconds, I even believe what she's saying is the truth. I can see the faint stretch marks marring my stomach and thighs. The thighs that, although they're far from being skinny, are no longer touching. The cup of my bra that's slightly too big for my breasts.

"Seriously, you should wear it together with those knee-high black high-heel boots. It'll look amazing and show off your legs."

Oh, you mean my three-hundred-year-old trunk-sized thighs? Why wouldn't I want to show those off to the world?

I want to roll my eyes at her and tell her to stop blabbing gibberish, when my gaze becomes blurry and I can feel sweat rise on my skin. When I blink, it's a completely different picture I face.

My breasts are still super small, the only thing I ever liked about myself now completely ruined and gone, but my stomach is even bigger than before. My thighs press against one another and I'm scared if I move, I'll hear that awful squeaky sound that happens when they rub together.

"What's taking you two so long?" Maddaline calls from the doorway of her walk-in closet.

Lana turns around so we face both Maddaline and Nikki. "Look at our girl Jen here. She's been hiding on us. With all the baggy clothes she wears, it makes sense nobody noticed she's lost some weight."

"Dayum, girl. That dress looks hot on you," Nikki agrees.

I don't say a word. Are they blind or do they really enjoy humiliating me so much?

Maddaline's eyes take me in from head to toe before they settle on mine. She smirks, a knowing look in her eyes.

Does she know? Impossible. I've been giving my best so nobody would notice. Not even Max. But the way those blue eyes stare at me ... the way her lips curl into a knowing smirk, it's like she knows.

"Wear the boots with the dress," Maddaline says before she turns around and disappears into the bathroom.

In the end, I wore the dress and boots. It didn't seem like Maddaline left me much of a choice, not with the look she shot my way.

Shrugging off the feeling that she knows my secret, I try to concentrate on the here and now. I try to reason with myself, because if she knows ... if she really does know, I'm screwed.

The dress starts sliding up. *Again.* Irritated, I tug it back down.

"Stop fidgeting! You're making me nauseous," Nikki grits through her teeth.

The dress continues to slide up, and I can feel it barely holding on to the curve of my ass. My fingers itch to pull it down, but I hold back.

People move as we walk through the house. Two hours fashionably late.

There are whistles and catcalls as our little group strides about, with Maddaline at the center. I try to keep at the back and stay as invisible as possible, but I can feel all of their looks on me.

What do they see?

My heart starts beating harder as all these thoughts assault my mind. I can feel my body's temperature rising, a fine layer of sweat coating my skin.

"Look who finally decided to show up!"

The loud words snap me back to reality, the nervous breakdown withdrawing, if only for a moment.

Maddaline giggles, accepting a one-armed hug and a kiss to the cheek from Nicolas, another one of the hockey players and one of my brother's friends.

"Don't tell me you missed me already." Maddy winks playfully, her hand brushing against his bicep. "We aren't even that late."

"Well, as long as you show up looking like this." His eyes slide down her body and then back up, slowly taking her in. "You can be as late as you want."

She giggles again, shaking her head at his antics, but doesn't say anything.

"Did you girls ..." Nicolas turns his dark eyes in our direction. They slide over Nikki and Lana until they land on me. And then they don't move.

His eyes bulge out and his mouth falls open as he stares at me, not even trying to be subtle.

"Is that ... is that Little Jeanette Sanders?"

I shrug weakly, not knowing what to say as his eyes roam my body. Uncomfortable, I switch from leg to leg, but the only thing the motion does is help my skirt rise even further.

Dark eyes stay glued to my legs, and for a moment, I stop breathing. My heart beats faster and faster as he keeps staring at me.

I want him to stop.

I *need* him to stop.

Cold sweat coats my skin, and the only thing I can hear is my heart thumping wildly in my ears.

The bile rises in my throat, and just when I think I'm going to throw up in the middle of the party, his eyes finally leave my body and concentrate on my face.

"You're looking hot, girl!" The surprise in his voice is clear.

Girls' giggles break through the sound of my pounding heart. But only barely.

"We tried to tell her that, but she doesn't believe us!" Lana nudges me playfully with her hip.

"Who doesn't believe you on what?" Patrick joins our group, two Solo cups in his hands.

His smile is big, showing off his pearly whites as he looks around our group.

"Jeanette," Nikki offers, giving him one of her sweet smiles and innocently batting her eyelashes. "She's been hiding on us."

His blue eyes settle on me, his gaze holding mine.

"Keeping secrets," Lana chimes in.

"Does she now?" He lifts his brows, offering me a cup.

"Mhmm ..." Nikki takes the second cup out of his hand. "And now, she'll have to pay. Bottoms up."

She clinks our cups and brings the red plastic to her lips. Her eyes stay glued on me until I do the same. Together, we tilt our heads back and let the cool liquid slide down.

Regular folks get beer, but for Maddy and her group, only the best. Usually cocktails.

I don't know who makes them or what they put inside, but this time I welcome the slight bitterness of tequila—or is it vodka?—mixed with sweet orange juice.

I only manage half the cup before I start coughing. They start laughing, but at this moment, I don't have it in me to care. I'm concentrating on starting to *breathe* again.

A big, warm hand lands on my back, tapping lightly.

"Come on. Cough it all out," Patrick says, his taps steady on my back.

It takes a few minutes, but when I get it under control, I slowly lift my head. My cheeks are bright red, partly because of all the coughing and partly in embarrassment.

Looking at his blue eyes under my eyelashes, I find him smiling. "Better?"

I nod once, nibbling at my lower lip.

This is disastrous. What else can happen to make this day even worst? I'll trip over something and break my ankle? Or maybe I'll fall down and the material of this dress will finally give up and rise, baring my butt for the whole world to see.

"Don't worry, it happens to the best of us."

"I guess so," I say, my throat hoarse. "I think I should go and grab some water."

Patrick's hand lands on the small of my back. "Let's get you some, shall we?"

My whole body stiffens, but he doesn't say anything, although I'm sure he has to feel my discomfort.

Slowly, I take in one long breath, trying to will my body to relax.

As if he can read my thoughts, Patrick's smile widens. "Don't worry, I don't bite."

Nervous laughter parts my lips.

"That is, if you don't ask me to." He winks, and I can't stop the bright red from coloring my cheeks.

Not in embarrassment.

Not in discomfort.

No, this time it's something different.

This time it's in excitement.

Now

Shaking my head, I shove the memory back into the box where it belongs—one that's closed for good and if I never open it again, it'll be too soon.

Pulling my sweater over my chilled fingers, I see the bar is relatively empty, with most of the people scattered around the room. Some are sitting on the couches in the dark corner, others dancing on the make-shift dance floor.

Pushing through the people, I make my way to the bar.

The guy behind it is about to give drinks to a couple of girls giggling on the other side. He winks at them playfully before he turns his attention to me.

He's cute, I have to admit. Well over six feet, but kind of on the skinny side. His brown hair is shaggy and all messed up, but in a cute way. His big brown eyes sparkle with mischief as he looks at me, his lips curled in a big smile.

Slowly, he comes closer, leaning over the bar so he's in front of me. If I didn't know better, I'd say he's pulling one of the classic guy tricks. It-is-so-loud-in-here-I-have-to-push-my-head-into-your-cleavage-to-hear-you-better bullshit, but he doesn't do it in the sleazy way most guys do. No, he has a young, almost innocent air about him. Kind of reminds me of a younger, male version of Amelia.

"What can I get you, beautiful?"

"Oh, it's gonna be like that?" I laugh, shaking my head at his innocent grin.

"Don't know what'cha talking about." He scratches the nape of his neck.

"Pleaseee," I drawl, rolling my eyes playfully. When was the last time I did that? "Throwing compliments and nibbling at that lip playfully. How many hearts have you broken tonight?"

A husky laugh parts my lips, startling me completely.

How long has it been since I've laughed with a guy? Flirted? It feels foreign, but I'm quite sure that's exactly what I'm doing. Flirting. With a guy who's most likely younger than me.

"I'd never do that." He wiggles his finger in front of my nose. "I'm one of the good guys."

I lean forward, pursing my lips. "Mhmm ..."

He shakes his head like he doesn't know what to make of me, which makes me smile. "So ..." I wave my hand in the air, waiting for him to fill me in on his name.

"Liam."

"Liam." I smile. "Do you know how to mix fancy drinks or you do you simply pour whatever gets in your hand first?"

"Thought you'd never ask." He winks at me.

Taking a step back, he keeps holding my stare for a heartbeat longer.

"Jeanette," I say. "My name's Jeanette."

"Jeanette," he murmurs, trying my name on his tongue. "Got it."

Liam turns around, fishing a cocktail mixer out from somewhere and starts preparing my drink. I watch him as he works, a little surprised to find out he actually knows his shit around the bar. After expertly mixing a drink, he pours it in a Solo cup and hands it over to me.

"I'd put it in a fancy glass, but I think we're safer if we stick to these." He tilts his chin in the direction of the cup that's nestled between us, his hand still wrapped around the plastic.

When he doesn't remove it, I lift my brow in question. "Mind if I take that, or did you make it for yourself?"

Liam grins, his slightly crooked tooth flashing in the dim light of the room. That little imperfection making him look even cuter. Like someone's sweet little brother or that little Beast of Amelia's. Max's name for her dog, not mine.

"Come and get it," he taunts.

My smile widens as I lean forward, my still cool fingers brushing against his warm ones as they wrap around the cup.

"What the hell do you think you're doing, Rookie?"

The fine hairs at the nape of my neck rise at attention. My fingers flex around the plastic cup, but I will them to relax because the last thing I want is to spill the drink all over myself.

Slowly, I bring the cup to my lips, taking a long, calming pull before I put it back down on the bar, finally ready to turn around. What I don't expect to find is Andrew so close to me.

My chest brushes against his, my nipples instantly hardening at the feel of his strong chest touching mine. Traitorous little things.

Frustrated with myself, I puff out a breath of air and tilt my head back so I can look him in the eyes.

I'm tall for a girl, but Andrew still has a few inches on me, and with him standing so close in my personal space, I have to do anything possible to put him in his place.

"Need something, playboy?" I arch one of my brows in question, sarcasm dripping in my voice. "A bottle you can drown your arrogant, rich ass in?" Something behind his back draws my attention. A disheveled brunette, tall, lean and in a skimpy dress looks at us with interest. Her eyes find mine, and I can see anger rising in them. Typical Andrew ho. A smirk curls my lips as I return my gaze to his furious green eyes. "Or maybe you're just looking for a condom so your dick doesn't fall off once you dip it in one of your pretty, foolish girls?"

Andrew takes a step closer, his toes touching mine. His eyes narrow as he looks at me, his jaw clenching so tight I'm afraid it'll snap in half any second now.

"Jeannette." The low growl that comes from his mouth is a warning, loud and clear, and the vein on his forehead is throbbing. I never thought I'd see that happen to kids our age, but I guess I was wrong.

"Andrew." I fold my arms over my chest, not taking a step back.

Who does he think he is? The biggest manwhore in the whole town thinks he can give me a lesson in decency just because he saw me flirting with a guy?

He leans closer, completely caging me in against the bar. So close I can smell him, the clean, manly smell of pines and woods, mixed with alcohol and sweet smoke.

"You're playing a dangerous game, Princess," Andrew whispers in my ear, making goosebumps rise on my skin.

I lean closer, not letting him intimidate me. "I never invited you to tag along."

We stare at each other. Green eyes facing gray ones in a stare-off worthy of a high-stakes poker game.

After God only knows how long, his jaw relaxes and a small smirk forms on his lips. "Do you really think I'd sit around and wait to be invited?"

Small, devilish smirk.

"Fat chance in hell."

With that, his hand grabs the nape of my neck and his lips crush to mine.

Chapter 11

ANDREW

At the first touch of my lips on hers, I can hear her gasp. And what a sweet, sweet sound it is.

Delicate.

Feminine.

Her lips part, opening her mouth for me to devour it.

Devour her.

My hands cradle her cheeks, holding her hostage as my tongue slides into her mouth, relishing in her sweetness. I can taste whatever drink Rookie whipped up for her on her tongue as it slides against mine in our never-ending battle for control. Mixed with a sexy, exotic fragrance of perfume and something that's just her, it makes my head go dizzy with desire.

Need.

She overflows my senses completely, the only thing I can feel, see and hear, just her.

Only her.

Although I caught her off guard, she doesn't stay that way for long. Her fingers dig into my shoulders, her body pressing tight against mine.

One of my hands slides off her cheek and down her neck, caressing her shoulder in passing, the curve of her waist and hip until I reach her ass. I push her tighter against me, my bulging dick nestling against her lower stomach.

"Shiiiit," I hiss softly against her lips. Even through our clothes, I can feel her inviting warmth.

Enveloping me.

Provoking me.

Fucking owning me.

Trying to regain even a sense of control, my fingers dig into her hair, pulling her head back.

Her eyes snap open, but it's not frantic passion that awaits me in her gray eyes.

They're hard and cool.

Completely unfazed.

Before I can blink out of my daze, her hand connects with my face, the slap resounding hard in the room. Or maybe it's just my imagination. My hand touches my burning cheek, as I work my tender jaw.

For a girl, she has one nasty right hook.

"I'm not one of your Hill-hoes that you can use and dump as you please." Her voice is low, too low as she spits the words out. Completely disgusted. The only thing I'm not sure of is if it's with me or herself.

She wipes her mouth with the back of her hand before she pushes past me and starts walking away.

Frozen in my spot, I lift my gaze only to find big, round eyes looking at me from the other side of the bar.

"What do you think you're looking at, Rookie?"

Damn him, it's all his fault.

Dude lifts his skinny hands in the air in surrender. "Not going there, man."

"You better not." I give him one last warning stare before I turn on the balls of my feet, debating on what to do.

It's clear Jeanette doesn't want anything to do with me.

But for some crazy, fucked-up reason, I can't get her out of my head. She's messing with my mind, and I'm starting to think she won't go away. Not until I fuck her out of my system.

So although I know I most definitely shouldn't, I surrender to my crazy wishes.

I know I'll regret it.

I know it's fucked up and wrong on so many levels.

I know that Max will probably have my ass handed to me if he ever finds out. Which, from the little display a while ago, will probably be sooner rather than later.

Yet, still ...

"Jeanette," I call, running after her.

The music is loud, but I can still see some people turn their heads as I pass by. Let them look. It's not like I care.

"Andrew." Grabby hands scrape my forearm, but I brush them off, not caring in the slightest who it is or what she wants.

"Not now."

I storm out of the living room, where most of the people are, and continue down a much darker, quieter hallway.

Just when I think she got out of the house, I hear the rattling of a locked doorknob. Turning around the corner, I lean against the wall, looking at her. Frustration mars her face as she tries to open the door to John's study. Irritated, she punches the door before she presses her forehead against it.

"It's locked."

My voice startles her. Abruptly turning around, her stormy eyes meet mine.

"No shit, Sherlock."

I roll my eyes at her sass, but she doesn't find me amusing.

"I was looking for Max."

"The last I heard, he's in the game room." She pouts at my words.

Her lips call to me, so much so that I can't avert my gaze.

That little, taunting pout I want to suck off her face. The curve of her full lower lip that simply begs for me to nibble at it until she opens up to me.

I can still hear her little, barely audible gasp in my mind. So sexy. So needy. So provoking.

I've been with a lot of girls, I'm not even bragging, but not one of them ever twisted me up like Jeanette Sanders has. Not one of them could get me hard with a quirk of her brow. Maybe that makes me a masochistic asshole, but I can't help myself.

"Come with me." I extend my hand toward her.

"What?" She wants to take a step back, but she's already pressed against the wooden surface. "I'm not going back there. Hell, I'm not going anywhere with you. I just want to be left alone until Max is done so we can go home."

Her harsh words don't affect me in the slightest because I can see her mind working. The way her eyes take me in, debating on what to do. To go with me or not to go. If she doesn't go with me, she can either go back to the party, which we both know is not her scene, or go outside where, given the fact that she's dressed only in a thick sweater and jeans, she'll freeze her ass off.

White teeth flash in the dim light as she toys with her lip. The one I wanted to nibble at just seconds ago. My Adam's apple bobbles as I swallow, taking a step closer, my hand still outstretched.

"You know you want to go, Princess."

The nickname falls off my lips effortlessly. Never before have I ever had a nickname for a girl. I never cared or paid enough attention to call any of them by name, much less give them nicknames, but Jeanette... From the first time I saw her, sitting in the classroom all alone in her cool, collected glory, I knew she was nothing like the girls from Greyford.

She's different. High class and almost arrogant, with a

bitchy attitude. The nickname was supposed to be insulting, and maybe it was in the beginning. A way to taunt her. A way to get a reaction out of her. To see what's hiding behind her icy exterior and try to *figure her out*. But now when I call her that, it doesn't sound insulting.

Not even close.

A cute little frown appears between her brows again, her lips pressing together.

"Fine, but only for a moment."

Chapter 12

JEANETTE

My eyes roam freely around the big, messy room.

The last place I expect to end up when Andrew asked me to go with him is his bedroom, but here I am. Maybe this is where he takes all his conquests.

"No, I don't bring girls up here," he deadpans when he sees my face. I guess I didn't hide my disgust well enough.

"I didn't say anything," I defend, looking around so I can avoid his probing eyes.

The walls are bare, dark gray, and a huge king-sized bed is in the middle of the room with a messy deep-green comforter, as if he just got out of bed and was too lazy to make it again. The desk on the other side of the room is full of books and papers, backpack thrown on the floor close by and completely forgotten. The same goes for his hockey duffle. A few sticks randomly lean against the wall or furniture, one even peeking out from underneath the bed. Two doors lead to the en-suite bathroom and walk-in closet. And, of course, there is a huge television plastered on the wall.

A total guy room.

The only thing that surprises me is that it doesn't smell half bad. With all the hockey equipment, you'd think there would be a stale, locker room smell to it, but nope. The only thing I can smell is his fabric softener and something that's completely Andrew.

"You didn't have to, your face says it all, Princess."

The frown on my forehead deepens. "Why do you insist on calling me that?"

"Because I can." He shrugs, a mischievous smile curling his lips. "And because you hate it. Did you know a special sparkle appears in your eyes when you're pissed off?"

Andrew starts coming closer, his grin only growing bigger with every step I take backward to put some distance between us.

"First your eyes widen in surprise. Then they narrow. Ice melts and becomes fire. Raw, angry, all-consuming fire."

I swallow hard, not saying a word. Taking another step back, I find a hard surface behind me. The bed. The unexpected obstacle makes me stumble, but I don't fall because Andrew leans forward, his hands wrapping around my wrists and holding me tight.

Tilting my head back, I look at him. He's standing close. So close I can feel his hard body against mine.

He puts my hands on his chest.

Hard.

Steady.

Warm.

Green eyes look down at me, searching my face for God only knows what. The now-familiar scent of pines and greenery surrounds me.

His lips part, tongue darting out and swiping over his lower lip as he studies me.

Waiting.

I feel my own lips react, parting slightly. The silent *whoosh* of air leaves my mouth and touches his skin.

His eyes grow darker, pupils dilating, and my heart kicks up a notch.

What is happening right now? Only a few minutes ago I was pushing him away and slapping him just to convey my message properly, and now we're at it again?

"I enjoy watching you melt, Jeanette."

The back of his hand brushes against my cheek.

"Watching you melt in my arms."

I want to protest, but he doesn't give me a chance. His lips crush against mine firmly, demanding I open my mouth, and I do. I fucking do. Not to return his kiss, but to put him in his place, only he doesn't know or care. His touch becomes firmer, tongue brushing against my trembling lips, and my traitorous body gives in.

Just like he said, my body melts in his arms as his lips swipe over mine. My mouth parts, letting his tongue probe inside and making me moan.

Arms that a minute ago were trying to push him away now clench around the thick fabric of his hoodie and pull him closer as we both assault each other's mouths.

Faster.

Harder.

Sloppier.

Our tongues mash together in a dance for dominance. His hands roam my back. They go down, down, down until they reach the curve of my ass. His fingers dip into my back pockets and give me a firm squeeze as he hoists me up.

"And—" I try to protest but am too startled with the sudden shift.

My legs wrap around his waist tightly, and I can feel his

hardness press into my center. My head falls back at the feel of him pressed so close to me, and I have to bite my lip to stop a moan from coming out.

Completely oblivious, he switches his attention to my neck. His nose traces the path from my collarbone all the way to the back of my ear, where he presses his lips in a kiss, the warm air tickling my skin.

"So soft," he rasps.

It feels good, so fucking good, the way his body molds to mine.

My fingers dig into his scalp, running through the soft, messy strands of hair. Tugging at the ends, I pull his head back so I can look into his eyes. His pupils are dilated, gaze hazy—but not with alcohol or any other substance—with lust.

What's left of those green irises looks at me like he wants to eat me alive, and my body shudders in his arms with need.

Why do I want him so badly?

There's nothing good or charming about Andrew Hill. He's everything I'm supposed to stay away from, everything that could be the cause of my fall, yet my body doesn't seem to get the memo. My body wants him. Even worse, *craves* him. And in this moment, I don't want to resist him.

But that doesn't mean I'll let him have all the leverage.

I softly bite into his lower lip, the unspoken warning making him groan into my mouth.

"You don't hold all the power, asshole," I whisper in his ear as my lower half brushes against him.

His fingers, still cupping my ass, hold me still, pressed firmly against him. The smirk that spreads over his lips, taunting. "We'll see about that, Princess."

ANDREW

You don't hold all the power, asshole.

Her words echo in my mind as my lips assault hers without mercy. My hands hold her body close although, for all her words, she's not trying to get away from me. If it's possible, she's trying to get closer. Her hand wraps around my neck as her legs squeeze tightly around my waist, my throbbing dick pressing even more into her heated center.

I groan in approval, my hand slipping inside her sweatshirt and caressing the soft skin of her back. When my fingers reach the clasp of her bra, I tug it open.

Breaking the kiss, my lips follow the path of her chin, neck and finally collarbone. Her head is tilted back, her eyes closed, and I can see her pulse hammering in her neck, the result of her rapidly beating heart.

A smug smile appears on my lips as my fingers wrap around the edge of her shirt, ready to pull it off.

"Don't." Her hand shoots forward, delicate fingers wrapping around my wrist.

I look up at her suddenly worried face. She's gnawing at her lower lip worriedly, and all I can think about is soothing her. The need to reassure her, make everything all right, is even stronger than the desire boiling in my blood.

What the hell is happening to me?

"What's wrong?" My hand cups her face, fingers brushing against her cheek.

Jeanette lets her lip go, the pouty flesh red and plump from our heated kisses.

Sexy.

Inviting.

Not able to resist it, I brush my lips against hers.

Once.

Twice.

"Tell me what's wrong," I murmur against her lips as I lower her to the bed.

She looks up at me with those dark eyes. So open and vulnerable. Her hair is spread over my pillows, shining against the crispy white sheets.

"Light ..." she says, but stops.

I frown. "What about it?"

Color flashes on her cheeks, and for the second time, I see something beneath the cool and composed mask she wears for the world.

I see that softer side that's hidden underneath the surface.

The one I saw that night when I caught her playing the violin.

"Can you turn it off?"

I look at her for a few seconds longer. I don't want to do it. I want to see her body react to my touch. I want to see her face when I enter her. I want to see her fall apart. But the worry in her eyes is evident. So for the first time in my selfish life, I comply and do as she asked.

I want her.

I want her so badly my whole body is stiff with need to have her.

Any way she'll let me.

When the room is safely clouded in darkness, except for the faint light of the moon, I return back to the foot of the bed.

Jeanette hasn't moved an inch, and I can see her playing with her lip again.

"Where were we?" I ask, my voice husky.

"You were just about to take off your shirt."

"I was?"

Her eyes glide over my body, so hot and intense. "Mhmm ..."

Reaching behind my back, I pull my shirt off and let it fall to the ground before I climb onto the bed, my body hovering over hers.

Instinctively, her legs fall open, making more room for me.

Inviting.

Needy.

I chuckle, my hand brushing against her side. Up and down, my fingers trace, tugging at the edge of her shirt. "I think it was something else."

This time when I try to pull her shirt up, she doesn't stop me. The material slides up, revealing her creamy skin. Throwing her shirt and bra aside, I let my hands caress her skin. Her tits are exposed, moonlight falling over them and accentuating her erected pink nipples.

My mouth waters at the sight.

My fingers trace a path up, over her tiny waist, and cup her breasts, pushing them closer, thumbs brushing against the sensitive tips.

Her eyes fall shut and she arches her back, pushing her tits further into my touch.

I lean down, my head hovering over her chest. "Eyes on me Princess," I murmur, my hot breath touching her exposed skin and making me shiver.

Reluctantly, she opens her eyes, dark gray orbs looking at me. "You don't get to tell me what to do, Hill."

There is a little bit of anger mixed with sexual frustration, and it's making me smirk wider.

"If you want some of this." I push my hips further into her so she can feel my hardness. "Then yes, I do."

Without giving her a chance to say anything, my mouth

wraps around the erected tip of her nipple, pulling it deep into my mouth.

Moaning, she pushes her boobs into my face, her hand running through my hair and holding me to her.

"An-drew ..."

Encouraged by her soft whimpers, I continue playing with her tits, switching between the two. My tongue swipes over the hard tip before I nibble at it. Sucking and teasing, I play with her body.

But it's not enough.

I want more of her.

Need more of her.

My hand goes down her stomach, flicking open her jeans and dipping inside. Her legs open wider, making more room for my hand. She's so hot, I can feel her heat radiate even with clothes on, but this close, it's like fucking fire. My fingers slide through her lower lips, opening her and feeling her slickness.

I groan loudly against her nipple when my fingers find her entrance.

Torture.

That's what it feels like touching her but not being inside of her. Like motherfucking torture.

She's so hot and wet.

So perfect.

I toy with her, teasing her entrance, as my mouth wraps tighter around her nipple. Her hands pull my hair as her body wiggles, trying to find its way to release.

"Soon, Princess," I chuckle against her skin. "Soon."

She pulls my head, inviting me upward. I kiss my way to her mouth, and when our lips mash together in another fervent kiss, I push my finger inside her.

Jeanette clenches around my hand, moaning loudly into my mouth.

Pleased, I work my finger inside, adding a second one. She's so freaking tight, but the way she responds to my touch is pure perfection.

She's melting in my arms, and I'm ready to be swept by her current.

Increasing the speed, I time the thrusts of my fingers with my tongue dipping into her mouth.

Her hands hold my head, angling it the way she wants it. Giving her a sense of control, when in reality she doesn't have any.

With my free hand, I cup her boob, my finger flicking over her nipple, pinching the soft flesh.

Jeanette whimpers, this time louder. Overstimulated, her body starts trembling beneath me as her pussy squeezes my fingers tightly. I finger her faster as she falls over the edge, her head falling back into the pillow as her body arches into me.

Slowing my caresses, I help her down from the high. My lips brush against her cheek. "You had enough?"

Weakly, she shakes her head no, making my smile widen. Scraping my way down her neck, I kiss the hollow of her throat. "Want more?"

"I want you." She kisses me on the side of my lips. "Now."

"Somebody is feeling needy," I tease.

As fast as I can, I pull my pants down, freeing my raging dick. Jeanette inhales sharply as she looks at me with wide eyes. I fist it in my hand, pumping slowly, letting her get her fill.

"Somebody needs to stop all the talking and do more fucking."

Laughing, I open the drawer of the nightstand and grab a condom.

"You sure?" I ask one last time as I tear open the wrapper and put it on. "Last chance."

Her hands wrap around my waist, fingers digging into my skin. "Now."

Spreading her thighs, I settle between her legs and plunge inside.

A slow, painful hiss parts my lips, my head falling forward. She's squeezing me so tightly, so perfectly, I can barely breathe.

My cock is pulsing in tune with her pussy clenching my length.

Gritting my teeth, I hold still, waiting for the first wave of pleasure to subside so I don't embarrass myself.

Her mouth takes mine. We kiss, hard and deep, her tongue plunging into my mouth as she starts to move slowly.

Following suit, I start moving, too, giving her time to adjust.

Our hands roam over our slick skin, mouths never breaking the touch as we start moving faster.

I pull my dick all the way out, the tip barely touching her entrance before I'm back inside. Every time deeper.

"More," she rasps, her glassy eyes pleading with me, and all I can do is comply.

My hands slide underneath her, gripping her hips and moving her up. The new angle gives me more leverage, making my thrusts harder, strokes deeper.

Her hands slide down my chest, nails scratching my skin. Shivers run down my body as I increase the tempo.

Her walls squeeze around me, and I can feel the pressure starting to build at my lower back.

Leaning forward, my lips brush against her neck. "I'm going to come," I pant against her skin, each word accompanied by a strong thrust. My teeth scrape her skin, and with one final thrust, her pussy grips me hard, milking me until there is nothing left.

I thought once would be enough. To have her just one time,

fuck her brains out and be done with it. But now, when I'm so deep inside her, I realize how wrong I've been.

How silly.

Once will never be enough.

Not with Jeanette Sanders.

She, in all her contradictive ways, has become a habit I do not want to break.

Chapter 13

JEANETTE

The door closes softly behind me, but I still cringe at the sound. Staying still, I lean my head to the side, listening carefully for any noise coming from the bedroom.

I left Andrew sleeping soundly, but you never know. Lying on his stomach, his hair tousled from my fingers, he looked so innocent and peaceful I didn't want to wake him. Or, if I'm being completely honest, what I didn't want is to face him. Not after what just happened.

Sighing, I run my fingers through my own hair, praying that it looks presentable. I put on my clothes as quickly and quietly as possible in the darkness of his room, but I'm sure whoever looked at me now would know what I've been doing. My lips still feel tender from his kisses, and I swear I can scent the smell of sex and Andrew all over me.

Once I'm sure I'm in the clear, I continue quietly down the hall. When I come to the stairs, I can hear the faint sound of the music. It's a little past one in the morning, so I guess there should be enough people downstairs not to be too suspicious.

When I return back to the ground floor, I decide to go to the bathroom before I go in search of my brother. I'm more than ready to go home, whether he wants to or not.

Keeping my head down, I speed walk through the crowd of people. Just as I'm about to turn the corner, I hear a faint whispering.

"What do you know about Jeanette Sanders?" a quiet, although clearly male, voice asks.

I stop in my tracks, listening.

"The Ice Bitch? What do you want with her?"

There is a slight pause, in which I imagine he gives the girl he's talking to whatever non-verbal response.

"She's one frigid bitch who thinks she's too good for this town. Daddy's princess thinks she's better than us. God, I hate her presumptuous fat ass."

I feel my temper rising in my veins, but I bite into my lip, preventing myself from speaking. My hands clench by my sides.

The guy laughs quietly. "If I were you, I'd be careful of what I'm saying. Turns out she hooked up with Hill tonight."

"Drew?" Her voice raises to a high pitch. Jealous and irritating, how fitting. "He's messing with her. It's probably 'cause she's taboo. Sister of his teammate and friend. The guy gets off on that shit."

A lump forms in my throat.

"I don't know, some of the guys told me he looked pretty pissed when he saw her flirting with the bartender. Someone even said jealous."

"Drew Hill? Jealous?" The girl bursts into laughter. "Are you fucking serious? The guy doesn't do jealous. What he does is four things: fighting, booze, weed and fucking. Not necessarily in that order."

I swallow hard, listening. Every word she says makes my heart pound harder in my chest. Because I know it's true. The guy is on the path to self-destruction. Even excelling at it.

That's why you should keep far, far away from him.

"Besides, even if he were into relationships, which he's not, she wouldn't be his type. He likes them skinny, preferably blond and with their mouths shut. If his cock is the one doing shutting, even better."

Her words sting. And even if I know I shouldn't, I feel my eyes drop down, assessing. Looking for every overly emphasized curve and imperfection.

You're not going there.

My hand slides over my stomach, tugging down the hem of my sweater.

Just half an hour ago, I was in Andrew's bed, feeling sexy and powerful, but now... the girl's words roam around my mind, bringing back my worst insecurities.

My worst demons.

"Anette!" Max's voice brings me back from falling deeper into my thoughts.

Deeper into my darkness.

I lift my eyes to find matching ones looking at me. "Max," I whisper, forcing a smile. "I've been looking for you!"

"Funny, 'cause I've been looking for *you*. Lia told me you disappeared somewhere."

What else did she tell him?

"Well, I had to use the bathroom, and since the downstairs one was crowded as hell, I went upstairs," I lie smoothly. "I think I'm ready to go home."

"You were ready to go home since before we got here," he teases, fluffing my hair playfully. "I'll grab my stuff."

I nod my head, watching him go, the girl's words still running through my mind.

"Anette?" Max looks over his shoulder, his eyes searching mine knowingly. "Are you okay?"

I want to laugh, but shut it down because I don't want to sound frantic, and the laugh that wants to come out? Crazy as fuck. So I push it down, willing my lips to spread into a smile.

"Yeah, I'm fine." The words fall off my lips easily, aid so many times, I've lost count. The fakest words ever uttered. The easiest lie said. "Just tired."

He nods his head, but his eyes stay on mine for a while longer.

Looking.

Searching.

But they don't find anything.

They never will, because I'm an expert at keeping things close to my heart.

"What the hell do you think you're doing?"

The door swings open with force, crashing into the wall. The sound is so strong, it makes me sit upright in bed just as he turns on the light, blinding me.

"What is wrong with you?" I almost whine at my brother, throwing myself back on my pillow and pulling my blanket over my head.

"What is wrong with me?" he yells, trying to pull the blanket away, only I manage to scoop it up and not let go. "What is wrong with you? Andrew? Really?"

My eyes narrow as I look at him. Completely pissed.

I hate being woken up. And he knows it. Of the two of us, he's the chipper twin who's always up with the first rays of the sun, while I sleep in as long as possible.

And now, not only did he wake me up, he's also throwing the biggest mistake of my life back in my face? Does he have a death wish?

"What about Andrew?" Giving up on going back to sleep, I fluff the pillows behind me so I can lean against them in a sitting position, blanket pulled under my chin. "He's your friend, if I recall correctly."

And my mistake.

But I keep that part to myself.

Last night when we came home and I finally settled in bed ready to fall asleep, I found out I couldn't. My mind was still full of Andrew.

His hands touching me.

How they traced my body, making my skin tingle in excitement.

His kisses.

How they made my heart race, and blood hum through my veins.

How he filled me, oh-so-perfectly.

Even now, my thighs tighten at the thought. I can still feel the soreness between my legs, yet I want more.

But I can't have more.

If the words of the girl from the hallway weren't a wake-up call, nothing is.

Andrew Hill is a world-class douchebag. He got what he wanted, he gave me what I needed and now we're done. Even though I wouldn't mind a recap of last night, I know that he's the type that goes for one-night stands only, and I'm not a girl looking for a relationship.

Any kind of relationship.

And then there is the fact that he and Max are teammates and friends.

Which would be a big no-no.

Not like he cared about it before ...

So, I'll do what I've been doing the last couple of years. I'll keep to myself, and with my stellar personality, everybody will leave me alone.

"Then why are you fucking him behind my back?"

My heart stops in my chest, eyes growing wide.

How does he know? Did Andrew tell him? I'm gonna kill that fucker.

Surprise turns to shock turns to rage.

Hot and burning.

"Excuse me? And you think you're one to talk?"

"Jeanette ..." he growls in warning. Actually growls.

"I don't know what the fuck you're talking about," I grit defensively through my teeth, not ready to say anything else until he tells me exactly what he knows.

"I'm talking about this!"

Max comes closer, pushing his phone into my face. I blink a few times, clearing away the raging haze clouding my eyes, and look at the screen.

He doesn't know, I want to sigh in relief, but then he would definitely know something's going on, so I hold it in.

The photo is a shitty quality because it's dark, but I can clearly see the outline of the bar. I'm pressed against it with Andrew caging me in, his hands cupping my cheeks as he devours my lips.

They tingle as I look at the photo, remembering last night.

"That's what you call fucking?" I spat, throwing away the phone in disgust.

Maybe if I don't look at him, the feeling will go away.

"He kissed you, Jeanette!" Max howls, his hand running through his hair in frustration. "He kissed my baby sister."

"I'm hardly a baby." I roll my eyes, playing it off. "And he was drunk."

"Did you like it?" His eyes narrow as he takes me in, looking for some kind of clue. Something that will help him figure me out, see the secrets I'm hiding.

"What? No!"

"You're lying!" He points his finger at me.

"Oh, please! You're delusional, Max!" I throw my blanket off, getting out of bed, suddenly feeling cornered.

"I know you!"

"You don't know shit. I don't like Andrew. The guy is the world's biggest douchebag! What is there to like?!"

I open my closet and start going through my stuff, needing some kind of distraction.

"Exactly!"

"He's your friend, not mine," I deadpan.

"He's not a bad guy, Anette." Max sighs, sitting down on the edge of my bed. "He's angry and misunderstood. He's broken and damaged like ..."

Max stops mid-sentence, catching himself before he says something he won't be able to take back. My head falls forward.

"Like me," I finish for him. "He's broken and damaged like me."

"I just don't want to see you hurt, Anette."

I can hear the sheets rustling, and then he's there, behind me. His strong, reliable arms wrap around me as his head falls to my shoulder.

For a few seconds, I let myself stay in his arms. For a few seconds, I welcome his warmth and strength before I wiggle free.

"You don't have anything to worry about. There is nothing going on between me and Andrew. Nothing will ever be going on between us."

"Anette ..." Max sighs, but I shake my head no.

Then I take my stuff and go to the bathroom, shutting the door firmly between me and my twin.

Chapter 14

ANDREW

"Where the hell is he?" The loud roar comes from the foyer. "Don't even try to pretend he's not here. I already stopped by his house, and it's empty. And since nobody can stand the fucker except you ..."

"What did he do this time?"

This comes from Derek, but there is no answer. Only the sound of the footsteps against the tiles.

I take a swig from my beer bottle before I put it safely on the table. No need for the good stuff to fly all over the floor unnecessarily just because I managed to piss off one of my friends.

"You!" Max storms into the living room, and I turn around just in time for his fist to connect with my jaw.

"What the hell, man?" Derek comes behind him in a hurry, panting slightly, his hand holding on to his ribs, but he still manages to pull Max off of me.

I work my jaw, trying to see if it's broken because the asshole has one nasty punch. I guess it runs in the family. Rubbing the itchy, swollen flesh, I quirk my brow at him. "Are you done?"

"Andrew ..." Derek warns, but I'm not known to be a good listener.

"What? He came in and punched me, not the other way around." I watch as Max crosses his arms over his chest, trying to intimidate me, I'm sure. I lean back in my seat, grabbing the beer off the table and taking one long pull.

I have a feeling I'll need it in order to survive this.

"You hooked up with my sister!" Max spats, coming around so he can look me in the eyes.

I run my hand through my hair.

Well, that took long enough.

The silence that spreads through the room is grave. Max looks between me and Derek, still standing somewhere close to the door, the realization drawing in his eyes. "And you knew!"

Derek winces, and I actually feel bad for the guy. It's not like *he* hooked up with Max's sister.

Nope, that would be me.

And to think she left me high and dry in the middle of the night. It's not that I'm a big cuddler, and usually I want them out of my sight before my dick's completely dry, but I wouldn't mind an encore of *that*.

If I close my eyes, I can still smell her on my sheets and feel her tight pussy gripping around my dick fiercely. Just the thought of it makes my cock stir in my pants. I shake my head, trying to cool off. The last thing I need right now is to get a boner in front of the pissed off brother of the girl who's making me all hot and bothered.

"Not my story to tell."

I hear Derek shuffling behind me, his footsteps slow and measured as he goes to his dad's liquor cabinet.

Thank fuck.

"I don't fucking care," Max growls, pointing his finger at me accusingly. "Out of all the fucking girls in this godforsaken town, you had to go and kiss my sister?! What's wrong with you, man?"

Sighing, I tilt my head back. "I don't know … she was there and …"

And what? I couldn't take my eyes off of her? I couldn't stop thinking about her? Fantasizing on how it would be if what happened in the library hadn't stopped when it did? Thinking of how it would feel to bury my cock into her pussy, feeling her squeezing around me as she pants my name against my skin? And have all those thoughts replaced with hot rage when I saw her flirting with damn Rookie?

"She's not one of your one-night stands, Andrew! Dammit!" He turns around, kicking the recliner with the force of his fury.

I cringe, happy it's the recliner and not me. This time, that is.

"She's been through enough. Suffered enough, and I don't want some douchebag on my team to break her heart again!"

His words make my shoulders stiffen.

"So what? I'm good enough to be your friend and teammate, but not good enough for your sister?!"

He looks at me, his eyes not missing a thing. I thrust my chin in the air, waiting for his response. Daring him to say it. To say out loud what he's been thinking all along. To call me on my shit and give me a reason to be an even bigger douche than I already am.

"No, the way you are right now, you're not good enough." He shakes his head in resignation. "Nobody will ever be good enough, but especially not you."

My jaw tenses, teeth grit as I get on my feet. My hands clench by my sides so hard my knuckles turn white. It would bring me immense pleasure to shove my hand into his face, but I hold back.

"Duly noted," I grumble and turn around.

"Andrew ..." I hear Derek calling after me, but I don't stop to acknowledge him.

I have to get out of here before I do something I'll regret. Because no matter how hard I want to blame this on Jeanette or Max, deep down I know it's my own fault.

And I can't blame Max for protecting what's his. If I had a sister, I wouldn't let her within a ten-mile radius of the likes of me.

She's been through enough. Suffered enough ...

What the hell happened to you, Jeanette Sanders?

JEANETTE

"What are you doing here?" I look over her wet, shaky frame standing on my front porch.

She's like a mouse. Her brown hair is flat and sticks to her head, a shade darker than usual. Her clothes are soaked, and I can see her trembling.

It's nighttime in the middle of November, so it's freezing outside, but the only thing protecting her from the weather is a worn leather jacket that is also wet from the rain.

Brook shifts uncomfortably, but her chin tilts up in defiance and I admire her for that. Not a lot of people would dare to say openly what they think of me, but Brook doesn't give a damn about what I think or say about her. She doesn't talk about it much, but I have a feeling she has seen too much of the world's ugliness to be bothered by my bitchy attitude.

"This was a mistake." She shakes her head and turns to leave, but I stop her just as thunder strikes. It's deafening and the light illuminates the dark, angry sky for a second before we return to darkness.

"Get inside, Brook." I open the door wider, inviting her in.

Her green eyes widen for a second. Whether in surprise or relief I don't know, and I don't bother to figure it out.

Closing the door behind her, I lock it and turn on the security alarm. My parents are out of town, and I haven't seen Max since our argument this morning. When I got out of the shower, the house was empty, Max nowhere around. Still angry with him, I skipped breakfast and went straight to the gym, where I spent a better part of the morning. Now it's evening and still no word from him.

"I don't want to intrude."

I roll my eyes before I turn toward her. She looks even more pitiful in the bright light of the foyer than she did on the front porch.

"Do you see anybody else in here beside me?" I give her a second to answer, but she doesn't. "Take off your shoes and jacket. Do you have anything to change into? You'll get pneumonia if you don't get out of these wet clothes."

"I don't need ..."

"You'll leave a wet trail all over the house and you'll destroy Mother's precious, designer furniture. And although I'd like to see her face if you did, she's not here and it won't be half as fun without you around so ..." I deadpan, not giving her an option to contradict me. Brook pales, her mouth hanging open. "Come on up, I'll give you something of mine to change into."

"You don't have to do that."

This time I don't hide my eye roll from her. "I'm not doing it for you."

"Then why are you doing it?"

A heartbeat passes in silence before I snicker. "Didn't you

hear what Max said? Beneath all this cool exterior maybe lies a heart."

Brook gives me an exaggerated eye roll of her own, but she peels her shoes off and follows me upstairs. We walk in silence, her wet feet squishing against the floor and the storm raging outside the only sounds in the house.

Once we get to my room, I grab a pair of leggings, a sweatshirt and a pair of socks that should fit her before showing Brook to my bathroom.

In the harsh light of my room, I can now see what I couldn't in the dim light of the foyer. Her lip is swollen, and there is a faint red mark on her cheek. I swallow, suddenly uncomfortable. Brook notices my gaze lingering on her face.

Green eyes darken, and I can see her shift from one leg to the other. "I wanted to go to Lia's, but she's at Derek's since ..."

She offers as an explanation.

"I see ..." I nod my head in understanding.

The few times Max has dragged me along to Lia's, Brook has always been there. These two are more like sisters than friends, and Lia's parents treat Brook like their own. But I get it; it's not easy to ask for help. And now that Lia's dating Derek, it's normal that she isn't home as much as she used to be and that part of the time she spent with her friend she now gives to her boyfriend. Lia's house has been Brook's safe haven, but without her friend there, she doesn't feel comfortable staying at Lia's house alone.

"You earned those at home?" I tilt my chin in the direction of her face.

"If you don't want me here, I'll go." Brook's voice is steady and clear, her arms crossed over her chest. Partly to show her badass attitude and let me know loud and clear she'll be okay on her own, and partly to help her hide the shaking of her drenched body.

I've never tried to pretend we're friends. I wouldn't even call us acquaintances, for that matter. We simply go to the same school, and except for Max shoving me in their direction a few times, I keep to myself, so for her to come here ... I don't even want to think what it cost her.

For a while, we just stare at each other.

Her dark green eyes meeting my cloudy gaze.

Two stubborn, opinionated, too-smart-for-their-own-good young women facing each other, both trying to come out as winners in a fight that's non-existent.

Sighing in exasperation, Brook hangs her head. "I don't have time for this shit."

She starts toward the door, but my fingers curl around her wrist.

"You're not going anywhere."

My parents are far from winning the award for the Parent of the Year, but at least they never beat me. They just leave me in this big-ass house all alone. The least I can do is give somebody else shelter.

I may not be looking for a friend, or even company, but I can't let her walk away. Not when she is in a shitty situation like this. Not when the storm is raging outside.

I'm a bitch, but not like this. I'd never put another person, another *woman,* down.

There is a special place in hell for people like that, and with all my faults, I haven't fallen that hard. Not yet anyway.

"I'm going to order some takeout." I turn around and start walking away, giving her privacy to change.

"Jeanette?"

"Hmm ..." I tilt my head to the side, letting her know I'm listening without turning around. Like I said, this doesn't make us friends.

"You want to watch *Teen Wolf?*"

I shrug. "Sure. Come down when you're done."

Definitely not friends. Just two girls with a love for the same paranormal TV show.

My obsession with Isaac Lahey started way before the play date—that's what I call the night my brother ditched me at Amelia's doorstep—not that I would admit it out loud.

It's girly, childish and totally not like me.

But he's still my secret crush.

Sue me.

"Are you going to be okay here?" I ask, looking at Brook standing next to my brother's bed. In his room, so big and masculine, she looks even smaller than before. "I would have put you in the guest room, but Mom still hasn't had time to decorate."

"I'm okay." She runs her hand through her hair. "I could have slept on the couch."

"Well, he's not home, so why sleep on the couch?"

"I just hope he doesn't come in during the night. I don't think he'll find it amusing that I'm in here."

The picture makes both of us laugh out loud.

"If it gives you any peace, I'll text him and let him know to either find another place to sleep or to crash on the couch when he gets home."

"Jeanette, I can ..."

I lift my hand in the air to stop her. "Not a word. Serves him right anyway."

"Did you guys have a fight?"

Her words make me stop in my tracks. Brook's been here for hours. After she took a shower and changed into a clean set of clothes, she joined me in the living room where I have already opened Netflix on *Teen Wolf*. We were halfway through the first episode when the food came.

We ate watching television in comfortable silence, only commenting on the show and even that rarely. Both of us loved the easy quiet that settled upon us. She didn't ask unnecessary questions, and neither did I. On some subconscious level, we understood each other.

"Something like that."

She nods in understanding, although I don't really think she can understand.

"You know where the bathroom is, and if you need me, I'll be in my room."

"Okay." Brook nods once again, and I leave her to it, closing the door behind me.

Once I get to my room, I grab my pajamas and start toward the bathroom, when the little light on my phone catches my attention.

When Brook got here, I completely forgot about my phone. Worried that maybe Max tried to contact me, I grab it and unlock the screen.

Only it's not Max's message that awaits me.

It's Andrew's.

Dread washes over me. Swallowing hard, I tap the message and look at it.

Asshole: It's too late to send your big bro to save your honor now, Princess.

Well, fuck me. Could this get any worse?

Chapter 15

ANDREW

It's official. Jeanette Sanders is avoiding me.

Something I should be doing right back if I don't want to get on Max's bad side, but I can't seem to get it into my head.

She's been through enough. Suffered enough ...

The words he told me last week still haunt me. They're rolling in my mind on repeat, torturing me day and night.

When I don't hear the words, I can see her in my mind.

Taste her on my lips.

Feel her on the tips of my fingers.

She's everywhere and nowhere at the same time.

Close yet far away.

I don't even know why I'm stressing so much about her. She should be out of my mind by now. Hell, she was supposed to be out of my mind as soon as the deed was done, but no.

Not her.

Everybody but her.

It's driving me crazy.

A small, equal parts pained and frustrated sound comes out of my mouth. Quiet, yet loud enough so that a few people who sit close to me can hear it, and they lift their gazes to look at me with probing eyes.

I meet their stares head on, daring them to say something out loud. Not only am I going crazy, but I'm also agitated, which is never a good combination. Thank God it's Friday. We have a game to play later today and then a party to let loose.

My leg starts jumping up and down nervously. Lifting my gaze from my notebook, where I pretend to write while in reality my mind is otherwise occupied with thoughts of her, I find myself looking in her direction.

Seated in the middle of the class, she's always looking for a space to blend in, only she can't. She wouldn't be able to blend in even if she became invisible.

She did something with her hair. It's not straight like usual, but wavy, barely touching her shoulders. She's wearing another sweater form her arsenal, this one formfitting and dark gray that I'm sure makes her eyes stand out even more.

I let my eyes drink her in because I know this is the only chance I'll get. Max is watching me like a hawk when we're in a close proximity. That is, when she shows up at all.

The whole week she's been avoiding the cafeteria for lunch. The girls said she's busy working on some project for school, but I know better than that. Jeanette is avoiding me. And with Max in almost all of our classes, this was the only chance I had to get her alone.

Not that it's made a difference because she's an expert when it comes to avoiding. Sliding into the classroom just as the final bell rings and running out as soon as class ends, with most of the kids still seated.

If that's not the definition of avoiding, I don't know what is.

Sliding my hand into the pocket of my jeans, I take out my phone. Holding it out of sight, I lift my eyes to scan the room. Mrs. Wright, our AP English teacher, hates when we use our phones in class. If she catches me, not only will she take my phone, but she'll also give me detention. Something I can't risk, not with the game after school.

She writes something on the board, so I decide to use this opportunity to type out a message.

Me: You can run, but you can't hide.

When I hit send, I lift my gaze and look at her. For a few heartbeats there is nothing, and then I see her shoulders tense.

Her hand slides under the desk, although her eyes are still glued to the front of the class and our teacher, who's now turned around, talking animatedly.

I look at her, pretending to listen, but I don't hear a word she says because my mind is concentrating on the girl sitting a few rows in front of me.

Finally, Mrs. Wright turns back to the board to write some more. Jeanette's head falls forward, and most would think she's writing down notes, but I know better. She's reading the message.

Her whole back snaps up, rigid, and I can feel her angry attitude all the way from here. For some reason, it gives me joy. My lips curl in a half-smirk, and I can finally feel myself breathe again.

She doesn't turn around. She doesn't acknowledge me in any way. But I simply know.

She read my message, and it pissed her off.

And for some reason, that makes everything right in my fucked-up world again.

JEANETTE

The bell rings and I'm on my feet, dashing out of the classroom. I'm so glad it's Friday because I'm not sure how much longer I would be able to keep it up. Running away all the time ... it's tiring. But there's nothing much I can do about it.

If my fight with Max and his warning weren't bad enough, seeing Andrew's hateful message on my phone the day after was an eye-opener in itself.

What happened last weekend shouldn't have happened. For various reasons. One of them being that Andrew is Max's friend and teammate, and the last thing I want is to cause my brother trouble during his last year playing in high school. He's good at playing hockey, better than good actually, and he needs to end this year on a high note so all those prestigious colleges with division one teams notice him and offer him a spot. That has been his dream for years, and I'm not going to take it away with my selfishness.

But there is also the fact that Andrew is a screw-up just like me. Max was right; we're both damaged goods. Two jaded, broken people, with fucked-up pasts who will only bring more pain to one another. So completely wrong for each other.

Why did it have to feel so damn good though?

Just as I'm about to turn the corner, a hand wraps around my wrist. The door I'd been passing opens, and I'm ushered inside quickly before it closes firmly behind us, throwing us into darkness.

"What the—" I try to get my hand out of the steel grip, but it's useless. The hold is too strong.

I'm pushed against the wall, both of my hands pressed up by my head against the hard surface.

"Not so quickly, Princess," he whispers against my ear, his warm breath sending goosebumps down my skin as the smell of pines and wood surrounds me. "I think we have some unresolved business."

"Kidnapping will not get you what you want, Hill," I spat, trying to get out of his hold, but no matter what I do or how hard I try to resist him, I can't get him off of me.

"*Tsk* ..." Andrew shakes his head playfully, his nose rubbing against my exposed neck. "Such harsh words. I'm simply *borrowing* you for a bit. You're a hard person to track these days, Jeanette."

"Maybe that's because I don't want to be found. Ever thought of that?"

Andrew lifts his gaze, his green eyes easily finding mine even in the dark classroom. "It didn't cross my mind."

His fingers brush against a strand of my hair, pushing it behind my ear. "I like what you did with your hair."

I shudder at his touch; my eyes fall closed for a second as I bite into my lip to stop myself from saying anything.

Stop myself from uttering a sound.

"Eyes on me, Princess."

These words. These damn words throw me back to that night.

The night I try to forget with everything I have in me.

The night I keep dreaming about night after night.

Eyes on me, Princess.

They snap me back into reality. My eyes shoot open, throwing daggers at him.

"You need to leave me alone."

I can't do this. Not again.

"Or what?" He quirks his brow in question.

Such a daring gesture. It irritates me to the point of no return. I grit my teeth, angry at him and at myself. How does he do it? Getting the better of me, making me feel all these things? Irritating little shit.

I struggle against his hold on me, but he keeps strong. His grip lethal, unmoving. So much bigger, so much stronger than me.

Yet, I'm not afraid. Only pissed off.

"C'mon. Show me." He taunts me, his grin growing bigger.

I push and I pull, doing my best to get out of this. To get free of him. I struggle and struggle as he watches me, laughing in my face, but then the hold on my wrists loosens. Surprised, I gasp loudly and fall forward.

His green eyes widen in surprise as I trip over my feet, losing balance. I expect to fall. I expect to stumble into him and throw us both to the floor in a mess of the intertwined limbs, but I'm wrong.

Because Andrew is there. Hard and steady, his arms curl around me as my body connects with his.

My legs wrap around him, a silent shriek leaves my lips as he sways on his feet but somehow manages to regain his balance, and then I'm back where I started. My back pressed against the wall, only this time ... this time my legs are wrapped around him tightly, cradling him into my center and holding him close.

He breathes hard, chuckling. "If you wanted to get into my arms, Princess, all you had to do was ask."

I open my mouth to protest, but nothing comes out.

His lips brush against mine, hard and fast.

I breathe in, a current of electricity running through my whole body at the first touch of his lips against mine.

A slow, quiet moan erupts from my throat, and my hands that are wrapped tightly around his neck dig into the soft strands of dark hair, tilting his head to the side and deepening our kiss.

So good.

So damn good.

My tongue swipes over his, pulling it deeper into my mouth. There is a low rumble in his throat, his hands gripping my ass tighter and pulling my lower half away from the wall. I grind my hips against his, feeling the delicious bulge of his cock pressing against my center.

God, how I missed this.

Hard and hot. I rub against his lower half as he tongue-fucks my mouth, conquering it like a warrior conquers the land, not showing mercy or weakness.

Andrew breaks our kiss, his mouth following the line of my chin and down my neck, nibbling gently at exposed skin, his light stubble scratching the soft flesh.

"I love your hair," he whispers against my skin. "It's girly but doesn't get in my way, leaving your neck wide open for me to kiss. I don't know what's so sexy about your neck, but I could kiss it for hours. Nip and nibble until I make you come."

My heart kicks up a notch as he does exactly that. He sucks and nibbles, making me squirm in his arms. And I know, I simply know, it'll leave a mark.

"Andrew," I whisper, my fingers running through the mess of his hair.

"Mhmm ..."

He keeps up his work, and although I know I shouldn't, I can't help myself. I tilt my head to the side, giving him a better access. "We shouldn't."

"Says who?"

Leaving one final peck in the hollow of my shoulder, his nose traces back up my neck until our eyes meet.

He presses his forehead to mine as his green eyes stare into me. His dark lashes are long, and there is a ring of amber circling those green gems. Even a couple of small amber dots in his right iris, invisible if you're not standing nose-to-nose.

Still breathing hard from our make-out session, he stares at me intently, waiting for an answer.

"Says me. Says Max. Says everybody," I protest, shaking my head and trying to wiggle out of his arms.

This was a mistake.

Only he doesn't let me go. The dumbass tightens his hold on me, one hand cupping my cheek and making me stare at him.

"Fuck everybody. I'm not done with you yet."

"We can't."

The bell rings in the hallway, letting us know we don't have much time left.

I shake my head, but he doesn't move an inch.

"It's nobody's damn business what we do and who we do it with."

"So what do you suggest? That we hide?"

I couldn't do that. I *wouldn't* do that.

Or would I?

Another bell rings, and with resignation, Andrew lets me slide down his body.

"Tonight, come to the party." He takes a step back, his hand outstretched, still holding on to mine. Another step back and our fingers barely touch. "Come and I'll give you what you need."

With those words, he takes one final step back, breaking our contact. We stare at each other for a heartbeat longer.

Just a second longer.

Then I turn around and run out of the classroom, not once looking back. If I do, I'll accept everything he offers. If I do, I'll give in to my weakness. I'm so good at forming bad habits, and Andrew Hill? He'll be the worst habit of them all.

Chapter 16

ANDREW

Me: 1 hour. My room.

I type out the message and hit send. Locking the screen, I lift my gaze. My eyes scan over the packed living room until they settle on her. Completely on the other side, hiding in the corner with Brook and Amelia is Jeanette. Both she and Brook have been standing against the wall, but Lia pulled them closer to the crowd and made them dance.

A smirk forms on my lips as I observe her. Taking a pull from the bottle in my hand, I let my eyes roam over her body. Her hair is still a disheveled mess of loose curls that bounce as she moves her body to the beat of the music. It's sensual and sexy as hell. All I can think about is going to her, pressing my hand into her stomach and pulling her back close to my front as I bury my head into the hollow of her neck.

She changed since the game and is now wearing dark tights with a gray sweater dress and ankle boots. A dress with a high neckline and some kind of sleeves that go from being ultra-tight on her upper arm to being loose around her wrists.

Quiet, almost unnoticeable sexiness, that's what she is.

She doesn't try too hard, and she knows who she is. She isn't preoccupied with fashion or her looks. She almost downplays it, just to stay as invisible as possible. Like that's gonna happen.

"Do you have a death wish, dude?" Derek slides into the recliner next to mine, shaking his head in disappointment.

"I'm not there, am I?" I shrug my shoulders nonchalantly, disrupting the girl next to me.

I don't know her, haven't invited her, but I didn't exactly tell her to screw off when she came and nuzzled her way next to me. Her hands wrap around me, fingers tracing patterns on my chest as she nibbles at my neck, whispering God knows what into my ear.

I look down at her, suddenly irritated by her presence. She looks up at me through her thick fake eyelashes, as she licks her bright pink lips seductively. "Maybe we should ..."

Disentangling myself from her, I shoot her a hard stare. "Get lost. Now."

"But ..." She bats her eyelashes, completely confused, but I tune her out, turning toward Derek.

"Do you have to be such an ass?"

"Don't get all judgy on me now, King. Just a few short months back, you were the same heartless douchebag as me."

"All I'm saying is, you probably shouldn't be sitting here with some random co-ed hanging all over you while at the same time eye-fucking one of your teammates' sisters." For the last part he leans forward, whispering quietly so nobody can hear him. "I mean really, and then you wonder why he thinks you're not good enough for her."

His words sting for some reason, but I wash it away with a gulp from my nearly empty bottle.

"I want to fuck her, not date her. Regardless if other girls are part of the equation, I doubt he'll like the idea." I roll my eyes at him, leaning back in my seat. My tired muscles sigh in relief.

Tonight was a tough game. We managed to pull a win, but

barely. Everything was off today. Derek being sidelined for two games was hard enough on the team, but add to the mix the strained relationship between Max and me ... well, let's just say that the team could feel it, and it affected the whole game.

Like he can read my mind, Derek murmurs against the water bottle in his hand, "Well, you'll have to figure it out and soon, because it's not just affecting the two of you."

My eyes go back to Jeanette, only she's not there. Taking a swipe of the space, I see a glimpse of gray darting out of the living room.

Showtime.

"All in due time," I murmur, jumping to my feet. "All in due time."

Derek looks at me, then back at the corner where the girls were. "Andrew ..." he drawls in warning, but I wave him off.

"I'm going to take a piss, Mom. May I?" I taunt him, daring him to say something out loud.

"Your funeral." He shakes his head, but I don't stay to drown in his disappointment.

I've got places to be.

JEANETTE

Asshole: 1 hour. My room.

Right, like that's gonna happen. Fuming, I turn on the water stronger than necessary and end up splashing myself.

"Great," I groan loudly. "Just great."

The fucker says one thing and does something completely

opposite. Oh, I saw him sitting on that love seat with one of his Hill-hoes. Everybody did.

Did you really think he'd change? Yeah, right.

Is it too much to expect a guy who wants something long-term with you, even without any strings attached, to give a fuck-off to everybody else? Is it? I don't think so.

You think I'm getting attached? Don't. I just don't want to get an STD.

Grumbling, I take the towel and try to dry off when the door bursts open, then closes loudly.

Turning on the heels of my feet, I narrow my eyes at him.

"What do you think you're doing?"

"You should consider locking the door." He smirks, leaning against the surface like he has every right to be here. Which technically he does, but you get my point.

"I would if I didn't know for a fact that the top floor is strictly off-limits to everybody." I dab a few more times against the wet stain on my dress, not meeting his stare on purpose.

"Yet, you're here." He lifts his brow. "Why is that?"

Throwing the towel to the counter, I cross my arms over my chest. "I think we already established I'm not *everybody*."

He *tsks*, shaking his head. "Are we back at it? I'd hoped we'd moved on. 'Playboy' does have a nice ring to it."

"That isn't a compliment," I grit.

White teeth flash at me as a grin spreads over his lips. "I know, but it does sound endearing."

Tilting my head back, I look at the ceiling, inhaling deeply and praying for patience. This guy will drive me crazy and bring the grays to my hair before I leave high school.

"You see, you're not even denying it."

"Because there's no point. It wouldn't get through your thick skull anyway."

As soon as the words leave my mouth, I know I made a huge

mistake. His grin turns wicked. "My skull isn't the only thick thing about me, baby."

"No, your ego is even thicker."

He throws his head back and laughs. A full belly laugh. It's deep and husky, and I can feel it in my bones.

"Only you." He shakes his head as he takes a step toward me. "Only you."

"What only me?"

"Only you can give me a figurative kick to the nuts and make me hard at the same time."

I gulp down hard.

Why do I suddenly feel like I'm in so much trouble?

Chapter 17

ANDREW

I watch her gulp down, her throat bobbing with the effort as I stalk closer to her. Gray eyes widen as she stares at me nearing, my tongue darting out to wet my lips in anticipation.

"Any special need for you to wear this?" My finger traces the collar of her sweatshirt.

"You know there is, jackass."

Soft chuckle leaves my lips and I pull the hem down to reveal one big bruise on her neck surrounded by a few smaller ones.

There is no girl out there who'd ever dare to talk to me like that. They're all overly polite and indulging, ready to do whatever it takes to gain my attention and please me in any and every way possible just to keep me for a few minutes longer. Not that it ever worked out for any of them, but that didn't stop them from trying.

Jeanette is their complete opposite. She sees me for the jerk I am and isn't afraid to call me out on it or slap my hand if I cross a line. That in itself is refreshing and arousing.

Dick, jackass, douchebag, jerk, asshole ... she can call me all that and more, and I'd laugh in her face just to see her get pissed off. Every time she gives me her stubborn pout, I want to lean down and kiss the irritation off her face. Every time she crosses her arms over her chest, pushing those perky tits closer, I want to run my hands over her body and pull her into me. Every time she tilts her head in annoyance, making her hair sway, I want to lean in and burrow my head into the hollow of her neck and mark her.

It turns me the fuck on.

Everything she does.

Everything she says.

Everything she is.

It's a fucking turn-on.

A madness.

A madness I don't want to escape.

A madness I'll spiral into with my eyes closed if it means she'll be there waiting for me.

A habit.

She's become another one of my bad, bad habits, and I don't want to give it up.

I don't want to give her up.

"Such a shame," I whisper as I lean forward, my breath touching her skin and making her shiver. "Such a shame you have to hide them."

I run my hands up and down her sides, caressing her.

"You're a Neanderthal, Andrew."

Jeanette shoves me away, but there is no real force behind her push. I'd know; it still rings in my ear from the last time she slapped me. This time she doesn't want me to leave her alone.

Another soft chuckle leaves my lips as I brush my nose up and down the side of her neck. "Yet, you still like me."

"Like you?" She shudders under my arms, her fingers circling around the loops in my pants. Pushing away only to pull back closer, that's our constant. "I can't *stand* you. You're arrogant, petty and down-right mean. A daddy's boy who thinks the world revolves around you. The biggest manwhore this state has seen in the last fifty or so years. You're a cynic dick most of the time. Oh and did I mention a manwhore? How could I forget that?!"

She rolls her eyes at me, sobering up, and takes a couple of steps back, only to bump into the counter.

"You saw me with that girl downstairs." I nod my head in acknowledgment, I figured as much.

Taking a step forward, I look at her intently.

She crosses her arms over her chest. "You're imagining it," she deadpans, sarcasm dripping off her words. "The whole school saw you."

I watch her carefully, the hard line of her lips. A sliver of something, I'm not sure what, flashes in her eyes, but it's soon gone.

My eyes narrow. "Are you jealous, Princess?"

"Me? Jealous? Of what? Not getting an STD?!" She throws her head back, laughing, but it doesn't reach her eyes.

"I'm sorry to inform you that we already slept together. Welcome to the dark side," I deadpan, annoyed.

"Ugh ... do not remind me of that."

"Why the hell not?!"

Why is she resisting this so much? I know she wants me, craves me even. Just like my body craves hers. Standing here like this, so close I can touch her, I feel her body respond to me.

Jeanette shakes her head stubbornly. "It was a slip. A moment of weakness."

I give her a knowing look.

Who are you trying to fool, Princess?

She keeps pouting, her hands crossed under her breasts in defiance. But I see it for what it is—a weak attempt at holding back. Nibbling at her lip, I see her shift from one leg to the other.

"And at school was another slip?" I take a step forward, my hands caressing hers softly. "Coming here to the party, too? Just a slip?"

I take another step forward, bringing us chest to chest. My leg slips between hers, her center brushing against my thigh as she tries to adjust to my intrusion. But not objecting. Never objecting. Never pulling back.

Jeanette tilts her head back, her eyes meeting mine. Wide and slightly glossy.

"Yes!"

"What yes?" I murmur as my head bows down, my lips tracing the column of her neck.

Kiss after soft kiss, I taste her sweet skin on my lips, brushing over tender flesh.

"Just a s-slip ..." Her voice gets lost as I nibble the place behind her ear. She shudders, her fingers gripping my forearms.

So responsive.

I pull back just enough to see her face. Her cheeks are flushed, her breathing heavy. Brushing a strand that has a will of its own behind her ear, I let my hand slip into her hair, my fingers tangling with her wavy strands.

"Well, you're slipping an awful lot, Princess."

Guiding her head to the side, I slowly bow down and take her lips with mine, the kiss slow and demanding. Thorough. She moans loudly, the sound filling the small space and going straight to my dick, making me even harder than just a few seconds ago.

Apparently, Jeanette likes it because she starts grinding against me, the movement steady and sensual. Her hands go up my arms and around my neck, her full tits pressing against my hard chest.

She slips her tongue in my mouth, making me groan. I meet

halfway, our tongues twisting and twining while our hands roam over each other's bodies.

Up and down.

Down and up.

Her hand slides down my chest and underneath my shirt, her fingers brushing against the bare, taut skin of my stomach. Her nails are softly scraping over my abs and making my dick twitch in my pants, the hard length pressing against the zipper of my jeans.

My eyes fall closed at the sensation, my hand at the nape of her neck tightening. She nibbles at my lower lip, biting softly into the sensitive flesh and tugging at it.

I groan again, breaking the contact. I free my hands to slide them down her sides. My fingers curl around her hips, and in one swift movement, I lift her in the air and place her on the counter.

A puff of air leaves her lungs at the sudden movement. Yet still, her legs fall open wide.

Inviting.

Jeanette looks at me from the counter, melted eyes calling me.

"Still think this is just a slip?" I ask, licking my raw lips.

Her hand slides from underneath my shirt and goes lower, caressing the bulge contained in my pants. She bites into her lip as she feels the hardness of me, her eyes getting all hot and heavy.

"In this moment, you could be the devil himself and I wouldn't care."

Her hands work rapidly at unbuttoning my pants, the sound of the zipper lowering the only sound in the room except our heavy breathing. Once my pants are wide open, her little hand slips inside, curling around my hot length and pulling it out.

I hiss through clenched teeth as her hand works my length expertly. Her hold strong, strokes long and sure.

This time she's the one demanding a kiss, hectic and sloppy.

My hand sneaks up her inner thigh, up and up until I find her hot center. My fingers stroke her through her tights and panties, only it's not enough.

Irritated with all the material between us, I nudge my hand past the barrier and slip one hand inside, looking for the source of all that heat, and when I find it, all I can do is groan loudly in approval.

So hot.

So wet.

For me.

Only for me.

I stroke her through her wet folds, my finger gliding easily. Two strokes around her entrance, teasingly just so I can retreat and hear that needy moan of distress.

Her hold on me tightens in warning. "Don't mess with me, fucker," she utters, her voice low and husky.

"What do you want me to do?" I tease her some more, this time with my thumb circling around her clit. Slow, leisurely circles that make that little bundle throb under my touch.

Her head falls back, bearing her delicious neck to me. I lean forward, running my tongue down the exposed surface.

Her body responds to my touch, her hands digging into my hair and holding me close.

"I want you. In me. Now." Her response is short and breathy.

Chuckling against her skin, I slide my hands out and let my fingers find the hem of her tights.

"Ready for some slipping?" I tease her, Cheshire-cat smile spreading on my lips.

"Shut up and fuck me."

In a hurry of movements, we get her out of her panties and tights, pulling them down roughly. As soon as she's free, her fingers wrap around my dick again, pulling me between her spread legs.

A jolt of hunger and need shoots through my system at the first feel of my dick sliding through the heat of her lower lips.

I grit my teeth, hissing softly, my forehead touching hers.

"C-condom," I stutter. "We need a condom before I throw it all to hell and fuck you so hard you won't be able to walk straight for days."

Jeanette shudders—from the intensity of my words or from the feel of bare skin touching bare skin I'm not sure.

Our mouths touch, tongues mingling together until I'm not sure where one ends and the other begins.

One of my hands goes to my back pocket, fishing out the square wrapper. Breaking the kiss, I bring it to my teeth and tear it open. She takes the rubber from the wrapper, and after a few more teasing strokes, slides it down my hard length.

Taking a step closer, the tip of my dick slides through her folds, coating me into her wetness. Her breathing hitches, and it takes every bit of willpower I have not to burst even before I enter her.

"Ready to slip?" I ask, taking my dick into my hand and circling her clit teasingly with it.

Her hands grab my face, bringing me close for a kiss.

Hot.

Heavy.

Kiss.

"Fuck me, Andrew."

So I do. My dick slides down her wet pussy, until it nudges at her entrance. Her sharp intake of air fills the room as I penetrate her slowly until I'm completely inside, her walls stretching to accommodate the intrusion.

"T-tight," I breathe against her lips. "So freaking tight."

Light sweat coats my skin, but I still, letting her adjust. Although it pains me, I hold back until she gives me a sign, just a small nudge, coming closer and pulling more of my dick inside. Then all bets are off.

I pull out, only to slide back in.

Over and over again I thrust into her, slowly speeding up. And like before, Jeanette doesn't hesitate; she matches me thrust for thrust, demanding her own satisfaction.

Her own release.

Her hands grip my shoulders, nails digging into my skin.

"F-faster," she pants, her inner walls clenching around me.

My hands go to her ass, squeezing her cheeks and readjusting the angle before I give her what she asked for. My hips move rapidly, our mouths sloppily kissing.

And then we're slipping.

Hard and fast.

Her pussy clenches hard around my dick, and the familiar tingling in my lower back starts. I thrust three more times, each time trying to get deeper inside of her, and then we both burst. The grip of her inner walls around me is strong, milking me completely as her whole body trembles in her release.

We're slipping, falling into the darkness, and there is no way out.

We're lying on that counter in the silence until our breathing goes back to normal, my dick inside her the whole time. I'm pretty sure that's not the wisest idea, but I don't give a fuck. The feel of her around me is so good, too good to give up.

When I feel her shift under me, I pull out, making quick work of disposing of the condom and readjusting my clothes.

Jeanette does the same, because when I turn toward her, she's almost presentable.

Who am I trying to kid? The girl looks thoroughly fucked. Her clothes may be in place, but her hair is all messy, her cheeks flushed and her lips raw and puffy from our kisses.

I run my hand through my hair, trying to get my own mess in order. "Still think this is just a slip?" I lift my brow in question.

Her eyes narrow at me. "If I admit to it, will you stop harassing me?"

"Only if you agree to keep on slipping."

Jeanette purses her lips, thinking. "Nobody can know about it," she says finally.

I lift my hands in the air. "I'm not one to kiss and tell."

"Tell that to somebody who believes in your bullshit, Hill." She rolls her eyes, hopping off the counter. "Oh, and if I see any more of your hussies hanging on you, the deal is off."

Then she walks away without giving me a second glance.

Chapter 18

JEANETTE

"Do you think people are beyond redemption?" I ask suddenly, going through the stack of clothes in front of me.

All the movement around me stops, making me lift my gaze and face my companions.

"Where is this coming from?" Lia asks, a small frown marring her face.

I lift my shoulders in a shrug. "Just wondering."

"Some heavy wondering for a silly shopping expedition." The sarcastic answer comes from the other side me.

I turn around to give Brook a nasty stare. Things between us have been somewhat better after the night she came to my house drenched as a mouse, but that doesn't make us best friends. I don't think we'll ever be. We're both too fucked up to be the type of besties you see in movies, painting each other's nails while spilling secrets and gossiping about boys. Yeah, I think not.

"Not all of us wander around with nothing deep on our minds." I roll my eyes, but my words don't have their usual bite.

Maybe I'm not ready to call them my friends; we all know how that turned out the first time around, but they sure are getting on my soft side.

They're like puppies, cute and overly eager to please just so they can get a tummy rub.

"And here I thought the only thing on your mind was figuring out the best way to ice people out."

Ouch.

Her words sting, but I lift my chin higher in the air, not letting her get to me.

"Brook!" Amelia exclaims in warning, coming to stand between us. "Can we please concentrate on getting the job done? Derek's parents invited me for dinner this weekend, and I need to look my best."

"What's wrong with something in your closet?"

"Nothing." She shrugs, going back to searching through stacks of clothes. "I just want to look pretty, B."

"You're always pretty, Lia." She interrupts her. "Don't let anybody convince you otherwise."

"I know, but I want to wear something extra pretty, like the dress Mom got me for my date with Derek. He has never brought a girl home, Brook. I want them to like me."

"They're going to like you, Amelia." I come closer, my hand touching her shoulder in reassurance. "Everybody likes you."

"You don't like me."

There is no malice in her words, only the truth.

"I'm different," I say simply, shrugging. My hand falls from her shoulder, and I take a dress out of the stack. It's not something I can imagine Amelia wearing, but I have to do something with my hands.

"Why?"

That one word is filled with so many questions.

Why don't you like me? Why are you different? Why are you even here? Why don't you care? Why don't you have friends? Why are you still hanging with us despite that?

Why?

"You remind me of someone." I swallow hard, a small, barely visible smile appearing on my lips. "Someone I used to know."

Before

"Higher, Max!" I squeal in delight. "Push me higher!"

My big brother, bless his soul, does exactly that. We're only five, but he'd do anything to see me happy.

To put a smile on my face.

Pulling all the strength his five-year-old body can muster, he pushes me harder, the swing going up, up, up in the air. I outstretch my legs, feeling like I'm touching the sky. The light breeze kisses my cheeks as my hair swings with the wind.

Weightless.

That's how I feel.

Weightless.

And so happy.

Like I could do anything, be anything in this moment.

Only the sky is my limit.

And nothing bad can happen. Nothing bad can touch me.

How wrong I was... how wrong...

Now

"Look who we have here."

The screechy words bring me back from the walk down memory lane, something that has been happening a lot lately. I blink a few times, focusing on the present instead of the memories.

"The trash boutique is over there." Diamond waves her hand, trying to indicate God only knows what. "You should check it out. I'm sure you'll find something of your liking."

Her friends burst into hyena laughter around her.

Lia nibbles at her lip worriedly. The girl doesn't have a confrontational bone in her body. She's not meek, but she avoids fighting and conflict as much as possible.

How she ended up being friends with Brook, I have no idea.

Brook grabs her hand, taking Diamond in from the top of her bouncy hair to the bottom of her stiletto heels, then swipes the store with her gaze. "Oh, that's why we couldn't find anything here ..." She nods her head knowingly and starts walking her friend out of the store. I follow behind, waiting for the blow. "Hooker clothes don't actually suit you, Lia. No worries, I'm sure we'll find something less trashy somewhere else."

I burst into laughter, not able to contain myself. Brook turns around, giving me a playful wink over her shoulder.

No, I can understand why they're friends. Similar yet different, they're the opposite other one needs to feel complete. Brook is strength and grit to Amelia's gentleness and kindness.

We keep giggling on our way out, but my laughter is cut by Diamond's harsh, angry words.

"Stupid, fat bitches."

I turn around, my eyes narrowing on Diamond, but it's not her face I see. Not even close.

It's dark hair and blue eyes that look back at me. Only darker, more intense, not Diamond's watery shade.

Fingers wrap around my wrist, tugging me.

"Ignore them," Lia whispers. "They're just petty and jealous."

"Right," I mutter, as we finally get out of the store.

But no matter how hard I try, I can't shake it off.

Fat.

Later that day, when I finally get home, I let the door close shut behind me, not bothering to lock it.

Taking two steps at a time, I get to my room quickly.

I don't look around, my mind set on one thing and one thing only.

Restless.

That's what I'm feeling.

Restless.

And I know it won't change until I get down to the gym and work it out of my system.

Fat. Fat. Fat. Fat. Fat. Fat.

The word is on repeat in my mind.

Sometimes it's Diamond's voice I hear.

Sometimes it's the voices from my past.

My demons and insecurities trying to crawl back to life.

I enter my room, pulling my clothes off.

Jacket.

Sweater.

Tank top.

"You're home already?"

I turn around, facing Max. His hair is disheveled and he

looks tired. He's most likely been working on his homework after his usual morning workout.

"Yeah, just got in," I say, going to my wardrobe to get my workout clothes.

"Had fun?"

"Mhmm..." I answer non-committally, grabbing the first pair of leggings and sports bra I see.

Ignore the mirror.

Fat. Fat. Fat.

"You're talkative." I feel him shift behind me. "Everything okay?"

"Yes." I turn around, plastering a fake smile on my face, but trying to make it look as real as possible. "It's been a hassle trying to find something perfect for Lia, but we did it. Now I just need to let off some steam. You know me and shopping don't mingle well. Reminds me too much of all the times Mom dragged me shopping with her."

He cringes.

No shit, buddy.

"Well, once you're done, I could do something for dinner and you could maybe help me with some of my math problems..."

I sigh, pushing closed the lid of the box that opened in me. For Max. I have to get my shit in order for Max. So he can't see, can't figure it out.

You'll slip, the voice whispers in my ear.

Not today, Devil. Not today.

"No problem." I give him a small smile. A real one this time.

Max is not dumb, far from it, but school has never come easy to him. More times than I can count, I spent afternoons and nights working with him on his homework or helping him study for an exam. I always wondered if he has some minor form of dyslexia, but I never uttered it out loud.

"When I finish my workout, I'll help you with whatever you need."

He breaths out in relief, his whole body relaxing.

"Thanks, Anette. Waffles? You'll probably be hungry once you're done."

I cringe.

Fat. Fat. Fat.

Around three hundred calories. Each.

Fat. Fat. Fat.

"We had a big lunch, so I'm still pretty full."

"You don't know what you're missing," he jokes, walking backward to his room.

I only wish.

Chapter 19

ANDREW

"What did I tell you about the stupid parties?"

I groan loudly at the sudden noise. It's making my head throb even harder. "Can you please be quiet?"

The bang of the door and the sudden light illuminating my room don't help either.

What the hell did I do? Drink the whole cabinet downstairs?

My throat is like a desert, making my voice weak and raspy.

"No, I cannot, Andrew!" He bellows. "I asked you for three things. Three fucking things and you can't even do that?"

With each word, the level of his voice rises, and if I opened my eyes, I'm sure I'd see the vein in his forehead throbbing.

"It wasn't that bad?" I offer weakly.

"Wasn't that bad?"

I cringe at his roar, my fingers massaging my painful forehead in hopes to dull the throbbing. So far no luck.

"Downstairs is a disaster. You'll get your ass out of bed this very moment and go clean up your shit. No more parties, I mean it."

Just the thought of getting up turns my stomach, the bile rising. "The cleaning crew should be here soon."

"They won't." He pulls the covers off my body, the cool air touching my naked skin. "Get your ass out of bed and clean your shit. I have investors coming in an hour."

I groan loudly, pulling the pillow over my head.

Shit doesn't even begin to cover it.

"Oh, and Andrew?" Sighing, I remove the pillow to look at his retreating form. "The charity gala is this weekend. You better be on your best behavior."

Irritated, I yell after him, "I didn't sign up for that!"

"Not going was never an option," he throws over his shoulders. "Now go and clean up that mess before the investors come."

Sneaking my stick past Derek's defense, I steal the puck from right under his nose. Two powerful pushes of my legs and he's left in my dust as I glide the black rubber over the smooth ice. Harder. I push myself harder until the net comes into view. Making a short swing, the stick connects to the puck, sending it flying into the goal.

"Suck it, loser." I turn around to face a slightly breathless Derek. "Two weeks off the ice and you're all winded like some grandpa."

He shakes his head at me. "Try having a concussion and then let me know, dickwad," he says, but there is no bite to his words.

"What has your panties in a twist anyway? You never come to the rink early, much less put this much effort into it."

You'd think I'd get offended by that, but you'd be wrong. The guy is telling the truth. As much as I enjoy hockey and it lets me lose some steam, it's not my dream to play with the big boys. I'm leaving that to Derek, and well, Max.

"Can't a guy just want to shoot some shit with his friend?"

Derek gives me a pointed look. I guess he knows me better than most people and can see right through my shit.

"Dad's been riding my ass about the partying."

"Mr. Hill? What for? I thought he wasn't around much ..." He leaves whatever he wanted to say hanging in the tense air between us.

"Apparently, he's ready to play daddy dearest." I shrug, like it doesn't matter, when in reality it does.

When Mom left us, it crushed me. For weeks, *months*, I waited for her to come home. Waited and hoped that she'd change her mind and come back to us and we'd be a family again. I needed her, *we* needed her, and she just up and left.

For *months* I asked myself what I did wrong. Did I do something to make her leave? Would she have stayed if I had better grades? Or maybe if I cleaned my room more often? Maybe if I didn't spend so much time at practice and with my friends, she would still be here. But it's not just her I lost when she walked away.

No, I lost both of my parents, because after that day, Dad has never been the same. Gone were the days we would go and play hockey or he'd take me to watch our favorite team play. Gone were the days we'd go to the park or arcade together. No more staying up late to watch movies, or days when we'd stay alone and eat our weight in junk food. All of it gone in the blink of an eye.

She left us, and he left me.

I lost everything, all in one day.

And now he thinks that a few public stunts for his campaign and a charity event give him control over my life?

Where was he when I was eight, all alone at night waiting

for him to come home? In the end, I gave up on waiting and ate cereal for dinner by myself.

Where was he when I was ten and broke my hand while riding bikes with Derek? Oh yes, he was somewhere on the other side of the state saving some rich kid from prison time.

Where was he when I was twelve and almost burned the house down trying to cook something for dinner because our housekeeper was sick? Most likely somewhere fucking his very personal assistant of the month.

Every time I needed him, he wasn't there.

Yeah, we shared the house, but he was hardly around and I was left alone.

Going to the goal, I fetch the puck, and then start skating toward the other side of the rink.

Hard and fast, I'm sliding from one side of the rink in what seems like seconds. I'm pushing my body, muscles tensing, the rage boiling my blood.

Taking a swing, the stick connects with the puck, sending it into net so hard I'm surprised it's not broken, but not even that slows me down.

Missing the goal by just an inch, I let my body collide with the Plexiglas behind it, my gloved fist punching the hard surface.

"Now that he's decided to enter politics, the guy thinks we can be one big happy family and everything will be alright again," I say when I hear the familiar *whoosh* of skates nearing.

"I'm so sorry, man. That sucks."

I give the glass in front of me another frustrated hit before I turn around. "Yeah, well... it's not like talking about it will change anything."

Derek opens his mouth to say something, but just then, the rest of the team enters the rink.

Practice. That's what I have to concentrate on, and tune out everything else. Only that way I'll be able to keep the last bit of sanity I have left.

Chapter 20

JEANETTE

"What the hell is this supposed to be?" I shove the hanger into my mother's face.

She blinks a few times before her eyes concentrate on me and the offending object in my hand.

"It's a dress."

"That I realized for myself," I say dully, looking at her taking a sip of her wine. A half-empty bottle sits on the table beside couch, all before five o'clock in the afternoon. I guess it's all about perspective, right? It has to be five o'clock somewhere. "It's a sorry excuse for a dress, fit for five-year-old playing dress up. The real question is, why is it hanging in my closet?"

Another sip followed by a wave of her hand. "It's for the party."

"I'm not going to any party."

"Oh, yes you are." She wiggles her finger in my direction, giggling.

Frowning, I look at her more closely. Her usually composed hair is messy, her eyes glassy and there are frail mascara smudges under her eyes. Not only is she drinking before five in the afternoon, she is *drunk*.

Reaching a new low, I see.

"Both you and Max are going. It's the annual charity event here in Greyford. Red and black Christmas gala. All the donations go toward your father's new hospital. And since we had to move here because a certain someone ..."

"Okay," I grit through my teeth, not wanting to listen further. "I'm going. But I'm not wearing this."

I let the hanger fall off my finger, then I turn on the heels of my feet and storm out of the room.

After all these months, she still resents me.

Better.

Moving here was for her and Max's benefit more than mine. They don't even know half of the truth behind our moving.

Better.

Let them believe in lies.

After all, they're prettier than the truth.

Looking at myself in the mirror, I add another swipe of red lipstick.

I went with neutral, nude eye shadow, but winged black eyeliner and red lips give the whole look a dramatic tone and go well with my red dress.

A *new* red dress.

No way in hell I'd put that fluffy, girly monstrosity on myself and wear it to bed, much less in public.

If I had to play Cinderella for the night, at least I'd do it on my own terms.

So I ignored the fact that I hate shopping, dressing up and dresses in general, and went to buy myself something I actually like.

It took a while, but in the end I found it. A dress I not only like but feel confident in. Instead of typical red, I choose a deep burgundy color. It drapes into a front tier and transitions into cape sleeves that trail out at the back alongside the sheath skirt. The front looks pretty modest, that is until I turn my back, which is completely bare.

Arranging my locks one last time, I call it quits.

Bypassing the full-length mirror, I close the bathroom door behind me, slip into simple black stilettos and take my clutch off the bed.

When I shut the door, I see Max doing the same on the other side of the hall.

His gray eyes swipe from the tips of my shiny heels to the top of my head.

"You look beautiful."

Smiling, I take him in. He's wearing a two-piece black suit, a crisp white dress shirt with a burgundy tie that matches my dress. I can't have my date looking sloppy.

"You clean up nice, too."

He chuckles, looping our elbows together. United front for tonight.

"No date?"

"Who would I bring?"

There is no amusement in his tone. As far as I know, the closest he came to hooking up since we moved to Greyford is Lia, and we all know how that turned out. And then there is Brook. You have to be blind not to feel the tension between the two of them. The only thing I'm not sure about is if it's chemistry that sparks between them or plain frustration for having to share the same air.

"I'm sure you'd have found *someone*." My insinuation is clear and he knows it, but ignores me, shaking his head.

"And bring that *someone* into the crazy that is our family? Yeah, right."

"I was just saying." I shrug.

"What about your date?" he counters. The look he gives me is more than enough for me to understand to whom he's referring.

"That was a one-time thing," I grit, my shoulders tensing.

"I really hope so."

"He's not *that* bad."

"He's bad enough, Anette," Max contradicts, turning toward me. "I don't want you to get hurt again. And although I like the guy, he's n..."

"Not the guy for me," I interrupt him, suddenly sick of this conversation. "Too damaged. I know, Max. I know."

Why does it seem that all we do lately is fight, fight, fight?

Once we were one being, one person. We couldn't spend five minutes apart. Now on some days we barely tolerate each other. When did it change? *Why* did it change?

Before more questions form in my mind, I dismiss them.

I know *when*. I know *why*.

There is no sense in opening old wounds.

I slip my hand out of his and continue walking down the stairs, my mind all over the place.

I know Max means well, and it pains me to lie to him about this, too.

Lies, lies and more lies.

It seems like when you start, there is no going back.

"Oh, here she is." I snap out of it when I hear my mother's voice, my eyes slowly lifting until I meet her gaze, and then I see him.

Dark blond hair perfectly styled so it doesn't get in his face. Light blue eyes surrounded by long eyelashes. Clean-shaven square jaw. Lean body dressed in a custom-made three-piece black suit and black tie to match.

"Jeanette." My mother smiles sweetly. Too sweet. "Meet Ethan. Your date."

Chapter 21

JEANETTE

"I'm going to kill her," I spat when I get to Max, who's leaning against the bar. He hasn't left this spot since we got to the Greyford Country Club, where the charity gala is taking place, while I had to play nice with my *date*.

Taking the glass of bubbly champagne in front of him, I tip my head back and down the whole thing in one go.

"Why? It's not a big deal."

Is he for real?

Slowly, oh-so-slowly, I turn around to face him. "She didn't set you up on a blind date!" I whisper-scream, sticking my finger into his chest.

"And it wouldn't matter either way if she had." He shrugs. "Why does it matter to you?"

"Because I hate it when she tries to mess with my life. I didn't want a date! If I wanted one, I would have found one. But I didn't. Why doesn't she leave it alone for once in her miserable life?"

Max takes my waving hand in his. "It's just a few hours."

He looks calm and composed, but I can see a glimmer of amusement in his eyes. "You're so happy to see me agonized."

"Me? Never!" But he laughs, so I know I'm right. "Where did the lover boy run off to anyway?"

He looks around, presumably searching for Ethan fucking Williams.

"Don't look for him. Don't think of him. Don't even dare to whisper his name," I whisper-yell at him, looking around and searching the crowded room for him.

This makes my brother laugh. "Come on! He can't be that bad."

"You don't know the half of it!" I protest, crossing my arms over my chest and lifting my chin in the air.

"Then, by all means, enlighten me." He mimics my pose perfectly.

"The dude is a know-it-all. All he does is talk about himself and check his looks in every reflectible surface. The leader of debate club, speaks Spanish and German, straight-A student with early acceptance to Yale to study law and, listen to this, a leader of Greyford High's oldest and fiercest opponent—St. Jonah High."

Gray eyes bulge out. "No way. She didn't."

I roll my eyes. Of course *that* got his attention. Who the fuck cares about his sister being miserable by being put on the spot, when the guy she's forced to date is the enemy on the ice? "Yes way, she did. And he's a shit dancer. After the tenth time he stepped on my foot, I stopped counting."

"Well, he can't be *perfect*. Now can he?"

"Who can't?"

In unison, we turn around. The fine hairs at the back of my neck rise as an uneasy shudder runs down my body. Light blue eyes take me in, a smirk curling his lips.

I guess it's supposed to be one of those arrogant, I'm-the-man smirks that popular boys wear like a second skin, but the only thing it does is make my skin crawl.

"Nobody." I force out a smile.

Ethan looks between the two of us for a second. He opens his mouth to say something, but decides to let it go.

Smart boy.

"Sorry for that." He removes an invisible curl from his forehead. He does that often, and it's irritating as hell. How much can one guy be obsessed with his looks?

A lot, apparently.

"My dad wanted to introduce me to some people around."

"Don't worry about it." I wave it off.

You could have stayed with him the whole night and made this easier for me.

"Wanna go dance again?"

Max tries to hide his chuckling, but when I elbow him in the gut, it soon turns into a cough.

That bastard will hear it from me later.

Swallowing the real answer, I make myself meet his gaze and smile. "Yeah, sure."

Kill me now.

I slowly start walking toward the dance floor. There are a good number of couples, young and old, dancing to the quartet playing softly in the corner of the room. Round tables are scattered around. People are sitting and standing, talking in small groups, champagne flutes in the hands. The warm light illuminates the space, accentuating red and gold details.

Ethan falls in step behind me, his big hand settling on my lower back.

Low.

Too low to be considered appropriate.

The same feeling of unease returns in full force, but I keep my lips shut tight. It would be so easy to tell him to keep his creepy, too-soft paws to himself, but causing a scene in a place like this will only piss my mother off, and I'm not in the mood to deal with her attitude.

It's one thing to cross her in the privacy of our house, but to do it in public surrounded by all her high-class friends and Dad's colleagues ... yup, that wouldn't go well. So I suck it up. I'll do one more dance. Just one more, and then I'll *kindly* explain to him that my feet hurt from the heels I'm wearing and go sit down at my table for the rest of the evening. That should do the trick.

We finally find an open spot. I start to turn around to face him and get this over with, but his hands land on my hips and pull my back to his front. His chin lingers over my shoulder, and I can feel his hot breath against my skin. It's more like panting than breathing, and it makes me shudder.

My lips press in a tight line.

Just a little bit more. You can do it. Just a few more minutes and then you're done. No more dancing. No more sleazy touching. No nothing. Done.

I repeat those words over and over again as the music continues playing. It feels like we've been doing this for an eternity, when in reality it's probably just a minute or two.

Suddenly, he turns me around in his arms, pulling me closer. His face lowers, the tip of his nose touching the crook of my neck, inhaling me in as one of his hands caresses my naked back.

I want to scream in frustration. Why is he doing this? His touch feels all wrong, and his nearness makes me feel cornered, uneasy.

I swallow hard, getting ready to push him away.

Enough is enough.

But a hand wraps around my wrist, pulling me away.

Max.

I want to sigh in relief. That is, until I hear *his* voice.

His *growl.*

"Get your fucking hands off of her!"

Chapter 22

ANDREW

Taking a sip from the flute in my hand, I wish, for the hundredth time in the last hour, that it was something stronger than the bubbly shit they distribute around here like water.

Kid throws a party for his classmates and is judged by adults, but out here those same adults are giving alcohol without the blink of an eye. What a bunch of hypocrites. The biggest of them being my father.

The asshole smiles at the old dude he's talking to, schmoozing him to empty his pockets and fill his budget for the campaign.

I tuned him out twenty minutes ago. He wanted me to be here, fine, but he didn't say anything about having to interact or play nice.

I take another long sip, imagining it's Scotch, the strong, smooth liquid sliding down my throat burning just right. But there is no burn, only the tickle of the bubbles.

Where is the real booze?

Looking around for the bar, I hear my father calling my name, but I wave him off without even throwing a backward glance. He can deal with the old guy just fine on his own. I'm here to show people that we're one big, happy family. I did that by showing up. Mission accomplished, time to get buzzed if I plan on surviving the next few hours here.

I tug at the neckline of my shirt, trying to loosen the red tie around my neck. I tried to ditch the tie, but Dad insisted. I guess part of the black-tie even means you have to actually wear a tie.

Huh, go figure.

The crowd is not as big around the bar as it is around the tables and the dance floor. I guess the rich like to be served more and think drinking champagne makes them fancy as shit. I slide onto the open stool, signaling the bartender to give me a double Scotch. The night is long and if I plan to survive it, I'll have to get buzzed. Hell, maybe I'll even sneak out and have a smoke. There is nothing like a few puffs of sweet Mary to calm you down. Just thinking about it makes my blood buzz. I could slip out for a while; it's not like anybody would miss me.

A guy in some classy penguin suit the waiters wear pours me a generous two fingers of their finest and slides it my way. My hand wraps around the cool crystal as I lift the glass in the air in thanks and take a sip.

"Well, well, well ..."

Slowly, I lift my eyes to meet the gray ones as he slides into the seat next to mine.

We haven't spoken since he came to Derek's house to tell me I'm not good enough for his sister. Not that his opinion matters.

"What brings you here, Sanders?"

Out on the ice, we're as good as always. Now that Derek is back in the game after his concussion, we're playing fiercer than ever, yet ... there is still tension between us that didn't exist before.

Tension I put there when I kissed his sister. *Fucked* his sister. Not that he needs to know about that part. If he does find out, I'm sure he'll cut my dick off so I won't be able to fuck anybody ever again.

"Better question is, what brings *you* here? This doesn't seem like your scene. Who's hosting the party?"

I shrug nonchalantly, taking another sip from my glass and signaling the waiter to bring him a drink, too. "No party. Daddy dearest needed family to join him while he charms everybody in this room into thinking what a great mayor he'd make. Honest. Charismatic. Family man and a single father. You know the drill."

"So the rumors are true?"

"Apparently."

Not that it interests me in the least. Next year, I'll be far, far away from here, and I'm not coming back. I'm not particularly interested in playing hockey professionally, but I know some scouts are looking at me. And if playing hockey takes me away from here ... why the hell not?

I tilt my chin in his direction. "What about you?"

"Dad works for the hospital, and since this is a fundraiser for the hospital ..." He leaves the rest of the sentence hanging in the air, taking a sip from his own glass. I know what he means. Just like me, he's here for his *family*. The only thing I'm not sure about is—is he doing it because he has to or because he wants to?

And if he's here for his family that also means ...

I turn halfway in my chair, letting my eyes slide over the crowd, looking for her dark hair.

"She's with a date, you know."

Max doesn't even bother to turn around. Leaning against the bar, he's swirling the amber liquid in his glass.

My whole body goes still, jaw set tight.

A date? She's here on a fucking date after specifically prohibiting me from fucking around while I fuck her?

My fingers shake with rage, and I'm not sure if I want to

shove my fist into Max's face or take the half-empty glass in front of me and throw it at the nearest wall.

"He's the son of our family friends ..."

He keeps talking about the dude Jeanette took to this fancy event, but I tune him out. His words, although unclear, bring images of the guy into my head.

Family friend's son, I guess they must be good friends if he approves. The dude is probably everything I'm not. Refined and *whole*. Not an asshole like me who carries a chip on his shoulder everywhere he goes. Not some lunatic who gets a thrill out of kicking guys stronger than necessary around the ice. Not a guy who looks for oblivion in the sweet smoke and booze.

Somebody not *damaged*.

Somebody not *destructive*.

Somebody who's not *me*.

I'm not sure when I wrapped my hand around the glass, but I'm squeezing it so tightly my knuckles turn white. I throw what's left in the glass down my throat, letting it burn me from the inside out.

Maybe it can burn my demons along the way.

Take them to hell where they belong.

Too bad this is my life and there is no escaping it.

I chuckle bitterly. "Why are you telling me this? You made your point more than clear."

You don't have to throw it in my face. I get it, dude.

I'm not good enough.

"I just want you to ..." His eyes dart somewhere over my shoulder, the gray irises darkening to the stormy color his sister wears like a cloak. Intense and gloomy. "What the hell?"

I turn around before he can finish his sentence, my whole body alert. My heart kicks up a notch as I'm looking for whatever he saw.

Whoever he saw.

Looking for her.

My eyes scan the mass of people, reds and blacks, long silky dresses and suits that could feed a small country for a year. Until they land on her.

I don't know how I didn't see her the first time around, but now I can't take my eyes off her.

Jeanette is wearing a short dark red dress that touches her knees. The bottom part is tight, but there is some kind of wavy thing that covers her upper body. She turns around, swaying on her heels. And her back.

Exposed.

All that silky skin bared for everybody to see.

A hand slides up her naked flesh, fingers spreading against her backbone.

My whole body tightens in rage.

Seeing another guy's hand on her feels wrong.

So fucking wrong.

She doesn't belong to you, dude. Chill out.

I try to hold back. I try to make myself take a step back.

Leave, that's what I have to do.

Leave.

Only my body has other plans.

My eyes lift up, up, up.

I have to know.

I have to know who this guy is that's worthy of Jeanette Sanders.

The guy who is the complete opposite of me.

Broad shoulders, he's tall, taller than her, but not as tall as me. Light, preppy hair moved out of his face. Light blue eyes. Arrogant smirk on his stupid face.

A smirk worse than the one I'm usually wearing, if that's possible.

"Ethan-fucking-Williams?" I roar, turning toward Max.

His eyes narrow even more looking at me, the fists by his sides clenching and unclenching fast.

"What do you know about him?"

"Enough to know he's a douchebag."

"Coming from an asshole himself. You don't have to ..."

"Right, and when I say he's worse than me, I mean it. Anybody but him, Max." I let my eyes meet his so he knows I mean what I say. "Anybody but him."

Then I'm gone.

I push through the mass of people, not caring who I shove away, as long as I get to her fast. As long as I get her out of his arms, out of his reach forever.

Of all the guys in this damn state ...

I shake my head, trying to calm down.

I can't cause a scene. Dad would have my balls if I do, but I'm not backing down. Not on this one.

She's leaving his stupid, arrogant ass behind—with or without me. Her choice, but she's leaving him now.

I hear Max behind me, but somebody calls his name. I'm not sure if he's still following or if he stayed behind, but it doesn't matter either way.

This is my problem to deal with.

Mine.

Just like her, for as long as we're fucking.

Mine.

Ethan's hand keeps caressing her skin, his face so near hers that it's making me crazy. If he doesn't stop in two seconds straight, I'm going to pull his damn hands out and there will be no surgeon who'll be able to put his body back in one piece.

His face is coming closer and closer to hers.

My teeth grit tight. So tight I'm sure I can hear them breaking.

I outstretch my hand–close, so close—wrapping it around her wrist and pulling her away.

Away from him and into my open arms.

"Get your fucking hands off of her!" I growl low at him.

Her body stiffens, then relaxes, then stiffens again, but she doesn't back away.

Ethan seems startled for a second, but soon regains his wits. His lips curl in a smug smile. "Hill, long time no see."

His voice is all cheer, loud enough to draw attention from the people standing close by.

"To see you never again in my life would be way too soon," I whisper just loud enough for him to hear me.

He chuckles, well aware of the fact. If there's one person I hate in this world more than my old man, it's this douche.

Jeanette's hand wraps around mine that's still holding her wrist, her thumb drawing little circles on my skin.

Calm and soothing.

"I see you've met my date." His sleazy eyes go back to Jeanette, taking her in.

I press my lips into a tight line, doing my best to resist his taunt. I know what he's doing and I'm not going to fall for it, not today anyway. No matter how hard I have to try.

He'll cross my path soon enough, probably on the ice, and then all bets are off.

His eyes linger on our hands. Still touching. Just barely, but enough for him to notice.

I break the contact, taking a step around her and coming toe-to-toe with Ethan.

"You stay the hell away from her." I speak so low I'm sure not even Jeanette can hear me. "Fair and only warning, Williams. If you touch her again, hell, if you come within a five-mile radius of her, I'm breaking every bone in your body."

Without waiting for his response, I turn around, grab Jeanette's hand and start pulling her out of there.

Away from him.

Away from all of them.

Chapter 23

JEANETTE

"Andrew, stop!" I pant, trying to get my hand out of his hold.

After he said, or more like threatened, Ethan, he took my hand in his and started to break through the crowd that gathered around us. Oh, they were all politely minding their own business, but you could see them lean just a bit to the side, their ears carefully listening to everything spoken so they have something to gossip about during dessert.

These people live and breathe drama like this.

Andrew's steps are long as he conquers the distance with determination, pulling me behind him. My legs, still slightly wobbly from the way Ethan touched me and the whole encounter between the two of them, trip over each other.

What the hell was that anyway? I've never seen Andrew so ... angry before.

He's usually cold, hiding behind his snarky remarks and sarcasm. Yes, he has a temper, but he usually saves it for the ice instead of unleashing it outside the rink, but right now he's furious.

He stops suddenly, his hands leaving mine, rubbing his face before they run through his hair, dark strands sticking out in every direction.

"What the hell happened in there?" I ask, my hand waving in the general direction of the building behind us.

My whole body shudders with cold, and I realize that we're outside in the cold and snow, and the only thing I'm wearing is my light dress.

Green eyes find mine. "You're cold," he states, as if he just now comprehends that he brought us outside in freaking December when it's cold as fuck.

Shrugging out of his dress jacket, he takes those few steps that separate us and wraps it around me. My arms slide inside and the warmth of his jacket surrounds me, the scent of cut grass and pines entering my every pore.

I burrow my head inside, pulling the material closed over my chest in hopes of keeping the warmth as I inhale deeply, savoring his scent.

The anger and frustration I was feeling only a moment ago deflates because of his sweet gesture.

The jacket is big, too big for me, falling all the way down to my knees. Wrapping it around me as not to let the cool air underneath the material, it almost feels like he's hugging me.

"What the hell happened inside, Andrew?" I repeat, my voice soft. "How do you know Ethan?"

"The better question is—" He leans closer, eyes narrowed and jaw set tight. "What the hell are you doing with him on a *date*?"

The last word comes out as an angry, irritated growl. He's leaning into my face so I can see every dot in his eyes and every line marring his forehead, including the vein throbbing furiously.

He's pissed.

But so am I.

How dare he? He's the one who's been hooking up with other girls ever since I've known him. I stopped counting the number of different girls hanging from his hand between our hook-up in library and now. He fucked a girl at the Halloween party, kissed another one in the cafeteria just to piss me off, lets them hang off him like they're accessory simply because he gets a thrill of knowing they find him irresistible.

Fucking idiotic douchebag.

I shove him away, putting all the strength behind that one push. "It's none of your business, Hill," I spat. "You don't get to come out here, cause a scene and then demand answers from me, like I'm the one in the wrong here!"

"No? You went on a fucking *date* with my biggest enemy and asshole ..."

I roll my eyes at him. "You're the one saying ..."

"While we're..." He stops, opens his mouth, but no words come out. Andrew is so close to me, panting hard, puffing little clouds in the air on every exhale. "While we're ..."

"While we're ... what?" I don't let his nearness and height intimidate me. Taking one step nearer, I'm now so close our chests are brushing.

Inhale.

Brush.

Exhale.

"Whatever the hell we are."

"Nothing." I let my eyes meet his and hold his gaze. "We're nothing. Fooled around a few times, had sex twice. Aren't you the ultimate love-'em-and-leave-'em guy?"

"Maybe I am, but listen to me carefully, Jeanette." His cool fingers brush against my cheek, untangling a strand of hair and pulling it back as his fingers slide between my strands. He tilts my head just slightly, and I can feel the tingly sensation run through my body as he fists my hair.

Excitement.

Even when I'm pissed and fuming, he can make my body react.

His green eyes are wide, almost haunted, but also intense. So, so intense. And they're looking straight at me.

My tongue darts out to wet my dry lips.

"Fuck whoever you want to fuck, date whoever you want to date."

I swallow hard, my irritation growing and I don't even know why. He's giving me exactly what I expect of him, exactly what I want, but ... "Then why ..."

His fingers tighten their hold on me. "But don't ever go near Ethan Williams again. Understood?"

"Why him? What did he do to you?"

Some of the intensity in his eyes dies as he disentangles his fingers and takes a step away from me.

My body shudders as the icy night air surrounds me again. For a few seconds, I forgot where we were and how cold it is outside, but now that I'm not wrapped up in Andrew's heat, it's back in full force.

Once again he runs his fingers through his hair, the distant look in his eyes remaining until they fill with suppressed anger and rage.

For a slip of second, I actually feel afraid of the look on his face, the look in his eyes, until I realize it's not directed at me.

No, it's directed toward Ethan.

"He's partly the reason why my family fell apart."

ANDREW

I regret the words as soon as they leave my mouth, but there is no taking them back now.

"What?" Jeanette's mouth opens in surprise.

"Forget it." I turn around, raising the barrier between us. I saw the fear on her face, and it wrecked me. She's actually afraid.

Of me.

I'm used to it. People fear me because of my name, my popularity and my dickhead attitude. But never her. Since the moment she stepped her tiny little foot in Greyford, Jeanette Sanders has been my equal. Not once has she tolerated my attitude, and she always calls me on my shit, twisting my balls if and when I take it too far. And in some bizarre way, I like it. I like her determination and her confidence. I like her strength and sense of right and wrong.

But I guess one can only take so much, and this is her breaking point.

Swallowing hard, I take a few steps away from her and the party, but I'm soon stopped in my tracks. Her delicate, icy fingers wrap around my hand, tugging hard.

I look over my shoulder at her, lower lip wobbling with cold but a determined look in her gray eyes.

She lifts one finger in the air. "I'm not going to forget it," soon followed by the second. "And you don't get to leave me here on my own."

Sighing, I turn around. "Let's get you inside. You're going to freeze to death."

Why did I bring her outside in the cold when I know damn well she's so sensitive to it? She's always wearing those sweaters and big socks to keep warm. I didn't think, that's why. I let my rage overtake me, and not only did I help her freeze, but I also made her scared of me.

How big of a fuckup can one person be?

"No." Jeanette folds her arms over her chest to keep herself warm probably as much as to keep them from shaking. "Tell me, right here, right now."

"You're going to get pneumonia."

"I don't fucking care. Now tell me."

Throwing my head back, I exhale in exasperation. Jeanette Sanders and her stubbornness will be the death of me. And herself, because I'm sure if she doesn't return inside soon, she'll end up in the hospital.

"When I was eight, I came home one day to see my mom had packed her shit and left," I say matter-of-factly. It's been a long time since I resigned myself with her decision. "No explanations, no goodbyes, nothing. Just one lousy Post-it note attached to the divorce papers saying she's feeling asphyxiated by her life and that she needs out, so she left. She didn't mention where or leave a way to contact her. Nothing. It's like she erased us out of her life."

"Andrew ..." she starts, but I stop her. I don't need or want her pity. And if I stop now, I'm not sure I'll be able to start again.

"She left, and for the next few years I didn't hear from her. Not once did she call to ask about me. To hear how I was doing, to wish me happy birthday or any other holiday. It was like I never existed, yet still ... yet, still I hoped. I hated her, but I loved her, because she was my mother. And mothers are supposed to love their kids, right?"

I laugh bitterly.

"Then one year, I was twelve or thirteen, I found her. I just started using social media, and I googled her. Turns out, she didn't move too far away, just the next town over."

Jeanette's eyes soften, crystal liquid forming in them. I know she'll interrupt me once again, but it's like I'm on a roll and I can't stop.

"Turns out she wasn't asphyxiated by the family life; she was asphyxiated by us. She left us and found herself another family.

That afternoon when I found her, I took my bike and rode like crazy. Ten miles, but I would have done anything to see her. To hear from her what I did wrong for her to leave us. Because it had to be my fault, you know? I must have done something for her to leave us. For her not to even want to talk to me."

"Oh, Andrew ..." Her voice is a whisper. A beautiful, broken, pained whisper.

I try to stay away, to keep my distance, but she doesn't care. She comes to me, her arms wrapping around my middle as she pulls me closer, burrowing her head into my chest.

My hands hang by my side; it's like I don't have it in me to lift them up, but she doesn't seem to care. Clearing my throat, I continue. "When I got to her house I was so sweaty you'd think I spent hours doing drills on the ice. My breathing was hectic, heart beating hard in my chest, partly from exhaustion and partly because, after years, I was finally going to see her. My mother."

Her image from that day resurfaces in my mind. My eyes fall shut as I try to fight back the memories. Push back the pain of that day.

She was wearing jeans and a casual, light pink sweater. Her brown hair was lifted in a high ponytail that swayed through the air. She wasn't wearing a lot of make-up, just a bit of mascara to accentuate her blue-green eyes and shiny gloss on her lips.

"I climbed the steps to the door and rung the bell. It seemed like forever. Waiting there, shifting my weight from one leg to the other nervously as I rubbed my sweaty palms on the sweats I was wearing, but it was probably seconds."

I clear my throat, overwhelmed. It feels like it's happening all over again.

"I heard the hurried steps behind the door, followed by the laughter. I remember thinking how there was no more laughter in my house. Just silence. Then the door swung open, and there he stood. Ethan Williams. Even then, he was my biggest rival. We always seemed to play the same sports and compete in the same competitions, only on opposite sides. Baseball and hockey, debate and math competitions, he was always there. Sometimes winning, sometimes loosing, but always present. And now, the door opens to my mother's new home, and he's there.

"We were staring at each other, silent. I didn't know what to say, and neither did he. I was confused, thinking maybe I got it wrong, maybe this wasn't her house. But then there she was. Apron on and a trace of flour on her cheek. She was laughing. She was fucking laughing and calling him honey. 'Ethan, honey, who's at the door?' That's what she asked. And like a bucket full of cold water had been thrown over my head, I woke up from the daze. Her eyes connected with mine. I remember them growing wide in surprise, her mouth opened as if she'd say something, but I didn't want to give her a chance. I didn't want to listen. She erased us from her life? Very well, she'll be dead to me."

Absentmindedly, I rub my chest, the pressure behind my breast bone making it hard to breathe.

"I turned around and ran for my bike. Even though I was tired, I pedaled so hard, just in case she decided to follow me, but of course she didn't. Why bother with the son she never wanted when she had a newer, shinier version in her new family?

That evening when I got back home, the house was empty. Nothing new about that. Dad didn't bother coming home much after she left. He was always too 'busy' with work to bother with me. I broke every single thing on my way from the front door to the living room. Vases and sculptures, frames and whatever else got in my way. I was so angry. And then I saw the bar. The image of my dad finding solace in alcohol when he did bother to come home flashed in my mind. That was the first time I got drunk. I got so drunk I was puking half the night, and when I woke up, I was so sick I couldn't get out of bed. But I learned two things. One, my mom is a selfish, lying bitch who doesn't deserve a bit of my remorse and guilt. And two, alcohol brings oblivion. Even if just for a few hours, it helps you forget. So I kept on drinking."

Chapter 24

JEANETTE

My hands tighten around him, and somewhere along the way, his hands curled around me, too, returning my hug.

Harder.

Stronger.

Tighter.

We hold on to each other for dear life.

Until our bodies are molded together to perfection.

Until there is no space left between us.

"I'm so sorry," I whisper softly.

Just once.

I murmur those words just once. My voice barely audible, but it's enough. He knows it, and I know it.

On some level that only we understand, this is enough.

Broken, misunderstood boy finds solace in the arms of equally broken and fucked-up girl.

In this moment we let ourselves feel the pain of our pasts wash over us.

Just for a little while.

It won't change anything.

The wrongs won't be rewritten and the present will still be the same, but in this one moment, we let ourselves feel the sadness of what might have been.

His forehead presses into mine, and I close my eyes, letting myself feel.

All of it.

All the possibilities and choices.

All the paths we could have taken, the paths the people around us could have taken, and maybe if they had, maybe if *we* had, we wouldn't be as broken and jaded as we are.

Irreparable.

What might have been if his mother had stayed and they were still a family. What might have been if that day I didn't give in to Maddy and her friends. What might have been if his dad spent more time with him, instead of working long hours and avoiding his home and son. What might have been if I didn't give in to the pressure of my peers.

What might have been ...

So many what ifs. So many possibilities, so many options. But at the end of the day, what mights are just an illusion. Just a lie. Beautiful, but a lie nonetheless.

We are who we are because of the choices we made.

The paths we took.

If things were different, if his parents had stayed together or if I hadn't gone through what I did, would they have led us to this moment?

To this now?

His hands cup my cheeks, rough fingertips brushing over my cheekbones. I flutter my eyes open, looking at his deep greens.

"Don't you dare pity me, Jeanette Sanders."

I let the small chuckle part my lips. "Do I look like somebody capable of that? Besides, there is nothing to pity. You had a fucked-up childhood, boo-fucking-hoo. You're not the first one, and you most surely won't be the last. Hell, you didn't even see the worst of it. Don't you dare think that excuses your shitty behavior and asshole attitude."

Andrew laughs, and it feels good. It feels good to laugh. To let go of all the bad surrounding us, all the tension and hard memories and just *be*.

"What about you, Ice Princess? Or is it Queen? I'm never sure."

I shove him away, rolling my eyes at his playful tone.

"What about me?"

"What's your story?"

Flashbacks run in front of my eyes. All the things that have happened in the last few years. Too many things. Too many memories. My smile falls, but I try to hold on to it.

"It's a story for another day," I finally say. "After your emotional vomit, I think we've both had enough."

He shakes his head. "Brat."

"You still like me."

Green eyes look at me attentively. I hold his gaze, letting him take his fill, but also taking in mine.

The way his eyes are just a tad darker and mossy. The way his tawny hair sticks out in all directions, making him look like a mischievous little boy. The pout of his lips.

"Yeah, I kind of do."

I nibble at my lower lip as his words settle. My heart skips a beat and I inhale sharply. Andrew Hill just said he likes me.

The whole concept feels foreign, yet my skin buzzes with anticipation.

His eyes lower to my lips before they return to mine.

A flash of white teeth, and then he's kissing me.

And it's like nothing I've ever felt before.

Soft, almost tender, he nibbles at my lip playfully.

My fingers dig into the soft material of his dress shirt as I lean into him, getting on the tips of my toes to be closer to him.

Our lips mash together, sliding slowly.

He pulls my lower lip in his mouth, sucking softly.

I moan, my lips parting and letting his tongue slide in.

Hot, wet, sensual, his touch makes me beg for more.

Just as soon as it began, the contact breaks. He pulls away, and with one final, close-mouthed kiss, he takes a step back.

"You're shivering." His hands slide up and down my arms in an attempt to make me feel warmer.

"Just a bit."

"Let's get back inside, or you really will catch pneumonia and your brother really *will* kill me then."

"Max!" I turn around dumbfounded, as if I'm expecting to see him jump out of the frozen bushes or something.

"Somebody stopped him from coming after me."

"I'm not sure if that's a blessing or a curse."

Andrew's hands wrap around me, pushing me back in the direction of the country club.

"Either way, he knows you're with me."

She looks over her shoulder at me. "He thinks you're not good enough. Too broken, just like me."

"Maybe he's right." He takes the baggy out of his back pocket and starts rolling a joint.

"He thinks you'll hurt me. Fuck me up beyond repair."

The sharp flame of the lighter illuminates the night.

"How can I break something that's already been broken?"

His words should make me feel at ease, but they don't because a small voice at the back of my head gives me the answer I don't want to hear.

You put it together, only to break it apart. This time, beyond repair.

Chapter 25

ANDREW

Princess: Stop staring at me. People are starting to notice. M is starting to notice!

I chuckle lightly, not able to hold it in as I type back quickly.

"Who're you texting, dude?"

Lucas, one of the guys on the team, tries to look over my shoulder, but I lock the screen swiftly, putting the phone back into my pocket. I pick a fry off my tray and pop it into my mouth.

It's lunchtime, and we're all sitting together in the cafeteria. Derek and Lia are doing their lovey-dovey thing while the rest of us sit and talk hockey, at least the male part of the group. Winter holidays start this weekend, so there are no games until school starts back in January. But the coach still wants us to come to practice every day, which is more than fine by me. It's not like I have anything better to do anyway.

"Yeah, who're you texting?" Max asks, his eyes holding mine for a while before he looks pointedly at his sister sitting on the other side of our table.

He's been doing it a lot since the charity ball. After Jeanette and I got back inside, we were both swept away in different directions, but I could feel Max's probing eyes on the back of my head for the rest of the evening. He knew something was up. We were together outside and he saw us walk back inside together. Only an idiot would let it slide.

"Just some chick."

Now that Max's attention is back on me, I can feel her piercing gaze staring daggers into my skull. I know I'll pay for this one later, but it's that or let them know the truth. I'm not sure what exactly the truth is, but things have been different since the party last weekend.

"You hooking up with that cheerleader chick again?"

"Nope, definitely not the cheerleader."

"Dude." Derek lifts his gaze from Lia's neck for a second. "Like he'd do the same girl twice. That would practically mean he's engaged to her!"

I open my mouth to say something, but the scraping of a chair against the floor makes us all lift our heads.

"Already done?" Max asks, looking at Jeanette's half-eaten lunch.

"Yeah, I have some studying to do before my math exam. I'll see you later."

Max opens his mouth to say something, but Jeanette is already gone. His gaze follows her for a while and I think I can see worry written on his face, but even if that's the case, it's gone in the blink of an eye.

The guys return back to talking hockey, my marital status thankfully forgotten. I join in when needed, but my thoughts are elsewhere.

A few minutes later, my phone buzzes in my pants. I check it under the table so these nosy assholes can't see it. Quickly reading the message, I put the phone away and get on my feet.

"If you'll excuse me." I pick up my tray and grab my shit off the floor.

"He's going to get some," Derek teases.

"Maybe he'll stop being such a pain in the ass," somebody else adds, and all the assholes around him burst into laughter.

Chuckling, I give all of them the finger and walk away. Let them think what they want to think.

JEANETTE

I'm leaning against the wall, looking at my nails. The black color is chipped at the tips, and I make a mental note to take it off later tonight. With the holidays just around the corner, I suppose I should look presentable. Sighing, I let my hands fall by my sides.

Just then the door opens and a person enters the room, closing it quietly behind him.

Spinning around quickly, my hands wrap around his wrists, pinning him to the smooth surface.

A cunning smirk curls his lips. "Would it be weird if I said that this just made my dick twitch?"

I roll my eyes. "Everything is always about your dick."

Andrew leans forward but doesn't even try to break free. His lower half brushes against mine. "He's just trying to salute you. Nothing wrong with being polite."

"Why are we talking about your dick in the third person?"

"Don't be like that, Princess." He leans forward, whispering, "You're going to scare him away."

Andrew tries to kiss me, but I shove him back. "You're incorrigible."

"I think we already established what you think about my incorrigible ways."

"You mean, what *that chick* who's not a cheerleader thinks."

"Oh come on!" he groans, running his fingers through his hair. "I had to say something."

As I turn my back to him, his hands wrap around me from behind, and my body relaxes instantly at his touch.

"I know. That was low. Sorry."

And I do know it, but it still rubs me the wrong way hearing him talk about me that way.

"You're the one who doesn't want Max to know, not the other way around. For all I care, they can think whatever the hell they want. I don't care either way."

That's the one thing I admire about Andrew. His ability to not care about what people around him think. They can love him or hate him, and he won't give a damn either way. He's just so disconnected. So ... unfazed.

I look down at his hands wrapped around my middle, holding me close. His embrace is warm, our bodies molding together perfectly.

"He can't know. I won't put you or him in that position."

"You'd rather lie to him?"

I find it unnerving, how well he knows me. Or maybe he's just good at reading people. Reading *me.* No matter which one it is, he can see through my defenses, and that in itself is scary.

"I'm already lying to him," I murmur quietly. So quiet that only I can hear it. "So what is one more lie?"

Turning in his embrace, I tilt my head back so I can look at Andrew. "I'm not risking fucking this up for anybody."

Something flashes in his eyes, but he shakes it away. His hand brushes against my cheek, his finger tangling with the strands of my loose hair.

"Whatever you want."

Slowly, one side of my mouth tugs upward. "Anything?"

My hands, which are pressed against his chest, slide upward until they curl around his neck.

Andrew returns my half-smile with one of his own.

"Anything you want is yours for the taking, Jeanette."

I stand on the tips of my toes because, although I'm tall, he's taller. My grip on his neck tightens and he lowers his head.

So close.

Our breaths mingling.

Our noses brushing.

Our lips parting.

A slow, delicious tremble runs through me at his proximity.

At his touch.

"Even you?" I whisper against his lips.

I can feel the heat radiating all around him.

The warmth of his breath against my skin.

The roughness of his fingertips on my cheeks.

"Most of all me."

His words are all the push I need. Closing the barely visible gap between us, I press my lips against his.

He meets my gaze as my tongue slides over his lower lip and finds its way into his mouth.

At the first touch of velvet against velvet, Andrew groans loudly. His eyelashes flutter closed as his grip on me tightens. My tongue plunges deeper, and a needy moan vibrates in my throat.

So good.

Why does it always feel so good to kiss him?

My whole body turns into one giant nerve that's pulsing with all this energy, and it feels like I'm going to burst if I don't get just a little bit more of him.

One more kiss.

One more swipe.

One more touch.
More. More. More.
Until this ever-growing habit is satisfied.
Only it never is.
There is always more, and I'm not ready for it to be over.

Chapter 26

JEANETTE

"Granny!" I squeal in excitement as I open the front door and find my favorite family member on the other side.

"Jeanette Ann." She smiles brightly. Her hands wrap around me, pulling me in for a long hug. Kissing both my cheeks, she takes a step back, looking at me. "You look beautiful, baby girl."

"It all comes from the Wilson-Davies side of the family." I wink playfully at her. And I'm not lying. Both Max and I got most of our physical attributes from our mom, who's a carbon copy of Granny. Her hair is styled in a trendy bob and colored religiously to keep it its original midnight black color. Even in her late seventies, her crystal-blue eyes hold the sharpness I remember from a young age.

"Let me help you with that suitcase." I usher her inside, pulling the middle-sized Louis Vuitton suitcase behind me before closing the door. A shiver runs through my body. I thought it was cold before, but I was wrong. So wrong. It's downright freezing outside, and my sensitive Californian skin can't take it for too long. "You should have called and somebody would have gone to the airport to get you!"

"Oh, shush! I'm not that old."

She takes off her coat, scarf and gloves, and I grab them from her to put them away. She's wearing one of her many pants suits. This one dark gray with barely visible silver stripes and a white silky shirt underneath it.

"Where is everybody?"

"They're around here somewhere." I wrap my hand around hers, taking her with me to the kitchen to prepare some tea to warm us up. "Dad is in the office, finishing some paperwork for the hospital. And Max is downstairs in the gym."

"On Christmas Eve?" She looks at me skeptically.

"Patients don't get better on holidays, and Max ... well, he said he has to work out so he can eat all he wants later. He got a starting position on the Wolves, and the team is just a few short games away from entering the playoffs. He's really serious about winning that thing and getting a hockey scholarship so he can play on the next level and possibly going pro later on."

Granny shakes her head, but I can see a smile tug at the corner of her mouth. "Hockey has always been Max's first love. What about you? Are you still playing violin?"

I put the pot on the stove.

"Occasionally."

Margaret Wilson Davies doesn't beat around the bush. She says it as she sees it and doesn't feel shame for doing so. I guess it's another trait I took from her.

"You should practice more. Did you apply to Julliard? I'm sure they would feel honored to have you as their student. Or are you still thinking about going to Harvard?"

"Granny ..." I turn around to give her a pointed look. She knows very well how I feel about discussing my future; she just likes to ignore it. After everything that happened almost two years ago ... it's hard to make a decision like this one.

"Alright," she sighs, letting the subject be. "How are you

holding up?" Her sharp eyes take me in from head to toe, not missing anything. "You look skinny, but then again ..."

Then again, that's my new normal.

"I'm fine, Granny. I've been doing eve—"

I don't get to finish because Mom bursts into the kitchen, startling us both. At the same time, the water starts boiling in the pot, so I move it and start working on our tea.

"Mom! When did you get here? Why didn't you call us to come and pick you up at the airport?"

They hug stiffly, exchanging air kisses. I'm not sure how their relationship was before, but since Mom married Dad, it has been strained. Grandpa, God rest his soul, and Granny took it really hard that Mom wanted to marry a "commoner." The Davies family comes from old money and thinks their blood is blue instead of red. The men work in politics, law and economics, while their female counterparts are responsible to keep up public image, produce heirs and do charity work. Old fashioned and sexist, but those are my grandparents. They even tried to set her up with one of their family friend's son they deemed suitable, but it didn't work, so they had to accept the fact that she married Dad.

"I'm old but not immobile, Jane Elizabeth."

I muffle my giggle as I pick the tea cups. "Earl Grey, your favorite."

"Thank you, dear."

Sitting by her side, I carefully stir the hot liquid in my cup.

"Still, you should have said you were coming today."

"Is there a problem with me being here, Jane?" Granny lifts one of her perfectly shaped brows in question.

Mom's cheeks glow red. "Of course not!"

"Then, it doesn't matter." Granny shuts her down. "Once we have our tea, Jeanette and I can help you with dinner."

Mom looks at us for a second in silence. I'm sure there are a lot of things roaming around her mind, but she keeps her mouth shut.

No matter their relationship, Grandma has always treated Max and me with love and respect. She's never pushed her wishes and judgment on us, never tried to convert us into something we're not.

"No need, I have it all under control."

Granny looks around the spotless kitchen. "Oh really?"

"The delivery should be here around six thirty."

Grandma huffs, but doesn't say anything. Mom waits for a bit, but when nothing comes out, she nods her head. "If you'll excuse me."

The two of us exchange a glance. "Welcome home."

After our tea and chat, Granny decided to go to her room to "freshen up" and have a nap before dinner since there was nothing to help with.

I wanted to go and play violin for a bit, but even if I tried to be really quiet or went on the other side of the house, I'd probably wake her up, so in the end I decided to Netflix and chill.

It's been a while since I've binge-watched *The Originals*. I can't decide who's the sexiest, Joseph Morgan or Daniel Gillies. They're complete opposites, both their personality and physical attributes, but they both have so much charisma it's impossible not to like them.

Just when I was immersed in Klaus's killing spring, my door flies open.

Not lifting my eyes from the bloodshed happening on the

screen, I take one of the pillows on my bed and throw it in his direction. "I told you to knock, dickhead."

Max chuckles, his hands gripping the pillow he caught mid-air. Of course he did.

"Do you knock before going into my room?"

"I don't go into your room." I frown.

Why is he here again? Getting between me and the love of my life.

"Only when I'm not home so you can steal one of my hoodies."

Gasping exaggeratedly, I look at him. "I do no such thing!"

Gray eyes keep staring at me.

"Okay, maybe on weekends."

Shaking his head, he jumps on the bed.

"Whatcha watching?" Max looks over my shoulder at the show that's still playing on my laptop. "Is that the vampire dude?"

I pause the show and close the screen of my laptop, turning around to look at him. "He's not just some vampire *dude*. He's Klaus-freaking-Mikaelson, the vampire king himself. Show some respect, dude."

"Whatever." Max ruffles my hair before jumping off the bed. His own hair is messy and still slightly wet from his shower. "The caterers are here. I suggest you put on some *presentable* clothes, Mom's words not mine, and come down."

Sighing, I look at the laptop with longing. "Later."

Dinner goes as smoothly as can be expected. Things are pretty tense in the beginning between Granny and my parents, but after a while the conversation starts to flow easier, mostly thanks to Max and his chattering between huge mouthfuls of food.

I nibble at my own dinner—turkey, mashed potatoes, cranberry sauce and lots of vegetables—listening to them and participating when necessary. The caterers did a good job on the food, I have to give them that, but maybe it would have been fun if Granny, Mom and I had cooked dinner together. It's been such a long time since we've done something together because we *can* instead of because we *have* to.

The image of Amelia and her mom from the first time I visited her house flashes in my mind. I can picture them together this time of year. Decorating the house, wearing those obnoxious Christmas sweaters, baking cookies and preparing dinner for family.

Their relationship is so easy, so natural. I've never seen anything like that. Never felt anything like that. Not with my mom. There was a time ... a time when my dad and I were inseparable. A time when he was my hero and I wanted to be just like him when I grew up, but that has changed.

After dinner, we went to the living room, which was professionally decorated for the holidays. All the decorations are white and pale gold.

Classy and perfect.

We have red velvet cake before settling down and exchanging presents. And when everything is said and done, we retire to our rooms, too tired from the constant need to pretend everything is all right, while in reality, everything is falling apart.

Asshole: Merry Christmas, Princess.

My finger traces the words on the screen as a smile curls my lips.

Me: Merry Christmas to you too.

Me: What are you up to?

I leave my phone on the bed, rubbing my wet hair. I'm too lazy to dry it, but I know if I don't, my head will hurt in the morning and I'll have a nest on my head, so I grab my dryer and quickly work on drying it.

Ten minutes later I'm done. One of the benefits of having shoulder-length hair.

The light on my phone blinks, signaling a text message.

Asshole: Same old, same old.

Frowning I type back: **Not doing anything special with your dad for the holidays?**

Three little dots appear on the screen, and I wait for him to type back.

Asshole: He's supposed to be here for us to do something.

I reread the message over and over again, the frown on my forehead deepening.

He's all alone in that big-ass house of his? Where is his dad?

I think back to all the times I've been to Andrew's house or just around him in general. If I don't count the brief glance at him at the charity party a couple of weeks ago, I don't remember ever seeing his dad around.

How could he do that? Leave his son alone for Christmas? My family is fucked up, but even we spend the holidays together.

Looking out the window, I see that the snow has slowed down a bit. I tilt my head to the side, listening carefully. The house is quiet. Shortly after exchanging presents, Grandma went to her room, saying she was tired and everybody else followed suit.

I nibble at my lip, thinking.

I shouldn't do it.

It's insane.

Really insane.

And if somebody hears me ...

I shouldn't.

My eyes fall down to the dark screen of my phone clenched in my hand.

No, I shouldn't ...

Chapter 27

ANDREW

I walk through the dark house, a glass of whiskey in my hand, just an occasional dimmed light turned on to give the illusion that somebody is home.

Taking a slow sip from the glass, I let the liquid burn in my throat.

Well, I guess *I'm* home, but to anybody looking from the outside, it would look like the house is empty.

Covered in darkness and silence.

Asphyxiating.

If it was any other day, I'd get out of here or invite somebody over. Anything to avoid this deafening nothingness.

But it's almost midnight on Christmas Eve. There is no escape for me tonight.

I look at my phone, expecting a slight glow indicating a text message, but there is nothing. Only blackness.

Unlocking the screen, I go through Jeanette's messages. We've been texting a lot lately, and I've actually been looking forward to our banter, hoping it would take my mind off the loneliness, only she never texted back.

My last text stares at me accusingly.

Me: He's supposed to be here for us to do something.

I shouldn't have said it. I should have kept my mouth shut and maybe she wouldn't feel like she has to say something to make this better. Because there is nothing that can be said. My mom hated me so much she left me, and my dad can't stand the sight of me, so he'd rather spend his time outside these four walls.

Leaning against the window, I take a sip of whiskey, watching the snow fall. It's not a full-on snow storm, more like a glide of fluffy bits from the sky.

Peaceful.

The whole backyard is covered in untouched whiteness.

Pure and whole.

Everything I'm not.

Sighing, I debate between lighting a joint to de-stress or simply crashing in bed, when I hear the faint sound of a car nearing.

"What the ..."

Turning around, I leave the now-empty glass on the bar top and start toward the foyer. Dad decided to go to some Christmas dinner with his associates. He wanted me to come, but I brushed him off. I didn't have it in me to spend one more evening pretending to be something he wanted me to be. Not tonight.

Derek and his dad joined Amelia and her family for dinner since his mom was working the night shift. Or was it the other way around? Either way, it can't be him.

Not bothering to look through the window, I unlock the door and walk out to the front porch.

White puffs of air come out of my mouth, and the cold makes my skin tingle.

From the doorway, I watch the gray SUV approach,

recognizing it instantly. My heart kicks up a notch, but I don't move a muscle. Bright lights blind me for a moment when the car stops just in front of the house, but then they're off and I can finally see clearly again.

The door opens, and one toned leg comes out after the other.

"What are you doing here?" I ask, my eyes looking at her messy hair and make-up-free face.

God, she looks beautiful.

Her chest lifts as she inhales deeply. "Nobody should spend Christmas alone," she finally says, shrugging. "And I come bearing food."

We look at each other from a distance. Her cheeks and nose are red from the cold, and she's shivering even in her thick winter jacket.

Sighing, I run my fingers through my hair. What the hell am I going to do with her?

"Well, if you come bearing food, by all means, come inside."

* * *

"This is really good," I mumble happily over a mouthful of turkey. "Want some?"

Shaking her head, she smiles softly from the other side of the couch. "Nah, I'm good. Mom ordered dinner from some fancy catering service."

I nod my head in understanding, swallowing. "No cooking?"

"Granny wanted to, but Mom is ..."

Jeanette waves her hand in the air, trying to come up with the right word to describe her mother, but she doesn't have to because I understand her completely. My family is the same.

Or, well, *was* the same.

We still have a housekeeper who comes around every day. She cleans the house, does the grocery shopping and prepares the meals. Most days she's the only other person in this house besides me.

Eating the last of the food, I put the box on the coffee table and take a sip of water, mostly to give myself something to do while I try to settle my mind.

What is she doing here?

The question has been roaming around my mind since I recognized her car coming up the driveway. The last thing I expected when she didn't answer me back was to see her on my doorstep, but I guess I shouldn't be surprised.

Jeanette Sanders might be tough on the outside, but underneath her cool exterior there is one very compassionate, although bitchy, heart. I've seen it before.

She hides it well. Her walls are so big and strong, but for some reason, I can see through them.

"You didn't have to come, you know," I finally say.

Jeanette shrugs, tucking a strand of her hair behind her ear. "It's not like I had anything better to do anyway."

"What about your family?"

"They went to bed, or whatever the hell they're doing. They won't even notice I'm gone."

I nod, observing her. Her cheeks are still flushed, although she's been inside for a while now. White teeth flash in the dimmed light of the living room as she nibbles at her lower lip. Soft flesh turning red.

"So I suppose you don't have to go home anytime soon?"

Jeanette shakes her head, silky strands shaking with the motion. "Nope."

My eyes zero in on that plump lip, tongue darting out to wet my own. "Anything specific you'd like to do?"

"We could probably find some cheesy Christmas movie on TV." She shrugs, but a small, playful smile tilts her lips.

"Christmas movie, huh?"

Taking the remote off the coffee table, I turn on the TV. Then I relax into the couch, my hands spreading over the back and my fingers brushing against her shoulder.

Gray eyes find mine. "What do you think you're doing?"

"You wanted to watch a movie, we'll watch a movie."

She pointedly looks at my hand thrown over her shoulders before they return to my face. "Just like that?"

"Just like that." I shrug, not wanting to make a big deal about it.

When we're together, we usually mess around. Kissing, touching, fucking ... whatever we're in the mood for. But we're never just together. We don't go out on dates or do other coupley shit together, so tonight's a first.

First dinner.

First movie.

First cuddling session.

When the fuck did I become that guy?

Jeanette stares at me for a while longer. I'm not sure what she's looking for or if she found it.

"Okay," she finally says, snuggling into my side as I scroll mindlessly through Netflix waiting for her to point out something she might like.

"That one."

I press play, not really interested in what's on TV.

The movie starts, and although my eyes are concentrated on the screen in front of me, I don't see a thing.

I'm just happy I'm not alone. That there is something, *someone*, here that's diverting my attention from all the loneliness that was haunting me only minutes ago. And that it's her.

Her little body is snuggled into my side, her legs thrown over mine as my hand brushes her arm.

Up and down.

Down and up.

Slow and steady my fingers caress her body.

It's actually *nice*. Sitting here and doing nothing with somebody else. Kicked back and relaxed. I've never done this before with a girl.

Obviously, there were other girls before Jeanette. A lot of them. But with them, it was all about the physical. Touching and teasing and fucking. Lots of fucking. Chasing the high to find oblivion. To find peace. No matter how temporary. But then I was out of the bed and running before my dick even got the chance to empty properly.

When she's around, it's the complete opposite.

I crave her.

I crave to touch her. To wrap my hands around her and feel her body mold to mine. The way she sighs just before she leans her head on my chest is music to my ears. I crave her hands on my body. The sound of her laugh and the glow in her eyes when she looks at me.

"Will you stop it?"

Jeanette turns toward me so abruptly, she knocks me flat on my back. She almost falls off the couch, so I wrap my hands around her, her chest pressing against mine. The impact is strong enough to knock the wind out of our lungs.

I look at her, eyes wide and lips slightly parted.

"If you wanted to play dirty all you had to do was ask." I flash a grin at her, watching her cheeks turn pink.

"I-I ..." she stutters, a mix of confusion, shyness and what's left of earlier irritation.

Pressing my finger against her lips, I shush her. Her mouth opens like she's going to protest, but I kiss her on the lips.

Once.

Twice.

Thrice.

Our lips barely brush before I pull away.

She moans, dissatisfied and needy, which only makes me chuckle more.

"You were saying?"

I nibble at her lip, pulling it into my mouth.

Her fingers grip my shirt tightly and push me away. Finding her balance, she shuffles in my lap straddling me, her pussy rubbing firmly against my dick and making us both groan loudly.

"As I was saying—" Her fingers dig into my scalp, pulling me closer. "Shut up and kiss me."

Not giving me a chance not to obey her, her lips land on mine.

Hard and needy.

Lips part, tongues tangle with so much intensity and desire I can feel my whole body burn with need. Want like no other runs through my veins, making me burn from the inside out.

Kiss her.

My lips slide against her, a low moan vibrating in the back of her throat as I plunge my tongue deeper.

Touch her.

My fingers slide up her thighs, grip her slim waist, before they lower down her back and on her ass.

Feel her.

They squeeze the toned flesh, helping direct her grinding hips to the painful throbbing in my cock, her heat enveloping me completely.

Take her.

I want to bury myself inside of her so deep the only thing

she can feel is me. Hear my name fall from her lips as I claim her over and over and over again.

"My room," I growl as I jump on my feet with her in my arms.

I have to have her. In my room, on my bed, on my terms. With my cock buried so deep in her pussy we won't know where one ends and the other one begins.

"Andrew," Jeanette shrieks, completely startled. She barely manages to grab a hold on me before I run toward the stairs.

Chapter 28

JEANETTE

As soon as we climb to the second floor, my mouth is back on his. We kiss greedily as he advances blindly toward his room. Lips clashing, teeth nibbling, tongues plunging.

It's hot. It's messy and almost desperate, but I can't help myself around this guy.

Once he's in my proximity, I need him to touch me. I need his hands on my body and his lips devouring mine.

It's insanity.

Pure and simple.

But I'll take this kind of crazy any day of the week if it means having him.

Having his lips on me as his hands play my body like the most beautiful of symphonies.

Making me feel wanted.

Making me feel alive.

Making me feel *whole*.

My legs tighten around him, and I can feel the pulsing of his dick nestled between our bodies. Even behind all these clothes separating us I can feel how hard he is.

Sliding my hands down his shoulders and chest, I dip them underneath his shirt. My cool fingers touching his feverish skin.

A low hiss parts his lips and I bite slowly into his plump, swollen lip, pulling it into my mouth and sucking lightly to relieve the sting as my hands trace his lower abs.

"This has to go," I murmur, slipping his shirt up his chest and over his head, throwing it away in the darkness of his room.

As soon as the shirt passes his head, his lips are on mine again. Heated kisses drive me insane, so insane I almost miss the flick of the switch and the dim light turning on.

"Andrew," I plead.

He knows what I want, but he shakes his head lightly, not once stopping the kiss. His hand grips the edge of my shirt.

"Please." I try again, feeling vulnerable.

During all of our hook-ups, we were clouded in the darkness. Hiding from other people. Hiding from each other. Hiding from *ourselves*.

I gulp down, trying to calm the panic that's boiling underneath the surface.

I'm not ready.

I can't let him see my body.

I can't even look at my body; how can I expect him to look at it? To like it?

"Princess," Andrew whispers, his forehead pressing against mine, panting slightly. "It's just me."

His green eyes gaze into mine with so much tenderness and sincerity, something in me breaks open.

I believe him.

I *trust* him.

Just me.

It's just Andrew. There is nothing to be afraid of.

Slowly, I nod my head once. The movement barely visible, but he sees it.

Like he sees me.

His mouth presses against mine.

One. Two. Three times.

Tender, closed-mouthed kisses.

Then he resumes the work of taking my shirt off. I lift my arms in the air, helping him slip it over my head.

He lets it slide off his fingers, his eyes still staring into mine.

"You're beautiful."

I chuckle nervously. "You didn't even look at me."

The tips of his fingers caress my cheek. "I don't have to see you to know how beautiful you are."

So many mixed feelings cluster in my body. Unresolved, messy feelings that make me choke up.

How does he do it? How does he go from a complete jackass to the sweetest of guys in seconds?

This time when his mouth connects with mine, his touch is light. Almost tender. His lips swipe over mine slowly as he tastes my lips on his. Simple, tentative, chaste kisses that make me shudder.

I sigh, one of my hands going to the nape of his neck, my fingers running through his hair, the brown strands soft at my touch.

His hands cup my cheeks, thumbs brushing against my cheekbones as he suckles my lower lip.

My mouth parts, eyes snapping open and landing on his. Green globes, hooded with lust, watching me.

His lips are puffy and red from our kisses.

I swipe over his lower lip with my thumb, but don't get far because he sucks my finger between his lips.

Moaning softly at the sensation, I let my eyes close and my head tilt back.

"Eyes on me, Princess." He bites softly into my finger.

Those words ...

The tender nibble makes me shiver as warmth spreads through my body. I blink my eyes, barely holding them open.

My hand slides down his chest, feeling every ridge and valley. Strong yet lean. Just feeling his chest under the palm of my hand makes my mouth water. I let my hand brush over his peck, my finger twitching the flat nipple playfully until it hardens.

I wet my suddenly dry lips, and then I bow my head, pulling one nub into my mouth and sucking lightly.

"Jean—"

His sudden hiss makes me chuckle. Empowered. He makes me feel empowered.

I switch to the other side, repeating the same thing. I can feel his dick jump up in excitement, pressing harder against my pussy.

I swallow the needy moan at the touch of him against me. I want him. I want him so badly, but not just yet.

My fingers go lower, tracing every ab separately, and then I come to soft, light trail that leads into his jeans. Taking my lip between my teeth, I let my fingers trace down, down, down ...

"Not yet, Princess," Andrew grumbles, his voice low and rough as his hand wraps around my wrist, stopping me just before I can reach the edge of his jeans. "If you touch me, I'm going to burst and we don't want that."

"I think we esta— ..."

He cuts me off with a kiss. One long, hungry, greedy kiss.

It's wet and sloppy, but oh-so-good.

He sucks at my lip until I open up, letting his tongue enter my mouth. We swirl and dance, playing the game only known to us.

The dance of two desperate people, looking for release.

Looking for oblivion.

His hands find a way between the strands of my hair, tilting my head to get better leverage. His tongue dives deeper, making my legs shaky.

I moan loudly into his mouth, the combination of rough touch and soft lips a turn-on like no other.

My hands dig into his shoulders. Hard. So hard, I can hear him hiss.

Andrew bites into my lip.

A mute warning, before he breaks our kiss completely.

He lays me down on his bed, his big form looming over me. His chest rises with sharp breaths, and I can see his heart hammering rapidly in his chest.

He lowers over me, holding his weight on his elbows as he kisses all over my body. My neck. My collarbones. My chest. Each globe of my breasts.

Slowly, one of his hands sneaks backward, unhooking my bra and pulling it off. All the while, his eyes stay glued on mine.

The need to cover my chest is strong, but I don't do it.

I don't hide.

Not in front of him.

With eyes still on mine, his free hand slides down my side and over my tummy.

Can he feel the stretch marks? Can he feel the muffin top that no matter what I do I can't get rid of? Can he? Is he disgusted? What if he ...

He kisses me, tongue sliding into my mouth, making my head fall back and my eyes close.

"Eyes on me," he whispers between kisses, his hand cupping my breast, slowly squeezing the soft flesh as his finger rubs my nipple, making it harder than it already is.

"You're beautiful, Jeanette Sanders." Each word is accompanied with a kiss and a caress. "Beautiful and mine."

Tears gather in my eyes.

The way he looks at me, the way he touches me ... it's all just too much.

I squeeze my eyes shut, holding back the tears, and press my lips against his in a frenzied kiss.

Pushing him back, Andrew falls on his back and I straddle him.

There are no words to describe what he just gave me. The gift of acceptance, confidence in my own body, in my beauty and worth.

No words, only actions.

So I show him.

I kiss him like there is no tomorrow.

Only today.

Only now.

Only this moment.

They belong to us.

Only us.

I kiss him like he's my air and my water and everything in between.

My hand slides down his chest, fingers dipping into the waistband of his jeans.

"I need you," I whisper, almost desperately. "I need you, Andrew."

He helps me pull down his pants and kicks them off the bed.

As soon as his cock is free, I wrap my hand around it tightly. I work his length, putting the pressure just the way I know he likes it, my thumb swiping over his angry red head and smearing pre-come around it.

His head falls back as he moans. I kiss down his chest, ready to take him in my mouth, but he doesn't let me.

He throws me back on the mattress gently.

"Inside," he grits through clenched teeth. My legs fall open. Waiting. Anticipating. I can see a faint sheen of sweat on his forehead and determination shine in his eyes. "I need to be inside you."

His hands tangle in my hair as he kisses me almost desperately.

I can feel his body weight press into mine and I welcome it with open arms, and then he's inside of me.

I whimper, a mix of pain and pleasure as he enters my body in one swift movement. My legs wrap around him, heels digging into his ass and pulling him closer.

So good.

So perfect.

Andrew keeps kissing me as he moves inside me.

All over my face and chest, his hands touch everywhere he can. He plunges inside, hard and fast, hitting just the right spot, and I match him thrust for thrust.

"More," I breathe, pressing my lips against his. "I need more."

Over and over again, he gives me what I need. He retreats, only his tip brushing against my entrance, teasing, and then he plunges inside.

Harder.

Deeper.

My back arches off the mattress, yearning for his touch.

"Andrew ..."

I force my eyes open, so I can see his face. Brushing a damp strand of hair off his forehead, I press closer against him, and our lips touch, trembling.

He understands the need that's hunting me. Increasing the speed, we climb higher and higher.

We climb, our bodies shaking in need.

Climb until we finally break free.

ANDREW

Jeanette sighs contently as she shifts next to me, blanket tightly wrapped around her, keeping her body hidden from my eyes.

Leaning on my forearm, I look at her sleeping form. There is still a slight flush on her cheeks, and her lips are still raw and swollen from all the kissing. Her plump bottom lip sticks out ever so slightly, begging me to kiss it again.

A strand of messy hair falls over her face, and my hand darts out. Slowly, as not to wake her, I brush the lone strand behind her ear.

She looks happy, almost peaceful, and I can't help myself but brush her cheek with the very tip of my finger, the touch so soft there is no way it'll wake her up.

Beautiful.

Sleeping like this, in my bed, with her hair spread over my pillows and curled in the sheets where we just made love ...

The words hit me like a fucking train. Hard and brutal. I pull my hand and my whole body back abruptly, so abruptly I almost fall off the bed. My mouth hangs open in surprise as I try to figure out what the hell is wrong with me. We just fucked. Not made love, *fucked*. The orgasmic bliss is still in the air, my hormones raging. It has to be that. There is no other explanation.

There is no way I have fallen in ... I shake my head, trying to clear my mind.

They're all the same.

But are they? Are they really?

Jeanette murmurs something, her hand reaching out.

Reaching out toward me, but before her fingers can touch me, I'm already slipping out of bed.

Away from her.

I'm standing next to the bed, naked as the day I was born, looming over her. She murmurs something again, this time unintelligible. Her hand is still outstretched on the wrinkled sheets.

Calling me.

My body yearns to go back to bed, to slip between the sheets and wrap my arms around her while her head rests on my chest, but just the thought of it makes bile rise in my throat.

I cover my mouth with my hand and rush into the bathroom. Falling on the floor, my knees hit the hard, cold surface of the tiles as I loom over the toilet dry-heaving. My breathing speeds up and a cold sweat coats my skin.

This isn't happening.

It's just my fucked-up brain playing games with me.

Post-orgasmic bliss.

Hormones.

Whatever you want to call it.

It's not real.

My fingers dig into the toilet seat so hard my knuckles turn white. One lone drop of sweat slides down my nose and onto my lip, its saltiness grounding me to this moment. Closing my eyes, I will my lungs to slow down. Years of training help me zone out and concentrate on one thing at a time.

Slow inhale, controlled exhale.

In through the nose, out through the mouth.

I repeat this motion over and over again until my lungs start working at a normal speed, until my heartbeat returns to its steady beat and my skin isn't a nervous, wet mess.

When I'm sure I won't throw up my guts, I relax my fingers and collapse onto my ass. Sighing, I rub my face, spent.

I have to get my shit in order and figure out what ...

I don't get to finish my thought because the door slowly opens and a messy, dark head peeks through the crack.

"Hey, why are you up?" Her voice is low, husky. She rubs the sleep from her eyes.

"Just ..." I swallow, not sure what to say.

Jeanette opens the door wider, stepping into the bathroom. She slipped on one of my shirts, but I could bet you there is nothing underneath it, and just the thought of it makes me want to have her again.

Strong.

Overpowering.

Irrepressible.

That's how deep my need is for her.

But every coin has two sides, and on the other side, matching that desire for her is fear. The fear of the power she'll hold against me if I give in to it.

If I give in to her.

"You should go home," I blurt out finally.

Jeanette stops in her tracks, a frown marring her forehead.

"Now?"

"It's getting late."

I feel like a complete dick, but I can't help myself. I need her gone. Far, far away from me. Away from this house. Away from this goddamned town because if she stays here, if she's close ...

Those dark gray eyes look at me carefully. There are confusion and irritation written on her face, battling for which one will win. Which face she'll show to me.

We're all wearing masks. That's what she told me once.

Finally, she nods, her eyes looking somewhere over my shoulder. "You're right."

Look at me.

"It is getting late."

Look at me, Princess.

She gives me one final nod and turns on the heels of her feet.

I start to get up, my hand outstretched, but she's already out, the door closed firmly behind her. A physical barrier she erected between us to add to the emotional wall she has around herself.

You're the one who put up the wall first.

I fall back down on my ass, my hands clench into fists, and I pound on the hard tiles, welcoming the pain.

Jeanette never comes back inside. I can hear her shuffle around the room, picking up her stuff and getting dressed, and then as silently as she came, she leaves my house.

Leaves me... alone.

Chapter 29

JEANETTE

"She's in her room," Max says to somebody on the other side of the closed door. "She's been in there for the last few days. I tried talking to her but ..."

Tightening my grip around the pillow, I refuse to lift my gaze off the screen. Klaus is just about to rip someone's throat out, and I'm in the mood for some bloodshed.

"Has she started getting ready for tonight?" The voice is low, almost tentative. Lia.

"Nope, she said she isn't going anywhere."

"What? Then I'm out too..."

"Brook! You're going, and Jeanette is going, and everybody is going!" Lia's voice rises with every word. I can feel her frustration all the way from here.

"Obviously not," Brook says, and I can imagine her rolling her eyes. Then she continues loud enough so there is no way I can*not* hear it: "Her royal bitchiness is too busy to spend some time with peasants!"

I cover my mouth to muffle the laugh that wants to erupt from me. She's good, I have to give her that. Quirky almost. The way she always finds something new and creative to say to mess with somebody, but I don't have to admit it out loud.

After that night she showed up on my doorstep drenched like a rat, our relationship has been ... strange, to say the least. We aren't friends, but we aren't enemies, either. Once Lia jokingly said Brook and I are the definition of frenemies, and I guess she might be right.

Clearing my throat so there is no trace of amusement in my voice, I yell, "I heard that!"

"You were meant to!"

Soon after, the door bursts open and there she is, standing in the doorway in her stupid ripped jeans and hoodie with her arms crossed over her chest. "Get your scrawny ass out of the bed, Princess."

I shoot her an annoyed glare from my position in bed, pulling the blanket tighter around me. "I don't think so. I'm fine the way I am now."

"You said you'd go to the party with us." Lia's head peeks over Brook's shoulder, her strawberry hair pulled in a messy bun on top of her head.

"Well, I changed my mind." I shrug my shoulders, my way of brushing them off while actually being *nice*.

Lia's shoulders slump, but Brook's prudent green eyes keep staring at me. I return her stare, not backing down. I lift my brow, challenging her to say whatever's on her mind or leave me the fuck alone. She smirks slowly at me, making me narrow my eyes.

What does she think she knows?

Turning on her heels, she shoves Max in his chest. "Off you go, this is a girls' zone only."

Max opens his mouth to protest, but she shuts the door in his face. Rubbing her hands together, she turns toward me. "Now, spill it. What did he do?"

Ignoring her, I turn my attention back to the screen. "I don't know what you're talking about."

She can't know, can she? The smirk on her lips and almost satisfied tranquility mixed with the knowing gleam in her eyes make me think otherwise, only there's no way ... nobody knows, not for sure. I haven't been going around telling people my business, and I can't imagine Andrew sitting down for tea and gossiping about our sex life.

Brook comes to my bed and yanks the blanket off of me.

"Hey!"

"Something must have happened for you to close up in your room and avoid Andrew's house like a plague."

"Mhmm ..." Lia nods her head in agreement. "Just remember what happened the last time I tried doing that."

Ignoring Lia because there is no way her and Derek's situation can even compare to me and Andrew—not like there actually is me and Andrew—I give my full attention to Brook. "Why are you even going over there? I thought that wasn't your crowd."

"Derek's going, which means Lia's going, which means ..." Sighing, she waves her hand. "It's beside the point. What did that asshole do?"

Pulling the pillow in front of me, I hug it tight to my chest. She took my blanket, but at least I still have this.

I lift my chin in the air in defiance but don't bother with a response.

"You're acting like a spoiled brat, Jeanette. Even Lia noticed there is something going on between you and Hill, and she's as clueless as they come."

Lia elbows her best friend. "I'm still here, you know."

"I'm telling the truth and you know it. Since you and Derek became official, you've been in a rose-colored world where everybody is happy and in love."

"Maybe that's why I *did* notice the thing between Jeanette and Andrew."

"We're not in love!" I protest in a hurry, sitting straighter.

Well, shit. There goes my immunity. No way will I be able to convince them they're wrong now that I hastily blurt out something like that. I should have ignored it. Why didn't I ignore it?

Both girls exchange a knowing look.

"She didn't deny there is something going on between them," Brook says, and then they walk to either side of my bed and sit down.

"We're not. In love, I mean."

"What are you then?"

"We're nothing." I try to act as nonchalant as possible. Salvage the situation any way I can.

"Try again." Brook gives me a condescending look, while Amelia puts her hand on my knee.

"Anybody with two eyes can see something is going on between you two." There is so much sympathy in Lia's voice I want to barf. "The way you look at each other when nobody is looking."

"Like we want to murder one another?" I suggest, but the two of them ignore me.

"They're looking at each other like they want to jump each other's bones, Lia. No need to sigh dreamily about it." Brook, always the voice of reason. "Besides, didn't you notice how they disappear conveniently one after the other? What do you think they're doing, huh? I'm not sure Hill has the patience of a saint like some guy we all know."

Lia's cheeks burn instantly and so brightly, you'd think we caught her reading one of her kinky books.

"W-well, i-it's n-not a-always about s-sex," Lia stutters nervously.

"Don't judge it till you try it."

Brook gives me a knowing look, and we share a quiet laugh.

"It's always the quiet ones," I agree.

Lia looks between the two of us, completely confused. "W-what?"

This time we don't try to cover our laughter. "Forget it."

Irritated with the two of us, she puffs her cheeks. "Well, if it's just about s—" She gulps down hard. "S-sex, why are you hiding in your bedroom and he's angry at everybody who dares glance his way?"

Sighing, I rub my forehead. I can feel the headache looming behind my temporal bone.

"If you must know, he was being a dick, and I don't want to be around to listen to his bitching."

"I can't still wrap my head around it." Brook shakes her head, stupefied. "Andrew Hill and Jeanette Sanders. Presumptuous Asshole and Ice Queen. Together."

I give her a sour smile. "It's so good to know you think so highly of us."

Brook shakes her head, completely ignoring my sarcasm, her green eyes sparkling with a special kind of glow I'm not sure I even want to decipher.

"Just think about it. If you two actually did end up together, it would be like an earthquake. You'd never know how fast or how hard it would hit and how much destruction would be left in its wake."

"Then it's a good thing we're *not* together. So no need to worry for your poor little town and its people."

"Prove it." Green eyes meet mine dead on.

"Brook ..." Lia warns, but Brook ignores her.

"Prove it. Prove you're not together. Prove you're closed off in your room just because you're PMSing or some other shit and come with us to the New Year's party at Andrew's house."

I lift my chin in the air and look at her down my nose, my "Ice Queen" attitude in full effect.

"What do you get out of it?"

"I either get the satisfaction of knowing I was right and there is something more between you and Hill, or some company at the stupid party I promised Lia I'd go to even though I know she'll spend most of her evening slow dancing and sucking face with her boyfriend, not having any actual time to spend with me. No matter how you look at it, it's a win-win for me."

Lia crosses her arms over her chest and purses her lips in annoyance. "We don't suck face."

Brook and I exchange a look before we both turn toward Lia and say at the same time, "Yes, you do."

Together we burst into giggles, and the tightness around my chest loosens a little bit.

Sitting back straight after getting herself under control, Brook looks at me. "What do you say, Princess?"

I look at both girls. So different, yet still best friends sitting on my bed and waiting for my answer. Why do they even bother with me? Again and again I ask myself that question, because I have yet to find the answer.

We're not friends. We're not enemies. We're just ... us.

Frenemies.

"I say, game on."

"You look like you'd rather be anywhere but here," Brook comments casually. "Seriously, what did he do to piss you off royally?"

"This isn't the time nor the place to talk about it." I look pointedly at Max's back. He's not necessarily close, but close enough that if he paid attention, he could hear what we're talking about. Or at least bits and pieces, which can be even worse than hearing the whole thing.

"Oops, my bad."

I roll my eyes at her.

"You've been in an exceptionally good mood lately. What's with that?"

"Nothing much. Just happy to be away from my shitty life for a few hours, drink some good booze and maybe find oblivion in the hands of a handsome stranger."

I quirk my brow at her.

Most people would probably pity her. Not me. I guess that's why she feels so at ease saying that in front of me. Acknowledging her shitty life. Knowing somebody won't feel sorry for you gives you space to open up and just be yourself. You don't have to worry about what to say or not to say to avoid awkward situations.

"What?" Brook shrugs, grinning. "A girl can hope, can't she?"

I shake my head teasingly, my wavy hair brushing against my naked shoulders. When the girls got me out of bed, I went to my closet and found an old cross-back, covered in rose-gold glitter slip dress to wear to this party. It wouldn't have been my first choice, but since I hadn't planned on going, I didn't go shopping, so I had to make do with what I've got.

"So what's the plan?"

Brook is wearing a tight leather skirt and red sparkly top. I even let her borrow my knee-high black boots to match the outfit.

Like Brook predicted, Derek snatched Lia as soon as we got to the party and they were nowhere to be found. Better that than have them be obnoxiously in love in front of our eyes the whole night.

"First drinks, then dancing and then ... I guess we'll have to wait and see."

Together we push through the crowd of people and make our way to the living room and bar. This time there is another guy managing it, not the cute rookie who flirted with me a few weeks back, but Brook shushes him away and starts making our pinktails. I don't know what she puts in them. Probably cranberry or raspberry mixed with vodka, or is it gin? I'm sure there is a trace of rum, but it could be something else. What I do know for sure is that they're yummy. And that's the only thing that matters.

Last time we had them was for Lia's birthday, and we might have gotten a little buzzed. Especially Lia since she's not used to drinking, but that night she wanted to forget Derek, so we had to help her. Chicks before dicks and all that. I guess tonight is a good night to have them.

Brook produces fancy cocktail glasses from somewhere underneath the bar, adds some ice cubes into each and pours the liquid from the shaker into them. She gives me my glass and we clink them together before taking a sip.

I let the cool liquid slide down my throat and close my eyes to savor the sweetness of it.

"This is so good."

"It would have been even better if we had some sugar to dip the edge of the glass in, but..."

"The drink is already getting to you, Brook." We both laugh at that, but she stops abruptly.

"What?"

Her eyes dart over my shoulder before they return back to my face. "You might not wanna ..."

I look over my shoulder.

"... look over your shoulder."

And I wish I haven't.

Andrew is standing there flirting with none other than Diamond-fucking-Morgan. Her blond hair is curled and falling down her back. Her lips, painted red, smile at him as she laughs at what exactly I'm not sure since the guy doesn't have a funny bone in his body. Her short, red velvet dress, the same color as her lips, is molded to her body.

I swallow hard, my hand gripping the back of the chair so hard my knuckles turn white. Relaxing my fingers, I loosen my grip and turn back around.

Brook pushes the now-full glass of pink liquid my way. This time I don't take a moment to savor the drink before I gulp all of it down.

Her eyes look at me with sympathy, but I ignore it. "I think we'll need something stronger than that."

For a second she's reluctant, but then that second is gone and she disappears underneath the bar. When she pops out again, she's holding a bottle of Jack Daniels victoriously in her hands.

"That'll do."

I grab it from her, unscrew the lid and bring the bottle to my lips.

Chapter 30

ANDREW

"You better come and take your sister off my bar," I hiss in Max's ear, barely holding it together. "I think people have seen enough of her lacy panties to last them years."

Max turns around immediately, gray eyes turning into slits.

He's been playing poker with some guys from the team, puck bunnies around them. Not that the guy would notice it. He's as celibate as the pope. Apart from his puppy obsession with Lia and his hate-hate relationship with Brook, I haven't seen him look at a girl for more than two seconds.

"What did you do?" he spats, but doesn't wait for my answer before he gets up and strides toward the living room and Jeanette.

When I saw her up on that bar, dancing and laughing, throwing her head back and revealing all the gorgeous skin that the guys around her were drinking in hungrily, I wanted to jump up there and throw her over my shoulder and run. Run far away so nobody could look at her.

Because she's mine.

Mine to watch.

Mine to touch.

Mine to have.

Only she isn't.

Not really.

She has never been mine, and she never will be.

I want to tell him I didn't do anything, but that would be a lie.

In all the months since the Sanders twins came to Greyford, I've seen them at a bunch of parties at my house, yet I've never seen Jeanette so drunk. Maybe it's presumptuous of me to think I'm the reason behind her sudden stripper behavior, but there is no other explanation. Not after everything that happened on Christmas Eve and her not returning even one of my texts after that. Not one.

Even through the loud music and chatter, you can hear the whistles coming from the living room. Hoots and hollers that make my blood boil. Make me so irrationally angry I'm barely holding on to my sanity. My hands are clenched into fists by my sides, ready to swing and break some skin and bones.

You have no right.

The need to get my hands around her waist, pull her down and hide her where nobody would be able to see her is strong, but I rein it in. Jeanette wouldn't appreciate it, and I didn't want to make a scene. Not with Jeanette drunk and Max close by and still watchful.

You're the one who threw her away.

Thankfully, Max is there in a heartbeat, pushing through the crowd like a man on a mission. He stops in front of the bar and tries to reason with Jeanette, while at the same time telling the gathered crowd to fuck off. But of course Jeanette doesn't listen.

She and Brook keep dancing, wiggling their asses and bursting into fits of giggles when they sing the wrong lyrics. Another turn results in an almost slip, not that you can expect anything more from a drunk girl trying to dance in high heels on the bar. Just when I'm done with it and take a step to get her down, Max wraps his hands around Jeanette's waist and pulls her to the floor.

"We're going home," he grits through his teeth.

Anger radiates off of him in waves, but he's trying to stay calm.

Brook starts to climb down, and she'd fall on her ass just like Jeanette if Max hadn't caught her and put her down.

"Buuuuut, Max!" Jeanette's protest is followed by a giggle. "I'm having fun!"

Irritating, annoying, drunken giggle.

"Home. Now."

Max picks her up again and throws her over his shoulder. He's holding on to thin strings of sanity that will burst soon and then all hell will break loose.

I open my mouth to call after him, but Max is already taking her away. Not that I know what to say. I went to him to take care of her, and he's doing just that, so what now?

Jeanette starts pounding at his back, but there is no real force behind her punches.

"Broooooook! Save me, will ya? We can have another drink, and then we can go back to dancing."

"I'm sorry, girl." Brook stumbles behind them.

Max gives her a stern look over his shoulder. "You should be sorry! It's all your fault!"

"My fault?" Brook shoots him a death glare, her cheeks turning pink in anger. "She's old enough to know how much she can drink. Besides, she had a shitty evening." Her eyes turn to look at me accusingly. "Can't blame a girl for having one too many."

"She had more than just one too many drinks!"

Brook starts to say something, but Jeanette's slow murmur stops her. "My head is hurting."

"I know, J. I think it's time for you to go to bed."

Jeanette looks at her friend, her nose furrows. "Why are you upside-down?"

"You're the one who's upside-down, silly."

"M-me?" Jeanette hiccups, her face growing pale.

"Yes, you ..."

Brook is too concentrated on figuring out Jeanette to see it, but I do. The little color she had in her cheeks drained out completely, leaving her skin unnaturally white. Her irises grow wide, and a faint layer of sweat covers her skin as her hands dart to cover her mouth.

"Turn her over!" I warn, hurrying to help Max set Jeanette on her own two feet and push her out the door.

Thank God we're close, and I get her out of the house just in time for her to reach the first pot and throw up the contents of her stomach.

My hand slides up and down her back in a soothing motion as I help her pull back her hair so it doesn't get in her face.

Jeanette heaves over the pot for a while after she emptied her stomach, and I wait it out next to her, my hand not stopping for a second.

My brain is yelling at me to stop, take a step back and leave her alone, let Max handle it. She needs somebody who cares about her, somebody who loves her. Not me.

You love her, you fool.

I shake my head in protest.

I don't. I can't. I'm not capable of loving anybody.

My brain tells me to run, but my body ... my body doesn't listen.

"There, it'll be okay," I murmur softly, only for her to hear. "Everything will be okay."

It's like it has a will of its own, and it doesn't want to leave her side.

Finally, she straightens, the back of her hand brushing against her lips, her face twisted in a grimace.

"Are you feeling better?"

Slowly, her eyes lift to meet mine, and although they're still glossy from all the alcohol, there is some clarity in them. Recognition.

Jeanette pulls away abruptly, almost missing a step and falling down, but even that doesn't stop her from glaring at me. "Don't touch me," she snarls, her finger lifted in the air in warning.

"What the hell?" I try to reach out to help stabilize her, but she pulls back again.

Her harsh words are like a slap to my face.

"I said, don't touch me."

I turn around looking for some kind of explanation, but all I find is an angry and disappointed Brook and a suspicious Max.

"Take me home?" Jeanette's voice is a soft whisper, and she looks small. So small and breakable.

Max nods his head in agreement, and as he walks around me, his eyes never leave mine. Once he's by her side, he wraps his arm around her.

"Let's go home."

"Brook?" Jeanette looks over her shoulder.

"Let me just ..." She goes through her bag I didn't even see her carrying and lifts her phone in the air.

"We'll be in the car."

Brook types something as I watch the two of them walking down the stairs and away from me. Max turns around once more to give me a warning glare over his shoulder.

He'll get to the bottom of it, and when he does, somebody will pay the price.

That somebody being me.

"Well, you screwed this up royally."

Putting her phone back in the bag, Brook looks at me.

"Who asked for your opinion?"

"Nobody." She shrugs. "Doesn't mean I'm not going to give one."

For somebody who was dancing her drunken ass away just a few minutes ago, she seems like she sobered up pretty quickly.

"Well can you give it to somebody who might actually want it?"

"Nope. Look, I'm not even going to try to act like I know what's going on between you and Jeanette ..."

"What's the point of this conversation again?"

Brook gives me a stern look. "But you better get your shit in order and stop playing games."

"I'm not playing any games."

"No?" One shaped brow lifts in question. "What was that scheme with Diamond then?"

"You're delusional."

I start to turn around, done with this conversation, but her hand on my wrist stops me. For a small thing, Brook Taylor sure has a strong grip and big attitude.

"Am I really?"

I let my mind go back. I was drinking with the guys, still pissed off that Jeanette didn't answer any of my texts, although I'm the one who threw her out.

I said I was sorry. Doesn't that count for shit?

Just as I was ready to get drunk and forget about everything, Jeanette entered the room in her short, flirty dress. She was talking to Brook, laughing and drinking, like everything was completely fine.

Why is she fine when I'm anything but?

Jeanette has me all twisted up from the inside out, and yet she's there *laughing*. So of course when Diamond came to me, being her flirty, needy self, I didn't tell her to fuck off and leave me alone. Not initially anyway.

I let her get close to me, let her flirt and maybe even flirted back. Hoping, no, not hoping, *wanting* Jeanette to see us. Wanting to make her feel all those feeling she's stirring up inside of me. Fifty shades of confused and fucked up.

"Fuuuuuck." I cover my face with hands, rubbing hard.

"Mhmm." Brook pats me on my back. "You're a dick, Andrew. And although some habits do die hard, you'll have to do better than that. Stop playing your games and get your shit under control. Then you might have an actual shot. God help us all."

Her hand falls from my back, and I can hear her heels clicking as she walks down the stairs.

"You think you're so much better than me?" I call after her, a part of me not wanting to let her have the last word.

"Not really, but if you can get your shit under control, maybe there's hope for the rest of us."

As her words hang in the air, I watch her walk away, my mind more confused than ever.

Chapter 31

JEANETTE

After my drunken striptease debacle, I don't just wake up with a hangover, I wake up with a hangover and the flu.

My head is pounding, my throat is like the driest of deserts but at the same time pulsing and burning strongly. I can barely cough properly, and my whole body hurts when I do. And don't even get me started on trying to talk. I can barely open my mouth without my throat hurting, so speaking is out of the question.

Most of the night I spent either throwing up or hanging over a bucket *thinking* I was going to throw up, so I'm not really surprised when I wake up and it's already late afternoon.

There are a bunch of notifications on my phone, but I'm not interested in any of them. I swipe my thumb over the screen, removing everything, but one particular message catches my eye.

Asshole: I'm sorry.

Just that. No explanation, no excuse, no anything.

Two words.

Seven letters.

I'm sorry.

I still stare at it, when the door to my room bursts open.

"You're awake."

Removing the message, I lock my phone and slide it under the pillow.

"Yeah," I rasp. My throat is so dry I have to clear it a few times so it's somewhat understandable. "Just got up."

I sit up straight in bed and turn on the bedside lamp to illuminate the dark room. A shiver runs down my body, so I pull the covers up to keep the chill away.

Max nods. "I made you some soup."

Just the idea of putting something in my mouth makes my stomach roll. "A bit later?"

Max gives me a long, hard stare. "Jeanette ..." My name is an exasperated sigh.

He enters the room and slowly starts walking toward my bed, like he's afraid I'll run away. And maybe I will. Maybe I should.

Max sits by my side, taking my hands between his. We both look at our joined hands for a while, not speaking a word.

Finally, he breaks the silence. "What was yesterday all about?"

Sighing, I tilt my head back before I concentrate on his face. "I'm fine, Max."

"But are you? Are you really?"

Gray eyes look over my face intently. Observing, watching, looking for signs. I know those eyes; I saw them for months and months after everything happened the first time around.

I give him a reassuring squeeze. "I. Am. Fine." I look him straight in the eyes as I say those words, hoping he'll be able to see it. Feel it. "Really."

"You don't look fine, Anette. You look like somebody ready to spiral out of control again. All these months I keep looking at you, wondering if I'm missing something again. Are you really fine or are you pretending? Will I be able to see it this time around? If you fall back to the darkness, will I be able to see it? Will I be able to pull you back out before it's too late?"

Every word comes out faster and faster, like he can't say them fast enough. Like they've been haunting him for a while, and now that the first one is uttered out loud, there is no stopping the rest.

His eyes are wide, looking at me with so much fear and hurt. Panic.

How long has he been holding this in? How long has he been afraid?

His hands hold on to mine tightly, so tightly it's starting to hurt, yet I can't make myself ask him to let go.

"Max ..."

"I can't lose you, Jeanette." He shakes his head desperately. "I can't. That time you broke. So small. So pale. So *fragile.* You'll never understand the fear I felt as I watched you literally fall apart in front of my eyes. I don't think I even realized until that moment how breakable, how mortal you are. The fear, the panic ... it's like nothing I've ever felt before. You and me, Anette. We're a team. We're one person. Losing you would be like losing a part of myself. I almost lost you once, and I barely survived it. To lose you for real ..."

He chokes on the rest of the sentence, and the only thing preventing me from throwing myself at him is the hold he has on me.

"Max, I'm fine."

"But are you really?" His eyes look over my face, my exposed hands. "You look skinnier than you did a few weeks ago. I saw you barely touch your lunch a few times at school."

His words make a knot grow in my throat, making it hard to breathe.

"Did you know I always notice it? Even when I'm not consciously looking or listening, I always see when you leave something on your plate. Or say you don't feel hungry. Every time you give yourself a critical look in the mirror I wonder—what does she see? Will this be the time the monster comes back and makes her see something that doesn't exist?"

"Oh, Max ..."

This time there is no stopping me. His pain is so real, so raw, that it feels like my own.

How long has he been feeling like that? How long has he been suffering like that in silence? And more importantly, how come I didn't notice it before?

Pulling my hands out of his, I throw myself at him, wrapping my arms around his shoulders and pulling him in a tight hug. At first he's like a statue, all sharp edges and hard muscle, but then his arms wrap around me, too. I lean my head on the crook of his neck.

"I missed this," I whisper, inhaling his familiar scent.

How long has it been since we hugged each other? And I'm not talking about Max bullying me into submitting to him, but a real hug?

Four years ago, everything changed, *we* changed, we lost our way, and it seems like we never found it back to each other.

His hands run up and down my back in a slow, soothing touch, and it makes me remember last night.

Last night and Andrew's hands taking that same path on my back.

His fingertips run up my spine. "You're skinnier." His words are a barely audible whisper.

Sighing, I pull back so I can see him. There are tears in his eyes. I've never seen my big brother cry, but seeing the tears well in his eyes breaks something inside of me.

"I'm trying, Max. I really am, but sometimes ..." I inhale sharply, trying to get enough air. My eyes are blurry with tears, so many tears there is no holding them back. "But sometimes, it's hard. There are days I can fight it, days I can look at my reflection in the mirror and say, 'Screw you,' and move on, but then there are days when nothing I say or do will ever make it better. Days when all I want to do is rip my skin off my bones and hide. Days when just the slightest of comments will ruin weeks of good days and make all the light submit to the darkness lurking underneath.

"I want to be strong, Max. I do. And not for you or anybody else, but for myself. I want to be confident and happy and *whole*. And some days I can be just that. But some days ... some days it's just too much."

"Is it Hill?" His sudden angry tone makes me jump back.

"Andrew?" I frown. "What does he have to do with anything?"

Max gives me a knowing look. "I'm not blind, Jeanette. And your sneaking skills are shit. Only a fool couldn't see through the two of you."

Sighing, I lean back against the pillows and look at the ceiling, trying to collect my thoughts. "It's not Andrew."

"For a while you seemed happier, J. Content. What changed?"

What did change?

It would be easy to say it's Andrew's fault, but it's not. Not really. When we started sneaking around, we both knew this was just something temporary, two people trying to escape reality by finding pleasure in each other. And did we find it.

Andrew can be a lot of things. Cold jackass. Insensitive asshole. Presumptuous dickhead. But not once did he do me wrong. He got as much as he gave, and with him, for the first time in a while, I felt like myself again.

Carefree.

Liberated.

Whole.

Being with Andrew Hill made me feel whole, but it also brought back a lot of insecurities. Maybe that's the problem. We both have a lot to work through right now, is it really the right time to juggle a relationship as complicated and fucked up as ours on top of everything?

I look at my brother sitting on the other side of me. "I was happy. *He made me happy*. Maybe that's the problem. Maybe I should start learning how to be happy on my own."

Chapter 32

ANDREW

Princess: We need to talk. Meet me at our spot in the library?

School just started back again, and this is the first time I've heard back from Jeanette since the party, or technically even before that.

I thought about going to her house but didn't want to risk stumbling upon Max. To be honest, after how everything ended on New Year's Eve, I expected him to come to my place to get to the bottom of what happened, but he never did. I'm not sure what to think of it. Had Jeanette said something to him? Did something happen so he couldn't come? I wasn't sure what to think or do, but since I hadn't heard of anything happening to either of them, I just accepted it and moved on, figuring I'd see them when we returned back to school. Only today when I entered the cafeteria and there was no sign of either of them, the worry returned in full force.

And then the cryptic message.

What did she want to talk about? Me being an asshole on Christmas Eve? Her getting drunk on New Year's? I wasn't sure, but I guess I'll find out sooner rather than later.

The library is quiet when I go in, just a student here and

there, all too immersed in their own work to pay me any attention.

I walk through the quiet rows, going all the way back, where the space is a little darker and the dust is just a tad thicker because nobody really comes around much.

Staying alert, I watch around in case anybody's following me or just seems lost between the shelves of books in search of something. Whatever Jeanette wants to talk to me about, I'm sure I don't want anybody around to hear it.

Finally, I get to the very back corner of the library. The place I took her and everybody else—Derek, Max, Lia and Brook—while we were staying at the school for the senior sleepover. She's sitting on the floor, cross-legged. Her dark hair is straight today, falling over her face as she looks down and writes something in the little notebook in her hand.

Stopping in my tracks, I take a few seconds just to look at her. The way her hair throws a shadow over her face and how the very tip of her tongue peeks out as she concentrates on whatever she's writing.

She looks so beautiful it hurts. I want to extend my hand and let my fingers brush the strand of her hair that's falling in her face behind her ear so I can lean down and press my lips against her soft skin. The feeling is so real, I can almost taste her on my lips.

But the last time I touched her, she ran away.

I inhale deeply, trying to calm down, but her smell fills the small space. Jasmine and orchid mixed with the dust and the smell of old books.

Strong.

Overwhelming.

My exhale is long and shaky, making her snap out of her world.

"Oh, hi," she says, looking up at me.

Closing the notebook, she lets it fall in her lap, and one of her hands reaches out to brush the hair behind her ear.

"Hi," I rasp, holding back the urge to touch her.

"You came."

I shrug, leaning against the shelf. "You wanted to talk."

"Yes, yes I did."

Her gaze falls down to the notebook in her lap, and suddenly a sense of dread washes over me.

Is she going to break up with me? Are we even together? Were we ever actually together? Or did I fuck it up? I always fuck shit up. My mom left me, and my dad is barely around and now ... now she'll leave, too. I can feel it.

My throat constricts, and it's hard to breathe.

"I know we ..."

"I'm sorry," I blurt out, but I can't hold it inside anymore. I can't. "I know I've said it a dozen times before. I never say sorry to anybody else, but when it comes to you it seems like I'm always doing the wrong shit, which leads to endless apologies, but I mean it, Jeanette. I really mean it. I'm so sorry. I shouldn't have acted the way I did, I shouldn't have asked you to leave that night, but you were there. In my space, space that has always belonged just to me, and you fit so perfectly I got scared. I got scared and I chased you away by doing what I do best–hurting people. Hurting *you*.

"And I most definitely shouldn't have let Diamond come and flirt with me, but we both know I'm a stupid jackass when it comes to stuff like that. I do things I shouldn't because I don't think, and in my selfishness, I hurt the people I care about. So, I'm sorry."

I run my hands through my hair, looking at her. "Please, say something."

Her beautiful eyes look at me, and there is stillness in them, so much stillness something in me snaps.

"You asked me here to break things off with me."

I turn my back to her, my hands pulling the strands of my hair.

What the hell is happening right now? Why does my chest hurt so bad?

Soft fingers touch my shoulders. "Andrew ..."

I turn around and there she is, standing so close I can touch her, yet she seems so far away.

"You can't leave me." My hands grip her forearms, holding on to her.

"I'm not going anywhere."

"Maybe not, but you're *leaving me*," I accuse. "Just like she did. Just like they both did."

"Nobody is leaving anywhere. I just think I—" She stops to correct herself. "*We both* need some time alone to figure things out."

"I have my shit under control."

"Do you? Do you really? One day you're throwing me out, and the next you're scared of me leaving. That's not having shit under control, Andrew."

We look at each other without saying a word. I don't know what to think, what to say. Part of me knows she's right, but the other part wants to call bullshit. She just wants to leave, just like everybody else.

Just like my mom left, and then my dad decided his work is more important. Just like Derek barely has any time for his friends now that he's with Amelia.

Jeanette's hand reaches out, brushing against my cheek. "They were right about us all along."

"They don't know shit, Princess. Nobody knows shit about us."

"They do. Max figured us out, Brook, hell even Lia, and I bet they're not the only ones. And they were right." She shakes her head at me, and I can see the sadness in her eyes. "We're not good together. We're too intense, too destructive for each other, too broken."

"Maybe, but we belong together." I cup her cheeks. "You can't deny it. We might be broken, but it doesn't seem like that when we're together. It's like all the broken pieces fall into place and are glued back to life."

"But that's the problem. We glue each other back together, but the glue is just a temporary fix. It's not permanent. It's just a matter of time before everything falls apart again. And this time, there will be no way of fixing anything. We'll be broken, this time beyond repair. And I don't want that, Andrew. I don't want to break you beyond repair. I do *not* want to be broken."

Tears gather in her eyes, but she's holding them at bay. Seeing her like this, trying to stay strong, breaks me.

"Don't say that. You're not broken beyond repair. I won't let you break."

"No, I won't let myself break. That's why we need this. We need to figure our shit out on our own. You have to deal with your demons, and I have to deal with mine. And then maybe, maybe we stand a chance at something."

"Don't do this." I close my eyes, not able to look at her anymore. If I do I'll lose it, and I can't. I just can't. "Don't, just don't."

Her hands grip mine, as she presses her forehead against mine.

"I have to. I have to choose what's good for me. I have to choose *me*. You make me happy, Andrew. So happy and confident and strong, but then you do something to piss me off, and the world is shaking around me. All the doubts and insecurities start to return, and I can't handle it. It's all just too much. I have to learn how to be happy on my own. How to be strong and *whole*. On my own. And you have to do the same."

"We can do it together," I insist. "I know we can."

One of her hands slides over my arm and brushes against my cheek. "Look at me, Andrew."

I shake my head, refusing her. If I open my eyes it'll be over. I know it'll be over.

"Look at me."

"I can't."

"You have to. Please. Eyes on me."

Eyes on me, Princess.

I can't deny her. Not when she's like this. When she says the words that belong to us.

Reluctantly, I open my eyes.

"You'll be okay. I wouldn't do this if I didn't know for a fact that you'll be okay. We have to do right by ourselves, Andrew. We have to."

"You know the shit that's haunting me, but what's haunting you? What's so fucked up you think I can't help you get through it?"

This time she's the one who closes her eyes.

Just for a few seconds, she shuts me off. I can see her throat bobble as she swallows hard. I can see the wheels turning in her head as she tries to figure out what to say, how to say it.

Her fingers grip mine tighter.

She's scared. I can feel her fear like it's my own, and it scares me. Because I know, whatever she tells me, it won't be good.

I open my mouth to stop her, but she's faster.

"I have anorexia," she whispers, opening her eyes and looking straight into mine. "Anorexia combined with slight body dysmorphic disorder."

"What?!"

I'm so stunned I don't know what to say. Jeanette has anorexia? My eyes scan her body looking for a clue as my mind does a rewind of all the months we spent together.

Did she avoid food? Did I see her sneak into the bathroom after eating? Did she seem worried as she ate, as if she's counting all the calories she's consuming?

"Some things happened back in freshman year, back in California. Things that made me question the way I look, things that lead me to start excessively exercising and skipping meals. At the beginning it was just dinners, but suddenly it was eating altogether. I didn't even realize it because the image in the mirror, it just became worse and worse. My parents were hardly around and Max was busy with hockey, his friends and other ... *things*. So nobody paid attention, until it escalated and I ended up in hospital."

"But you're better now?"

I can't stop staring at her, looking for clues that something is off. Her clothes fit her body perfectly, and although she looks thin, she doesn't seem overly so.

"I was, or I thought I was, but it never really goes away. The distorted reflection in the mirror, avoiding food, overthinking everything I put in my mouth. It didn't get to the point where I'm back where I was three years ago, but I can notice it. Max sees it, and I can't ..." She stops, taking a deep breath in. "I can't put him through that again. I can't and don't want to put myself through it again, either."

"Jeanette I don't know ..."

"You don't have to say anything," she interrupts. "I didn't tell you to gain your sympathy or because I think it's somehow your fault. It isn't. All the fears and insecurities, they're all on me. They're my problem and I have to learn how to deal with it, how to get it under control. That's why I started therapy again. I want to get better. I want to find a way to heal. You showed me how good it can be to feel whole again. Now I have to do it on my own."

There is a light in her eyes, determination that I haven't seen before.

"What if I can't do it? What if I can't face my demons? Can't face her?"

Jeanette brushes her thumb over my cheekbone, and then I feel it. One lone tear that rolled down, but she didn't let it fall. One lone tear of the little boy who's scared to lose somebody he cares about.

"You can, and you will."

Her lips brush against mine in the most tender of kisses. I pull her closer, my hands wrapping around her shoulders.

"I know you can, because I know you, Andrew Hill. Strong, but stubborn. Self-centered, yet gentle. Full of yourself, occasionally mean, but underneath it all ... underneath it all is a good heart that only a few can see. It's that heart that's making me fall for you. Even when they told me I shouldn't. Even when I knew if I opened up, you could completely break me. Even when I was supposed to stop my bad habits, you—the worst habit of all, I couldn't give up. I don't want to give you up, Andrew. But for now, that's what's best for me. And this time ... this time I come first."

Chapter 33

JEANETTE

"How are you today?"

I want to roll my eyes at the woman sitting on the other side of the big mahogany table, but I keep it under control. She's just doing her job, after all. And apparently she's good at it, the best in this part of the state.

Dr. Allison Mitchell is in her mid-thirties, not that anybody would give her that much. Her pale-blond, almost white hair is pulled into a messy bun at the nape of her neck. Big brown eyes are surrounded by long eyelashes barely covered in a layer of mascara and hidden behind big, nerdy glasses. They're light pink and match the lipgloss she always wears.

To be completely honest, the first time I entered her office I wasn't sure this would work. She looks my age. Ripped jeans, Chucks and T-shirts with smart-ass comments don't give the most professional first impressions.

Tilting my head back, I look at the white ceiling, trying to imagine I'm somewhere else and not getting my brain checked.

"Fine, I guess."

"You guess?"

"I still struggle to look in the mirror, afraid of what I'll see once I do, but I think I'm getting better. Every day I make myself look at my reflection a few more seconds than the day before, trying to hold on to the real image and not what my mind wants me to see. I'm also keeping tabs on what and when I eat. Max helped me come up with a weekly menu and helps me keep to it."

There is a slight pause. I nibble at my lower lip as I think and Doc lets me have a moment. It's something I've noticed about her. She knows when I'm done saying what I have to say and then probes me for more information, but she also has a sixth sense on when I need more time. She actually leaves me in peace to sort it in my mind before saying it out loud.

"I miss Andrew. I didn't even realize what a big part of my life he'd become until he's not there. We used to text a lot, nothing extremely important, but those texts made me smile. Now it's just radio silence."

She hums non-committedly. "Wasn't that what you wanted?"

My brain shouts yes, but my heart isn't in it.

"I guess." I shrug. What's there to say? "I think I needed it more than I wanted it. I need to know I can do this on my own and for myself. I want to get better. When I stopped therapy just before we moved to Greyford, I really thought I had it under control, but I guess I was wrong."

Dr. Mitchell leans back in her chair, folding her hands in her lap.

"The disease you have is chronic, Jeanette. It'll always be a part of your life. A constant struggle. You'll have to fight it day in and day out for the rest of your life, you know that."

"I do."

"The way to do it is to let people in. Admit you have a problem and work on it. There is nothing to be ashamed of. You have anorexia. For a while you had it pretty rough, but you *are* getting better. Nobody can take that away from you. It's *your* victory and you should be proud of it. But sometimes it's okay to feel weak. It's okay to need help from other people to keep you sane. If Andrew is one of those people, why push him away?"

I let her words settle in.

Why push him away? Why really? When I told him about my struggle, he didn't seem grossed out, not like people in my last school. When it got out that I was hospitalized and treated for anorexia, everybody started to look at me differently. Like I was a freak or something. All those people who didn't notice for *months* that something was wrong. All those people who were envious and wanted to know how I'd lost weight just a few months before were then giving me ugly looks and talking behind my back.

Not Andrew.

"Because I'm not the only one who needs to fight her demons. He has to do it, too. If we don't, we'll only bring more pain to each other down the road."

ANDREW

"You skipped the practice again today."

Leaning against the back of the chair so much that I'm rocking on the back legs, I slowly release cloud after cloud of smoke in the air. I watch them disappear before taking another pull, the sweet smoke entering my lungs and running through my veins relaxing my whole body.

"You have to stop with this shit, Drew!" Derek says angrily. There is some stomping, and the joint is pulled from between my fingers.

"Hey!" I lean forward, ready to grab it back, but Derek is faster. The front legs of the chair hit the floor with such force I almost fall off. "Give it back!"

"No, I'm done watching you self-destruct, Andrew. This shit has to stop."

I narrow my eyes, watching him put out the blunt. Why do I see two of Derek? Both of them look at me with blue eyes filled with a mix of fury and weariness.

"Nobody asked you to come, so go the fuck away and leave me alone," I yell at his stoic face, then murmur more quietly, "Everybody else does."

I turn around, as not to see the look in his eyes. The judgment. The worry. But my big, fat fuck you is ruined because I trip over the chair, almost falling down and knocking my jaw on the edge of the coffee table.

When did that get there?

Shaking my head, I laugh at my own clumsiness as I try to stand up.

Strong hand wraps around my forearm, helping me get back on my feet. "You're stoned."

"I just didn't see the chair." I pull my arm out of his hand. "I need something to drink."

"What you need is a cold shower to sober you up, that's what you need."

Hands wrap around my arm again and turn me in the opposite direction of the bar.

How am I going to get my drink if not from the bar? The old man stashed all the good stuff there.

"I need a drink..." I protest again, trying to get out of his hold, but he's not letting me.

"Of coffee," Derek finishes. "You need a drink of coffee. It'll bring a little bit of clarity to your foggy brain, you jackass. I'm not sure there is any chance at saving your sanity though."

"N-no." I shake my head, but it feels heavy. Why is it so heavy? And why is the whole room spinning?

"Yes, you've been like this for far too long. It's time to sober up and get your shit under control, Andrew. We have a game coming in a couple of days, and we need you if we're going to win it. Coach was so pissed that you didn't show up to practice yet *again,* and I took half an hour of him drilling my ass, threatening he'll bench you before I managed to calm him down and get you another *last* shot. You won't mess it up. I won't let you."

"I can't. I just can't." I shake my head again. The panic washes over me, making my heart beat fast and my lungs close up. Cold sweat coats my skin, and I tug at the neckline of my shirt. Why is it so hot in here?

"Yes, you can," Derek insists, half carrying my body up the stairs toward my room. "I don't know what caused your latest freak-out, but whatever it is, we'll deal with it once we get you sobered up."

"You c-can't," I pant. Why is it so hard to breathe in here? I need air. "S-she..." I try to open my lungs, but they're just squeezed so tight. "...l-left."

My legs wobble underneath me, and for a split second, Derek loses his hold on me. I fall to the ground, my knees hitting the cool, hard floor, the impact resounding in the empty house.

"Andrew!"

Derek tries to get me back on my feet, but I don't have it in me. I shake my head, telling him to leave me alone, to let me be, but he doesn't get it.

"S-she l-left m-me..."

Chapter 34

ANDREW

"Do you feel better now?"

"Will you leave if I say I do?"

Derek throws himself in the recliner opposite me, getting comfortable. I guess that answers it. He's here to stay whether I want him to or not.

"Not so fast, buddy."

"Figures," I mutter, busying myself with finishing the burger in front of me.

After Derek got me to my room, he put me under an ice cold shower until my balls froze to death and my mind cleared from all the substances. Or as much as you can get rid of with the shower from hell. One thing is sure, a cold shower is a wake-up call like no other and one I don't wish to repeat anytime soon.

"Want to talk about it?"

"Not really."

"Andrew..." he drawls, a warning note in his tone.

"Talking about my feelings won't change a thing; it'll only piss me off more." I roll my eyes and take a sip from the cup he put next to my plate. My throat feels dry and itchy, and although I'd love to get up and pour myself a glass of whiskey from the bar, I know as long as Derek's here that's out of the question.

When the tasteless, bland liquid touches my tongue I can barely hold it in.

"What the fuck is that?" I yell as soon as I swallow the disgusting drink.

"Green tea. I think I saw somewhere that it helps with detox. God knows you need it."

"That tastes like crap."

"That's your body's way of telling you it feels like crap," he muses, sipping from his own cup. "Shut up and drink it. When you return, there is a high chance you'll get tested for substances, and we can't have you benched because you decided to drown yourself in booze and weed. We're playing St. Jonah's, it's the last game of the regular season, and if we don't win..."

He doesn't have to finish. We both know what's at stake—we win and we go to the championship tournament; we lose and we go home. Easy as that.

Gripping the cup between my hands, I force myself to take a big gulp of the damn tea, the frown constant on my face. I can be a big boy and guzzle it all down like a champ, but I don't have to pretend I like it.

The things we do for the game.

It would be too presumptuous of me to think the team depends solely on me. Both Derek and Max are way better players who have so much more to lose than I do, but hockey is a team sport, as our coach often likes to say, and in order to win we have to play like one. Since Max joined the Wolves, something just clicked between the three of us and we've played better than ever, but even that doesn't save us from occasional defeat. Hence the need to win the last game so we can progress further in the competition.

"Now." I shoot Derek a warning stare, but he ignores it. He

wiggles in his seat until he's happy with his position—legs spread just enough, leaning against the few lone pillows in the armchair, his hands resting on the armrest. The most casual of poses and the most dangerous one. "Will you get the stick out of your ass and tell me what has your panties in a twist or will I have to get it out of you by force?"

The side of his lips twitches upward in silent amusement as our eyes lock in a stare off.

Seconds tick by, I know because the silence is so profound you can hear the old clock ticking loudly. The ancient monstrosity belonged to my father's grandfather and has been passed down from father to son for generations. If it ever gets to my hands, I'll take a hammer and crush it to pieces.

"Fine," I finally say, pushing the food away from me. Suddenly I don't feel hungry at all. Actually, I feel sick. My stomach is rolling around my belly, and I can feel my heartbeat spike up. The palms of my hands are so sweaty I have to rub them against my pants.

Derek leans forward if only slightly, curiosity shining in his crystal blue eyes.

"You want to know what happened?"

The question is rhetorical, but he still answers. "This should be interesting."

"Jeanette-fucking-Sanders and I started hooking up. We've been going on and off since the senior sleepover, until it became..." I swallow down hard and force myself to clear my suddenly dry and raspy throat before I continue. The words are on the tip of my tongue. So clear. So true. So hard to utter out loud. "More. But then she left me. She left me like my mother did all those years ago. Like my dad does constantly. She just... left."

JEANETTE

"I'm so sorry I'm late," I say as I run into Amelia's living room and sag onto the couch.

"Yeah, yeah, the queen is never late. Everybody else is simply early."

"Brook!" Lia scolds her, but Brook barely tilts her head to the side in acknowledgment. She's too busy with scratching the Beast, better known as Lia's King Charles spaniel, Lola.

"Next time I'll make sure to arrive in a chariot so I can have my grand entrance," I deadpan, taking off my jacket and scarf.

The little beast finally notices me and jumps to her chubby little legs, running like crazy toward me. Her big ears fly through the air as she barks happily. I roll my eyes, ready to push her assault away, only she's faster, jumping in my lap and attacking my face with her slobbery tongue.

I was actually surprised when her barking didn't welcome me at the door, but I guess when you're in puppy heaven nothing else can be expected.

"Geeez, chill." Brook rolls her eyes at Lia. "I was just messing around. J knows that. Right, J-J?"

Finally pushing off the beast, I give Brook a death stare. "Call me J-J one more time and you might find yourself in need of a plastic surgeon."

Brook *tsks*. "So sensitive."

"Let's get down to business, shall we?" I grab my bag and fetch the books I'll need. I put them on the coffee table, neatly organized. Brook leans over my shoulder, and we discuss one of the tasks we had to complete for our homework when I feel a curious stare probing at the nape of my neck. "Lia?"

Big brown eyes look between the two us sitting side by side. A little frown appears between her brows. "Why do you always have to bicker like an old married couple? Can't you two just act like normal friends for once?"

Brook and I exchange a dumbfounded look. "Hell, no!"

Lia stares at us for a few seconds longer, shaking her head before she finally shrugs. "Whatever."

Then she joins us on the floor, and the three of us work on our Spanish. It's one of the only classes, except for homeroom, that we have together.

Señorita Rodrigues is one small thing, but she's feisty. She's ruling the class with an iron fist, intent on making everybody learn how to speak Spanish, if only the basics. Next week we have an exam on past tenses, of which there are many, and they all have a bunch of confusing irregular verbs and different uses you have to memorize.

We're in the middle of a heated discussion on whether we should use *pretérito imperfect* or *indefinido* when the doorbell rings, waking up Lola from her slumber. Barking, she runs toward the sound of the noise with Lia on her heels.

"That's the delivery guy," she throws over her shoulder. "I'll be back in a bit."

"I seriously think that *tuviera* makes more sense in this sentence."

I shake my head. "It's a description in the past. Something that's been going on for a while... It just seems logical to put *tenía...*"

"The food's here," Lia says loudly as she returns, putting the plastic bag on the coffee table. "If I hear one more conjugation, just one, my head will explode."

Sighing, Brook and I exchange a look.

"I guess a dinner break won't kill us," I agree as she tears into the bag and takes out the little white boxes.

"I wasn't sure what you were in the mood for, but we had an urge to eat Chinese so..."

Lia keeps on talking, but I tune her out. From the corner of my eye, I can see Brook closing the books and notebooks to make space for the food. Lia opens the carton, and the spicy smell of chicken, rice and vegetables fills the room, intensifying the queasiness in my stomach that I've been feeling all day.

Gulping down, I feel bile rising in my throat suddenly and I barely get enough time to cover my mouth before I'm on my feet, dashing out of the room and down the hall where I know the downstairs bathroom is located.

I don't even bother with turning on the light. Tumbling down in front of the toilet, my shaky fingers grip the seat as I lean forward and empty everything that's inside of me.

My whole body is shivering, in complete contrast with my heated skin, as I try to get it all out.

I hear hurried footsteps nearing. The light turns on, and then there is a soft touch on the nape of my neck, a cool hand pulling back my hair so it doesn't get all messy.

"Jeanette, are you okay?"

Wiping my mouth with the back of my hand, I stay seated for a moment to assess my body. My heart is slowly starting to slow down, and my breathing is deep and steady. My clothes cling to my still sweaty skin, but all in all, I don't think my stomach will rumble in protest if I move.

Slowly, with the help of Amelia, I get to my feet. "Yeah... just feeling a little queasy. That's it. I think it's a bug or something. I'll just..."

I wave my hand in the direction of the sink. Taking a small sip of water, I rinse my mouth as best as I can, washing away the lingering stale taste.

"A bug?" Brook asks from the doorway. "You were fine just a few minutes ago."

"I've been feeling off the last few days. It just comes and goes…"

Brook chuckles, making Lia frown.

"If I didn't know better I'd say you're…" she stops mid-sentence her eyes growing wide.

"Brook, seriously stop it. Can't you see she's not feeling well?" Lia huffs, her grip on me tightening as my legs give under me.

It can't be. Simply can't.

My heart starts beating faster again as panic spreads through my veins, icy cold and terrifying.

This can't be happening.

"Jeanette?" Lia asks worriedly, but I can barely hear her through the hectic thumping in my ears. What is that noise?

My lungs constrict and it's hard to breathe. I try to open my mouth to inhale, but the only thing that comes out is low wheezing.

My vision blurs, and I have to close my eyes to regain my footing.

"No, you won't."

Strong hands grab my chin, shaking me slightly.

"Jeanette? Jeanette, open your eyes."

My eyes? I want to protest, but can't. The hold Brook—at least I think it's Brook—has on me is so strong. I try to flutter my lids open, but they're so heavy. Why are they so heavy?

"C-c-can't," I rasp.

"What's wrong with her?"

This is not the same voice. It's softer. Terrified and completely panicky. Lia.

"I think she's having a panic attack," says the first voice.

Brook. Then she turns her attention back on me. "Jeanette, open your eyes."

I try again, only nothing happens.

"Why? Because she has a bug?" She sounds so confused that if I wasn't in this state of shell shock I'd probably laugh at her.

"No, because she's pregnant."

Chapter 35

JEANETTE

"Are you sure you're feeling better?" Brown eyes look at me in the rear-view mirror with weariness. "You scared us to death."

I nod my head once, trying to tilt my lips even if only in a half smile, but my attempt fails miserably.

What the hell am I going to do?

As if she can read my mind, Brook lifts her gaze, too, before she returns it promptly to the road. "Maybe you're not pregnant."

When I got my shit under control, the girls decided we should go and figure it out now. Like right the fuck now. Lia helped me clean up while Brook went back to the living room to pick up our things before we all got into my car and left.

There was no way in hell I could have kept us on the road, and Amelia, the worrier and empath she is, wasn't in much better condition, so that left us with Brook behind the wheel.

"Maybe," I agree, although I'm not certain of anything anymore. How could I be? My life is a mess, and this is just the cherry on top.

We drive in silence for a while. The only thing I asked them when we got in the car is not to go to any store where we could run into somebody we know, so we decided it's better if we drive to the next town over.

In the end, it's Lia who breaks the silence. "How late are you anyway?"

"No idea ..."

"How can you have no idea?" Brook grits through her teeth. "It's the most basic thing a girl should ..."

"Brook!" Lia interrupts her. "That's enough."

"I always had a pretty irregular cycle due ..." My throat bobbles as I swallow, this time harder, my fingers fidgeting in my lap nervously.

What will they think of me if I tell them the truth? Will they hate me? Judge me because of my weakness? I haven't shared this secret with anybody except Andrew. I couldn't bring myself to do it, not after everybody turned their backs on me when they found out. They thought I was some kind of freak when, in reality, the only thing I wanted was to belong.

A part of me knows they're not like all those people. Even Brook with all her snarky comments and irritating attitude isn't bad, not really. I know they don't gossip or wonder about other people's lives, yet a part of me ... a part of me can't help but wonder. What if, when they find out, they do think I'm some kind of freak?

I look down at my lap, my fingers trembling with nerves, and I have to grip them into fists to get them to stop. Clearing my throat, I finally whisper, "Due to the fact that I have an eating disorder."

Lia gasps loudly, her hand covering her mouth, and then silence. Louder than any yelling or screaming, more ominous than any words can be.

Wide, green eyes find mine in the rear-view mirror. "Jeanette, I ..."

"It's okay," I laugh quietly, but there is no humor in the

sound. "You couldn't have known. Nobody does. I didn't even think ..." I look out the window. "When I was in therapy, the doctors told me some of the consequences my actions may have caused, one of them being irregular cycles and infertility. But this is the first time I haven't had it for this long, maybe more than two months. My period is usually late, but not *that* late. Not since ... not since the last time things got out of control."

There is another long pause.

Silence fills the cabin of my car, while at the same time thoughts rage in my mind.

What are they thinking? Why are they not saying anything? Are they disgusted? Do they think I'm a freak? A weirdo? Or even worse ... do they pity me?

"Have you—" Brook clears her throat. "Have you been sick lately?"

"Have I been eating, you mean? You can say it. I know how my disease works." I run my hand through my hair. "It's been ... rough. Some days are harder than others, but I'm trying to eat regularly. Healthy."

Lia turns around in her seat, her hand gripping mine tightly in support. "We'll figure it out. Together. We'll figure it out."

Her kind, brown eyes are even bigger than usual, tears pooling in them, but Lia's holding them back. Strong. She's trying to be strong for me.

I open my mouth, but no words come out.

Another hand sneaks back gripping my knee, giving it a hard, reassuring squeeze before it loosens and returns back to the steering wheel.

No judgement.

No unnecessary questions or probing.

Just support and reassurance.

Just ... love.

I exhale slowly, and for the first time in so long it feels like a weight I didn't even know I was carrying has lifted off my shoulder. For the first time in forever, it feels like I can breathe.

"So ..." Lia drawls. "How are we going to do this?"

The brown paper bag is sitting on my desk, and we haven't touched it since we got back to my place.

When we finally got to the next town over—thankfully the rest of the ride passed in silence since I needed some time to get my thoughts under control—Brook pulled into the closest drug store. We looked around for a bit, trying to pretend we were just browsing the aisles when we damn well knew what we needed. Finally, I gave up on pretending and went straight to the pregnancy tests.

The funny part? They're right next to the condoms. Maybe if I was looking for condoms and not the test, I'd have been laughing. Then again, maybe not.

I took one in my hand and checked it out. What if I'm pregnant? What if I'm not?

I'm not sure which option scared me more.

"Are you going to take it?"

Brook's quiet question returns me back to the present moment.

I intertwine my fingers in my lap, holding tightly. "I don't think I can. I'm just so scared."

"Of being pregnant?"

"That," I agree. "But ... what if I'm not?"

"What?" Brook yells surprised, startling us all.

"What if I'm not? I'm nowhere near ready to have a baby, but what if this is my only chance? The doctors were pretty forward with me; the chances of getting pregnant are low. What if this is my only chance and I've blown it somehow?"

Lia and Brook exchange a worried look, at a loss for words. Not that I can blame them. What seventeen-year-old wants to be pregnant? Only a crazy one, that's who.

Restless, I jump off the bed.

I want to know, but at the same time I don't.

"Come on." Brook loops one of her hands through mine, the other one gripping the brown bag as if her life depends on it.

"What? What are you doing?"

"We're doing it. And we're doing it now."

"We?" I pull my hand out of hers, stopping in my tracks. "Brook, are you feeling ..."

"We're going to take it together. God knows you bought enough for the whole senior class of Greyford High."

I roll my eyes at her. "I didn't buy that many!"

"Mhmm... let's go."

"Do you even know what you're doing?" I ask, skeptical.

"How hard can it be? You pull your pants down, unclasp the stick, squat over the toilet and pee on it. It's not quantum science."

"When you put it like that ... But you go first."

Brook lifts her finger in warning. "You're going to pee on that stick today whether you do it on your own or I have to force you to do it. Clear?"

"Crystal."

Brook nods and then stomps into the bathroom like a woman on a mission. The door closes behind her and I turn around, sighing in relief.

"You two really have a strange relationship," Lia mutters, shaking her head disbelievingly.

She's so quiet, I almost forgot she was in the room.

"You want to take one, too?" I gesture over my shoulder in

the direction of the closed door of the bathroom. "Apparently we have plenty."

Lia pales, her freckles standing out even more before she bursts into laughter. She's laughing so hard that tears pool in her eyes, and I can't help but laugh, too.

It's intense and slightly panicky, but I welcome the outburst. It feels good to laugh, forget my worries and insecurities if only for a moment. Liberating.

Once my breathing returns to normal and I wipe the tears from my eyes, I feel better. Relaxed.

Lia straightens from her bent position, wiping her own tears. "Thanks, but I don't think I'll need them anytime soon."

"Nothing like a pregnancy scare to emphasize the importance of birth control." I turn around to find Brook standing at the doorway. Green eyes meet mine. "Your turn."

For a second, I let my eyes fall closed. This is it. I have to do it. I have to *know*.

Inhaling deeply, I open my eyes and nod decisively before I enter the bathroom.

My heart is fluttering in my chest. A steady *thump, thump, thump*.

Brook left the bag open on the counter. From the corner of my eye, I can see the white stick sitting neatly on the left side of the sink. Her test.

I dig into the bag, pulling out a new one. Carefully, I open the box and read the instructions, which tell me basically the same thing Brook told me before. Open the test, squat, pee, close, wait.

It takes some time for me to relax enough to actually do the deed, but once I'm done, I close the stick and put it on the right side of the counter and wash my hands.

"Are you done already?" Brook's brown head pops into the bathroom, not caring in the slightest for my modesty.

"Thank you for knocking," I say dully, but she ignores me and opens the door wider so the both of them can enter.

I close the toilet seat and sit down, looking at the counter and tests like they're a ticking bomb about to explode.

Brook and Lia murmur about something, but I can't hear them. My heart is speeding up and my breathing is growing labored. Panic and exhilaration. I can feel butterflies in my stomach, like little birds learning how to spread their wings.

What if it's positive? What if I'm actually pregnant? How am I going to do it? How am I going to tell my parents? Max? Andrew? How am I going to tell Andrew?

A new, stronger wave of panic assaults me.

Does he even want to have kids? Now? Ever? We're both so fucked up. So *not* ready to be in a proper relationship, much less have a *child*.

But what if it's negative? What if this was really my only chance to have a child of my own and it was just false hope? Will I ever be able to forgive myself? Will I ever be able to forget the pain and disappointment? I've never really given it much thought. Pregnancy wasn't on my mind, not even close until now, until there is a possibility of maybe actually being pregnant.

The beeping sound brings me out of the maze of my thoughts.

"Ready?" Brook looks at me worriedly, nibbling at her lip.

I gulp down. "Can we do yours first?"

"Sure." She nods, picking up her test. She looks at it, and even though she didn't have a reason to do it, even though she doesn't think she's pregnant, I can see her shoulders relax in relief. "It's negative."

She turns it around the show us the big fat minus. Then she throws it in the bin underneath the sink and turns around to look at me.

Lia comes closer, her hand falling over my shoulder and giving me a reassuring squeeze.

I give Brook a "go on" sign and wait as she picks up the test and looks down at it.

Her throat bobbles as she slowly lifts her eyes. Lia's hand on my shoulder tightens almost painfully, and if I wasn't already sitting, I'm sure my legs would give out on me.

Gradually, as if in slow motion, Brook turns it so we can see it.

"What are you going to do?"

Chapter 36

ANDREW

"Hill!" Coach shouts, stopping me in my tracks.

I exchange a quick look with Derek before returning my gaze to the man standing in front of the room. "Yeah, Coach?"

"Stay here for a bit, son."

"Sure thing, Coach."

All the guys slowly leave the locker room, the noise and banter going away with them down the hall and to the bus waiting outside to take us to our game later today.

I nibble at my lip nervously, shifting from one leg to the other. Coach looks through his papers and organizes his stuff until the last of the guys are out and there is only silence on the other side of the door.

"Feeling good, Hill?"

I rub my suddenly sweaty hands on the sides of my thighs, nervous, but more than anything else, confused. "Coach?"

He lifts his gaze, dark eyes as sharp as always as they zero in on me. His face is washed with age and cold, wrinkles around his mouth and eyes prominent and most likely the result of frowning on all the bad calls and stupid shit his players pull.

"I think my question is pretty clear."

"Yes, Coach. Crystal," I say in a hurry, then add, "I'm fine. Ready to get this show on the road."

Dark eyes narrow slightly as he looks at me, trying to find ... something. I'm not sure what. The last few days have been tough. The day after Derek came to my house to get me back on track, the coach gave me a verbal beating and then pushed me until I wanted to puke my guts out. Even now, I can still feel the smallest of muscles I didn't know existed from all the exercise he put me through.

I try to stay still and hold his gaze. Not show him that I'm nervous when, in reality, I can feel drops of sweat forming on my forehead.

Will he tell me I'm benched for the game? Why did he even let me come back then?

"You sure?"

I nod my head. "Yes, sir."

"Because if you're not ..."

"I'm ready, Coach."

"You've had your ups and downs this season, but you're a good player, Andrew. That is, when you're not acting like a little shit, which is often." His face relaxes, if only a little, and his mouth even tilts into something that can be considered a smile. "In case you were wondering."

The guy almost never smiles, so I guess I should just take it.

"Now grab your shit and let's go win this game."

I look at the seconds ticking by on the huge clock on the screen. Only five more minutes to go and the score is six to five in St. Jonah's favor.

Those snarky little bastards meant business today. Not that

they usually don't. God knows there is enough bad blood between Greyford High and St. Jonah's to last the lifetime. I don't even remember how or when it all started, not that I care. My problem isn't with the school; it's with one of their players.

As if he can hear my thoughts, jackass lifts his head, his eyes finding mine from the other side of the ice. Ethan-fucking-Williams. A taunting smirk curls his lips. Anger spikes in my blood, but I try to keep my face impassive like I've done for most of today.

A hand lands on my shoulder as determined eyes find mine through the protective face shield. "You cool, bro?"

Gritting my teeth, I grab the offered water bottle and take a pull from it, swirling the liquid in my mouth before I spit it. "Fine."

Playing fair or dirty, it didn't matter one bit to them as long as they take the win and go to the tournament. The stakes were high, but they were getting pretty desperate if you ask me.

From the corner of my eye, I can see Derek and coach discussing something, probably our next move once we get back on the ice.

My blood is still rushing through my veins, right leg bouncing nervously. I want to get back out there so I can unleash what's left of this pent-up energy inside of me and get this game over with.

"Hill, Sanders, King," coach yells over the noise filling up the rink. "You're up, boys."

Without giving him a backward glance, we launch back to the ice, making the exchange.

For the next couple of minutes the game is intense. Both teams are doing whatever is in our power to keep the puck on our side—we need to score not one, but two goals so we can win, and the only thing they want is to keep our sticks off the puck so we can't score and tie the game.

Currently we have the puck. Max stole it from one of the opposing players, to their distress, and we all chase it toward the goal. The guy following Max is close on his heels, and I put all of my energy into reaching him to either move the dude out of his way or get clear so he can pass me the black rubber, when I see a flash of red in the corner of my eye.

A shoulder runs into my side, making me stumble.

"Son of a bitch," I hiss, shooting my stick forward just in time. He trips over the stick, losing his balance and falling into the Plexiglas.

Take that, fucker.

Just when I turn to get back to the game, I hear the buzzer. Red light flashes as my eyes shoot up, looking at the scoreboard. Six to six. One more goal. Just one more, and we're going to the tournament.

Anticipation and adrenaline rush through my body, pumping me up. Max and Derek skate backward, waiting for the next play. They give each other a passing stick tap, but that's the only acknowledgment of the score because now we're tied, and if we don't want to go into overtime, we have a minute and a half to score another goal.

Jonah's players have the puck and they start the attack. We're running out of time. I skate backward, ready to stop anybody who wants to go through.

A tie or a win. These are the only acceptable options.

"Hill."

"Williams."

Even through his face shield, I can see his smug smile.

Play it cool. You have to play it cool. Think about scoring the goal and don't let him get to you.

"Still pining after that raven-haired bombshell?" he yells over the crowd.

I grit my teeth, trying to hold in my rage.

Don't let him get to you, I chant in my head, my eyes following the progress of the puck, but the dude doesn't shut up.

"She's stunning, that's for sure. But don't forget, she was mine first."

This time I don't even try to control myself. I launch at him, shoving his unprepared body away and pinning him against the Plexiglas. My hands curl around his jersey, pulling him off the ice.

"Don't you dare say her name." I shove him into the glass, making it tremble with the force I put behind the movement. "Don't you dare."

"Aww." He pouts his lips in exaggeration, taunting me. The guy has a death wish, that's for sure. "The little hussy has you wrapped around her little finger. How cute."

"You're a dead man," I murmur, my voice dangerously low.

I let him drop down and start pulling off my gloves when two sets of hands wrap around my forearms pulling me away.

"Think about the game."

"We need you to win this thing."

Both Derek and Max start pulling me away when the ref comes between us. His mousy eyes look from me to Williams, frowning as he assesses the situation. "All good?"

"Good." I nod stiffly as we get back to the game.

With less than a minute on the clock and the puck in their possession, the best outcome we can hope for is to go into overtime.

They push and pull, everything they can do to bulldoze through our ranks and get to our net. I can see one of our guys get shoved aside forcefully, making an opening.

As the guy holding the puck sees it and skates in that direction, I hold my own fort with Williams at my heels. He goes through the opening. Our goalie sees him and gets ready to defend the net when a flash of white skates between them, stealing the puck.

Fuck yeah.

Everybody notices the puck exchange. Jonah's defenders shoot to catch Sanders, while the rest of them try to stop us from coming forward.

"You're not going anywhere, pretty boy." Williams sneers at me.

"That's what you'd like to think."

I start right, which is the logical option, but instead go left. Using all the strength I have left in my legs, I shoot over the ice and between the players, making a half circle and coming from the other side.

The defenders are at Max's back. He shoves off one, his eyes meeting mine for a millisecond, and then the second guy's at him just as he slides the puck in my direction.

I watch the black rubber glide on the white surface toward me.

My eyes lift, staring straight at the goalie. He's glaring at me through his mask. Drops of sweat slide down the side of my face as everything slows down.

Seconds. That's all that's left. Seconds.

And I only have one chance. I cannot screw up.

My body moves on its own, muscle memory kicking in when my brain shuts down. I'm coming diagonally from the left side, so it would be logical to shoot left.

One shot.

I shoot right.

Red light flashes and all hell breaks loose.

Chapter 37

JEANETTE

"Yeah?" I mumble into my phone, not even looking who's calling. The stupid device started vibrating, and no matter how hard I tried to ignore it, it wouldn't stop and I couldn't concentrate on my calculus homework.

Not that I could concentrate to begin with. My mind was too busy trying to figure out the mess that is my life to worry about something as trivial as homework.

"Jeanette, honey, I need you to go to Dad's office. He left some papers on his desk and he needs them at the hospital." Mom's peachy voice comes from the other side of the line.

"And do what with them?" I groan, half my brain still concentrated on the problem in front of me.

"You have to take them to him."

"Can't you do that?"

The last thing I want to do is go to the hospital and see my dad. Surely somebody else can do it.

"I'm at the PTA meeting, and Max has that away game."

Forgetting about the problem in my notebook, I massage my temples, which suddenly throb painfully and it has nothing to do with math.

"Fine," I agree reluctantly. My headache will only become

worse if I keep fighting her on this, and it's not like I'm in a state of mind to actually try and finish my homework.

She tells me what to look for, the commotion of voices behind her growing louder, and then she hangs up on me.

Sighing, I set my phone down on the desk before I lean back in my chair, staring at the ceiling.

I don't want to go, but it can't be helped, so I get up, grabbing my bag before I go to the study to look for the damn files.

As soon as I enter the hospital, the smell of antiseptic and illness surrounds me.

Once upon a time I was addicted to that smell. I used every opportunity I could get to tag along with my dad to the hospital and watch him work. When people would ask me what I want to be when I grow up, I would always say, without a trace of a doubt, "I want to be a doctor just like my daddy."

I wanted to save people's lives. I wanted to make a difference.

Until everything changed, me included.

Until the moment I couldn't save myself. How am I supposed to save somebody else if I can't save myself?

Now, I haven't stepped foot inside of a hospital for more than a year. I haven't stepped within a five-mile radius of hospital. That's how much I despise it.

Yet, I'm here today, and the smell that once brought me comfort now makes me nauseous. But maybe that doesn't have as much to do with me being here as it does with my other state.

Breathing through the mouth, my hands grip harder the files in my hands, and my thumb brushes over my lower stomach. A small army of butterflies patters in my abdomen at the touch. I still haven't gone to the doctor for a check-up. I know I should have called, but I wasn't ready. Just as much as I wasn't ready to share this news with anybody else. Before Brook and Lia left my house a few days ago, I swore them to secrecy. If the news got out… I didn't even want to imagine the proportions of the shit storm it would cause.

Walking through the hallways, my footsteps resound. The chatter and beeping of different machines surrounds me, the smell of antiseptic a constant in the hallways.

It's always hectic and alive. Strange, considering the amount of people who die here every day. But to me, hospitals always represented life.

Life and hope.

The elevator chimes, and people slowly get out before I and a few others manage to enter. I press the button for the cardiology floor and hang back as the elevator slowly begins to climb.

People—patients, staff and visitors—slowly come and go around their business. Finally, when we reach my floor, I exit.

Walking down the hallway, I see a few people milling around, but not many. That's the cardiology department for you. One nurse is sitting at the station, and I can see another going through the medicine cabinet. For a second, the first nurse lifts her gaze, and I give her a nod in acknowledgment but don't stop to say anything. I've never been here, so I don't know her.

You used to know all the nurses, and they'd explain everything you wanted to know.

Not anymore.

That was in another lifetime.

With confident, long strides I walk down the hallway until I reach the door my mom said is my dad's office. I lift my hand to knock, but find the door slightly ajar.

It feels like déjà vu.

I know I shouldn't, but I can't help myself.

Swallowing the lump in my throat, I peek in the small space left open.

My father is seated in his chair. His dark hair, dappled with grays, is messy. His white coat is left open, wrinkled from the long shift.

I hear their murmured voices, but I can't decipher the words, the buzzing in my head growing louder and louder.

They both laugh, and I see the nurse that's inside with him —young, barely out of college, with long legs, a tiny waist and big bust—leaning over the table toward him. The motion opens even more of her shirt, exposing her ample chest that my father doesn't even pretend not to look at. His hand covers hers on top of his desk.

The bile rises in my throat.

This can't be happening.

Not again.

I take a step back, but when that's not enough to get them out of my sight, I take another and another before I turn around on my heels and hurry away.

When I pass the nurse's station, I remember the file in my hand.

That stupid file.

"Give this to Dr. Sanders."

I thrust the file her way and run out of there, not waiting for an answer.

She calls after me, but I ignore her.

I have to get out of here.

I have to escape.

The space, the sound, the smell... it's all too much. The picture of my father in his office with that nurse, etched in my mind. It brings memories. Memories I've spent a lot of time forgetting.

But the thing about the memories?

They usually come back.

Before

I run pass the nurse's station waving at Sally. She's the fifty-something head nurse of the cardiology department in St. James's Hospital. Sally gives me a short wave before continuing her phone conversation, probably with one of the patient's families.

Sally's the best nurse ever, and I've met quite a few since I started tagging along with my father to work. She's caring, emphatic, and so, so nice. She always smiles, and I've heard a lot of patients say that her smile brightens their day and makes them feel better.

Yes, medicine helps, it can save people's lives, but care and compassion are equally as important, if not more, in the recovery.

I walk down the hallway, greeting nurses and patients along the way to my dad's office. I didn't tell him I was coming, but since Max and I went to school in the same car today, I figured I'd stay in the city while I wait for him to finish with his hockey practice.

When I come to my dad's office, the door is closed, but like every other time, I don't knock before entering. If he was with a patient or family, Sally would have mentioned it to me on my way in.

Muffled sounds come from within, and then I hear something fall just as I open the door.

Standing there, in the middle of my dad's office and bent over the table, is a nurse with her pale, naked ass in the air and scrubs nowhere in sight. And standing right behind her, thrusting like his life depends on it, is my father. Thank God I couldn't see anything because of his coat, but clearly his pants are pooled around his ankles.

Their passionate moans fill the small space, and the smell of sex is etched into the walls.

I'm not sure what happens next. How it happens. I'm not aware that I moved or made a sound, but I must have, because both of them turn around abruptly, looking at me with confused, passion-filled eyes.

The girl, who can't be *that* much older than me, looks petrified and maybe even ashamed. My dad? He just looks shocked.

"Jeanette..." He breaths my name, his eyes wide.

I take him in, my skin crawling in disgust. Shaking my head, I take a step back. I keep retreating until I'm out of the room.

He calls my name again, but I ignore him. Turning around, I start running.

What is happening here? Dad is cheating on Mom? Does she know? Does Max know? How could he do this? To me? To us? How could he do this? Is this the first time or...?

Tears run down my cheeks as I take the stairs two at the time. The elevator is nowhere in sight, and I don't want to risk him catching up to me.

I need space. I need to think.

What am I going to do? How am I supposed to tell Mom, tell Max, that Dad has been cheating?

What am I going to do?

Now

A sob rips through my throat as soon as I get outside. The sky is a gloomy gray color, now almost completely dark. There is a slight chill in the air and I wrap my hands around myself tighter, running toward my car. I have to get out of here.

This can't be happening again.

Not after everything.

Not after all the secrets I kept and all the lies I told to keep my family intact. Not after everything I sacrificed so my brother and my mother would never find out the truth. Not after all the guilt. God, the *guilt*. It's been eating at me alive, but I've kept it all in.

I can't go through it again.

When I see my car in the parking lot, my hand digs into my purse to find the key. After some shuffling through all the shit I have in there, my fingers finally wrap around it, only for it to fall on the ground through my shaky fingers.

"Fuck."

Bending down I grab it again, my grip on the plastic strong as I press the button to unlock the door.

Tumbling into my seat, I let my tears fall.

Why is this happening again?

Why? Why? Why?

With every why, my clenched fist connects to the steering wheel in front of me.

That day when Dad got home, he confronted me. He wanted to know if I'd told anybody and if I planned to. Begged me not to. Like I had it in me to break Mom's and Max's hearts.

I inherited a lot of things from my father—his wits, his smarts, his love for medicine—but one thing I didn't inherit is his ability to willingly break people's hearts. I did, however, inherit something else, something even worse: his ability to betray. I betrayed my family by keeping his transgressions a secret.

But I would do it over and over again if it meant having my family together. Even as imperfect and fucked up as we are, we're a family.

That day the naïve little girl inside of me died. Wounded by the ugliness of society, surrounded by poisonous people, betrayed by her own blood and riddled with guilt, she died and the only thing that's left is a shell of the person she once was.

Figuratively and physically.

So I gave him an ultimatum. He would toss aside all the whores he was fucking and become the loyal husband and caring father everybody thought he was, and I'd keep my mouth shut.

Brushing away my tears, I take a few deep breaths to calm myself. I put on my seat belt and start the car, putting the heating on max to warm my numb hands before I pull out of the parking lot.

That day, Dad accepted my ultimatum. Of course he did, there was no other choice for him.

I thought that was the end, that everything would be over. But it was all just beginning.

Chapter 38

ANDREW

"Good shot, Hill."

One of my teammates pats me on the shoulder in passing. We just got back to Greyford, and everybody is grabbing their shit to go home, take a shower and change before the party later tonight.

And what a party it will be.

For the first time in years, Greyford High will participate in the Ice Globe Tournament, which is basically a high school version of what the Frozen Four is for college or the Stanley Cup Playoffs on the professional level.

You can still feel the buzz of excitement going through our group. Everybody is riding the adrenaline high from the game and victory earlier today, and I don't think it'll leave us anytime soon.

Even coach and his staff are wearing big smiles on their faces, and they didn't drill us too much after the game about taking it slow tonight, which would be a first.

Realistically, we all know there is still a long road ahead of us, but tonight we're celebrating our victory. Tomorrow we'll put it behind us and concentrate on practicing for the tournament.

"Look at them, worshiping you like a war hero." Derek stands next to me, his hockey bag thrown over his shoulder.

Those last few seconds of the game play on repeat in my head. It was insane. When I got the puck, time slowed down. I looked at it in wonder for a millisecond before I charged at the goalie, hoping I wouldn't mess it up somehow.

"If I'm their version of a hero, something is really messed up in their lives. It's just hockey."

"Do I hear that right, King?" Sanders joins our little group, looking perplexed. "Was that modesty actually coming out of his mouth?"

"Oh, shut up." I shove him away, if only to hide the slight blush warming my cheeks.

They both laugh at me.

"Look at him, blushing and all. Humbleness looks weird on you, Hill. Please go make a baby cry now so that balance is restored back in the world."

"You two are jackasses, you know that?"

They both laugh again, harder this time.

Frowning at them, I pick up my bag and start walking toward my car. "I have shit to take care of and a party to organize. If you two assholes don't want to help, get out of my way."

"Okay, okay," Derek runs after me, still laughing. "Don't get all sensitive on us. What do you need help with?"

Unlocking my car, I throw my duffle on the back seat before I turn to face them.

"I need you to go set up the party at my place. I have to go back."

Max looks at me, confused. "Back where?"

My eyes find his. Same as the eyes of the girl I'm falling for.

The girl I've *fallen* for.

The whole game I'd been looking in the stands for her,

trying to find her seated between thousands of fans, but she wasn't there. She's always there, supporting her brother, but not today. Was she busy or was she avoiding me?

I couldn't stop wondering where she was and how she was doing. Is she really trying to get her life under control or was she just sick of me and wanted to call it quits and this was the easiest way out?

Just the idea of Jeanette Sanders being done with me and cozying up to some random guy makes my chest squeeze painfully.

I don't want her to be done with me because I, for sure, am not done with her.

But she was right. I have to bury my demons so I can stop constantly comparing her to them. I have to figure out *why* so I can stop wondering about the past and concentrate on the future.

"Back to face my demons."

JEANETTE

I'm not sure how I manage to get home, but somehow I do. Memories of the past and present intertwine in my head so much that I'm not sure what's then and what's now, what's true and what's just an illusion.

Somewhere along the way, snow started falling, slowly at first, but by the time I get to my empty, dark house it's falling harder.

Not bothering with the lights, I go straight to the living room.

Mom is out with her friends somewhere and Max, I don't have any idea where he is. He was supposed to be home by now from his game, but I guess he stayed with his friends.

I turn on the fireplace, enjoying its warmth and the golden-orange light playing in the dark room. Then I curl down into the armchair and wait.

The fireplace is there more for the show, but it does look nice and I enjoy cozying next to it while watching TV or playing the violin. It gives a special, almost rustic charm to the room.

Only tonight I'm not here for entertainment, and there is no amount of heat that can make me feel warm.

My eyes set on the crackling, almost hypnotizing flame.

Flame that takes me back to the past as I wait for my present to catch up to me.

Before

For the next few weeks, everything returns to normal, or as normal as it can be when you're hiding the fact that you caught your father cheating on your mother in his office with a twenty-something bimbo.

Dad and I don't speak. Not at all. If anybody notices, which I don't think is the case, they don't call us on it.

He comes home on time, actually sits down to have dinner with us and sometimes even spends nights with Mom watching TV or going to Max's games. They seem happy. Mom and Max. I haven't seen her drink more than an occasional glass of wine with dinner, so there's that.

One big happy family.

Suddenly my appetite is gone.

"I'm done."

Pushing back my almost untouched plate of food, I get out of the chair.

"But you didn't eat anything!" Mom protests.

"Not hungry." I wave her off, not bothering to turn around. "I'm going to get ready."

Maddaline's parents are out of town, and she's organizing a party at her house. Not my favorite hang-out place, but Patrick will be there.

Since the party at his house, we've become a *thing*. We text a lot, he joins us during lunch in the cafeteria and we've even hung out and *danced* at a few parties between then and now. I know he wants more; I can see it in his eyes. Sometimes when we talk and he looks at me, his eyes darken with desire. I've been brushing him off for weeks, but... maybe soon I'll get the courage to actually let him do more than just kiss me here and there.

I take my time getting ready since Max is downstairs and it'll take a bit for him to be done. I choose a dark blue dress. It's casual and cute—knee-length, A-line with sleeves that reach my elbows. And for the first time in a while, I feel pretty wearing it.

I carefully put on my make-up and curl my dark hair just in time for Max to knock on my door.

As soon as we get to the party, he's snatched by his friends, and I wander around looking for Nikki, Lana and Maddy.

Just when I'm about to turn the corner, my face plants into a chest. Raising my eyes, I can't help but smile when I see the familiar blues looking back at me.

"Hi," I squeak, blushing.

"Hi yourself, pretty girl."

Patrick leans down, his lips brushing against the corner of my mouth.

"Just got here?"

I nod my head. "I've been looking for the girls, but I can't seem to find them."

He looks over my head, his eyes scanning the crowd. "They're... somewhere around."

"I presumed so," I laugh. "What are you up to?"

Patrick lifts his cup. "Refill. Want one?"

"Sure."

We chat on our way to the kitchen. He tells me about hockey, and I mention a project I've been working on for my chemistry class.

There are a few people in the kitchen, but my eyes narrow, looking at the just-closed door that leads to the terrace.

"Hey, was that..." I tip my chin in that direction.

Patrick looks through the window. "Oh, that..." He shrugs. "They've been at it for weeks now."

My whole body goes numb.

Blue eyes lift as he fills his cup from the keg, looking at me worriedly. "I thought you knew."

I open my mouth to say something, but no words come out, so I settle for a shake of my head. No, I didn't know. I had no idea.

Weeks.

He's been hiding it for weeks.

They both have.

Patrick keeps talking, but I tune him out as I walk toward the window. It's one of those huge floor-to-ceiling windows designed to bathe the room in natural light.

And there, on the other side of the glass, even through the darkness of the night, I see them.

Max and Maddy.

Kissing like their lives depend on it.

I guess she finally got what she was after.

"You want something?"

My whole body jerks when I hear Patrick behind me. Composing my face as best as I can, I turn my back to the window. If I look at them one second longer, I'm going to puke.

"Sure."

He leaves his cup on the counter and starts gathering things for my usual cocktail. When his fingers wrap around the bottle of clear liquid, I make up my mind.

I put my hand over his, stopping him. There is confusion in his blue irises.

"I'll just have this."

Chapter 39

JEANETTE

The front door slams closed, disrupting my trip down the memory lane, but not before a whiff of cold air enters the house. Rustling comes from the foyer, and I can imagine my dad putting his briefcase on the table next to the door. He empties his pockets, leaving his keys and loose change in the bowl on the table before he takes off his coat, scarf and shoes. Always in the same order.

Then he takes his briefcase to the office.

I can hear his soft footsteps nearing. He almost passes by the living room, but the light of the fire catches his attention.

"Jeanette?" From the corner of my eye, I can see him look inside the living room. "Why are you sitting in the dark? I thought the house was empty."

He flicks on the light, the sudden brightness blinding me temporarily, but I don't turn around to look at him.

Not yet.

I'm not even sure I *can* look at him.

"Are you okay?"

"You promised," I accuse softly.

"Jeanette?"

He comes closer, almost like he's nearing a wounded, scared animal, unsure if his sudden movement will upset me.

"You promised." This time I accompany the accusation with a slight shake of my head. "And the worst part is I actually believed you."

How does the saying go?

Fool me once, shame on you. Fool me twice, shame on me.

Guess I can't blame anybody else for my foolishness but myself.

"What are you talking about?"

There is a weariness in his voice, but is it because of the fact that I found out or because of the fear of what I could do with this information? What I *will* do with this information. Because I'm done. I'm done with keeping secrets and lying for other people. I'm done with putting other people first while at the same time breaking my own heart.

Inhaling deeply, I do my best to keep a stoic expression as I face him despite the fact my whole world is breaking.

"I was at the hospital today."

He runs his hand through his hair. "I know, I asked your mom to bring me the file, but she said she'd send you. The nurse gave them to..."

"I saw you," I interrupt him, not interested in the least in what he has to say. Not anymore. He can save the excuses for somebody who wants to listen to them. That somebody isn't me. "I came to your office. The door was slightly open, and there you were." A humorless chuckle parts my lips. "With the nurse. Again."

His eyes, so much like my own, grow wide.

"Jeanette..." He wets his lips, trying to find the words.

Words, lies, I don't want to listen.

"I'm done, Dad." I shake my head. "I'm done with the

secrets and lies. I'm done with feeling guilty because I'm hiding this from Mom and Max. I can't do it anymore."

The ache in my chest grows stronger and stronger. And although I didn't want to, I can feel the tears gathering in my eyes, making my vision blurry.

"I can't. I've protected you for too long. Now I have to think about somebody else, too. Not just myself and my selfish wishes."

"Jeanette, please. Just let me explain."

He tries to grab my arm but I pull away, walking around him. I need to get out of here.

"Spare us both from your lies; what little trust I had in you is gone. I'm going to tell them. I'm going to tell them, and there is nothing you can do to stop me."

"Jeanette, it's not what you think!"

He goes after me, his voice full of panic.

I laugh almost manically. "Isn't that what all cheaters say?"

"Jeanette!"

Once again his hand wraps around mine, but I pull it away before his grip tightens. I can't do this anymore.

"I'm going out. I can't deal with this now."

I see the keys to my car on the desk. Grabbing them, I slip into my sneakers and run outside in a hurry so he can't reach me.

The icy air attacks me as soon as I'm out the door. Big, crystal snowflakes fall all around, sticking to everything in their way.

Not bothering to remove the fine dusting of snow that's covering my SUV, I unlock the door and jump inside. I turn on the ignition, quickly pulling the seat belt over myself and turning on the lights.

Dad is running down the stairs, yelling at me frantically, the front door wide open behind him.

Putting the car in reverse, I turn around and start driving away.

That's when I let the first tears fall.

When did everything start falling apart? Why didn't we see it in time? Why didn't we stop it?

The only thing I ever wanted was a normal family. Parents who love and care for each other. A sibling I could play with and confide in.

And I had it for a while. We weren't perfect, but we loved each other.

Then we grew up. The differences between us became so obvious, and as time passed, we moved further and further apart.

Mom with her high-class expectations and drinking problem.

Dad with his workaholic ways and cheating.

And Max... he became his popular, outgoing self while I drew more and more into myself. Until the expectation of the people around me became too much to bear. But I wanted to do it nevertheless, to make the people around me happy.

I carried the weight on my shoulders for so long until it broke me.

Before

The world is dizzy. I giggle loudly as I watch it go round and round.

"You're cheerful tonight," Patrick whispers in my ear, his nose tracing the column of my neck.

"I'm always cheerful," I protest, pouting.

He laughs at me. "You're so cute when you're drunk."

"I'm not d-drunk." I hiccup. "I never get drunk."

Patrick shakes his head, but the smile remains on his face. "If you say so."

We're dancing, or more like swaying, on the make-shift dance floor Maddy had the hockey players create in the middle of her living room.

Patrick's arms are around my waist, holding me close to his hard body with mine around his neck. Closing my eyes for a second, I press my forehead against his chest, his spicy scent surrounding me.

It's nice. Having his arms around me. Feeling the warmth of his body.

His hand slides up and down my back, shivers going through my skin.

I lift my head and find his dark eyes looking at me.

So intense.

So hot.

He wants me.

He really wants me.

His tongue darts out, wetting his lips, and I don't wait a second longer. Rising onto the tips of my toes, my fingers dig into the skin of his neck, pulling him down. Our lips touch, and I lose myself in the feel of his mouth on mine.

The spark of surprise is soon lost, and his mouth is attacking mine.

Clumsy, eager, open-mouthed kisses.

I return them with the same fervor, enjoying the feel of his hands roaming my body.

After a while, we break our kiss. Our breathing is hard, labored. His forehead presses against mine, his warm breath tickling my skin.

"Want to go up?"

I don't even think about it; I just nod.

The sound of the door opening and closing wakes me up. Groaning softly, my hand lifts to massage my throbbing forehead.

What the hell is wrong with me?

Why does my head hurt so much?

Where am I?

Shifting, I hear the sheets rustle under my bare skin. Why am I naked? My eyes fly open, but then swiftly shut when they're assaulted by the light of the bedside lamp.

So bright.

Groaning in pain, I take a few deep breaths, trying to hold it at bay. The second time, I open my eyes much slower, letting them adjust. It's not even that bright, but my head hurts nevertheless. My mouth is dry, but even the thought of drinking water makes my stomach turn.

The bottle with clear liquid flashes in my mind. Tequila. I'd been drinking tequila.

Lots and lots of tequila because...

When I remember the reason behind my sudden need to find the oblivion in alcohol, the bile rises in my throat. Pressing my hand against my mouth, I push it down, the sour taste burning my throat.

I stay motionless for a while, and when I'm sure I'm not going to puke, I slowly get into a sitting position. Holding the blanket to my chest to hide my nakedness, I look around the room.

Maddaline's house.

I'm in Maddalines's house.

One of her guest rooms. I know because she once invited me and the other girls to sleep over, but of course we all had to sleep in our own rooms.

I want to sigh in relief, but then my eyes land on the shirt at the foot of the bed.

Patrick's shirt.

So that means... my thighs press against one another, and I can feel the uncomfortable, slightly burning sensation between my legs.

Closing my eyes, the hazy shots of what happened slowly start returning.

Kissing.

Groping.

Undressing.

I swallow down hard.

Sex.

I had sex with Patrick.

Where is he then?

I look around the room once again, although if I didn't notice him before it's not like he'll jump out of the closet or something.

Quickly, I hop out of the bed. My legs are shaky. My whole body is, really, as I grab my clothes off the floor and start dressing myself.

He left his shirt, so he couldn't be that far. And he can't walk around naked, so he'll have to come back.

I can't be naked when he returns.

I can't let him see me naked.

He already saw you naked.

The panic returns in full force. I have to get out of here.

Giving the room one final look to make sure I have all my things, I start toward the door, only to find it slightly ajar.

My cold, shaky fingers wrap around the doorknob.

"I can't believe you actually did that!"

"Maddy..." There is a warning note to his voice, but there is also something else. Nervousness.

"When I suggested that you flirt with her and get her to fall for you, I never in a million years thought you'd actually succeed in doing it, much less take it a step further!"

The blood in my veins turns to ice, my racing heart slowing down until I can barely feel it beat.

"Maddy, I don't know what you have against her. She's nice and..."

"She's annoying," she snaps. "Acting all goody-goody, when in reality she's just like everybody else."

"And how is that?" Patrick challenges.

"Breakable."

"You hate her because she's ... whole?!"

"No, I hate her because she *acts* like she is. Like she doesn't hate her brother for stealing the spotlight and leaving her in the dark. Like her screwed-up family doesn't matter and she's fine being alone."

"Maybe she is."

"Nobody is fine being alone," she protests, her voice rising.

Her words hit the bull's eye. And the irony of this situation isn't lost on me. Because for the first time I see who Maddaline really is. How lonely and jaded she is.

"Coming from somebody who knows it first-hand, Maddy?"

"Don't you dare turn this on me! We're not talking about me here."

"Aren't we?"

"What about you? Playing with the little princess's heart, deceiving her, *fucking* her so you can come back to my bed? Don't you think that is a little fucked up?"

What? Maddy and... Patrick? Didn't she want Max?

My brain starts going through weeks upon weeks of time spent with her. Getting to know her. And in part, being her friend. But it comes up empty. Maddaline never mentioned Patrick. Not even once. But I guess that doesn't mean shit. Because Maddaline does what Maddaline wants, and that is everything.

My eyes fall closed as that realization washes over me.

Maddaline wants everything.

The best, cutest, most popular guys. Good-looking girlfriends. Popularity. People to love her. People to envy her. People to *fear* her.

Everything.

Including my brother, and the boy I was starting to fall for.

The boy who was hers to begin with.

A sob parts my lips, and I press my hand over my mouth to hold it in as the tears start falling down my face.

Stupid, stupid girl.

"Screw you, Maddaline," Patrick whisper-yells.

Because he's afraid of being found out? Because he doesn't want to risk *me* finding out?

I shake my head. I can't take this anymore. I need to go. I need to...

I don't get to finish my thought. Stumbling, I lean forward to try to balance my weight, but what I do is push the slightly ajar door wide open.

The silence filling the hallway is deafening. Patrick turns around, his eyes wide when he sees me. But when I turn around to look at the person I was actually feeling sorry for just mere moments ago, I find her with a knowing look in her eyes. Maddy knew I was there, listening. She knew it all along. Reading the realization in my eyes, her lips tilt if only slightly upward.

"Jeanette..." Patrick steps toward me, his hand outstretched.

I take a step back, wrapping my arms around myself. Why is it so cold suddenly?

Ignoring him, I concentrate on her.

The light pink dress she's wearing is molded to her body perfectly, showcasing her curves and tiny waist. High heels make her legs look even longer than they are. Her dark hair is curled, and her make-up flawless.

Perfect. Cold. Calculating.

"What else will you take from me?" I ask her weakly. Quietly. "Is there anything even left for you to take? You've got Max; that's what you wanted after all, right? You became my friend so you could get close to him. Everything to get the most popular guy to like you. Even including his ugly, fat sister in your company." Her eyes widen slightly, but that's the only reaction I get from her. "DUFF, that's what you call me. You thought I didn't know? Well I did, for a while now, yet I still stayed around. So much for not being fucked up. Anybody who is willingly friends with you has to be fucked up to tolerate being in your company. Why *this*? Why not let me be? Why not leave me alone?"

With every word, my voice grows louder and louder, words falling from my lips quickly. Frantic. That's how I sound. Frantic and crazy.

Tears are rolling down my face, and I don't even have it in me to care.

"Jeanette..." Patrick tries again, but I stop him.

"Don't touch me." My arms wrap around me tightly, holding my trembling body together. "Just don't touch me."

Patrick lifts his hands in the air in surrender. "I'm sorry, I didn't ..."

"I don't care." I shrug weakly. "I don't even have it in me to care anymore. I'm done. With all of you." My eyes meet Maddaline's. "Congratulations, you succeeded. You broke me. I hope you enjoy it as long as you can because that feeling won't last long. You'll need to destroy again and again to keep it."

I don't wait for her response. Willing my legs to move, I walk around them and hurry down the stairs.

The party is still in full swing. People laughing, drinking, dancing like nothing is wrong. And it's not, at least in their lives. Just a regular Saturday night with friends, where the worst thing that can happen is that they wake up with a raging headache the next day because they had a cup too much to drink.

I was just about to round the corner and get to the front door to get out of this house when I collided with somebody. Apologizing, I don't lift my gaze, just try to walk around him, but strong hands land on my shoulders.

"Anette?" The worried voice of my brother breaks through my loud, hazy mind.

Lifting my head, I look at him through blurry eyes. His matching set of grays looks at me, and when he sees the state I'm in, his whole body stiffens, his hands on my shoulders gripping me tighter.

"What happened?" he demands in his serious, no-nonsense voice.

More tears come to my eyes, and suddenly I can't take it anymore. All the lies and secrets, all the pretense and hidden agendas. I want it all to be gone.

My whole body trembles as fat, ugly tears fall down my cheeks, washing what's left of my make-up with them. My nose is all snotty, and I'm sure I'm a mess, but I don't care.

I can't find it in me to care anymore.

My heart is thumping loudly in my chest, and it's getting harder and harder to breathe.

Shaking my head, I try to walk around him, but his hands are holding me in the spot, his grip so strong I'm sure it'll leave bruises.

"Jeanette, tell me what happened," he repeats slowly, his voice hard.

I try to get out of his grasp once again, but when it's no use, I decide on a different approach, done with people wanting to control me. My fingers tighten into fists, and I start punching his chest.

If he doesn't want to let me go, I'll make him.

"It's all your fault!" I yell, accentuating every word with a punch. His grip on me loosens in surprise, but only barely. "I thought you were different. I thought you cared. But you're just like them. Just like everybody else. We should have always had each other's backs, Max. You're my twin! Instead you betrayed me."

My voice is growing louder with every word, drawing attention to us. I can feel people's curious eyes on my back. Watching. Assessing. Judging.

"What the hell are you talking about?" My eyes are even blurrier than before, but I can still see his growing wide.

"You and Maddaline fucking behind my back, that's what I'm talking about. My so-called best friend."

"Anette..."

But I'm not done. Not even close. "Did you know she actually hates me? She's only been hanging around your ugly, fat sister so she could get into your pants! But don't worry, you're not the only guy she's been fucking. Turns out Patrick is one of her boy toys, too. I guess I'm not the only Sanders who she fucked over."

His hands fall from my shoulders, and I want to sigh in relief, but he reaches for me again.

"Jeanette..."

I take a step back. "Don't touch me. Don't you dare touch me!"

The hurt flashes in his gray irises, but I don't let myself feel sorry for him.

"I'm going home."

I take a few steps around him, careful not to touch him. Not to touch anybody. Just the thought of it makes my stomach queasy. But I don't get far.

With the first step, I notice my legs are weak and wobbly, barely holding my weight.

With the second step, I see that the world around me isn't only blurry from my tears, but also dizzy.

With the third step, I try to reach out to regain my balance, but I don't find anything.

Only darkness.

Now

A sob rips from my throat as memories of the past and present mix in my mind.

Fat tears roll down my cheeks like waterfalls, blurring my sight and making it hard to see. My breathing is hectic, fast inhales and shallow exhales make my brain fuzzy and my chest constricts with pain.

Out of nowhere, a bright light appears in my rear-view mirror. At first, it's only a small dot in the darkness.

A car.

A black SUV.

Just like the one my dad has.

The car is approaching fast and the light becomes brighter and brighter, reflecting in my rear-view mirror and blinding me.

I can hear my phone vibrating in the seat next to me, but I ignore it.

Why is he doing this? I can't talk to him right now. I need to be alone. Why doesn't he get that?

I press my foot harder on the gas, and my car speeds up. The light is still reflecting in my mirror, impeding me from seeing clearly through the dark and narrow road that leads from my house into town, and the snow doesn't help much, either.

When I finally think I'm gaining some distance between us, he's there again.

The buzzing stops only to start again. Sighing in frustration, I reach for the phone but it slips down onto the floor, still vibrating.

"Shit."

Holding on to the wheel with one hand, I try to reach for the phone with my other.

I'm going to throw this damn thing out the window.

My fingers wrap around the cool, buzzing metal, and I straighten in my seat when I suddenly feel the wheels give on me.

The phone slips through my fingers again, as I grip the steering wheel in a hurry so I can regain control of the car, but it's no use.

I slide on the icy, wet road. Instinctively, I start to break, but it only makes things worse.

There is a sharp light coming from the other lane.

Strong and blinding.

I open my mouth to scream, but nothing comes out. Metal crashes, my body moving with the impact and then... only darkness.

Chapter 40

ANDREW

"Care to explain to me why we're here again?"

I don't move my eyes from the house standing before me. It's not as big as I remember, but it sure is as terrifying. Not that I would ever admit that out loud.

We've been sitting in my car for almost twenty minutes because I haven't mustered enough courage to get out and get this over with.

"You could have gone with Derek. Nobody asked you to come with."

The lights are turned on on the ground floor, and I can see people mingling around the house.

What is she doing? Is she preparing dinner? I don't remember seeing her much in the kitchen when I was younger.

"And look at him grope Lia the whole time?" From the corner of my eye, I can see Max roll his eyes. "No, thank you."

I tilt my head to the side. "Jealous?"

"Of what? Derek and Lia? Please, I knew they were destined to be together from the first day of school. I think it was the way Derek stared at me like he wanted to launch at me and break every bone in my body when Lia and I entered the classroom. But don't go getting off topic here. We were talking about you."

Busted.

I scratch the nape of my neck, not knowing what to say. Or even if I want to say anything.

When I said I had shit to take care of, the last thing I expected was that Max, of all people, would be the one to offer to go with me. But then again, I shouldn't be surprised. Max offered to help Derek win back Lia, even though I would bet he had some kind of feelings toward the girl during that time.

It's always the quiet, cute ones who wrap you around their little finger the tightest.

Or in your case, sexy, raven-haired girls with sharp tongues.

"I'm here to ask my mother why she left and never looked back," I blurt out.

Tense silence fills the car.

My eyes are still zeroed in on the house and the shadows moving around inside. Two silhouettes come closer. They talk for a while, I suppose, and he must have said something funny because she throws her head back, laughing.

Did she ever laugh in our house?

His hand reaches forward, tucking a strand of her long hair behind her ear.

Uncomfortable, I turn my head in the other direction.

"Andrew, I ..."

"You don't have to say anything. You're not from here, and it's been ages, so I suppose you haven't heard." I shrug nonchalantly. "I don't need nor want your pity."

"Pity you? You're too big of a douchebag for anybody to pity you." Max is trying to lighten the mood; I can see it in his eyes. He laughs it off, but when the laughter slowly dies, his face grows serious again. "You don't visit her?"

I chuckle. "As far as everybody else is concerned, I don't even know she's here."

I throw a quick glance at the window. The shadows are nowhere in sight, but the light is still on. I should probably use this opportunity and get it over with. Still, my body stays glued to the seat.

"You didn't want it ...?"

"She took her shit and left," I interrupt him. "She left, and she never looked back. I found out by coincidence later on that she moved back here."

It feels like the temperature has suddenly dropped drastically in the car, white puffs of air coming out of our mouths as we breathe.

"Why visit her now then? You resent her so much, blame her for leaving you and fucking up your life, so why now?"

"I want to know why. Why did she leave? Why did she never look back? Did I ..." I shake my head, dismissing the last question. "It doesn't matter. I came to get my answers so I can move the fuck on and forget about her."

Max opens his mouth, most likely to say something that should make me feel better. Reassure me that it's not my fault. But what if it is? What if she left because I'm so fucking unlovable?

"I'll be right back."

I open the door with force and let it close behind me. With long steps, I stride toward the front door, not once looking back. If I look back, I'll never find it in me to finish what I started.

As soon as I climb the few stairs to the front porch, I press the doorbell and wait as it rings inside the house. Even through the closed door, I can hear the sound of the TV playing somewhere in the house.

Inhaling deeply to calm my raging nerves, I will my fingers

to relax. The palms of my hands are sweaty, so I rub them against my thighs.

The phone rings somewhere and pans clatter before I hear a low, "I'll get it".

Shifting my weight from one leg to the other, I contemplate running away. If I put real force behind it, I could probably get to the car before she opens the door. It's not that far. That way she'll never know I was here. She'll never ...

The lock turns in the doorknob and the door opens suddenly.

"How can I ..."

The words get stuck in her throat as her gaze lifts to look at my face.

For a moment, or maybe it's an eternity, we look at each other. She looks the same, yet she doesn't. She's older, but it doesn't take away any of her natural beauty. Her rich brown hair is pulled in a high ponytail, just a few runaway strands curling around her ears. There are wrinkles around her eyes and mouth. Wrinkles that tell the story of her life and maturity. Dark eyelashes stand out on her otherwise make-up free face, accentuating her green-blue eyes.

"Andrew ..." She looks at me with shock and surprise written all over her features. Her lips are parted in a slight O, her eyes wide.

"Cassandra."

"What ..." Tears gather in her eyes, and she outstretches her hand as if she wants to touch me, but I take a step back. There is no way in hell I'll let her touch me. Realizing her mistake, she pulls back, letting her hand fall. "What are you doing here?"

"I'm not going to bother you for long, so don't worry."

"I'd never ..."

"Let's cut the drama, shall we?" I can see the hurt flash in her eyes, but I don't have it in me to care. Did she care when she left me ten years ago? Did she have tears in her eyes and her heart broken? I think we both know the answers to those questions. "I just need you to answer one question, one question only, so I can finally move on with my life in peace."

"Okay." Her throat bobbles as she swallows, brushing away her tears. "What do you want to know?"

"Why?" I look her straight in the eyes. I need to know that what she's telling me is the truth. My heart squeezes painfully in my chest. "Why did you leave and never look back?"

Why did you leave *me*? Why wasn't I enough?

Why? Why? *Why?*

Her eyes soften as they look at me. It's like even though I haven't outright asked her, she still knows the real question hiding behind it. Like she can read it from my eyes alone.

I blink, breaking our connection and regaining some of my composure.

"My leaving had nothing to do with you. Ever. You have to believe me ..."

I laugh in her face like the asshole I am. The asshole she made me. "I'm sorry if it takes me a while to believe that."

"It's the truth." She takes a step forward but doesn't reach out to touch me. "It was always about me. Your father and I ... we were never happy. All he ever wanted was a son and a career."

"Of course." This time I can't help but roll my eyes at her. What a bunch of bullshit. "If my father was so interested in having a son, why did he stop coming around the moment you left the house? Both of you are the same. Self-centered bastards who only think about themselves."

"I wanted to stay, for no other reason than you, but I couldn't. Being with your father had become too much. When he was home we always fought, and when he wasn't I always wondered who he was with. It was a never-ending cycle of destruction, and I couldn't keep doing that to myself. I was unhappy and depressed, and the last thing I wanted was to take you down that road with me."

"Why didn't you call then? Come by when you got back?"

"I wanted to! I wanted to so badly, but your father wouldn't have let me. It took him some time, but he tracked me down to serve me with the divorce papers. I asked about you, begged him to let me see you if only for a little while, but he laughed in my face and told me I lost you the moment I left and if I ever tried to come close to you, he'd take me to court to strip me of my parental rights over you."

"You should have at least tried!"

"And what? Cause you more pain and confusion? Make a circus of what was left of our broken family?"

"Anything, dammit!" I turn my back to her so she can't see the rage playing on my face. I grip my fingers into fists, and all I can think about is punching something until all these fucked-up emotions drain out of my body. "Anything would have been better than the constant loneliness. For years, *years,* I've wondered what I did wrong for you to stop loving me, for you to leave me. I hated you and I hated anybody who even tried to show me love and kindness. You left me, and then Dad left, too. And I did the only thing I knew how to do. I built walls so nobody could ever again do what you two have done to me—break my heart."

When I turn around to look at her, I find her crying silent tears. They're rolling down her cheeks and making her eyes look red and raw. She's looking at me with so much sorrow, I can barely stand to look at her.

Stop looking at me like that! I don't need your pity. When I needed you, you weren't there and now it's too late.

I open my mouth to say just that, but a loud roar stops me.

"ANDREW!"

I turn around instantly, my mother completely forgotten. Half of his body is out of the car, but the other half is stuck inside. His face is pale, curled in pain and fear like nothing I've seen before.

Cold dread washes over me, entering my veins and freezing all on its way.

Something's happened. Something must have happened to make Max go frantic like this.

My heartbeat slows down until I can barely feel it.

Something is wrong.

Really, really, wrong.

"It's Jeanette."

And then it stops.

His mouth keeps moving, he's saying something, but the buzzing in my ears is too strong to decipher the words coming out of his mouth.

Everything slows down—my breathing, my movements, my heart.

Jeanette.

It feels like I'm stuck in a bubble where time and space don't matter and I'm just hanging there, those two words going on repeat.

The light is not as bright. The snowflakes are stuck in the air, just fluttering around me. The sounds are just background noise. Nothing and nobody is moving.

Not me.

Not my lungs.

Not my heart.

Jeanette.

I can see Max still talking on the phone with God knows who. His lips are moving rapidly, but no sound comes out. Or maybe I simply can't hear it from the buzzing in my ears.

Jeanette.

His pupils are dilated, swallowing the gray eyes completely as panic and fear overtake him. All the color has drained from his cheeks, leaving only an ashy whiteness.

"I have to go."

Those words snap me out of the bubble I'm stuck in and I run.

I don't turn back, not even to sneak one last glance at the woman standing there.

She calls my name, but I ignore her. Everything that a few minutes ago seemed important lost all value. My past and my future. Nothing matters anymore.

I run hard and fast, my legs eating the distance between me and the car.

And when I jump inside, I don't wait. I press the gas and drive like my heart will be ripped out of my chest and cut into pieces if I don't move.

If something happens to Jeanette, it just might.

Chapter 41

JEANETTE

Noise wakes me up. I want to groan in protest, but can't find it in myself to move, my limbs feeling numb and heavy. I try to blink, but even my eyelids ache.

Why does my whole body ache?

Murmuring voices and beeping machines fill the otherwise silent space.

"Will she be all right?"

Dad?

I frown, trying to hear better. Trying to understand what's happening. His voice seems distant. Panicked and stressed out.

What's going on?

Where am I?

I try to turn my head, but something's preventing me from doing so. Sharp pain shoots through my neck and into my skull, making my entire head throb.

"It's hard to say. She fractured her forearm, a couple of ribs and she has a concussion because of the hit to her head. That's if we don't count all the scrapes and bruises. We're monitoring her brain in case the swelling increases."

Who are they talking about?

Did something happen?

I force myself to open my eyes. Is it me? Are they talking about me? What happened? My brain is screaming at me in pain, but I push it back, forcing my lids open. I manage, only barely, but the bright lights and white ceiling are just too much.

My headache becomes worse, so much worse. It feels like somebody is banging my head with a hammer.

I want to scream because it hurts. It hurts so much. And maybe I do. Maybe they know because soon after, there is nothing. Only blackness.

Before

"What the hell is wrong with my sister?" Max demands quietly, but with no less force and authority in his voice.

I try to relax my muscles, keeping my eyes closed. My whole body is tense, stiff. My head is throbbing painfully.

Where am I? What happened to me?

"She's stable right now. We gave her IV fluids to help stabilize her condition," the other voice says calmly. "I need to ask you a few questions. Did you notice anything strange in her behavior lately?"

"Strange like what?"

"Anything unusual, really. Did she seem stressed to you? Under a lot of pressure?" He stops for a few seconds, his voice growing softer, tentative. "Depressed?"

"Depressed? Is that what you think is wrong with her?" There is a slight pause. "Jeanette is not depressed!"

"What happened tonight?" the first voice asks. The doctor.

"We went to a party. She probably had a few drinks. When

she came down … I guess she got into a fight with one of her friends. She found out we were having a … thing. We didn't tell her. She got upset."

"That's all?"

Another slight pause.

"Is your sister eating properly?"

"I guess. What does that have to do with anything?" The exasperation is clear in his voice.

"Did you know your sister weighs less than one hundred pounds?"

"What?"

"She has an eating disorder, Max. Poor nourishment, add alcohol and emotional …"

I don't hear the rest because I fall back into the darkness.

My eyes flutter open, but fall closed from the brightness of the lights illuminating the room.

The hospital.

I guess it wasn't just a dream.

"Do you like punishing me that much?"

Opening my eyes, I find the judging gaze of my father seated in the chair next to my bed. He looks tired, disheveled. His hair is a mess, and the bags under his eyes are dark.

"It's not all about you." Not able to look at him, I let my eyes close again.

"Then what is it about?"

I shrug, but the movement is barely visible.

Tired. I feel so tired.

"Why didn't you tell us? Why didn't you tell anybody about your struggle?"

His words make my blood boil. Snapping my eyes open, I narrow them at him. "When? How? How do you tell somebody you can't make friends? And then when you do find them, it's because they want something from you and not to actually be friends with you. How do you tell somebody that those same friends everybody is so ecstatic about, bad-mouth you behind your back? Calling you clueless and fat, laughing at you."

"Jeanette ..." His eyes grow soft, but I brush it off. I don't need his soft words and compassion now. I don't need anybody. Don't want anybody.

If you're all alone, nobody can hurt you.

Nobody can break you.

"How do you break their illusion? Tell me!" I scream at him, the tears I tried so hard to hold back finally falling down. "How? How do you deal when you find your father, your *hero*, the person you worshipped above everybody else is cheating on his family? How do you deal with the guilt of having to hide the secret so you don't break apart your family? How do you deal when you see your brother kissing your so-called friend behind your back, not knowing how she hurt you so many times and on so many levels you eventually stopped counting? When you find out that the guy you thought liked you for being *you* actually did it to get back in the previously mentioned girl's good graces? Just tell me—how?"

My words are loud and angry, filled with so much repressed hurt and vulnerability. With the back of my hand, I brush away the tears streaming down my face, the tears I didn't even know were there.

Tears of anger.

Tears of disappointment and resignation.

When I look at my father, I see the tears in his eyes, too.

"So I'm sorry I skipped a few meals and spent hours in the gym trying to blend in, trying to have them like me. I'm sorry I had a few drinks more than I should have because I was frustrated and angry and disappointed. I'm sorry you have to be here because the guilt from all the lying and secrets became too much. And this..." I wave in the direction of my body. "Doesn't match in your perfect life."

Dad gets out of the chair and sits on my bed. He reaches for my hand, but I pull it back.

"You're perfect, Jeanette. The way you are now and the way you were before. You're perfect and brilliant, and if they can't see that, it's their loss."

I swallow hard. "Then why did you cheat on us?"

"Jeanette." My name is a sigh falling off his lips.

"I can't get it out of my head. I can't forget and the lies ... they're killing me." I shake my head. "I'm afraid to go to the hospital anymore because if I see her ... I'm not sure what I'd do, but it wouldn't be pretty."

He nods his head in understanding. "Then we'll move."

"What?"

"We'll move. Start from the beginning, but you have to stop this ... this self-destructive behavior. It has to stop. You have to start eating again, we can see the doctors, the best specialists, start the therapy ..."

"Okay," I agree. "Okay, we'll start again."

Chapter 42

ANDREW

"What the fuck happened?" I ask as soon as Max hangs up.

My fingers are curled around the steering wheel, holding so tight they've turned white, and I'm surprised I haven't pulled the damn thing out. I don't move my eyes from the road, my foot pressed on the gas as we fly through the streets as fast as possible.

I don't care that snow is falling and the roads are slick. Or that if the cops found us, they'd probably ban me from driving forever, but they'd have to catch me first.

Nothing matters, except getting to Jeanette.

She has to be alright.

She better be.

Alive.

There is no other option.

Max runs his hand through his hair, pulling at the strands.

"Did she ..." I swallow hard, unable to form words. My eyes fall shut just for a moment before they're back on the road. Just a moment of desperation and panic I allow myself. "Did she stop eating again?"

Abruptly, Max turns in his seat, his eyes probing the side of my face. He's still as pale as a ghost, but his eyes are narrowed.

Worry, suspicion and anger shine brightly from his dark eyes. The eyes of a person ready to snap any minute.

"How do you know about that?"

"She told me."

The tension between us skyrockets.

"You're lying."

I shake my head. "She told me, just after ... just after she broke up with me."

The silence that follows is deafening. So deafening you could hear a pin drop. My hands grow sweaty in nervousness, and I have to grip the wheel tighter if I don't want to lose control over the car.

I let it drag on for a while, but when the silence and anticipation become too much, I finally snap.

"Will you tell me what the fuck happened, Max? I need to know. Is she okay? Is she hurt? Did she ... did she *hurt* herself?"

Apparently he can hear the desperation in my voice and has mercy on me. "She's been in an accident."

"What kind of accident?"

Did she fall? Did someone hurt her? Was she in a car accident? What the hell happened? A thousand scenarios run through my mind at once, each one worse than the one before.

"Car accident."

The sound of screeching tires and the images of bent metal run through my mind. So many terrible images I can barely breathe. I can see her fragile body stuck between the metal. All alone and cold, begging for somebody to help her.

Bile rises in the back of my throat, and it takes everything in me not to throw up.

"Is she okay?" I ask, but the thing I'm actually wondering is: *Is she alive?*

The possibility that something might have happened to her, that maybe I'll never see her again ... never see her smile, never get a chance to kiss her, hug her, never hear her play the violin, never see that small frown between her brows when she's scowling at me or hear her voice as she puts me in my place, never get a chance to tell her I love her ...

My throat bobbles.

Max opens his mouth, but the phone buzzes in his hand again.

We both look at the device, and I can see Max's reluctance. If I were him, I wouldn't want to answer either.

Because what if ...

No, I'm not going there.

She's okay.

She's strong.

She's alive.

There is no other possibility.

No other option.

"D-dad?" Max's voice is low and rough as he picks up. His fingers grip the device and hold it close to his ear.

There is silence as he listens to whatever his father is telling him.

He sighs, rubbing his forehead. "Yeah. Sure. I'll do it. Bye."

"What did he say?" I ask as soon as he hangs up, giving him a quick glance. Just a little bit more and we're back in Greyford. Just a little bit more, and we'll be there.

Just hang on, Princess. Hang on.

"The doctors said she's as stable as she can be. Broken arm and ribs. Concussion. Bruises."

Every word he says is like a punch to my gut.

"But she's alive?"

You have to be alive. You promised. We get our shit in order and we can be together. You promised.

Max nods his head. "She's alive."

But she's not in the clear. I know it because if she were, there wouldn't be a dark shadow falling over his face.

"Dad wants us to stop by our house and grab some of her things.

"I-"

No, just no. I have to see her. I have to see that she's okay with my own two eyes. I have to take her hand and see her chest rising as she breathes, and I need it now.

I want to protest so badly. Throw a temper tantrum, demanding we go straight to the hospital to see her. But I can't do that to Max. His fear is so strong I can almost taste it mixing with my own and making the air in the cabin of the car so stiff, we can barely breathe.

"I know, but she'll feel more comfortable when she wakes up if she has her own things."

She'll feel scared and miserable if she wakes up and we're not there.

The words burn in my mouth, but I swallow them down. I know this is not his choice. He's doing what his dad thinks is best, so when we get to Greyford and I see the turn that leads to our houses, I take it.

MAX

Andrew parks the car hastily, and I jump out before it even stops completely. Without saying a word, I run inside. The hallway is lit, and I can see light coming from the living room, but I ignore it as I climb two steps at a time.

What the fuck happened, Anette?

When I get upstairs, first I go to my room to grab a bag. I don't want to lose time going through her shit trying to find one. The last thing I wanted to do was be here while Jeanette was lying alone and broken in a hospital bed again.

Fucking broken.

When Dad called and said she's in the hospital, all I could do was remember that day two years ago. I saw her collapse over and over again. At first I thought she just lost her balance because of the alcohol, but she never got up. For months after it happened I had nightmares. The image of her small, fragile body in the big hospital bed still makes my stomach turn. I picked her up in my arms and called 9-1-1.

That was the first time I realized how small she was, how skinny. She was always wearing baggy clothes, and to be honest, I was too preoccupied with what was happening in my own life to notice she was withering away. My own twin.

And now she's back there again.

Why does this keep happening?

Anger flows through my veins and I can barely keep myself from falling apart. I want to curl my fingers in a fist and punch something. Anything.

Grabbing the first duffle I can get my hands on, I leave my room and go across the hall.

Jeanette's room is the same. The bed is messy, pillows thrown all over. Books on her desk are open. She was probably doing her homework. Violin box is carefully leaning against the nightstand. Some of her clothes are thrown over a chair, and one pair of boots is left scattered in front of her closet.

Normal.

I open her closet and start pulling things out. A pair of pajamas. Make it two. Some T-shirts, leggings, sweaters. That girl is always icy cold. I throw in some socks and underwear. Charger and her iPad.

My eyes scan the room for anything else she might need when she wakes up.

You have to wake up, sis.

Still going through my mental list of essentials, I walk into her bathroom.

There is so much girly shit on the counter, I don't even know where to begin. I run my fingers through my hair in frustration.

Deodorant, shampoo, toothpaste ...

I start opening the drawers. More make-up, all the girly shit, wipes ...where the fuck does she keep unopened toothbrushes? I squat down to open the last drawer and there they are.

I throw one in the bag.

"I think that's it."

I start to get up when something in the trash bin underneath the sink catches my attention.

There is a carton, wipes and other garbage, and between it all, a white stick.

Two white sticks.

Mother-fucker.

Chapter 43

ANDREW

I stay seated in the car for a while after Max runs into the house. He didn't ask me to come inside, and I don't think I could take it right now. I haven't been here a lot, but it still reminds me of her.

The way she gets lost in her music.

The tender expression on her face.

Our bickering.

Those beautiful, shiny gray eyes looking at me.

Her laughter.

It's all there.

It's all there, and she's not.

Not able to sit still for a second longer, I get out of the car. I pace, rubbing my face in frustration.

Why is this happening? Am I cursed or something? People I care about either leave or get hurt. Is this my destiny? To lose all the people I come to care about?

Angry, I kick the tire with my foot.

Over and over again.

Is that it? Is she better off without me? I should probably leave now and not look back. Maybe then she'd have a chance. Maybe then ...

"You fucking piece of shit."

I turn around just in time to see Max storming toward me. He's a blur until he's right in front of me, his eyes dark and bloodthirsty. I barely see his hand lift in the air, and then my head snaps back.

A hollow throbbing spreads through my cheek, skin tingling as his fist connects with my face.

"What the ..."

I don't get to finish the question because Max starts punching me again, throwing insults. "You stupid ..." Punch to the face. "... fucking ..." Another one to my side. " ... son-of-a-bitch."

His knee lifts, connecting with my gut, making me double over and knocking the air out of my lungs.

I curse, stumbling backward. My hands wrap around my middle, holding on to tender flesh. My stomach hurts like a bitch, and I can already feel a nasty bruise forming on my middle.

"... t-the f-fuck?" I hiss.

Max's hectic breathing accompanies my shallow, breathless inhales. Every breath hurts, and my lungs burn with the effort.

"This is all your fault!" He throws something at me, and I barely have time to dodge it. "I knew it! I told her you're not good enough, but did she listen to me? No! Of-fucking-course not. She never listens to anybody."

"Cra-zy," I wheeze out.

"I told her you'd destroy her. You two are too fucked up on your own, so how the fuck are you supposed to be together? But instead of listening to me, you did it anyway. Instead of listening to me, you made a mess of everything. You fucked things up and now she's back off the wagon and was in a fucking car accident. You broke her."

"I broke her?" I spat out, furious. "She broke up with me! I asked, no I *begged* her to reconsider, but she wanted time. So I gave her time."

"Time? Is that why she's lying in a hospital bed pregnant?"

Pregnant?

I stumble backward, his words worse than any punch he could have thrown my way.

What the hell is he talking about?

"Fucking pregnant." Max walks around my frozen body, picking something off the ground. "I found this in her bathroom."

He shoves a white stick in my face.

A white stick with a big, fat plus on the display.

This can't be happening.

"That's impossible," I breathe, barely audible.

"The test says otherwise."

No way, we were always careful. Always ...

Our last time flashes in my mind, the images so vivid it feels like she's back in my arms.

My fingers curl into a fist and I turn around, slamming it into the car. A sharp pain shoots up my arm.

"FUCK!"

What if she's pregnant? She was in a car accident, for fuck's sake! What if something happened to the baby? What if ...

All the blood drains from my head, and I can feel my body begin to shake.

On autopilot, I open the door and stumble inside.

"Where the fuck do you think you're going?"

Max grips the door, preventing me from closing it.

I grit my teeth, barely containing my anger.

"Either get in the fucking car or get out of my way."

"You can't leave her alone, Hill. I promise you ..."

"I'm not leaving anybody alone. Now GET. IN. THE. CAR." I speak through clenched teeth, trying to keep what little is left of my sanity. "Or I swear to God, I'll run over you on the way to the hospital."

He's still infuriated, but so am I.

And right now, he's the one standing in the way between me and the woman I love, so if he puts up a fight, I won't be the one falling down.

Quietly, he runs to the passenger seat and slides inside.

With my sweaty hands, I turn on the car and press on the gas.

How long did she know? Why didn't she tell me?

Questions. So many questions. I want to be angry at her. I want to scream and punch something, but the worry, the fear for her, for the *baby*, is worst of all.

Is there even anything left to say?

Chapter 44

ANDREW

I take every shortcut I know, driving like a crazy man, and get us to the hospital in record time. Parking the car in front of the emergency exit, I stumble outside and start to run.

People call after me, cursing and yelling at me, but I ignore them. They can take the car, tow it away or do whatever the fuck they want with it. I don't care.

Bypassing the elevators, I go straight to the stairs and climb two or three at a time. Max's dad texted, saying they admitted her to the trauma ICU.

My lungs burn, and my muscles ache, but I don't let it slow me down. I probably look like a mess and slightly insane, too.

Once I get to the fourth floor, I go straight to the nurse's station. Two nurses—one older, one younger—are sitting behind the desk, chatting happily.

What the fuck are they so happy about? People die here; they shouldn't be so chipper.

"Jeanette Sanders," I pant as I reach them.

My hand flies to my burning ribs. I'm not sure if it's the strain from Max's beating and running up the stairs or if the fucker managed to break my ribs. He has a strong punch, so I wouldn't be surprised if he actually did break them.

The nurses turn around, and when they see me, they exchange a short, worried look.

My tongue darts out to wet my lips and I can feel a coppery taste. Blood.

"Are you a relative?"

"She's my girlfriend."

"I'm so sorry," the older one finally says. "Relatives only."

Frustrated, I run my hand through my hair, pulling at the ends. I must look like a mess, but I don't care.

Is she okay? Are they both okay?

Worry has been eating at me the whole way here, even more so since I found out it might not just be Jeanette who's in danger.

"Screw you. I'll find her myself."

I turn around on the heels of my feet and start walking down the hallway, looking left and right for Jeanette's room.

"Sir, you can't ..."

Her chair scrapes back, and I know she'll soon be at my feet, so I hurry up.

Nobody is getting in my way.

There are patients walking around on crutches or using a walker. Quiet chatter and beeping of machines fill the air and give a sense of normality. The smell of antiseptic is strong, like in all hospitals, and it makes my already queasy stomach turn.

I peek inside the rooms. People are lying in their beds, some entertaining themselves while others have visitors, but there is no Jeanette.

Just when I think I took the wrong hallway, I see the slightly ajar door.

My heart beats furiously in my chest as I slowly push the door open.

Unlike other rooms, this one is quiet. Only the silent beeps of the machine resound in the sterile space.

Whiteness and stainless steel, and in the middle of it all, a bed.

I take one step forward, just one step. That's all it takes. If I didn't have to touch her to reassure myself she's still here, still breathing and still very much alive although not conscious, I'd probably be on my knees.

Her dark hair is messy, and there is dried blood sticking to the usually silky strands. Her face is a mess of colors. There are a few purplish-blue bruises covering her skin, some red scrapes and the rest is ashen white. There is a collar around her neck that prevents her from moving her head and possibly causing more damage. One of her arms is in a cast and strapped over her chest for support.

So fucking small.

Small and breakable.

Lying like this in the big hospital bed, without a trace of consciousness and her fierce, determined spirit, she's nothing like the girl I know.

The girl I *love.*

My feet are glued to the spot, but I force them to move, blinking away the blurriness in my eyes.

One step at a time, I move closer until I'm standing right next to her. My hand wraps around hers carefully so that I don't move the thing stuck to her finger.

"Jeanette ..."

Her hand is ice cold, but I don't let it deter me. I haven't met a person who's colder than her. She's always wearing big socks and sweaters.

Leaning forward, I press my lips to her forehead, inhaling what's left of her scent. My eyes fall closed as relief spreads through my body, making me shudder.

I can see her chest slowly and evenly rising.

"You'll be okay, Princess," I whisper, pressing another soft kiss against the crown of her hair. "I'm here, and I'm not going anywhere."

Pulling back, I let my finger softly trace her cheek, my eyes scanning her body. Butterfly tape is holding a scrape over her right brow, and her lips seem to be swollen.

"You scared me to death, Jeanette, but the only thing that matters is that you get better. You hear me? Get better and open those beautiful eyes for me, Princess. I need to see those crystal grays on me, even if only to see your rage. I ..."

There is a loud stomping down the hallway, and I can hear the nurse hiss something, but then the door bursts open and Max enters, panting hard. "Are they okay?"

His eyes scan the room frantically until they settle on her. When he sees his sister in the bed, I hear him sob loudly. "Anette."

Max joins me on the other side of the bed. He lifts his hands, wanting to touch her, but lets them fall when he sees her up close, his hands gripping the railing instead.

"What ..."

His head falls back and he rubs his face. I can hear his shaky inhale as he tries to calm himself.

"Is she ..." he starts, but the door opens again. This time it's an older, dark-haired man. He looks tired and beaten.

"Max, you're here." Surprise flashes in his eyes, then they move to me. I can see his assessing gaze take me in. Silver gray eyes matching the twins', looking at me with curiosity.

"Yeah." He gestures in my direction. "Dad, this is Andrew. He's one of my teammates."

Mr. Sanders takes a step in my direction, extending his hand. I don't bother with pleasantries. Barely lifting my chin in acknowledgment, I concentrate on the girl lying in bed. My thumb traces Jeanette's hand in mine. There is no way I'm letting go. If I wasn't so scared of hurting her, I'd get in that bed and wrap my arms around her, holding her forever.

"And Jeanette's boyfriend," I add, mentally willing her to wake up.

If only for a few seconds.

"Oh, I didn't know she had a boyfriend."

I shrug. What else is there to say?

"Has she woken up?" I question.

"Not a peep since she got here."

"What the hell happened, Dad?"

Max's eyes are still glued to Jeanette. Tenderly, he brushes her hair, the only part of her that's undamaged. My teeth clench and I want to tell him to back the fuck off, but I keep my mouth shut.

He's her *brother*.

"She lost the control of her car. I tried to stop her, warn her not to drive. She's not used to driving in the snow, but you know your sister ... she was driving fast, and the roads were icy and slick. The other car came from the opposite direction, blinding her temporarily, and she started to slide. I guess she got scared, because she tried to brake, but the only thing it did was make her car spin off the road."

We'd seen her SUV on the way to her house, abandoned on the side of the road standing upside-down.

"That just doesn't make any sense." Max shakes his head. "Jeanette doesn't drive fast. And she's always nagging me about ditching my demon motorcycle."

His dad's face pales. He opens his mouth to say something, but a low moaning makes us all turn around.

"Princess?" I lean down, still holding her hand in mine.

Max joins me on the other side, his father and their conversation forgotten. "Anette, can you hear me?"

"Open your eyes, beautiful," I urge her.

Her body slowly starts to stir underneath the blankets, and I can feel her fingers wiggle in my hand. I tighten my grip a little, just enough to let her know she's not alone.

"Open those beautiful eyes for me, Princess."

Please, please, please.

I hold my breath, watching her eyelashes flutter. It seems like an eternity until they finally open.

The gray color is dull and they're glossy—from pain or from the drugs they gave her, I'm not sure—but they're open.

They're open and they're looking at me, slightly confused. A little frown appears between her brows as she looks between Max and me, probably wondering why we're acting like a lunatic duo.

"D-drew ..." Her voice is raw, but it's the most beautiful sound I've ever heard.

"Shhh ..." I press my finger against her dry lips as my eyes fall closed so I can get my emotions under control.

She's awake. She's finally awake.

When I open them, I find her looking at me worriedly. I shake my head.

Later, I try to convey my message with my eyes. *We'll talk later. This is about you.*

Only you.

I love you.

I love you, Jeanette Sanders, and I'm not letting you out of my sight ever again.

Chapter 45

JEANETTE

Soft voices start pulling me out of the darkness. I don't know where I am or how long I've been here, but as they gradually grow louder, I slowly start to perceive more and more of what's happening.

Like the fact that I'm lying flat on the bed and my whole body is throbbing. The pain in my arm is the worst, and my whole body is stiff.

Where am I? And who are the people talking?

Open those beautiful eyes for me, Princess.

That voice ... how do I know that voice? And why does it sound so sad?

I try to move my body, but it's useless. Every limb I try to lift stays glued to the bed, not moving an inch.

Why can't I move?

What happened to me?

I try to remember, but the only things that come to my mind are sudden brightness, a crash of metal and then blackness.

My head throbs. It feels like somebody is stabbing me repeatedly in the head. *Make it stop!* I want to cry out, but my throat is so dry the words won't come out.

Open your eyes, beautiful.

There it is again, that voice.

Who are you?

It sounds familiar. From where do I know it? And why does it make my heart pitter-patter in my chest?

I try again, this time harder. It almost seems impossible, like somebody glued my eyelids shut and I'll never open them again.

Open those beautiful eyes for me, Princess.

Princess? Only one person calls me Princess.

With one last effort, I finally feel my eyes flutter open. The bright light blinds me, and my eyes fall shut again. I want to scream in frustration, but then a shadow falls over me and this time, slower, I try again.

It feels like it takes forever, but when I open my eyes, I know all the effort has been worth it.

The most beautiful pair of greens looks down at me. Fear and tenderness mix together in those pools that suck me in and leave me breathless. And the breathlessness doesn't have anything to do with the pain in my chest, and everything to do with the guy standing in front of me.

"D-drew ..." My voice comes out shaky and weak. I want to reach my hand to cup his cheek but find that I can't because my hand is glued to my chest.

"Shhh ..." His finger touches my lips, shushing me effectively as I watch the proud, cold-hearted, nothing-can-affect-me boy give in to his emotions. His eyes fall closed and I can see his shaky inhale. His hand grips mine tighter, maybe a little too tight, but no amount of discomfort will make me pull away.

"How do you feel?" A big, warm hand brushes my hair, and I try to turn my head to the side to look at my brother, but realize I can't. There's something preventing me from moving my neck, so I turn my gaze to him.

He looks terrible. His skin is pale, and there are big circles underneath his eyes. Worry and fear are etched in every inch of his face as he studies me.

"L-like ..." It hurts to speak, so I clear my throat before trying again. "L-like a ... t-train ran me o-over."

My joke is lame, but it gets me a little huff of laughter.

"Don't joke like that," Andrew scolds me lightly. "Or I'll have to tie you to me so I can keep my eyes on you at all times."

I want to roll my eyes at them, but movement from the corner of the room catches my eyes.

Dad is standing there, watching the three of us. His hair is messy and his clothes wrinkled. There is blood on his shirt.

My blood, I realize.

Flashes of what happened come to my mind.

A call. Going to the hospital. Seeing my dad with the nurse. Driving home. Waiting for him. The fight. Running away. Accident.

The freaking accident.

As the memories come back, my head starts to hurt more and more.

"Jeanette?"

I can feel both Max and Andrew's worried eyes on me, but I can't move mine from my father.

"Y-you ..."

"Jeanette, I'm so ..."

"Out!" My voice is still raw, but I put all of the strength I can muster behind that one word. "G-get o-out."

He shakes his head, crying. His eyes beg me to let him explain, but I don't want to. I can't.

"Dad?" I can hear the confusion in Max's voice, but I feel too weak to explain. Tears come to my eyes. Tears of hurt, pain and betrayal. Tears of guilt and resentment.

Andrew's thumb wipes underneath my cheeks, brushing

away the tears. He looks at me carefully for a moment before he turns around, cold eyes starting at my father.

"She wants you out, so get out." There is no emotion or tenderness in his voice.

"Who do you think you are ..."

"You're upsetting her and making it worse," he grits through his teeth. Anger rolls off of him in waves, but he's holding it in. "She's been through enough. I won't let you upset her anymore."

Then he stands in front of me, his face softening as he blocks my view of my father. "I'll call the nurse. They have to check you out."

I nod in agreement. He presses the call button and leans against the bed next to me. His hand is holding on to mine, not letting go.

Never letting go.

We wait in silence, each one of us lost to our own thoughts. My brain is going through the snaps of memory from the last few days.

Was it just days? It feels like much longer.

First the pregnancy test and then the ...

Pregnancy test.

The panic returns in full force, stronger than before.

"Andrew, I ..." I grip Andrews hand strongly, not knowing how to say it. Not knowing how to ask. What to ask.

In that moment, the doctor enters the room, followed by the nurses. They rush to my side, checking monitors and observing me. I hear one of the nurses ask the guys to leave.

Reluctantly, Andrew starts to pull away, but I grasp on to his hand, holding for dear life. "S-stay."

"Princess ..."

"Miss Sanders ..." the doctor starts, but I stop him.

I don't care about what they want or what the protocol is. I need him by my side. "I need you here with me. Stay."

His green eyes grow soft, and he returns back to his position next to me, his hand holding mine.

I hear the door softly close behind Max. The doctor gives me a disapproving look, but I don't let him scare me.

They check my vitals and ask dozens of questions. I try to answer them all, when in reality the only thing that interests me is the baby.

What happened to my baby?

Is there even a baby anymore or did I ...

"Everything looks good, Miss Sanders. You should try and rest now. If you're in too much pain, the nurses can give you some pain reliever. The bruises and scratches should be gone soon, but it'll take a while for your ribs and hand to heal properly."

I nod my head in understanding. Gulping down, I wet my lips. "Doctor, I ..."

"What about the baby?"

Andrew's quiet question leaves me breathless and stupefied. His hand grips mine tighter, but that's the only indication that he's nervous. I don't dare look at him, afraid of what I'll find if I do.

How does he know? Did the girls tell him? Did he ...

The doctor looks between the two of us, his bushy brows furrowing. "What baby?"

Andrew's whole body stiffens next to me. Turning to the side as much as I can, I look at him, my eyes wide.

What does he mean 'what baby'?

"I ..." The words get stuck in my throat, and I have to clear it before I continue. "My period was late so I took a pregnancy test. It was positive."

Did I lose it? Did I lose the baby in the accident?

How could I be so careless? How could I ...

"We had to do different tests when you came, including blood work." Brown eyes soften as he looks at us. "I'm sorry, Miss Sanders, but you're not pregnant. The test must've been a false positive."

Chapter 46

ANDREW

You're not pregnant.

After those words, the doctor exits the room, reminding Jeanette to take it easy and ask for pain meds if she needs them.

The test was a false positive.

I rub my face feeling ... empty.

Why do I feel empty? I should be happy. Ecstatic even. I love Jeanette, I really do. But we're only teenagers with so much in front of us before we have kids. This feeling is completely unreasonable and batshit crazy, but for a little while, this was real.

This baby, *our* baby, was real.

The acceptance and love, the fear of losing it, was real.

And now it's all gone. Just like that.

"How did you find out?" Jeanette asks softly from her bed, breaking the quiet that settled over the room once the doctor left.

We lifted the back of the bed a little to help her into a more relaxed position. A bit of color returned to her face, and her voice is clearer after sipping on water.

"Max." When I see her surprised face, I explain, "Your dad

asked him to go home and grab some stuff for you. While he was packing, he saw the test."

"He was really pissed," she states, her eyes roaming over my beaten face.

I didn't bother looking at how bad it is. I can barely feel the pain, but maybe that's the adrenaline talking.

"Pretty pissed."

Her good hand lifts and touches my cheek. I wrap my hand around hers, taking some of the weight. I bring her palm to my lips and kiss the inside of her wrist.

It still doesn't seem real.

She's okay.

She's awake.

She's *alive.*

"Turns out it was all for nothing," she whispers. "Andrew, I'm sorry."

I shake my head. "You don't have anything to be sorry about."

"Yes, I do!" Jeanette protests. "I should have told you. As soon as I suspected, I should have told you. But I was so surprised and scared and ..."

She leans forward, her whole body shaking.

I sit down on the bed next to her, wrapping my arms around her, her shoulders trembling as she cries silent tears. "It's okay," I murmur, rubbing her back. "Shh, it's okay. We'll be okay."

"It's s-so s-silly. We're so young and I know we aren't ready to have a baby, but ..." Her voice breaks and it breaks me. It breaks me seeing her in so much pain without a way to fix it. And even if I could, I'm not sure I'd be able to, because her pain? I feel it, too. "For a while," Jeanette sniffs, looking at me through her tear-stained lashes. "For a while, it was real. When I saw that plus on the test, it was real. I was scared, terrified, but I wanted it. For a while, I *loved* that baby only to find out now that it never existed."

"I know, baby. I know. I feel it, too. I wanted it, too."

As I confess it to her, I feel her body shake harder. My grip tightens and I burrow my head into her neck, holding both of us together as we mourn the loss of something that never existed.

At some point, I hear the door crack open, but it closes almost instantly, leaving us alone.

I don't know how long we stay like that, holding on to each other for dear life. But after a while, her sobs stop and I slowly pull away, brushing the tears from her eyes.

"Maybe it just wasn't meant to be."

"What if it's never meant to be. With my anorexia ..."

"It will happen, Princess." I brush a strand of her hair behind her ear. "One day, when we're older and ready, we'll get our baby."

"You're saying it like it's a given."

"Because it is."

"You can't possibly know." She shakes her head stubbornly.

"But I do." My finger sneaks under her chin, lifting it so she's looking at me. "When my mom left, I became a detached douchebag. I was cold and mean to everybody around me, and nobody tried to stop me. They were either too blinded by my status or too afraid to say anything."

"Until me."

"Until you," I agree. "You don't tolerate my shit, and you put me in my place without blinking an eye. It was your fierceness and inner strength, strength you aren't even aware you possess, that broke my walls and made me start falling for you. It was your big, loving heart and your kindness, your spirit of a warrior and beauty that made me realize that I was doomed long before I even realized it. I love you, Jeanette Sanders. You and no one else, because let's be honest, no one else would be able to stand my irritating ass for longer than thirty seconds straight, so it's not like you have a choice."

"True," she says through hushed giggles. "So true."

"Don't you have anything to say to me?"

"Hmmm ..." She purses her lips, pretending to think. "Don't think so."

"Wrong answer."

I start tickling her good side until she laughs again. It's good to hear her laughter. She's been crying for far too long. I want to see her smile. I want those gray eyes to light up and melt into pools of silver. I want to be the one to make her happy.

"Okay, okay! I surrender."

"About time. So, care to share something, Princess?"

"Yes." She nods her head but keeps quiet.

"Well, don't let me hold you back."

"You, Andrew Hill, are the worst habit I could have chosen, but the one I don't plan to give up. I love you."

Her hand touches my cheek, beckoning me. Smiling, I lean forward, our lips brushing together softly.

"I love you, too, Princess," he whispers into my ear. "And one day, when it's the right time, we'll get a chance to do this again. I know we will."

Chapter 47

JEANETTE

"Jeanette, Andrew is here!" Mom yells from the foyer.

"In the living room!" I call back.

It's been a week since I was discharged from the hospital and things around the house have ... changed.

After the doctor told Andrew and me that I actually wasn't pregnant, followed by my meltdown and finally our lengthy talk and 'I love yous', I fell asleep, completely drained from everything that had happened to me the previous twenty-four hours.

When I woke up, both Andrew and Max were still in the room with me, each sleeping in a chair, head lying on the bed. I still don't know how they did it, but they did. Their sleeping position didn't look too comfortable, but it didn't last much longer anyway because Mom burst into the room.

That's when I finally told them everything, starting with what happened our freshman year of high school. From my social insecurities to the constant pressure to blend in causing my eating disorder. To finding out that Dad was cheating, our agreement, the guilt of keeping it a secret, with the highlight of discovering that Max was dating my so-called best friend and the betrayal of the boy I had a crush on. All of which ended with me in the hospital, being diagnosed and us moving to Greyoford, where it all started again.

Hands wrap around my middle from behind, bringing me back to the present, soft lips pressing a long kiss to my exposed neck. "What has you so deep in thought?"

I tilt my head to the side, revealing more skin for Andrew to kiss, and he complies. Scooting forward on the couch, I leave space behind me for him to sit so I can lean against him.

"I'm thinking about that day in the hospital." Andrew rests his chin on my shoulder. "Do you think he was telling the truth?"

As soon as I had finished with my part of the story, I saw movement at the door. Dad pushed it open, leaning against the doorway. He looked like he'd aged ten years in one day. And as I looked at him, I realized my heart ached for him. Even after his betrayal and cowardice, I still loved him. He was still my dad, even though I don't think I'll ever forget what he did. Forgive, probably, with time, but never forget.

I did a lot of selfish, unforgettable things. Things that hurt the people I should love most in my life, I won't deny it. I was a shitty husband and a lousy father, but after you ended up in the hospital back in California, I vowed I'd do better. What you saw in the office the other day was a reflection of the past. I did not *cheat once after you caught me that first time. I don't blame you for coming to conclusions like that. That's also my doing. I should never have asked you to keep my secret like that. Never. And I can understand that none of you believe me now, but I want us to be a family again. No secrets. No lies. A family. If and when you're ready.*

"I don't know, babe. I don't know him like you do."

"I think he actually might be."

I'm not sure what happened after that, but when I came home, Dad moved out. Mom needed some time to think and

Dad agreed to give it to her. He even suggested couples therapy with occasional family therapy in between. Once upon a time, they were madly in love with each other. How or when it changed, I guess I'll never find out, but I hope they get it back. No matter the end result, I hope they find their peace with each other and with themselves.

"Are you feeling better?"

Looking over my shoulder, I roll my eyes at him. "You don't need to baby me. I'm *fine*."

"Do your ribs still hurt?"

"Only if you squeeze too tight," I tease, but his hands let go instantly. "Hey! Put those back."

I wrap his hands around me again, snuggling further into his body.

"Princess, you better stop wiggling," he groans painfully. "If your brother sees us like this, he might break something of importance."

"Like your dick."

Andrew's whole body freezes behind me. I turn around to look at my brother standing in the doorway. "Nobody is breaking anything."

Max is the one who took all of this the hardest. Dad's cheating. Our parents' separation. My accident. And the role he played in what happened three years ago.

I tried to explain to him that I'm over it, and he should let it go and forgive himself. He insists he's okay, but I can see the constant shadow over his face. The moodiness. Spending time in the basement working out and boxing.

He hasn't forgiven himself for his part in what happened, and I'm not even sure he's forgiven me for keeping all the secrets.

"If you say so." He comes in to the room, kissing the top of my head. It's something he started doing again so I know that even if he's angry at me for keeping secrets, he still loves me but needs time. "You take it easy. And you." There is a warning note in his voice as he looks at Andrew. "You take your paws off my sister and treat her like the lady she is because the next time I won't go so easy on you."

"There won't be a next time. I'm not screwing this up again." His lips brush against the crown of my head.

"Better not." Max turns around. "You kids don't burn the house down while I'm gone."

We watch him walk away. His shoulders are stiff, the only indication that something's cooking underneath the surface of calmness he presents to the world.

"Do you think he'll be alright?"

Andrew's lips brush against my shoulder. "Yeah, I think he just might be."

When the door closes and I know we're finally alone, I turn around and straddle his lap.

"And you?"

Andrew's mom came to visit him the day after the accident. It was a coincidence really. Andrew didn't want to leave my side, but my mom told him to go home and take a shower, eat something and come back. Reluctantly, he listened, but when he returned, I saw he was in one of his moods. I guess anybody would be after being cornered with their past.

"I'll be fine, too." He leans in to kiss my cheek.

"Have you talked to her?"

I don't have to give him an explanation. He knows who I'm talking about.

"A few times. On the phone." He shrugs like it doesn't affect him one way or another, but I can see underneath the mask he puts on for everybody. He can't fool me.

The man he's turning out to be doesn't want to care, but the little boy inside him does.

"She wants us to meet for coffee or something."

I nod my head, brushing a strand of his hair away. "I think you should do it when you're ready. Small steps."

"Small steps," he agrees.

"And us?" My good arm slides up his chest and neck, fingers tangling in the hair at the nape. "Are we going to be alright?"

His hands grip my hips, pulling me closer. I can feel his hard length between my legs. Nibbling at my lower lip, I watch his eyes grow dark with desire. It's been a while for both of us, but I know he won't do anything until I'm all patched up.

But that doesn't mean we can't have some fun.

I pull him closer to me. His lips brush against mine, our breaths mingling.

"We, Princess, we're going to be perfect."

Epilogue

JEANETTE

The sound of the door closing echoes through the dark, silent night. My eyes scan around the almost empty parking lot. Almost, because although it's nearly eight in the evening, Andrew's black BMW and Derek's blue SUV are still parked there with a couple more cars I don't recognize.

Figured they'd still be here even though it's way past their usual practice time. They're so close to winning the championship, so everything is hectic. Long practices, extra gym time and the pressure of scouts from different colleges watching are getting to the whole team.

Locking my car, I pocket the keys. I burrow my head into the scarf so I'm protected from the wind and start walking around the school toward the rink.

Although it's almost the end of February, it's still pretty cold, and I can't wait for winter to finally be over.

Digging my fingers deeper into the pockets of my coat, I feel the cold, sleek metal under my fingers. A small smile curls my lips when I remember the message that was waiting on my phone when I finally decided to call it quits on my violin practice.

My Asshole: Meet me at the rink after the practice?

Seeing his nickname on the screen still makes my heart flutter in my chest and warmth spread through my body. Some couples would probably go for obnoxiously cute pet names, but we're not some couples. We're us, messy pasts, dysfunctional families, defects and all. Our love is jaded, hearts broken only to be put together again and mended, but that doesn't mean the wounds have disappeared. That the wounds will ever disappear. They won't, but that doesn't make our love less real. It's strong and fierce, burning bright and strong.

Running my hand through my windblown strands, I feel the now-familiar sting in my forearm. I got my cast off a couple of weeks ago and went straight into physical therapy, but it still feels pretty stiff. The doctors remind me all the time to take it easy and give my hand a chance to rest, but I missed playing the violin and I knew that the only way to get my hand back in the shape it was in before the accident was for me to practice. So, every day I take thirty minutes to play, but maybe I've gone a little overboard this time.

Sighing, I take in the facility in front of me. The lights are still burning brightly, and when I enter, I can hear the familiar swish sound of skates cutting through the ice. Sticks clashing, puck sliding, grunts and yelled orders that are an everyday occurrence in the rink make me remember all the times I spent waiting for Max to be done with his practice so we could go home.

My body shivers when a gush of cold wind enters as the door falls shut behind me. It's almost as cold inside as it is outside, but I don't let it stop me from going farther inside.

Two teams of three are having a scrimmage on the ice.

My eyes look over the boys in action, scanning through number eighty-eight and stopping at twenty-six. What can I say? I love my brother, but he's not the guy my body seeks out everywhere I go.

Yearns.

My body yearns for Andrew Hill.

He's always on my mind, no matter what I do or where I go.

And I hope this feeling never goes away.

Skating backward, he almost mocks the guys on the opposite team with his antics. And when one of them bites into his taunt, the puck is already across the ice, safely in Derek's hands. He skates toward the goalie, but another player gets in his way. Without removing his eyes from the opponent, Derek shoots the puck to Max. No matter how many times I see it, it amazes me the connection those two share.

Max angles his stick to shoot, but in the last second, both the player who was guarding Max and the one who was after Andrew launch at him. Max tries to shoot, but the puck bounces back, and they all lunge at him at once.

It's a mess of limbs and sticks in blue and white jerseys, and I'm not even sure who's playing with whom when the buzzer finally sounds and the red light flashes.

"Two to one for the white team," Coach yells from his spot on the ice. "Good game, boys. You can hit the showers. I'll see you tomorrow. Six sharp."

Grunts and murmurs of approval resound in the rink as players leave.

Moving toward the exit, I lean against the plexiglass, waiting for my boys to get off the ice.

"Puck bouncing off of somebody and ending up in the net," I tsk, trying to keep a straight face and even tone. "That can hardly be considered a win. You'll have to put more work in if you want to win that fancy trophy you all are aiming for."

The three of them exit and stand around me. With their

skates and full gear on, they tower over me even more than usual, and at five feet seven, I'm pretty tall for a girl.

Gray eyes narrow at me. "Wanna put on the gear and show us how it's done?"

The smell of both fresh and stale sweat surrounds me, and I can't help but burrow my nose deeper into my scarf, inhaling the familiar flowery scent of my perfume. Once I think I won't faint, I say, "And risk smelling like a year-old gym sock? No, thank you."

"Lay off of her." Andrew's hands wrap around me from behind, pulling me in. "You're just pissed that your shot at the goal got deflected."

"Hi, babe," Andrew whispers softly, his lips nuzzling at my neck. "Took you long enough."

I look over my shoulder so I can get a better look at him. His face is all sweaty and reddish from exercise and cold air. His musky smell reaches my nostrils, but there is no way I'd push him away. Not when his body is molded to mine perfectly and a sense of belonging and love settle in my soul.

"Sorry, I got carried away practicing."

He takes my hand in his, brushing his lips over my exposed wrist. "I hope you didn't overdo it."

Both boys snicker in the background, and if I'm not mistaken, one of them—probably my brother—coughs "pussy whipped", but we ignore them. Taking the hint, they both retreat.

"I'm fine. Really."

Since the accident, Andrew has been especially careful with me. My whole body hurt from the impact. My rib was broken, so it was hard to breathe, and I couldn't do anything with my hand. Overall, I felt like shit. Andrew was there as much as my mom allowed him. He'd come after practice to bring my homework and spend every free moment with me. He took me to doctors' appointments and to my first physical therapy appointment to assure they weren't messing anything up. But now I'm much better, yet he's still weary.

"Why did you want me to come?" I ask, hoping to change the subject, but also because I really am wondering.

He smiles, and for a heartbeat, I just stand and stare at him. It's not one of his mocking half-smiles he used to give to people, but it's also not one of his sexy smirks. He actually smiles, his green eyes shining brightly. He's excited. There is a happy twinkle in those field-green irises I love so much.

"I got you something." His fingers lace with mine as he pulls me wherever he's hidden his surprise.

I laugh at his enthusiasm. He's still so guarded and standoffish; I'm thrilled to see him acting so openly happy and excited. Like a little boy on Christmas morning.

"Couldn't you like... bring it to my house?" I tease. "You usually stop by for dinner anyway."

"Well." He stops. Looking at me, he rubs the nape of his neck, nibbling at his lower lip. "I think you'll be excited about the surprise. Your family... not so much."

I frown, confused.

What the hell are you up to now, Andrew Hill?

ANDREW

Kissing the tip of her nose, I pull away and continue back toward where I left my bag.

This was a really bad idea on so many levels I stopped counting, but when the guy called and told me it was ready, what could I do? He wanted to get it done as soon as possible, and I had no other choice but to comply if I didn't want my surprise to be ruined. Not like anybody would know it except me, but still.

I wanted to do this for her.

I really, really did.

And something like practice wouldn't stop me from it.

As I near my bag, I slow down my steps so I don't come off as a clumsy baby elephant and scare the poor thing.

Letting go of Jeanette's hand, I sit down on the seat next to my bag. When I pull the bag into my lap, I can feel it move.

"Shhh," I murmur softly through gritted teeth. "Just a bit more. Promise."

I probably look like an imbecile, but I don't care. Putting my helmet away, I take off my gloves and set them to the side.

"What is this?" Jeanette laughs nervously, pushing a strand of hair behind her ear. "You couldn't have left it in the locker room?"

"Not really," I laugh.

There was no way I was leaving this thing anywhere out of my sight. If it's anything like its owner, it'll get in trouble in no time, and I wasn't risking it. I still couldn't quite believe I'd come this far without being figured out.

"Like I said, I'm not sure if this is even okay or if your mom will hate me, but she doesn't matter. What matters is what you think and that you're happy." I inhale loudly, stopping the rambling. "I want to make you happy, Princess."

Her face softens as she comes near me. "You make me happy, Andrew. There is no need to..."

I press my finger against her lips, stopping her from commenting further.

"And I figured, if they do hate me because of the present, I can always keep it at my place. Gives me an excuse to have you at my house more." I wiggle my brows suggestively. "In my bed."

Gray eyes grow wide. She shoves me away before looking over her shoulder, for her brother presumably, but both he and Derek are already in the locker room, and the two of us are all alone in here. "Stop it!"

I grab her hands gently and pull her in for a quick kiss. But one kiss isn't enough. It's never enough.

Our lips mash together over and over again. At first slowly, barely brushing against one another. Then she sighs, her fingers dig into my scalp, and I can't help but groan at the sensation of her fingers running through my hair. My tongue darts out, and she opens to let me in.

My tongue obliges, velvet meeting velvet as we slowly glide together, deepening the kiss.

So sweet.

So warm.

I pull her closer, but instead of getting her in my lap, she stumbles over the bag.

Breaking the kiss, she pulls away. Her long lashes flutter, eyes slowly open, wide and clouded with desire. Then she blinks, desire turning to confusion as she takes a step back.

"W-why..." She waves in the way of my lap. "Why is your bag m-moving?"

I look down, also confused.

I left a small gap so air could get inside, but not big enough so my surprise could run away. The gap is now slightly bigger, and there is a little black snout peeking out from the hole as the bag wiggles. And now that the beat of my heart is not the only sound thumping in my ears, I can hear soft cries coming from my bag.

Sighing, I pull the zipper open as my hand digs inside, fingers curling around a fur ball.

Here goes nothing...

Jeanette looks at me, stunned, as I fluff small ears to calm down the noisy ball that wants to wiggle out of my hand.

"W-what..."

She points my way, her mouth hanging open as she stutters.

She actually looks cute when she's left speechless. I should do it more often.

"W-why..."

The fur ball wiggles, looking at Jeanette's stunned face. "Don't worry, Baby Black. Your mommy isn't usually this silly, but I think we surprised the hell out of her."

Big brown eyes turn and look at me with wonder. A little pink tongue darts out and licks my cheek, tickling me.

"She'll get over it soon," I whisper. "Promise."

"A d-dog?" She finally manages to form a full sentence. "You got me a dog?!"

"Don't yell, you'll..." I start but don't get to finish. Puppy jerks in fear, jumps out of my hands and starts running. "You scared her!"

"You brought a dog into the rink, Andrew!" she shouts. "What were you thinking?!"

"I was thinking that I wanted to surprise my girlfriend and do something nice for her." Puffing my cheeks, I discard the bag from my lap and get up. "Just don't let her..."

But the words fall flat as the little fluff runs past Jeanette's leg and straight for the still-open door of the rink.

Who was the dumbass who left the door open?

Jeanette runs after the dog, stopping at the door. "She's out there. I can't..."

She looks over her shoulder, but I'm already there. Standing in the middle of the ice, the puppy looks around herself in wonder, taking everything in. It's as if she just now realized where she is. Taking a tentative step, she looks down at the ice.

"She'll freeze to death!" Jeanette hugs herself, her eyes still zeroed in on the small fur ball. "She's so small, just a baby."

Sighing, I kiss the top of her head, and I move her to the side. "She won't freeze to death. It's not that cold. Besides, she's a dog. They're used to being outside in cold."

"Not baby dogs. Now go and get my puppy."

Chuckling, I shake my head and step on the ice.

The dog instantly lifts her eyes to look at me. I glide over the white surface slowly, so as not to scare her more.

"C'mere, love," I call out, extending my hand. "Mommy is done being silly and wants to meet you. What do you say?"

She tilts her head to the side, one of her small, fluffy ears falling open as she assesses me. I think I have her, but then she barks and runs away in a different direction.

"Come back!" I yell after the silly dog. "You little..."

In the background, I can hear Jeanette giggle, and I can't even pretend to be angry. I'd chase this fluff forever around the ice if it would get Jeanette to laugh like that all the time.

Turning around, I look at her. "Are you done, you little tease? I should have left you to figure it out by yourself."

"Nu-uh. Watch where you go and don't crash into my dog."

Laughing, I turn around just in time. The black ball runs toward me chasing... a puck.

I laugh even harder. "You know what? I changed my mind. This dog is obviously meant to be mine so..."

"No!" Jeanette protests seriously. "No take-backs. You said this was my present. You can't take it away anymore."

Making a circle around the rink, I come back to her. Leaning against the doorway, I lower my face so we're eye to eye. "I can't?"

She pouts. "Nope. Mine."

"You sure?"

"Mine."

"What about me?" I lean even further, our lips brushing. "Am I yours too?"

"Hmm..." She tilts her head to the side. "Maybe. If you bring me my dog. And fast."

"You little..." Lightning fast, I lean down and nibble at her lip. "I'll give you your dog, alright."

Grabbing the stick I left leaning against the wall, I turn around. The pup is still out there, playing with the puck. Sliding it, intentionally or not I'm not sure, and trying to take it in her mouth.

When she sees me coming, her little tail wiggles in excitement. She goes for the puck, but instead of taking it, she pushes it away, and I grab the chance to catch it.

"What are you going to do now?" I ask her.

I pretend I'm going to slide the puck her way, which makes her tail sway even faster, but then in the last moment, I start skating backward, pulling the puck with me.

Angry, she starts barking after me. Her little legs push as she runs toward me as fast as they can carry her.

I laugh because it's ridiculous, the tiny four-legged creature running across the ice on her chubby legs to get to me.

"Be careful!"

I'm not sure who that is directed toward, me or the dog, but still, I slow down as I near the exit until I stop.

Surprised, the puppy tries to break too, but she's going too fast and the ice is slippery under her paws, so it's not surprising she falls on her butt and slides over the ice, finally coming to a stop right in front of the exit.

"Did you have to make her chase you?" Jeanette mumbles. "I really hope she didn't get hurt."

She squats down, her hands wrapping around the fur ball and lifting her up in her arms. Jeanette scratches her behind her ears, and the dog looks at her with her big, dark eyes.

"He's a big meanie. Am I right or am I right?"

She licks her nose, making Jeanette giggle.

"I knew we'd get along. Are you precious or what?"

The two of them continue bonding as they bad-mouth me like I'm not in the room.

"What's her name?" Jeanette asks, suddenly looking at me.

"Just got her today." I shrug. "Figured you'd name her. After all, it's your dog."

She laughs nervously, pushing a strand of hair behind her ear. She always does it when she's nervous. "If Mom agrees with it. You know she doesn't like animals in the house, and there is no way I'll leave this little cutie out in the cold Michigan winter."

I come out, wrapping my hands around her. "She will let you keep her. But if she doesn't, I'll take good care of her for you."

"You'll even let her sleep in the house?"

"She can take over my whole bed if it'll make you happy."

"Famous last words."

"I'm not even joking. I'd do anything to make you happy. Even give up my own bed."

She shakes her head, laughing. "What about when we go off to college? Who'll take care of her then? I don't think they let dogs in dorms."

Jeanette says it jokingly, but I can see traces of worry on her face. Mostly we live in the here and now, but there is no escaping the future. In a few short months, high school will be over, and we'll be packing off to college.

Cupping her cheeks, I kiss her. "Screw them. Who wants to live in the dorm anyway? We can rent a place of our own, but then the dog is getting its own room. No bunking with us."

Because there is no way I'll let her go. Wherever she wants to go and as long as she'll have me, I'll be right next to her.

She laughs, and this time the happiness reaches her eyes, making them twinkle. "You're incorrigible."

I wiggle my brows playfully. "Sometimes a guy needs some time alone with his girl, and his girl only."

Jeanette gets on the tips of her toes and presses a kiss on my lips. "We'll see about that."

"They're here, Max!" Derek's voice echoes through the empty rink. He turns toward us. "What the hell, man? Coach wants us out of here, like twenty minutes ago."

Sighing, I let my hands fall. "I'm coming. I'm coming."

"Dude, stop cozying up to ... What the hell is that?"

I look down at Jeanette's hands and the puppy snuggled in her arms. "Oh... that's a Peekapoo."

"Peek-a-what?"

"I don't think I even want to know." Derek lifts his hands in the air in surrender. "I'm out. See you fuckers in the morning."

"He got me a dog." Jeanette lifts the puppy in the air for her brother to inspect it. "Isn't she cute?"

Max frowns at the dog for a second before his eyes find me. "You couldn't get her a plush animal? You really had to go for the real thing?"

"What my girl wants, my girl gets." I shrug. "Gimme a few minutes and I'll meet you outside."

I grab my stuff, and we all go toward the locker room. The door is left slightly open, but I don't get far, because Jeanette's delicate fingers wrap around my wrist, stopping me.

"Jeanette?" I turn around, confused.

"Thank you." She smiles shyly. "I know it probably didn't seem that way, but I do love my present." Her fingers brush my cheek, thumb swiping over my lower lip. "I love you, Andrew."

I kiss her fingers before I pull back. "I love you too, Princess."

Playlist

Nerv – Bad Habits
Imagine Dragons – Demons
Zayn – Pillowtalk
James Arthur – Say You Won't Let Go
Kevin Davy White covers George Michael – Fastlove
Sara Bareilles – She Used To Be Mine
Hailee Steinfeld – Rock Bottom ft. DNCE
Ashley Tisdale – Voices In My Head
Rita Ora – Falling To Pieces
Little Mix – Monster In Me
Demi Lovato – Warrior
Leona Lewis – Bleeding Love
Thomas Rhett Feat. Maren Morris – Craving You
Lindsey Stirling Feat. Lzzy Hale – Shatter Me

Acknowledgments

When I wrote "The End" to *Habits* after about a year of writing this book, I wasn't sure of anything. I didn't know if I liked the book or the characters. I didn't know if the story would flow effortlessly or if I managed to mix present events with past so that the story makes sense. Everything was a blur, and the only thing I felt was relief. I've done it. For better or for worse, this book is done. And that's exactly what I said to one of my friends.

She couldn't believe it. All this time spent working on something, only to finish it and not know if you're happy with the final result. Well, that's me. Writing the first draft is a long, emotionally and physically draining, *mechanical* work for me. But when I read it for the first time when everything is said and done, that's when all the feelings assault me. This time more than ever.

Reading it for the very first time, I knew this was the one. The story I'll love and cherish above them all. Yes, I love all of my books and characters; after all, I wrote them. However, there is something special about Andrew and Jeanette.

They're so imperfect, so real. You love them and you hate them. You want to strangle them one minute, and then hug them the next. They're jaded and broken, cold and arrogant, but beneath it all something more is hiding. Something that pulls you in and makes you feel everything they're feeling.

And oh, do they feel.

They feel for this world, and they feel for each other.

When I wrote *Lines* I didn't know this whole series would be more than just a series of teen books, but it turned out to be so much more. This series talks about more than just ordinary teenage problems like school, friendly quarrels and falling in love, although there is also that. This series holds a strong social message. Struggles that people both young and old have but feel like they need to hide because they don't fit into those neat little boxes society gives us to check. Bullying, eating disorders, emotional and physical abuse—they might not affect us directly, but they're always around us and we need to acknowledge them and show the people who are struggling that it's okay to open up. It's okay to ask for help. It's okay not to hide our pain. It's okay to be different. Being different is what makes us beautiful. Being different is what makes us unique. Makes us human. Never forget that.

Writing this book has been a rollercoaster, and I can't express how thankful I am to have the support of all the people in my life.

A big thank you to my beta readers—Nina, Andrea, Stephanie and Yasmin—for supporting me, listening to my complaints and worries until I make your ears bleed, because I know I do. Preparing a book to show to the world will never get easier, and I don't expect it to, but knowing I have you on my side makes me breathe a little easier.

Thank you to my cover designer, Najla. You did an outstanding job with the cover, and every time I fall more and more in love with your work.

Thank you, Tricia! Working with you has been an amazing experience I hope to repeat soon. I love your little comments and suggestions. Going through the edits has never been so fun!

I hope I didn't overwhelm you with all my questions and comments, I can't risk you running away!

To my Bookmantics and Supergirls, thank you all for being with me, loving my books and supporting me. You are the best!

And, as always, THANK YOU, readers. Thank you for taking a chance on this book and me. Thank you for supporting me and making my dreams come true.

Until the next book!

Xoxo,
Anna

Other books by Anna B. Doe

Greyford Wolves

YA/NA sports romance

Lines

Habits

Rules

Greyford High

YA/NA sports romance

The Penalty Box

The Stand-In Boyfriend

Blairwood University

College sports romance

Kiss Me First

Kiss To Conquer

Kiss To Forget

Kiss To Defy

Kiss Before Midnight

Kiss To Remember

Kiss To Belong

Kiss Me Forever

Kiss To Tempt

Kiss To Shatter

Kiss To Salvage

Kiss Me Tenderly

Standalone

YA modern fairytale retelling

Underwater

New York Knights

NA/adult sports romance

Lost & Found

Until

Forever

Box Set Editions

Greyford Wolves: The Complete Collection

The Anabel & William Duet

About the author

Anna B. Doe is a *USA Today* and international bestselling author of young adult and new adult sports romance. She writes real-life romance that is equal parts sweet and sexy. She's a coffee and chocolate addict. Like her characters, she loves those two things dark, sweet and with a little extra spice.

When she's not working for a living or writing her newest book you can find her reading books, binge-watching TV shows or listening to music while she walks her shi tsu puppy Tina. Originally from Croatia, she is always planning her next trip because wanderlust is in her blood.

She is currently working on various projects. Some more secret than others.

Find more about Anna on her website: www.annabdoe.com

Join Anna's Reader's Group Anna's Bookmantics on Facebook.

Printed in Great Britain
by Amazon

61900948R00212